The
Walnut Tree

Michael Pakenham

PublishAmerica
Baltimore

ISBN: 1-4241-0107-7
PUBLISHED BY PUBLISHAMERICA, LLLP
www.publishamerica.com
Baltimore

Printed in the United States of America

Adam,
with all the best,
Michael

To Jeannie with all my love

Author's Note

My thanks go to Richard Purdue for all his help as he gave me new hope when my resolve was weakening. To Caroline, who, being a kind daughter, assured me she'd greatly enjoyed the book. To Veronique Baxter of David Higham for her measured and polite criticism. To all those at PublishAmerica too numerous to mention. And finally to Jeannie for reading, reading and reading the manuscript and putting me right on so many things.

I hope my small band of loyal readers will enjoy the book, and thanks for buying it! There will be another one soon.

March 2006

The Beginning

The beat of the music, the hardness of his body, the excitement of his attention made her feel totally intoxicated. He glided around the wood-panelled ballroom, holding her close. She knew every eye in the room was watching them, and she felt thoroughly decadent. He stroked her bare back and looked down at her with his seductive steel blue eyes. "Later?" he asked quietly.

She moved comfortably against his chest and sighed. For months, she had waited for this moment. "Of course," she replied, hardly recognising her voice. Tonight, at last, she would make love with him.

PART ONE
2000

'Tis now since I began to die
Four months, yet still I gasping live;
Wrapped up in sorrow do I lie,
Hoping, yet doubting a reprieve,
Adam from Paradise expell'd
Just such a wretched being held.

Katherine Philips, *Upon Absence*

Chapter One

Jill Foster surfaced from her dream like a drowning woman. As reality hit her, she gulped for air and gradually released the tension on the pillow hugged across her chest. Her heart raced and her head pounded. That bastard Harry Sidenham had invaded her subconscious yet again. She'd never been able to erase him totally from her mind, which was not surprising considering the secret they had both shared for years. She adjusted her eyes to the half-dawn light and scanned the room for familiar shapes—her dressing table with its glass bottles of various perfumes and expensive face creams; her towelling robe abandoned through the night across an antique nursing chair; a small damp patch on the ceiling that resembled an elephant; and the hunched body of her sick husband Tim laying next to her.

She felt dirty and wretched at the thought of Harry being in their bed, even if it was only a dream. She needed a shower and a mug of tea, but she dared not move for fear of waking Tim. He would need pain killers as soon as he woke to deaden the pains that shot through his body.

He had started feeling ill a few months ago—just a tummy bug they thought. His condition was slow to improve and they suspected an ulcer as the pains in his back and stomach worsened. He'd been for tests and a scan at the hospital and they both feared he was suffering from more than an ulcer, but they didn't verbalise this to each other. It was as if by not talking about it they could prevent it from happening. Anyway today they would find out; they had an appointment with Mr. James, their consultant. Jill was scared and she couldn't begin to imagine what Tim must be feeling in his waking hours. At the moment his sleeping pills were working so she was careful not to disturb his drug-induced sleep.

The luminous dial of her bedside clock told her it was only four-thirty, at least another two hours before she could move. She closed her eyes but Harry was still there. He was an evil man, a viper with a deadly sting. If, God forbid Tim died, would Harry try to reenter her life? He had always been good at choosing his moments. They had parted years ago when he'd cruelly thrown her out of his house threatening, "One day I will come into your life again." Jill gave a low cry of despair and rolled over to be close to Tim. She smelt his sweat and felt the dampness of his skin. It was a body fighting disease and she felt totally inadequate to help.

••••••

The shrill tones of the alarm clock came as a relief. She eased herself away from Tim and slipped out of the bed hoping that he might sleep on. She hurried to the chair and removed her towelling robe and hung it up in the wardrobe. She slipped on a pair of white knickers and wriggled into her favourite pair of faded beige jeans before pulling a woollen green sweater over her head. That would have to do today—she hadn't the will to put on makeup. She ran a comb absently through her long blond hair and grimaced at her reflection in the mirror. She looked worn, and it distressed her. She glanced over at the bed and saw Tim was awake, his eyes following her as she moved. "I'm sorry Tim I didn't mean to wake you, but it's time for me to go and get breakfast. If you remember, your father is coming."

"I'd forgotten. Of course today's the day isn't it? I'd better start getting up."

"You have plenty of time. Just go slow and try not to worry"

Tim shot her a look of despair. "Well, that's asking a lot, given what could happen to us today."

"I know I know. It's going to be a shit of day for us both, but come on, we can cope." Even as she said it, she wasn't too sure she believed it. "Here," she said reaching for the glass of water and the two pills lying on her bedside table. "Take these. You're due them now."

He reached out with an unsteady hand and took the pills. She held his arm and guided the glass to his mouth. He did not complain. He swallowed and lay back against the pillows. "Thanks, I'll feel better in a few minutes and then I'll make a move."

"In that case I'll leave you, and go down and get breakfast on the go. I don't suppose you feel like eating much?"

"I'll see, but I doubt it."

"Okay." She moved away from the bed and looked drearily around their bedroom, a room where she'd made love, a room where she'd proudly held two daughters to her breasts, but now the room seemed suddenly depressing. She was jolted out of her depression by the sound of tyres on the drive. Max Foster always cheered her up. "Your father's arrived. I'm off. See you in a few moments, Tim."

She hurried down the carpeted stairs and walked into the kitchen. Standing in the middle of the room was her father-in-law. "Max," she said with a laugh, "don't you ever knock?"

"If the door's open, I walk in. If it's closed, I stay outside. Yours, as usual, was open." He rubbed his hands vigorously. "It's bloody cold out there."

"Warm yourself by the stove while I begin breakfast." She looked at the large man lovingly. He wore his age like old but untarnished armour. He was a little thick around the middle, hair up a couple of notches on his forehead, and wrinkles that had seen a lot of smiles radiated out from his eyes and mouth. This was a man that seemed to have told time to stand still, and time had listened.

She moved easily into his muscular arms, and kissed him lightly on his weatherbeaten cheek. She breathed in the familiar and comforting smell of cows. Ever since she could remember, he'd smelt of cows. Her father had once told her that when Max had held her in the church at her christening, the vicar had insisted on the doors being open even though it was a freezing cold February day. The memory always made her laugh. It summed up Max. She'd since learnt he changed for no one, not even God. He was his own man, with an infectious love of life and a wicked sense of humour, which at times got him into trouble. He had once told her that he thought the world far too serious a place. "You're only here once, so take my advice and milk it." Jill felt she'd never quite managed that, or that his remark stood up to scrutiny. Reluctant to leave his arms, she said, "Hey, this isn't getting the breakfast started and we haven't all day. Tim will be down soon."

Max's arms dropped by his side as he asked, "How is he?"

It was said lightly with a smile, but Jill knew he was deeply concerned. He'd lost a wife; she could not begin to imagine what the death of his only child would do to him. Shaking her head, she moved toward the refrigerator. "He's in pain, Max, and he's being so brave. He had another bad night— didn't get to sleep until after midnight. Those painkillers the doctor gave him don't seem to be working as well as they should. Oh, Max, I'm so bloody scared."

"That makes two of us. Hopefully after you've been to the consultant this afternoon we will be able to wonder why in the hell we were so worried."

"We can but hope."

"We must."

"Yes."

"This waiting hasn't been easy for any of us. It's frightening to live with the unknown. Always better to know your enemy."

He moved away from the warmth of the stove and dropped into his usual wooden chair at the head of the kitchen table. It was slightly rickety due to his habit of balancing his weight on the back legs, a habit Jill continually chided him about. There was no such rebuke this morning, a reminder to him that her mind was elsewhere. He admired her figure, only moderately impaired by the years. She was tall and slim, with blond hair that swung around her head in a pleasant display as she moved. He liked her face as well, intelligent and reserved, but sensual too.

"I know you're right, Max," Jill said over her shoulder, "and I am being positive, but wow that's difficult."

Max noticed her hand shaking as she put the eggs onto a plate.

"On top of that," Jill continued, "we've got this terrifying meeting with the bank this morning."

Max stopped swinging on the chair. "I have an idea."

Jill was wary of Max's ideas. "Oh yes?"

"I take your place. I go with Tim and you stay here."

She swung round to face him, a look of total incredulity crossing her face. "Don't be daft, Max. Of course I'm going. It's out of the question that you take my place"

His voice broached no argument. "Not this time. You're exhausted. You've had months of worry over Tim's health and even longer biting your nails over the dire state of the farm finances. You need a fresh brain to sort things out. So I suggest that you stay here and get some rest and then you will be in a better state for your visit to the hospital later. That is far more important than this little hiccup with the bank"

"Hiccup!" Jill exclaimed, putting a plate of bacon and eggs in front of Max.

"Yes, hiccup. I can deal with it—trust me."

Jill bit her lip. "Am I allowed to disagree?"

"If you want to, but think first, because I really want to do this."

Hiding her confusion Jill busied herself with making coffee. "I feel I'm jumping ship, Max."

"No, you're not, just being wise and sending a very able deputy. Take my word for it. Tim and I will do a very good job together, far better than the two of you with your minds on this afternoon at the hospital. So come on Jill, bite the bullet as they say. I suspect you know it makes sense."

She gave him a smile, rubbed her chin and shook her head. "I don't like this I really don't, but you could be right. I just don't think it's fair to ask you."

Max forked some egg into his mouth. "Delicious—much better than I could do, and you are a wise girl, and don't let me hear any more of this, 'its not fair rubbish.' I'm part of your family"

Jill sat down beside him, filled two mugs with strong black coffee and buttered a piece of toast "And very special."

"Not really, I just want to help."

"That's more than I should expect."

Max studied her face. "You look exhausted, aren't you sleeping either?"

"I dreamt of Harry last night."

"How very unpleasant. That man has an uncanny way of popping up when he's not wanted."

"You can say that again."

"The usual nightmare?"

"Yes, but it seemed more vivid than usual."

"You mustn't let it get to you."

She buried her face in her hands, and Max had difficulty deciphering the words that leaked through her fingers. "That's easier said than done." Then she laughed bitterly. "Wouldn't the bastard be enjoying himself if he knew how much it's getting to me?"

"You're probably right, but he will never know. Put it out of your mind Jill. Harry is history."

"How can you be sure? I wish I shared your optimism. If, God forbid, something terrible happens to Tim I can just imagine Harry enjoying driving a knife deep into my broken heart."

Max reached over and gently put the fingers of his right hand to her mouth. "Shush, little girl, stop worrying. You had a dream, okay, but that's what it was, a dream; treat it as such."

Jill blew out her cheeks. "I'll try, but it won't be easy. You know how much I distrust that man. For some reason, better known to himself, he blames me for all that has past. He would love to mess my life up."

Max nodded. "He's had many chances over the years. I really think you must put him out of your mind."

Before Jill could reply, Tim walked into the kitchen cutting off any further discussion about the threat from Harry. To say that he looked a little pale would have been an understatement. Both Max and Jill stared at him in horror.

Tim raised a hand as if guessing what they were about to say. "I know, I know, I look like shit. It's not one of my better mornings, but I look worse than I feel."

Max sucked in his breath and forced a smile. "Well, I'm glad to hear that son."

Tim gave a rueful laugh "I'm not done yet, Father."

"I'm sure you're not," Max said encouragingly. "You're made of tough stuff. Take more than a belly ache to stop you."

"I'm confident I'll be as right as rain after today is over."

Max nodded agreement. "I'm sure. No reason why we shouldn't have sorted out the bank and heard you've been given the all-clear by the doctors before the day is out."

"I would love to share your optimism, Father, and what's this about *we* I hear? Have I missed something?"

Jill spoke before Max could reply. "Your father is going to the bank with you. He knows a great deal about our financial plight, and as he reminded me he was once in the same position. If anyone can persuade the bank to hold off making us bankrupt, your father can. At first I wasn't keen on the idea, but it makes sense. At least one of you will be thinking straight."

In no mood to argue, Tim smiled. "Twisted your arm, did he?"

"Something like that."

"Thanks dad," were all the words Tim could find.

······

Jill reckoned she'd have two hours to wait until they returned. The two men she'd relied on for so many years had gone to fight for her future. There, she was doing it again—*her* future. So many times she was thinking that way now. It had to stop somehow, or she'd go nuts. She switched her thoughts to the two men she loved the most in the world, although for different reasons. Max because he'd been her father's best friend, and had always been there for her when she most needed him, and Tim because…well, just because.

She went upstairs and made the bed, moved to the bathroom and cleaned her teeth, and determinedly recombed her hair. It was not the time to play the pathetic act. Resolve was what she needed. She moved back to the kitchen and picked up the *Daily Telegraph* and forced herself to read a few pages. If anyone had asked what she'd read she couldn't have told them—her mind was on other things. She looked at her watch—half an hour had passed. *Time is dragging!* She dropped the paper back onto the table and stared out of the window at the frost-covered grass. It would be a cold wait, but she made a decision. She'd sit under the walnut tree—*her tree* as Max called it. She grabbed a warm coat from the hangers on the back of the kitchen door and ran across the lawn. She dropped onto the wooden seat that had been under the tree for as long as she could remember. She looked up at the barren winter branches, closed her eyes and wished with all her might that her worst fears would not be realised today. She opened her eyes and traced the familiar pattern of the branches. Whatever the season, the old tree always gave her a feeling of comfort. She huddled down into her coat and prepared for a cold and lonely wait.

......

She heard the Land Rover draw into the yard. By then, the pale winter sun had taken the bite out of the air, but she was shivering. She gave a halfhearted wave as the two men walked through the gate, and as she always did when she saw them together, smiled at the contrast between father and son. Tim, fragile, a little like his mother, modestly tall, just shy of six feet, with his neatly cut dark brown hair, his blue tie, tweed jacket and well-pressed cord trousers just touching the tops of his handmade polished brown shoes. Apart from when he was in his working clothes he was always well dressed. Max, a couple of inches shorter, deliberately looked as if he'd just dragged on some old clothes which happened to be lying on the floor. Whatever he wore—and he did possess some decent clothes—he looked rumpled, as if there were no clothes he couldn't overcome by the force of his personality. Today he was wearing baggy grey trousers and a threadbare tweed jacket. As usual he was not wearing a tie, his muscular neck sticking out from a wrinkled white shirt. His black hair, flecked with grey, was blowing untidily in the breeze, and his robust frame with its long arms and huge hands was hunched against the cold. At times, Jill laughingly told them they couldn't possibly be father and son. Her heart jumped when she saw they were smiling. Max's arm was resting affectionately on Tim's shoulder. Did she dare hope?

"Well?" she asked breathlessly, as they stopped in front of her.

Tim came close and stroked her cheek. "You're freezing!"

"Oh damn that! What happened at the bank?"

"Father has sorted it," he said quietly.

"Sorted it! Oh God I don't believe it. What have you both agreed?"

Tim spoke. "It was simple in the end. Father said he'd become a partner in the farming enterprise, then told that miserable bank manager how much money he was prepared to inject into the business, and bingo, the man was all smiles."

Jill's mouth fell open. "Oh my God, Max, I really don't think you should have done that. This farm is a bad bet."

Max looked her in the eye. "Not anymore, it's not, or at least no more than any other farm at the moment. Besides I made a lot of money from that outlying piece of land I sold to the supermarket and it's only burning a hole in my pocket. I don't need that sort of cash. My requirements are minimal, and my only hobby is hunting and that may soon be banned. So why not put it to good use, I asked myself, help a couple I very much love."

"But we needed a small fortune to pay off the overdraft, and I assume that is what you've guaranteed the bank?"

"Yes."

Jill threw herself into his arms. "Oh, you wonderful, extraordinary man. I should be furious with you, Max, and say we won't accept this unbelievably generous offer. I'm not going to though." She pulled away, tears staining her face, mascara stinging her eyes, but she didn't care. Perhaps after all she could hope that this was going to be her lucky day. "All I can say, Max, is exactly what Tim said a few hours ago, thank you. It's so inadequate, but I'm lost for a better word."

"That will be plenty," Max said with a smile, roughing her hair. "And now let's get you inside before you go as blue as an ancient Briton."

As they walked into the warmth of the house, Tim reached for Jill's hand. "Maybe this is going to be our lucky day."

......

Five hours later the euphoria had died. They sat in the reception area holding hands, oblivious to the other people round them, for however worrying their financial plight had been, it paled into insignificance compared with the critical situation that now faced them. This was mind-blowing stuff—a life could be under threat. Nothing came bigger than that.

This is not just about losing our livelihood; this is about losing my husband, Jill told herself, still not quite able to believe what had happened a few hours earlier. It was time to clear her mind of such good fortune and focus on the other crisis that was close at hand. She did her best to smile reassuringly at Tim. She squeezed his hand as much for her own comfort as his. For soon, very soon, they would know the answer and panic was playing jazz with her bowels. It was no good trying to bolster her confidence by thinking that millions of people had a health scare at sometime in their lives and most came out of it okay. Walking into the hospital had withered any confidence she had left.

Tim is dying. Until someone told her otherwise, that's what she would believe. That's what Tim believed as well although he'd done his best to hide his fear from her, but at nights, in pain, his guard had often dropped, and his eyes had said it all. She looked round the room. Clinically clean, a vase of white lilies on a table in the centre of the room, month-old magazines lying untidily on its polished top. Four large watercolours of the local countryside on the walls, and arranged round the room comfortable chairs now filled with other patients. Were they waiting to be told the worst? She caught a man looking at her, imagining she saw the hopelessness mirrored in his eyes and she quickly looked away. Three chairs away from him, on his left, sat a woman that Jill guessed was in her late seventies, her body covered by a long floral dress, her white shoes a little worn, and her skinny legs half covered by a pair of light blue socks. She was alone, her eyes darting round the reception area perhaps, Jill thought, trying to find a kindred soul. Was she counting her days, wondering how she would die, ticking off in her mind those that would come to her funeral? Jill felt a cold hand touch her heart. She felt that she was glimpsing the world of imminent mortality into which her husband was entering.

But this is something I can't share with Tim.

She leant over and kissed him firmly on the mouth. She felt a brief resistance—he was not at ease with public shows of affection—but then she felt the gentle touch of his tongue against her lips as he returned her kiss. "I love you," she whispered.

His eyes smiled at her, and for a brief moment, she saw the softness that had so entranced her years ago, and which had been missing these last few months. "And I love you," he said quietly.

She rubbed her opaline green eyes, fighting back the tears.

He saw her distress. "Hey, hey, remember what we agreed. No crying."

There was no time for Jill to reply.

"Mr. and Mrs. Foster, Mr. James is ready to see you now," the receptionist behind the desk called out. "Nurse here will take you."

Jill heard Tim gasp. This was it! Within the next half-hour or so they would know the results of the tests. She had felt an all-consuming terror once before in her life. It had been a long slow walk behind a nurse that time. Her legs had felt as if they were weighted down with lead and her heart had been in her mouth. She had wanted to run then, but the nurse had kept a firm grip on her arm. "It will be over soon," she'd assured her. "The first pregnancy is always frightening. It's the fear that something might go wrong. But it won't—you wait and see—just imagine the joy when you hold your child for the first time. You will wonder why you panicked."

What's changed?

She stared at the starched white uniform walking in front of her and felt that she was about to hand Tim's life over to a lot of strange people in white and green. People accustomed to losing patients, but who no doubt would smile at her and Tim and assure them that he would survive. Well, she'd take some convincing.

......

Michael James, tall, with white hair, kind brown eyes, and dressed as always in a dark pinstriped suit covering a light blue shirt, was standing at the door of his consulting room fiddling nervously with his yellow tie. It never came easy to him, meeting patients with bad news. Years of experience had not made a jot of difference. That's what set him apart from many of his colleagues. He still had a heart, which bled for those patients he knew he could not save. He still felt the same gut wrenching sickness whenever he told someone they were terminally ill. He knew he should be detached, treating each case like a carcass of meat to be butchered, but he'd never been able to think of a human being in that light. His colleagues had been taking bets for years as to when the strain would break him and he'd be forced into an early retirement.

He held a hand out to Tim and forced a smile at Jill. "Nice to see you both again," he lied. A quarter of his professional life was spent lying. "I'm sorry it's taken so long. It must have been a very worrying time for you."

Unbearable! Jill answered to herself.

"It has not been easy," Jill said as she followed him into the consulting room and sat down next to Tim. The chairs were green and soft. "Since we last talked, things have come to a head with our business and the problem with Tim's stomach is something we could have done without."

"I can understand that. I'm sorry to hear about your troubles. Farming is not looking too bright is it?"

"You can say that again," Tim said with a rueful smile. He leaned forward in his chair, working his intertwined fingers nervously.

Michael James nodded. "Yes, I'm sure. I know a little about it, because I come from a farming background. I have an older brother who farms. He tells me things are tough. But you haven't come to talk farming. You want to know about the tests."

"Do we?" Jill asked.

"I think it best, yes," James replied gently, opening a file in front of him. He'd read the contents an hour before. It was all gloom. No point in beating about the bush. He looked up at the two pale faces staring at him and experienced once more that awful sadness that he'd become so used too. "I'm afraid to say it's not good news. The biopsy indicates the presence of a malignant tumour."

"Oh, dear God!" Jill exclaimed, as the world collapsed about her shoulders.

Tim asked in a hushed voice, "How bad?"

"The tumour is well advanced."

"Is it treatable?" Jill gasped.

"All types of cancer can be treated, Mrs. Foster, but some with more success than others."

*It's terminal! I knew it I knew it…*raced through her mind.

Jill jumped up and knelt beside Tim as his head slumped forward. "Don't worry darling, please, this is the twenty-first century. Everything is curable, isn't that right Mr. James?"

"Let's put it this way, my dear. Modern medicine can perform miracles and give some people a chance, but," he said, turning toward Tim, "the cancer is in your pancreas and that can be difficult to treat."

Tim sat up straight and asked calmly, "So am I facing a premature death?"

"You are facing a big fight. I wouldn't like to say more at this stage. Let's get on with some treatment and see how things go."

"Is it worth it?"

"Of course it is. Your life is very valuable, Mr. Foster. You mustn't throw it away without a fight."

"No, no I understand that. So what you are saying?"

"Of course I can't give you any firm guarantees, but you have a chance. I will be able to give you a more precise answer once the treatment is finished, perhaps earlier."

"Well, at least it means you haven't given up on me."

"I would never do that to anyone Mr. Foster. I'm here to help, and I will do everything I can." James tried to give a reassuring smile to the couple in front of him. "A positive attitude can make a tremendous difference when fighting this disease. You may well look at me with doubt in your eyes, but it has been proven time and time again."

Tim smiled weakly and squeezed Jill's hand. "I'm no quitter, Mr. James. Don't you worry. I'll fight like hell!"

James knew Foster's chances of seeing two more Christmases were pretty slim, and by then he would most probably be glad to die. The treatments were painful and demoralising. But miracles had happened; he'd witnessed a few, and a fighting spirit definitely did help. He was not in the business of giving up on a patient however hopeless the case might seem. He'd witnessed some remarkable recoveries. He smiled and said, "That's the sort of attitude I like to hear. Here's a pamphlet I have put together which explains the treatments and their side effects. Any questions can be put to me when we meet next week." He stood up and held out his hand.

Taking it, Tim said, "Thanks for your frankness, Mr. James."

"I'm sorry it wasn't better news," James replied, walking them to his door." My nurse or I will ring you later in the day and tell you the next step. Now take care both of you until I see you again."

······

It was raining hard. The black slippery tarmac of the car park matched their mood. They walked the short distance from the hospital to their car in silence, oblivious to the rain soaking their clothes. Not until they were standing by their car did either of them speak. "I'll drive," said Jill, fighting to regain some semblance of composure. "The sooner we get home the better for both of us."

Tim handed over the keys without arguing. "Just look at my hands shaking!" He looked at them in disgust as he fumbled with the door handle.

"It's shock."

"Whatever, I've certainly felt better."

"I'm sure. Let me help you with the door."

"No! I can manage." As soon as he was sitting in the passenger seat, the thought hit him hard. He was dying, simple as that. No amount of reassurance from James was going to convince him otherwise. Suddenly, he felt very angry. He wanted to scream, to curse at God. What had he done to deserve such a rotten roll of the dice? He slammed a clenched fist against the window—winced from the pain, feeling thoroughly betrayed.

Jill drove fast. Probably too fast, but all she wanted were the comforting surroundings of their house and to talk to Max. She would have preferred it to be her mother with her calming ways, but that could not be. So she and Max would have to give mutual support and try to make Tim's life as bearable as possible in the difficult times ahead. He would have undivided attention twenty-four hours a day. It would be a struggle to keep cheerful, but cheerful she would have to stay, never letting him know that she was weeping inside. She glanced across at the man who had loved her against all the odds, and felt as if her world was falling apart.

······

The three of them sat numb—silent numbness—around the large oak kitchen table, at a loss for words. Max fiddled nervously with his mug of coffee; Tim stared at his mug of tea, watching the steam rise, and wondering why he should bother to ever eat or drink again. What was the point of keeping a rotting body alive any longer than necessary? Jill held a half empty glass of white wine, trying to focus on her next challenge—telling the girls when they came back for the weekend that their father was dangerously ill.

Tim broke the silence. "It's a bugger, isn't it? Fucking hell, what have I done to deserve this? Right this moment I feel like chucking in the towel. After all I'm probably going to die soon anyway."

Jill was gutted. She looked at his drawn face, his once animated eyes now so lifeless, and heard the bitterness. Who could blame him? She looked to Max for support.

"You must fight Tim!" Max begged him. "You have to believe you can beat this horror."

Jill added, "This is the moment when you grab yourself by the balls and don't look back."

Tim laughed at her vulgar metaphor, but it was good to hear the defiance in her voice. It changed his mood. "You're both right of course, and I'll fight; sure I'll fight. Just watch me."

Jill smiled for the first time since leaving the hospital. "You must believe you have a chance. I know you will have days of utter misery, but I will be here and we can work through them. As Morgan said to you, be positive and always remember that many people are cured of this shitty bloody awful disease these days."

"And I agree with that," Max said firmly.

"Okay, we start now. I'm not ready to die."

"You're made of tough stuff. Son, just like your mother, so I know you have the guts. With our help we will see this through." Max rose a little stiffly from his chair, his mug of coffee untouched. "Now I think it's time I left you two alone."

"You don't have to go," said Tim.

"I think I do. You and Jill need time to talk things over before the girls get back."

Tim nodded, agreeing with the decision of a wiser man.

Jill followed Max to the door. "Thank you, Max, thank you for everything."

"Go back inside now Jill and cheer up that young man. It will not be easy, but if anyone can do it, you can."

Jill grimaced. "I'll do my level best, but as I've already told you once today, I'm shit scared!"

······

They made love that night—the first time in weeks—desperately and hungrily, like two lovers about to be separated for good. When their passion had been exhausted, Tim lay sweating on top of her silently thanking God for bringing them together. She was so beautiful. Tall, lean and graceful, with her spectacular blonde hair spread out on the pillow. But she was a lot more than that to him. She was shot through with love, passion and restless energy. He traced his hand down the smooth flesh of her stomach appreciating, as if for the first time, the silkiness of her warm body perfumed with their lovemaking. He wondered if this would be the last time they would lie like this, the last time he would feel the heat of her skin. He felt her smile against his neck and gently pushed her to one side so that he could look into her eyes. "Oh, Tim," she whispered. "That was so beautiful!"

He couldn't speak. The burden was too great. He buried his head in her hair so that she couldn't see his tears.

······

The next morning she rose early. The children were expected later, and there seemed to be a thousand and one things to do. She'd neglected so much in the last few fraught weeks. Now it was time to get her head together. Tim lay propped up on his pillows looking frail and drawn. The pain had returned half way through the night, tugging them viciously back to reality. He smiled weakly as she handed him a cup of tea. "Last night—so beautiful, let's do it again soon."

Tears were never far away for Jill these days, and the thought that perhaps soon all the beauty, the softness, the sheer joy of making love with Tim might end brought the familiar pain to her eyes. "Yes, of course," she choked, "We will do it very soon again."

......

Emma nervously wiped the sweat from her brow and steered her car through the farm entrance. It was not a warm day but she was sweating with a hangover. She felt sick, a little dizzy and thoroughly disagreeable. She knew she was drinking too much, but coming home was never as easy as it should be, so she'd had a few extra glasses the night before. She'd never been able to rid herself of the feeling of not belonging. She'd first felt this strange intuition when she'd been a few days over five. Since then it had mystified her, but she'd learnt to live with it, no longer having sleepless nights trying to fathom why she felt distant from her family. Yet there was still this nagging unexplained question resting in the recess of her brain.

She drew up outside the house and turned off the engine of her new, dark-green MG coupe, hoping no one had heard her arrive. She knew that at some time she'd have to face questions about the car, but she needed a couple of Nurofen and a little time to compose herself before lying about it. She stared briefly at the front door and pleaded, *Please God, don't let me be sick in front of Mother.*

Before dragging her tall slender frame out of the car, she popped a couple of pills in her mouth and drank greedily from a bottle of tepid Evian water. She ate little these days, relying instead on vodka for her quota of calories. It worried her, because in her line of work her beauty was her greatest asset. She would have to watch the fucking vodka and force herself to eat more. She'd seen girls who had let themselves go, and the result had not been pleasant. Of course she could always throw in the towel, but she was not ready yet. "Just a few more years" was what she told herself and then "fuck you, boss," she'd be gone. Gone to a life of luxury, a life she'd craved for so long, and where a shiny new green MG would not be her only extravagance. She heard a shout from the garden and saw her mother hurrying towards her.

Get away from the bloody car! was her only thought.

Emma got out of the car and started running towards the garden, trying to ignore the thumping headache and the spots floating in front of her eyes. As she met her mother by the metal gate leading into the garden, she was doing a good imitation of a drowning fish.

"Darling, are you OK?" was Jill's first question.

"Fine, Mum, really fine. Just a heavy night," replied Emma, contriving to stand in such a way as to hopefully block her mother's view of the car.

Jill thought her daughter looked terrible. Half starved, no colour in her cheeks, and a definite glaze over her eyes. But she'd learnt to bite her tongue with her nonconformist elder daughter, and, contrary to what Emma had feared, there was no note of disapproval in her reply as she kissed Emma warmly on the cheek "I know the feeling, darling. Come and have a strong black coffee."

Emma hitched up her ankle-length brown skirt, exposing an elegant pair of Prada shoes, and slowly followed her mother into the house, thinking it wasn't coffee she needed—it was a bloody great slug of vodka.

"Thanks, Mum, coffee will be fine. How's dad? Got rid of that annoying indigestion has he?"

"Let's go into the kitchen then I'll tell you," Jill suggested, taking Emma's arm and leading her into the kitchen. They dropped down into the seats they always occupied when talking to each other. "He's not in the best of health, but I'll let him tell himself. He's looking forward to seeing you. He was complaining last night that he didn't see enough of you these days. It's such a pity you can't get down here more often; he misses you. But you're too busy, I suppose?"

"Well, you know, Mum, a journalist's work is never done and I have to earn a crust."

"A crust doesn't buy a car like that!" Jill exclaimed, spotting the MG in the yard through a window.

"Not mine," said Emma a trifle too quickly. "I've borrowed it from a friend."

"You're lucky to have such a wealthy and generous friend," said Jill with a 'pull the other one' look and making a mental note to ask more questions later. She was quite sure fledgling journalists didn't earn enough to buy expensive cars.

Emma gave her mother a weak smile and shrugged her shoulders. "I don't know why I bother to lie to you. If you must know, I've borrowed the money to buy it. Very extravagant I know, but it's great fun."

"As long as you don't get too deep into debt."

If only you knew! "I won't, and I think I'll pass on the coffee offer and go straight to dad. Tell you what Mum, why don't you bring two mugs to us. Where is he, upstairs?"

"In the sitting room," said Jill with some relief. She was in no mood to pursue the subject of the car.

Emma jumped from her chair and hurried out of the kitchen. Her mother's demeanour had her seriously worried. As she walked into the sitting room and saw her father she knew her concern was justified.

Tim was sitting in one of two chintz-covered sofas facing the French window that opened onto the lawn, giving him a view of the walnut tree and the vale beyond. Since the onset of his illness it was his favourite place to sit. The room was full of family photographs. Jill's father's watercolours and paintings of her horses shared the wall space. It was a warm, welcoming room, a room where Emma as a child had been at her happiest, but today she felt uneasy, about what she wasn't quite sure. It wasn't long before she knew the answer.

Her father looked thin, so pale, hunched up on the large sofa, smiling weakly at her. He looked old.

And he's only forty-eight! The words rang hollowly through her brain.

Without thinking she cried, "Dad, you look awful!"

Without speaking he patted the empty space beside him. "You don't need to tell me! Come and sit here and I'll fill you in on my health."

"I'm sorry, Dad, I didn't mean to say that."

"It doesn't matter."

Emma joined him on the sofa and leant over to kiss him. She was surprised how cold he felt. "You really aren't at all well." There was genuine concern in her voice when she asked, "Do you know what's wrong?"

He put a hand on her cheek.

"I do. Your mother and I saw the consultant yesterday."

"Oh God, I can tell it's something terrible!"

"I'm afraid so. There is no easy way to tell you...I have cancer."

"Oh shit! Is it bad?"

He told her everything then. All about the pains, his suspicions now confirmed by the specialist. The financial worries about the farm which he suspected had contributed in some ways to the cancer. And he poured out his worries about Jill."

When he fell silent Emma said in a hushed voice. "You will be cured, I know that."

Tim shrugged. "I'm in God's hands now."

"Well, I don't believe in God, but I do know a lot of people are cured these days," Emma assured him. "You hear about It all the time. I have a feeling right here." She touched her stomach, "that you are going to be okay."

Tim gave her a sad smile. "I wouldn't have a bet on it."

"Whatever. I've always thought you indestructible. No need to change my opinion now just because of some stupid lump."

Tim laughed. Emma's flippant outlook on life had always amused him. Perhaps it wasn't the right time, but what the hell—it cheered him up. "You're right. Some stupid lump won't get the better of me."

Emma grabbed hold of her father's hand, serious again. "And you better damn well believe that, Dad. We all love you and we're not ready to lose you."

Tim stared in some confusion at the tall girl looking at him, her hazel eyes wide with concern. He'd long held the rather disturbing view that Emma suspected there was something not quite right in their relationship. At times he'd tried to analyse where he might have gone wrong. But he'd never been able to put a finger on the reason for his unease, and had been tempted to believe Jill's assurances that it was all in his imagination. Looking at her now, with nothing but concern mirrored on her beautiful face, he was happy to believe Jill was right.

"Here's your coffee," said Jill, having waited until she guessed Tim had told Emma everything.

"Thanks, Mum. I think it's just what we need."

"You've heard it all now I presume"

"Yes, a real body-blow. I'm so sorry…Anything you want me to do, just ask. This is payback time."

"You're an angel."

"No, I don't think so, Mum, just a concerned daughter."

"And I love you for it," said Tim, wrapping his arms round her and smiling at Jill over Emma's shoulder.

••••••

There had been fleeting moments in her life when Jill wondered whether her decision to give birth to Emma had been the right one. There was a look about her that brought back painful memories. But now, as they shared their despair and fear of the future, any lingering doubt vanished forever. They sat silently holding hands, emotion transferring from one to the other, as they thought of the man they both loved. They heard him moving about upstairs as he got ready for another sleepless night and their eyes met as they both prayed he would not be too obstinate and refuse to take his pills. The silence was all embracing, even a little misleading, for it was easy to imagine that time was standing still and that it would never run out for Tim. It was, of course, an illusion. As they both knew, time stands still for no one.

••••••

Toria stood in the sitting room doorway, her blonde hair dishevelled by a gale blowing outside; a pair of jeans hugged her long shapely legs. "Mum," she cried, "You all right? You look shattered."

Jill rose slowly from the sofa and held out her arms. They hugged. "It's your father. Bad news from the hospital I'm afraid."

"Oh no! Tell me."

"It's cancer."

All colour drained from Toria's face. She rubbed her well-sculptured nose and her green eyes flashed concern. She pulled nervously at one of her earrings and shivered in her large woollen sweater.

"That's terrible!" She dropped onto the sofa next to her mother and covered her face with her hands.

"It's hard to believe I know," replied Jill fighting back the tears.

"Is he dying?"

Jill swallowed, brushed away an annoying tear and told her. When she'd finished there was a moment's silence while Toria digested the horror of what she'd just been told.

When she spoke, her voice was level and determined. "Right, for a start, I'm not going back to Durham University while Dad is ill, no way. He is far more important than my studies. I think I can defer for a year. I know several students who have done it. But if I can't, I don't care to be honest. Secondly, there is no way you can shoulder the entire burden. With me here full-time you will at least be able to have some time to yourself."

Jill was about to open her mouth to say Tim was going to make it without her messing up her college career but thought better of it. Instead she said, "I think that is a little drastic, but let's talk about it later after you've seen him."

"There is nothing to discuss Mum, my mind's made up." She rose to her feet. "Now I'm off to see dad. Is he in bed?"

"Yes, and probably asleep," replied Jill.

"I won't wake him. But I'd rather not wait until the morning to talk to him."

"He won't sleep for long—he's due more pain killers very soon."

"I'll sit by his bed and wait for him to wake. I just want to be close to him." Toria looked at Emma as she walked into the room. "Have you seen him?"

"Yes. I got quite a shock and wasn't very tactful, but he looks awful, so be prepared. I'll start supper while you and Mum go up."

"Thanks, Emma."

......

He opened his eyes as they came into the room. Jill looked worried. "Oh damn, I didn't mean to wake you."

Fighting the nagging pain that seemed to be enveloping his whole body, Tim mumbled, "I wasn't asleep, just waiting for the moment I could take some more of these useless pills."

"I'll talk to the doctor tomorrow," Jill promised. "You obviously need something stronger."

"Thanks" Then his eyes lit up as he saw his daughter. "Toria!"

She rushed to the bed and hugged him to her. "Mum's told me; I'm so terribly sorry." Then, gently pushing him away, she looked him up and down. She'd not been down from university for a month, and although her mother's frequent telephone calls had kept her informed of her father's illness she was shocked by how much he'd deteriorated in that time. His eyes were dull and sunk into their sockets. His brown hair was matted with sweat. His skin was pulled tight over his cheekbones and his shoulder blades were almost sticking out of his pyjama top. Just in time, she stopped herself exclaiming, '*God you look awful.*' Instead she said, "We'll have you right in no time."

"Of course you will," His voice betrayed his lack of confidence.

"No, I mean it," she said fiercely.

"I'm sure you do; now come and sit here," he said quietly tapping the bed. "It's probably not as bad as I imagine; sitting around plays hell with one's imagination. He reached out and stroked her hair as he always did when she came home. "This is just a little nuisance which will soon be over and then I'll be out hunting with you again."

"I'll hold you to that," replied Toria. "And I'm going to chuck in Durham and come home to help Mum."

"Oh no, you can't do that! You love it there, and besides you're doing so well. It would be a terrible waste to leave now and miss out on getting a degree."

"Nothing is more important than getting you better and Mum will need help. I understand how you feel, but what's some silly old degree in economics anyway? I may be able to get a deferment for a year. But really I don't care much. After all I'm going to farm, not be a high-flying financier in the city. No, I'm not going back for the time being. Nothing you or Mum can say will change my mind. You both need me here. I know Emma can't stay, what with her new job, so you've got me, like it or not."

"To have you here would be wonderful for your mother and me but I don't think—"

"Dad, just shut up. I'm staying."

Tim gave a resigned shrug of his shoulders. "I can see there is no point in arguing."

"You might as well save your breath."

A flicker of a smile crossed Tim's face. "You always have been a head strong young lady" He knew he should be firm and insist she went back to university, but the thought of her being at home was too tempting to be ignored. "Have it your way."

Toria turned to her mother. If she'd harboured any doubts about staying, the look on Jill's face wiped them away. "I've made the right decision," she declared, and her parents never said a word.

······

They sat in silence. There was no need to talk; their eyes said it all. They saw each other's sadness. Tim smiled every now and then, as he thought of Toria growing up—her tantrums—her youthful exuberance—her love of horses—her companionship, but above all else her gentle, giving disposition. Leaving Durham was what he'd expect of her. He studied her gratefully. Her fine cheek bones, her thin neck, her figure. She reminded him so much of her mother at the same age—long and lean and pretty, with life in her eyes. Toria sat very still, understanding that he was, perhaps, taking his last photograph of her.

"Penny for them?" asked Tim.

"I was just thinking how much I love you."

His face lit up with pleasure. "Just keep saying that won't you?"

"I suspect that's the easiest promise I will ever have to make, Dad." She drew him into her arms, shocked by the feel of his skeletal-like frame. She'd been blind to the seriousness of his illness for too long.

The voice of her mother calling from the kitchen cut into her thoughts and she pulled away from her father. "Better not keep Mum waiting, Dad; you know what she's like."

Tim chuckled raggedly. "Then you had better throw me my dressing gown quickly."

She picked the blue-striped woollen gown off the end of the bed and draped it over his shoulders. "Don't expect me to wait on you hand and foot, Mr. Foster."

"Oh, I will," he laughed. "And I will enjoy every minute of it!"

Once he'd struggled into the dressing gown (she was appalled to see how unsteady he was), she held out her hand and led him out of the room. "Now

I wonder what special dish Mum and Emma have done for us?" she asked, realising he was in pain.

It's at moments like this that I'll have to be strong and force myself to be cheerful.

She could not allow him to see or sense her distress. She had to convince him that he had a chance. She had to convince herself as well. Neither would be easy, but it would be her sole purpose in life until the last breath left her father's body.

Chapter Two

Jill was emotionally exhausted, glad to have a few moments on her own under the walnut tree. It had been nine months and three days since Tim had started the treatment. There had been moments of hope, like the blissful few weeks of remission when they both dared to believe that he was cured, only for that hope to be cruelly crushed by a fresh bout of pain. Now his fight had almost run its course, and Tim lay in a coma with only hours to live. Ever since they had walked out of the hospital the first time, she'd tried to prepare herself for this moment but with little success. Reluctantly, she tore her eyes away from his bedroom window, knowing that he was in good hands but still fearful that he might die without her by his side.

She played nervously with her fingers. At first she'd resented the presence of the nurse, feeling she was invading her private space, but the truth was that she and Toria could not cope, and the nurse had become indispensable.

Nevertheless it had seemed the final acceptance that Tim was dying. He would soon be buried in a teak box, deep in the damp earth, never to breathe fresh air again. Never to share a moment of love with her, never to enjoy a joke with his friends, never to see his children married. She moved restlessly on the bench, and once again looked up into the branches, as if for guidance. What would she do without the man she'd known for most of her life? The man who twenty-three years ago had rescued her from a nightmare and become her reason for living? How lucky she'd been; she must cling onto that thought for all it was worth. It would sustain her in her darkest hour, as the pain of parting and then the dreadful loneliness kicked in. He could so easily have married someone else. In fact, she was still surprised that fate had been so kind.

She stared at the branches gently swaying in the light wind, the swollen buds about to burst into life, and couldn't help comparing their freshness with the emaciated man lying in the house. She allowed herself a brief smile, remembering sipping her first glass of champagne with Tim on their wedding day, the tree's umbrella protecting them from the hot sun. It was the first of many important family occasions that had ended under this canopy. The girls' christenings, the birthdays, the Christmas photograph whatever the weather, and of course, the times she and Tim had sat and drunk to another year of marriage. The tree was an integral part of her life and thanks to Max's generosity would continue to be so. She stretched her weary body. She'd hardly slept more than four hours a night over the last three months. She looked at the mellow red brick of the house, the buds of the yellow climbing roses just showing the first signs of colour, and realised how lucky she and Tim were to have it as their home. At times her intense love for it surprised her, given the dramas that had been played out in its rooms over the years. Soon she would need its warmth and its familiarity to protect her from the shock of Tim's death. She sighed and rose stiffly from the seat. She'd been out of the house too long.

······

Jill glanced at her daughter's concerned face as she entered the room. She knew how she was suffering. Perhaps it had been wrong to leave her. "I'm sorry, darling. I didn't mean to be so long."

Toria threw her a weak smile. Don't worry yourself, Mum; you needed the break."

"Now it's your turn. Nurse and I can manage."

"Okay, but you will call me if he gets worse?"

"Of course I will. Are you going for a walk or what?"

"No, I think I'll go to bed and try to catch up on some sleep. Perhaps I should ring Emma first?"

"I've already done that. She's on her way."

"What about Max?"

"He'll be over soon."

"Then it's bed for me."

"I'll leave you as long as I can. And thanks, darling. You've given us such wonderful support."

"It was nothing. I would never have forgiven myself if I'd stayed at university."

"It was unselfish."

"It was only what any daughter would do."

Jill smiled. "Try and sleep."

"I will. See you."

Jill watched the door close before hurrying to the bed and reaching for Tim's hand. It felt cold, so lifeless, and she felt panic hit her as she threw a questioning look at the nurse sitting by the window.

The nurse read her thoughts and rushed to the bedside. She felt for Tim's pulse. "He's holding his own, Mrs. Foster."

Jill nodded. "But I don't think for much longer. Can you leave us alone for a while?"

"I'll go down to the kitchen and make myself a cup of tea. But let me say this before I go. I cannot diminish your overwhelming sorry and I hate my impotence. Always I am an outsider looking in on grief, but always I feel pain." The nurse ran her delicate hands through her short-cropped brown hair and gave a little shrug of apology. "I sometimes wish I could work miracles."

"I understand, Nurse. It must be terrible to watch other people's grief. I don't think I could do your job."

"Someone has to, and you get hardened. Anyway that's enough of that. Just give a shout when you want me back."

"I will, and when my father-in-law arrives ask him to wait, will you? He'll understand."

"I'll do that."

Once alone Jill climbed onto the bed and lay down beside Tim. She gently rested her head on his chest, feeling the familiar tickle of his hairs and hugged him close. There was no sign that he knew she was there. No movement of his body, or even a light touch from his hand as on other occasions. *The morphine has turned him into a vegetable,* she thought dismally. She clung to him like a limpet mine, praying that somewhere deep in his subconscious, he might know that she was there. The grief was like a living thing, invading her body and nestling deep within her marrow.

She didn't move until he died.

......

"It's almost impossible to believe he's gone," Jill said twenty-four hours later as she sat on the sofa in the sitting room with Toria and Emma curled up on the floor beside her. She'd said the same thing to a stricken Max a few hours earlier. He'd left an hour ago refusing her offer to stay. "I've been here long enough. If I don't go home I might never be able to leave," he'd confessed. "And you should have a little time alone with your children. Don't worry. I'll be fine."

"I arrived too late," said a distraught Emma.

"You can't blame yourself for that," comforted Jill.

"Perhaps not, but I would have liked to have said good-bye." Emma smiled weakly, inwardly cursing herself for the lost half-hour spent in the shower trying to sober up before leaving her flat. She laid her head on her mother's lap. "I'm sorry, Mum. I should have been here."

"Perhaps it was for the best. He wouldn't have recognised you. At least you have seen him at peace."

"I suppose."

Silence fell. There was nothing left to say. They had lost the man they loved and respected. The man that they sometimes had taken for granted, always being there to help them. They had thought he was indestructible.

······

The funeral was four days later in the parish church where Tim and Jill had been married and where their children had been christened. Her parents and Tim's mother lay buried in the churchyard. It was a church full of memories, and in spite of her devastation, Jill found a crumb of comfort from the familiar surroundings. Toria and Emma flanked her in the front pew. She stared as if hypnotised at the coffin resting on its plinth, the family's large bunch of white lilies lying on top of the polished teak. She felt very strange, almost confused, and utterly detached from the congregation behind her. She thought of her favourite poem by AA Milne that her mother had read her as a child. One verse in particular came to mind.

Wherever I am, there's always Pooh,
There's always Pooh and Me
Whatever I do, he wants to do,
"Where are you going today?" says Pooh...
"Well that's very odd 'cos I was too,
"Let's go together," says Pooh, says he,
"Let's go together," says Pooh.

'Let's go together.' Always, she and Tim had done things together. A perfect scenario would have been to die together, but Tim had departed on his own, and she was alone and very frightened.

"Mum," Emma whispered.

Jill started.

"The vicar's trying to catch your eye."

The vicar saw he'd got her attention at last and asked, "You ready, Jill?"

She nodded.

The vicar looked down at the packed congregation and began, "We are here today…"

Jill clutched her daughters' hands and felt them shaking.

Poor darlings, they are so brave.

They had had a tough ride but now it was about to end. The service was drawing a line between the past and the future. It was time to move on. She knew Tim would want it no other way.

......

The service over the congregation followed the coffin out into the strong sunlight. Tim was to be buried next to his mother. Jill stared into the hole, which seemed so threatening, so unreal. She wiped away a tear.

I said I wouldn't cry, I said I wouldn't cry.

But the tears rolled down her cheeks and she felt Toria's hand slip into hers. "Not long now, Mum," she whispered. "Then dad will be at rest."

"I hope so," she whispered back. She watched the coffin being slowly lowered into the ground and wondered if Tim could ever be at rest in such a dark, forbidding place. He'd so loved the sunlight, and the fresh air. He'd so hated being enclosed.

......

She stared blankly at the people milling round her—their words of condolence seeming hypocritical as they tucked into the trays of food and sipped at champagne with a gusto that appalled her. She knew she shouldn't be thinking like this. She'd invited them after all. She'd wanted to make them welcome and to thank them for their support over the last few months. But somehow it seemed unreal, rather like some charade being played out in front of her. She couldn't wait for them all to go home and leave her and the children in peace. She forced yet another smile at yet another couple voicing their sympathy, and noticed Max standing close by. As soon as she found a moment to be on her own she hurried towards him.

"Finding this a bit difficult?" he asked.

"Certainly am. Look at them, chatting away as if they were at a party. I wish I'd never asked them back."

Max put an arm round her waist. "You don't mean that."

"No, you are probably right, I just feel so down, not ready for this false bonhomie. Well, that's how I see it anyway."

Max looked round the room. "They're just trying to tell you that life goes on. Isn't that the way it's supposed to be?"

Jill inclined her head. "Maybe, but right now it seems so out of place. Oh, my God, look over there!"

Max saw the colour drain from her face and followed her eyes.

Standing in the doorway was a smiling Harry Sidenham.

"What the hell is that man doing here?" Max exclaimed.

Jill grabbed his arm. "I don't know, but I want him out of here pretty damn quick!"

"I'll get rid of him," growled Max.

"Dear God, he's seen me! He's coming over!" gasped Jill.

Max was shaking with rage. "Well, he's not bothering you!"

"It's too late, Max. I don't want a scene in front of all these people. I'll deal with him."

"Are you sure?"

She was far from being certain, but she said, "Yes, I'm sure."

"In that case I think I'd better make myself scarce. I might not be able to control my temper."

"I understand how you feel, but you know as well as I do that shouting at Harry only makes him more aggressive."

"I know, but he's beyond the pale coming here."

"Don't go too far away, will you?"

"I'll watch you," Max promised. "Now, here comes the toad, so I'm off."

As Jill watched Harry pushing his way through the chattering guests, she wondered if this was the moment Harry was going to choose to mess up her life. It would be in character to strike when she was at her most vulnerable. It was a chilling thought, one that made her feel her decision to face him alone was wrong. She looked round for Max, but she was too late. A hand clasped her arm. "Jill, don't run away, I've just come to say I'm so very sorry."

His voice sent a shiver down her spine. She swung round to face him. "You bastard Harry, what are you doing here?" Her heart thumped against her ribs, and she stood at bay like a hunted stag on Exmoor, her nostrils extended and her eyes radiating fear. "Get out, before I make a scene. You never liked scenes, did you, Harry? Let me assure you that this will be one hell of a bloody scene. How dare you come here today! You are not welcome."

Harry stared down at her, his eyes mocking her. As usual he was dressed impeccably; his slightly overweight body was dressed in a handmade grey pinstripe suit, blue striped Turnbull & Asser shirt, black silk Hermes tie, and Gucci shoes. His face bore the scars of too much drinking, red veins running from his cheeks to his eyes. Even in her state of panic Jill registered that he was going to seed.

"Brave words, Jill, but I know you better than you think. You wouldn't cause a scene and draw attention to me in front of all your friends."

"You are despicable!" She cringed and tried to back away.

"So you've said many times. Anyway this is no way to greet someone who has come to give his condolences."

Jill glared at his steel blue eyes and, gathering her fast diminishing courage, spat, "Oh, for heaven sake, Harry! Why lie? You hated Tim. You wouldn't be here if you hadn't an ulterior motive, and I have a nasty suspicion I know what that is."

Harry laughed. "What's this rubbish about an ulterior motive, what ulterior motive? Go on, tell me." He moved closer to her, his eyes glued to hers.

"Oh, Harry, Harry, don't play the innocent with me. You understand what I'm saying. Now, please get out. I don't want you around now or ever. Can you get that into your thick scull?"

Harry's face darkened dangerously. "Now, there's no need to talk like that Jill. Can't we be civilised about this? I'm genuinely sorry that Tim's died. I really am."

"You'd be the last person to shed a tear for Tim."

"How dare you!" he said in a level tone resembling irony.

"Oh, I dare Harry! Now for the last time, please go."

"Everything alright, Mum?" Toria's concerned voice asked behind Jill.

Jill turned with a smile of relief, (she was equally relieved it wasn't Emma.), "Yes, I think so, darling. We were just saying good-bye, weren't we Harry?"

Toria made no attempt to hide her dislike for a man she saw as a predator of married women and, as she had said to her mother, 'a total shithead.' She glared at Harry. "In that case Harry, let me walk you to the door."

Harry was boiling inside as he gave Toria an icy stare. "Very well, I'll go, but I don't need you to show me the door Toria. I know the way."

"But you were never welcome," Jill couldn't help adding as Harry turned to leave.

He whipped round quickly. If looks could have killed, Jill would have died on the spot. "I'll be back," he threatened.

"Don't even try, Sidenham," Max's voice came from behind Toria.

Harry turned a sardonic smile on Max. "Threats from you, Foster, don't frighten me." For a moment it looked as if he was going to confront Max. Jill held her breath; Max stood with his legs apart, his hands down by his side, daring Harry to move towards him. But then Harry shrugged and turned away.

Jill felt an overwhelming sense of relief as she watched him disappear. "God, Max, that was something I could have done without. That man is going to cause trouble."

Toria smiled sympathetically. "I'm sure he won't, Mum. I think you made it quite clear he's not welcome here. Whatever he once did to upset you must have been pretty serious."

"Oh, it was darling, it certainly was."

Toria didn't push the matter further, though not for the first time, she was thinking, *What is this thing with Harry and Mum?* Instead she said, "Well, you know how I feel about him—lecherous middle-aged Casanova. He may be around six-three, dress smartly, and no doubt is still very attractive to some women, but I find him disgusting."

"Which I hope Emma does as well," said Jill quietly, alarm bells ringing as she spotted her daughter through the window walking beside Harry.

I was right! This was the reason he came. It would be typical of the bastard.

"Don't worry Mum, Emma thinks he's an even a bigger scumbag than I do," Toria assured her.

Jill said nothing, but she asked herself, *I wonder what Emma would think if she knew?*

......

Emma had watched the confrontation with interest. Like her sister, she wondered why Harry got up her mother's nose. Jill was not the sort of person to bear grudges, but, boy, she sure held one for Harry. For as long as Emma could remember, his name had been taboo. Now perhaps, this was her chance to do a bit of detective work. She hurried to intercept Harry as he reached the front door. "Looks as if you were in a bit of trouble in there, Harry," she said amused.

Still boiling with anger, Harry snapped, "I don't find it very amusing, Emma."

"Well, never mind," she said unabashed by his obvious anger. "It would be rude not to see you off the premises and, besides, I hear you've got a new convertible Jag, which I'd like to see. I have always liked fast cars." *And you fascinate me and have a secret I want to know about.*

Harry's mood changed immediately. After all, Emma was the reason for his coming. Jill had been right on the button. He was delighted Tim had died. He smiled cheerfully. "Okay, come and have a look." They walked along the gravel drive to where he'd parked his shiny new silver Jaguar. "Like it?"

"It's cool, Harry, and although it may sound a little presumptuous, I'd love to have a drive in it sometime."

He favoured Emma with one of his most charming smiles, "Anytime, but probably not best to do it around here—you know, what with your mother watching. It would be nice to get to know you better."

"Well, we could meet up for lunch or something in Bristol where I work and I gather you have business interests there?"

Harry vaulted into the car. "Actually I only go there to see my accountant about three times a year, but it sounds a great idea. I can plan my next visit around you. Just give me a date."

"I'll ring you."

"That sounds brilliant. Here's my telephone number." He pulled a card out from his leather wallet.

Emma took it. "Thanks."

Harry blew her a kiss and gunned the engine. "See you, then," he shouted as he effortlessly slipped the car into gear and accelerated away from the house.

Emma watched the car until it disappeared, thinking that perhaps the next time they met she might dare to ask about the obvious bad blood that festered between him and her mother. But on second thoughts perhaps not—it might turn out to be something horrible, and if so she'd rather not know. The past was the past, and she had plans for her and Harry.

As for Harry, driving reflectively back to Sidenham, he deemed his afternoon to have been a great success. Jill had tried her best to humiliate him, the silly bitch, but what the hell. Had he ever cared about what people thought of him? What mattered was that he now had a chance to at last get his revenge. He'd waited a long time for the right moment to strike. Envy had eaten away at him for years. He hadn't expected her to be happy—to ignore him, to get on with her life as if he didn't exist. If it hadn't been for Tim, he was sure she'd have crawled back, prepared to do anything he asked, begging his forgiveness, and for as long as it pleased him he'd have kept her. Fuck Tim! But his death had changed everything—it had been a gift from heaven. Now he could start planning, and what better way to get at Jill than through Emma? He'd sensed her bold nature. She wouldn't be frightened to defy her mother—she was a risk taker, as she'd proved many times in the hunting field, tackling awe-inspiring jumps with a panache he admired. In the short time that he'd been able to talk to her, he'd sensed a certain electricity between them, and that, coupled with her attraction for danger might lead her to his door. He'd tread carefully. There was a lot more work to be done. One small mistake and he knew he'd risk losing her. The stakes were high.

His smile would have chilled Jill's heart. "Yes, yes, yes! He shouted as he drove up the long chestnut drive to Sidenham Hall. "It's payback time, Mrs. fucking Foster."

······

The champagne did little to calm Jill's nerves. Harry was not easily forgotten and his appearance had been threatening. There had been a message in his demeanour and it frightened her to death. Of one thing she was quite sure. In the not too distant future Harry was going to make a move. Harry would be better dead. She drained her glass and took another one off a passing waitress.

······

"**He**'s gone, Mum," Emma said quietly as she rejoined her mother in the dining room. "I thought it best if I saw him off. Wouldn't want him coming back here and upsetting you again, would we?"

Jill forced a smile, searching her daughter's face for a sign—a sign of what? Disquiet, anger, puzzlement? No, that was being paranoid. Harry wouldn't move so fast. He'd pick his time with care. He'd be far subtler. He'd worm his way into her affections and then strike like a cobra. "I don't think he'll come back in a hurry, darling," she said, steadying her voice with difficulty.

"No. I don't suppose he will," Emma said back. "I think he was pretty upset. A shame really Mum—after all, he is a neighbour."

Jill's eyes narrowed. This was not the sort of thing she wanted to hear, Emma hinting that Harry should be made welcome. Tim had made it abundantly clear to Harry that he was not welcome around his family, but he was no longer there to put a protecting arm around them all. It would be a different ball game from now on. She cursed silently under her breath. "He may be a neighbour darling, but an unpleasant one that is best avoided. Sadly, Harry takes after his father—selfish, amoral and dishonest. It's no good, him coming here and thinking he can make it up with me, now that your father is dead. I don't quite know how to put this without sounding like a bossy mother, but I would rather you didn't get too friendly with him."

Emma scowled. "I would understand better if you told me what's with you two. But I guess that's not going to happen?"

"It would serve no purpose. It all happened a long time ago. I would prefer to forget about that odious man as quickly as possible."

"He really gets under your skin doesn't he?"

"Yes. Now, can we move on to another subject?"

Emma felt a stab of irritation but decided to play it cool. She could see Harry anytime without her mother knowing, so why push it? "Okay, that's fine by me, Mum. It's no big deal. He's never had much to say to me, knowing how you and dad felt about him, but I can see why women find him sexy."

"I suppose he is—anyway to a certain type of woman. But as your father said, he's best avoided." Jill sighed. "And I could certainly have done without his presence today. Harry barging in like that has made the day worse than I ever expected."

"Well, the day is nearly over," Emma said, eyeing her mother's glass. Emma hadn't had a drink all day and boy did she need one. "And two fingers to Harry Sidenham," she lied with a smile. "And now I'm going to find a drink."

. . . . . .

At last they had all gone. The lingering smell of stale cigarette smoke hung in the down stair rooms, but the mess of nearly two hundred people had been cleared away. The drive was empty, the caterers' van on its way back home. With her shoes thrown off, Jill sat on the sofa in the sitting room wishing she'd asked Max to stay. The girls were curled up on the floor staring at a silent television set, drinking the remains of a bottle of champagne. Jill held a strong whisky in one hand. She was a little drunk and very emotional. It had been some day. All the sympathy, the smiles, the endless words of sadness had irritated her. It was totally alien to her normal sublime nature. She took another sip of her drink and thought of the man she'd kissed good-bye half an hour earlier. Like her, he was no doubt sitting alone and thinking of Tim. It was easy to forget how lonely Max would be. He deserved so much more, for no one had been a more devoted father or husband. But that was life, she supposed. Perhaps the farm partnership was just what she and Max needed two lonely people to keep their minds occupied. She shifted fretfully on the sofa and tried not to think of the future, which could have Harry worming his way into Emma's affection. It was at moments like these that she needed the calming influence of her mother. And thinking of her brought back memories—terrible, gut-rending memories.

Her life had been shattered a week after her sixteenth birthday, when her father had rung her school from the hospital telling her to get a taxi as quickly as possible as her mother had been seriously injured in the cross-country part of the three-day event at Badminton. It had never dawned on her that her mother might have been in danger. She'd competed all over the world for the British Equestrian Team and missed selection for the Olympics only because her horse had gone lame. Once at the hospital Jill had looked up into her father's red-rimmed eyes and said, "But she was such a good rider, Father."

"She was lying third after the dressage," he'd told her. "She thought she had a good chance of winning. So I expect she was pushing just a little too hard. You know how competitive she is. The horse fell at the Vicarage Ditch—tipped the top, and rolled on her. I'm afraid that even the best riders make mistakes sometimes."

Jill had sat by her mother's bed and watched her die.

It had nearly broken her heart. She'd lost her friend, her loveable, effervescent mother, and she'd dreaded the thought that she'd been left with her rather severe and autocratic father, and that all fun would disappear from her life.

Now she'd lost another friend, a man whom she thought would be with her for the rest of her life, there to protect her, love her, and see her through the good and the bad times. Suddenly he was gone. That was almost the worst, just a memory. One minute he was alive and laughing, touching and loving, and then nothing, just a heap of rotting bones. She gave a sad little smile, thinking that fate had not been kind to her.

PART TWO
1976–1977

Love is a universal migraine,
A bright stain on the vision
Blotting out reason.

Robert Graves

Chapter Three

The mist hung over the valley and the breath from nearly one hundred and twenty horses curled up through the still air to join it. Rain was forecast in the afternoon and Jill's excitement grew with the certain knowledge that scent at last would be good—it had been a disappointing month so far. There had been too many clear crisp days and in the dry conditions the hounds had struggled to hunt. She looked across at her father mounted on Churchill, his favourite black gelding. "It looks as if we might have a good day at last, Father."

"Certainly does, and about time too," Philip Bennett said with a smile. "This horse is getting a bit full of himself—needs a good gallop."

Jill felt his smile wash over her. She craved moments like these, when he forgot the world was going to pot, and that sinister forces he couldn't control were threatening his daughter. They were brief interludes to be savoured, and most occurred on the hunting field. She loved him, but wasn't sure he understood that. He was deeply aware that he could never take the place of her mother and Jill suspected he resented this. Since her death their relationship had been slightly strained, and as Jill spotted Harry Sidenham riding into the field she feared she was about to test their relationship to the full

As he spotted Harry, Philip scowled, his mood changing immediately. The lines in his rugged face squeezed in on his eyes. "Look at that young popinjay—surrounded by salivating women, all old enough to know better. The man is disgusting, and now Max tells me he wants to become joint master with us next season. Over my dead body, I say. I'm not having a fornicating immoral man like him sharing the responsibility of running the Hunt."

Jill suppressed a laugh, thinking back to the times when he'd told her she'd lose her tongue if she swore.

"What a disaster he'd be," Philip continued. "I blame him for a lot of what's wrong with this Hunt. Look at him now. All over the girls like a rutting stag. He should be castrated."

Jill reacted with unaccountable irritation. "Oh that's not fair, Father. I don't think you should be so intolerant of him. Look around you today. We're sitting in his field, drinking his port, surrounded by thousands of his acres, which we have the privilege to hunt over whenever we like, and tonight we come back to his magnificent house for the Hunt Ball. On top of that, he pours money into the Hunt, and although his friends may not be to your liking, he lends horses to loads of people in the area who wouldn't be hunting if it wasn't for Harry. Look how welcoming he is to the youngsters you keep telling me we need to encourage. He may not be your perfect gentleman, but he's a modern hunting man with new ideas, and we need a few more like him. So perhaps he has a right to apply for the mastership."

Jill watched her father's face redden. "I don't need your advice young lady. What do you know about him? Not a thing. So don't tell me what to do."

If only you knew, she thought. For a second she was tempted to tell him, her anger threatening to boil over at his intransigence. Harry might be a bit wild, but he wasn't pompous or boring, which at times her father certainly was especially when he was quoting the bible to her. But headstrong as she was, she bit her tongue, spotted Max, and rode towards him.

"That's right, just ride off," shouted her father, not caring that people were watching him. "Don't forget to come back here when hounds move off. We have a job to do."

She chose not to answer. Of course she'd be back. The annoying thing was he knew it. She squeezed her knees against the sweating flanks of Wellington, her fifteen-three bay gelding, and made her way over to where Max Foster sat talking to the Hunt secretary. "Morning, Max," she said, acknowledging the secretary's welcome with a smile. "This has the makings of a good day."

Max switched his full attention to his goddaughter. "Good morning, Jill. You look a bit flushed. Arrived late?"

"No. It's Father."

"Ah, say no more. He can be a miserable sod sometimes. But cheer up, it could be a good day and you've got Wellington looking splendid." He reached over and put a gloved hand on Jill's shoulder. "This mist, with rain threatening is very encouraging."

"I agree, and what fun it will be," said Jill, remembering when Jane, his wife had been killed in a hunting accident and Max had been tempted never to get on a horse again. It had been a close run thing. Seeing his wife killed in front of his eyes must have been horrific. "There are four things I love in life," he'd once said to a friend. "My farm, my hunting, my son and above all else, Jane. If I ever lost her, I don't know what I'd do." But Max came from tough Cumbrian stock, used to adversity, and after three months of mourning he knew exactly what he was going to do. "Carry on with life, which means hunting again, as Jane would want me to do," he'd told the same friend. "I'm not ready for the faceless man with the scythe just yet."

"And I'm back because of you," he'd said to Jill. She'd been too young to understand what he'd meant at the time. But when her mother had been killed, Jill realised exactly what Max had meant. She'd just been there for Max. He had been the same for her.

"Wellington could do with a good day," she said. "He's really getting a bit above himself."

"Which I hope that young man isn't," Max said, as Harry Sidenham rode up to them taking his hunting cap off to Jill and smiling at Max. "Morning Master," he said, before turning to Jill. "You look mighty pretty if I might say so, Jill Bennett. Hope you look as lovely tonight. You are still coming?"

"Of course, Harry."

"Good. I will expect a dance then. It might be fun to get a gang together for the reels as well. Will you join us?"

"Sounds a great idea, thanks."

"See you later, then. Enjoy the day." He dug his spurs into his chestnut thoroughbred and trotted off across the field, Jill noticing with an annoying stab of jealousy that he stopped by Cecilia Livingston who was reputed to have had an affair with him. She sighed loudly enough for Max to hear.

"You're still seeing him, then?" he asked, not slow to notice the electricity that had passed between them.

"Yes, whenever I can."

"Well, there's no good getting yourself into a lather every time you see him talk to a woman or you'll be a nervous wreck. If you fall for that type of man, you have to put up with his behaviour. Told your father yet?"

"No. It's a secret between you and me."

"Not for long, if you go on looking at him like that. Anyway, how long can you expect your father not to get suspicious? He guards you like the crown jewels, and how long has this been going on now?"

"Nearly six months."

Max shook his head. "Oh, you foolish girl, my advice is to come out in the open. No doubt your father will be very angry, but I'll try and talk some sense into him—but if he hears from another source…"

"He won't. We're very discreet, Max. We only meet when I'm in London, which as you know, is three days a week. As long as we keep it like that, Father need not know until Harry and I are certain about something."

"Which is?"

"Whether we want to have a permanent relationship."

"Dear God! You mean you're thinking you might marry him?"

"What's wrong with that?" asked Jill indignantly. "You are not being very encouraging."

Max shook his head. "No, I agree I'm not, because I just don't see Harry as the marrying type and settling down."

"He has to, one day, so why not with me?"

"You're wrong there. He hasn't got to settle down at all, and if he does I'd much rather it was with someone else." Max saw the disappointment in Jill's eyes. "I'm sorry, I shouldn't have said that, but you make sure he's not playing you along. Look at his record."

"It doesn't interest me."

"Have it your way. But let me ask you this question, and then I will shut up. Do you know how many girls' hearts he's already broken? Have you spoken to the two married women he enticed away from their husbands and then dumped, once the divorce came through? Do you know about his gambling and heavy drinking? Have you heard the rumour that he's short of money?"

Jill went deathly pale, replying, "I think you've said enough, and the answer is yes, I know he's wild. Yes, I know about the married women. Yes, I know about his drinking, and yes, I know some say he's short of cash. But I don't care—surprise, surprise I love him."

Max wanted to say, *Then you are a fool.* Instead he gave Jill a sympathetic smile and said, "In that case I'm wasting my breath. It's impossible to make a woman in love see sense, but watch him—please, please watch him. You're not the sort of girl I would expect to fall for a man with such a bad reputation. You're intelligent and normally sensible. So I must accept you think you're in love. But I also sense rebellion here—a sort of 'up yours, Father.' And that may be clouding your judgement. So don't jump in to the pot before you are sure, and don't be too proud to admit you were wrong. Although I've spoken frankly—maybe a little too frankly for your liking—I have only done so because I love you. Remember I'm always here for you."

"Well, I won't need you," Jill said defiantly. "It would have been nice if you'd found something positive to say."

Max smiled an apology. "I think we are about to move off."

"And I must go and find Father," Jill said, adding, "I know you mean well, Max—no hard feelings."

"Thank you, darling. Now, let's forget Harry for a while. We're here to have fun, and I must see to my duties. First 'draw' is the kale."

Jill saw her father coming towards her and she moved to join him, her disquiet forgotten. This was the moment she loved the best about hunting, when the adrenaline started to pump and the horse beneath her began to get agitated. No argument with Max was going to get in the way. Wellington snorted and pawed the ground eager to get on the move. Jill held him in check with some difficulty, as the mounted horses left the park. "The top left of the kale by the plantation?" she asked her father.

"Yes, you take that, and I'll go to the bottom right."

"I'm on my way." She dug her knees into Wellington's side. Hard muscle quivered, ears went forward in anticipation. She could feel the boundless energy beneath her. "This is it!" she whispered to him, and headed towards the kale just visible through the thinning mist. It covered an area of about ten acres, hard against a small plantation of beech and ash. It had been planted as kale for as many years as Jill could remember, and had always been the first 'draw' whenever the Meet had been at Sidenham Hall. Jill had hunted across the valley ever since she'd been five and knew it like the back of her hand. She cantered to her position. She looked across at her father fifty yards away, sitting motionless like a statue, his eyes already searching the dark green mass for a movement that might tell him a fox had been disturbed. Churchill, ears pricked, stood rooted to the spot, almost as if he knew any movement might ruin the day. She raised a hand to show her father she was in position and then turned to look down the valley towards the other end of the kale where the hounds were beginning to work. She could just make out the figures of Max and Harry sitting side by side eagerly awaiting the expected explosion of sound from the hounds as they scented their quarry. Not for the first time she was surprised that two men who reputedly loathed each other so much could forget all their animosity on hunting days. Behind them were the remainder of the horses, rippling muscles shaking, covered in glistening sweat, and wrapped in a cloud of steam. It was a sight that always brought tears to her eyes, and today was no exception.

Before turning back to stare at the kale, she allowed herself a quick glance at the enticing long line of cut and laid hedges behind her. She'd never forgotten the day her father had entrusted her to go on 'point duty' for the first time and she'd missed Charlie (the fox) coming out of the wood because she'd been watching two roe deer staring at her through the undergrowth. She had not been allowed to go hunting for three weeks. She watched two blackbirds fly low over the kale, saw a hare break cover to her right, and prayed that if Charlie was at home he'd come her way. She could feel the excitement building under her, and she gently put a gloved hand onto one side of Wellington's neck. "Easy, boy, easy," she whispered, knowing he was eyeing up the hedges, which she'd jumped so many times before. At first it had been on a flying little fourteen-two hands grey pony called Chester who hadn't known the word 'danger' and who'd dumped her in mud or wet grass many times when his enthusiasm had got the better of him. Then once she'd outgrown him, she'd been put on some of her father's mad thoroughbreds that had terrified the life out of her and 'buried' her heaven knows how many times. And then, at last, her father had said, "You're as brave and as mad as your mother was. You have earned my respect and a horse of your own." She'd never forgotten those words—it was very rare for him to compliment her on anything.

A week later, Wellington had arrived in the yard. She soon discovered he could jump like a buck, had brains (just a few), a healthy desire for self-preservation and the most wonderful eye for the country. She couldn't think of anywhere else in the world she'd rather be. Well—she smiled conspiratorially to herself—just maybe one other place.

She risked a brief look up to the top of the valley, remembering the days sitting on her pony with her mother by her side. "The best place to be, child," her mother had said. "You can see everything from here." Her mother seldom missed a thing. It had been the most wonderful education into the art of hunting that a child could want—watching hounds work, listening to the glorious sound of the huntsman's horn, and always her mother's voice explaining to her what was going on. On a good viewing day, when they could see for miles, her mother would sit quietly looking down into the valley for maybe half the day as the tabloid played itself out below them. Jill had learnt the art of patience, and it had been rewarded so many times by seeing nature at its rawest. It hadn't frightened her or tempted her to ask 'why?' Man had always been a hunter and so had the fox. They both understood the score and respected each other.

Suddenly there was no more time to think of her mother and her childhood; a hound 'spoke' not seventy yards from where she sat. She felt Wellington's flanks shudder and she stared at the kale. Soon the main pack picked up the pungent scent of the fox and the music echoed across the valley. It was a sound that stirred many a heart. She sat very still frightened to even move her head in case any movement might turn the hunted quarry back into the kale before he broke cover.

Come this way, come this way. Every nerve in her body tingled. She heard the music coming closer. Yes! Charlie was on the move! She glanced across at her father and saw him standing up in his stirrups. He'd seen something! She tightened her grip on the reins, as she saw the slightest movement of the kale leaves in front of her.

Don't move yet. He's coming.

The 'Halloa' when it came, was crisp and clear—unmistakably her father's. Charlie had moved up to the top of the kale and broken cover opposite him. She looked across and spotted Charlie twenty yards behind him moving down towards her. *He's not making for the plantation,* was her first thought. Her second was that if she moved she'd turn him back into the kale in front of the hounds and then it would all be over in seconds. She held her breath. Wellington stood frozen to the spot. His ears pricked and his large watery eyes fixed on the fox, which, in the matter of seconds, was within a few feet of them. He was a big dark dog-fox, totally unworried by their presence, his eyes shifty, aware of danger, but absolutely unperturbed. His back was wet from the damp kale and he glided past them without even a look in their direction. He didn't seem to have a care in the world. Jill waited until he was a hundred yards past her before she raised her hunting cap. Immediately, she saw the huntsman look up and turn towards her blowing *'Gone away'* as he cantered through the kale. "Follow me," her father shouted. "We'll try and cut him off. I know where he'll be heading." They flew across the old turf father and daughter charged with adrenaline, their horses at last free to do what they did best. Jill's father was making towards a small wood to try and turn the fox if he wanted to go that way. Today was not going to be a woodland hunt if he had anything to do with it. He wanted to feel the thrill of jumping hedge after hedge in the best grassland vale in the country. But Charlie had no intention of heading for the wood. He knew what he was about. With the scent good his best chance would be a quick dash across the grass and then weave through the flock of sheep at the end of the valley. Their pungent smell would confuse the hounds, and he'd make his escape. Seeing him cross over the first ditch, Jill knew what was in his mind, and she and her father reined in their horses to give the huntsman and the hounds time to catch up. Tempting as it was to go on alone they knew they might ruin a good hunt just for their own selfish pleasure.

Jill had had many exciting rides across the vale, but this one, with only her father and the huntsman in front of her was something different. The sheer speed that they took the hedges was breathtaking, but Wellington, as sure footed as ever was up to the challenge. Every time they landed on the other side of a hedge Jill gasped, "Good boy, good boy!" At times she would land level with her father and give a whoop of pleasure, which he answered by raising his cap and throwing her a quick smile before galloping on.

An hour and a half later they gave Charlie best. There were only twenty sweating horses left by then and Jill had jumped thirty-two hedges, two gates and six ditches. As she pulled up beside her father, breathless and shaking with excitement, she gasped, "Wow, that was quite something!"

"Best hunt this year. Wellington went well, I thought," commented Philip.

"Jumped like a buck. Wonderful horse—I was so lucky you bought him."

Her father grunted. He'd spotted Harry riding towards them. "And now my day's going to be ruined."

"Enjoy that Jill?" Harry asked as he drew up beside her, deliberately ignoring Philip.

He was breathing hard, his face red from the wind, and she thought he was the sexiest man she'd ever set eyes on. "Wonderful. Absolutely wonderful," she said, ignoring her father's scowls.

Harry gave her a broad grin and casually dropped a hand onto her knee, a gesture that her father observed with grinding distaste. "Well, the fox got away that time."

"Yes, and he deserved to," Jill added. She was secretly always pleased when he got away. In spite of the fox's reputation as a killer, she admired his intelligence and the crafty way he often escaped the hounds.

"Maybe, but the only good fox to my mind is a dead one," Harry said. "You can't afford to be too sympathetic. He's just a piece of vermin."

"Not much better than you then," Philip said, loud enough for the young couple to hear.

Jill glared at her father, certain that Harry would take the bait and start being abusive, which was just what her father wanted. But Harry chose to ignore the insult and continued, "And vermin need to be killed, that's the way I see it. Anyway, what about tonight, you going to dance with me?" He squeezed Jill's leg.

Her anger evaporated under his touch, and she felt quite sick with anticipation. She had a feeling that the next few hours were going to be something very special, and she wasn't going to let her father ruin the evening. "Of course, I'll dance with you Harry," she said, deliberately looking at her father. "No one is going to stop me."

With his blistering gaze rivetted to Harry's eyes, Philip moved his horse alongside his and said, "Lay a finger on my daughter Sidenham and I'll give you the beating of your life."

Harry laughed. "Just try it, old man, just you try it."

"That's enough, you two," cried Jill. "Can't you ever be civil to each other? You're both so bloody childish!" With that she turned away and spurred Wellington across the field. She'd ride home alone tonight—it was about two miles, and she'd not beat the light. But anything was better than driving home in the horsebox with her father. Damn him!

· · · · · ·

Jill watched Harry stride into the ballroom with a girl on each arm, and a smile on his handsome face. As he passed her on the way to his table, he pinched her bottom and whispered, "I like sassy women, see you later." Her heart nearly stopped. *Oh God, I could eat him alive!* She felt the now familiar stab of jealousy, as she watched him kiss one of the girls, but consoled herself with the thought that soon she'd be in his arms and have his full attention.

"Hi, Jill," a familiar voice said from behind her.

She turned. "Hello Tim, what a lovely surprise! Your father told me you were back, but I thought you were spending a few days with friends in London."

"I have been, but I wanted to come to the Ball. It's always such a good party."

Jill pecked him on a cheek. "Well, it's great to see you. How was Australia?"

"Great fun, but hectic and hard work. I'm glad to be home. I'm looking forward to working with Father on the farm. Anyway I've lots to tell you, and I want to hear all your news. How about if we sit together?"

"That would be great, and as far away from Father as possible. He really outshone himself with his rudeness today. I was wild. Quite spoilt the best day's hunting I've had for ages."

"Was it Harry?"

"How did you guess?"

"They are like two fighting cocks." Tim didn't add that he'd been told disturbing news whilst in London.

"I would call them childish. Anyway, can we talk about something else? I've really had a gut full today. How about telling me about the latest girl friend? Did you leave her crying in Sidney?"

Tim laughed. "I had no time for girl friends. Besides you broke my heart years ago. Don't you remember turning my marriage proposal down on your eighth birthday party? I'll be single for the rest of my life."

"Oh, Tim Foster, pull the other one! You only proposed because you'd just pinched my packet of smarties and wanted to stop me crying so that my mother wouldn't tell you off."

"I still love you, Miss Foster." It was said jokingly.

They both laughed. It had always been their way, lighthearted banter, quickly forgotten. But to his surprise, Tim couldn't dismiss what he'd just said so lightly. A year had changed her. She had blossomed into a strikingly beautiful woman. She had her long blond hair piled high on her head, showing off her delicate neck. He'd never seen her wear her hair in such a fashion. Her opaline green eyes seemed to have a little extra sparkle. He couldn't remember ever seeing her look so desirable. She seemed to glow. Was this what happened to a woman when she fell in love? Could she really have fallen for such a nasty piece of work? He felt a surprising stab of jealousy.

"Come on, Tim, let's sit down," Jill said. "My back's killing me after such a long day on a horse. If Father says he's got a seating plan, just ignore him. YOU are staying here. Apart from Father and Max, I don't know anyone on this table, and God forbid I land up next to Father! Next year, I think I'll bring my own party—I'm getting a bit tired of being guarded like a little girl. You'll come won't you?"

"You might not want me to."

She frowned. "Now what does that mean?"

"Oh, it's nothing really."

"You've never been one to be vague, Tim."

"No, really, it's nothing."

Jill decided not to pursue the subject further, instead asking, "You will dance with me won't you? That is, if I have any toes left after dancing with your father! I promised him the first dance."

Tim looked amused. "You poor thing, just make sure the band doesn't play too much rock 'n roll! But won't you be tied up with Harry after that?" He saw her go pale under her makeup, and silently cursed his stupidity.

Her eyes widened in surprise. "What do you mean? Is that why you went all vague on me just now?"

There was no way he could dig his way out of trouble. "Yes. I've been hearing things in London."

"Someone has been spying on me?"

Tim was quick to assure her otherwise. "It won't go further than me, but my friend Jack Gibbs, who I think you know, told me that he's seen you several times partying in London with Harry."

The constant hum of happy raised voices was in stark contrasts to how she suddenly felt. "Oh, I don't think so," she lied. "He must be mistaken." She fiddled nervously with her bag and looked over at where Harry was standing. He had a glass of wine in one hand—the other was stroking a girl's back. *Swine.*

"He was sure."

She couldn't take her eyes off Harry's hand. "As I've just said, he was mistaken. I've never been out with Harry. Yuck, he's a creep."

Her body language told Tim that Jack Gibbs had probably got it right, but he had no desire to push it further. He reached for a bottle of wine on the table. "Well, that's as it may be. Your life is none of my business. Want a drink?"

"Thank you."

He filled two glasses. "Jack always was a liar; he loves to stir things," he said lightly. "I'm sorry I mentioned it, and of course I'll dance with you later—*and* I'll come with you next year."

She managed to tear her eyes away from Harry and favoured Tim with a guilty smile. "I don't think you will want to."

"Meaning?"

"I shouldn't have lied to you, Tim. Jack was right. I am seeing Harry. I thought only Max knew. I assumed I was safe in London."

Tim's expression seemed to sour, as if the fun had gone out of their conversation. He took a long pull at his drink. "Does your father know?"

"Do you think I'm mad? I'm terrified of how he will react!"

He shook his head. "I don't think I would like to be in your shoes, and I'm so sorry, Jill—I'm totally out of order. It was very crass of me to mention Jack tonight or question you about your father. It just came out, and I can't even use alcohol as an excuse. Can we forget I ever brought the subject up?"

"Of course we can." She managed a laugh. "But make me a promise."

"That I keep my mouth shut?"

"Just that."

"You have my word."

She touched him lightly on a cheek. "You are a wonderful friend, Tim, and it's good to see you back. And I promise I'll dance with you right after Max has put me down—that is if I'm still in one piece!"

· · · · · ·

Max beamed with pleasure as he threw Jill energetically round the floor. That he was devoid of all sense of rhythm didn't discourage him. He danced the same whatever the tempo of the music, and that normally resulted in him hurling his unfortunate partners round the floor like dolls. He was totally oblivious to their discomfort. But tonight, Jill welcomed his madness, even though her toes were smarting. She needed the light relief, and soon found herself laughing in his arms, his enthusiasm irresistible and her concern evaporating.

"That's better," he panted as the music ended. "I didn't think you were quite your usual self to start with. Nothing to do with Harry, I suppose?"

"Tim knows about Harry and me. Apparently we've been spotted in London."

"Oh."

"That's what I said."

"So what are you going to do about it?"

Jill was about to answer, when the music changed to an old rock 'n roll number. "Ah, Jagger!" exclaimed Max gleefully, "No time for this sort of talk. Let's rock!"

Jill flew with him around the floor, glad to be at arm's length. At least her toes were safe. Max hurled himself this way and that, every now and then letting out whoops of joy and lifting Jill off her feet. Soon, he'd cleared the floor, and a crowd stood watching his antics under the shimmering lights of six massive glass chandeliers, clapping in time to the music and marvelling at Jill's agility. When the music stopped, a great cheer went up as they staggered back to their table.

"What an idiot," whispered Harry to a friend. "He should know better than to make a fool of himself in front of all these people. He should accept he's an old fool and stay firmly in his seat. He makes me sick. Come on let's go to the bar."

Back at their table, Max took out a large red handkerchief and wiped his forehead. "Exhausted?" he asked Jill.

"A little bruised," Jill laughed. "But that was great—just what I needed."

"So, you don't want to tell me more?"

Jill filled a glass with water, took a long drink, and smiled into his deep-set eyes. "I don't think this is the place. I shouldn't have said anything. Besides, it's sorted. Tim will say nothing."

"You're right, this isn't the place, but let me say one thing before you go off and dance with Harry for the rest of the night. If Tim knows, you can bet your father will hear soon. Nothing Harry does with a woman remains a secret for long."

"I thought we were being so discreet."

"You can never be discreet enough."

"No, quite obviously not," she said softly.

"So, tell your father."

"I'll try."

Max nodded. There was no need to warn her again. He'd said enough that morning. "You do just that; now come on, tonight we are supposed to be enjoying ourselves. What's it to be another dance or the champagne bar?"

"The bar," said Jill quickly.

Max laughed. "I hear Harry calling."

"Oh God, I'm sorry, Max. Is it that obvious?"

"Do I need to answer that?"

Jill smiled. "No, I don't think so." She picked her handbag off the table. "Are you coming for a drink?"

"I most certainly am—thirsty work this dancing."

Max took hold of her arm, and they wound their way through the crowded ballroom to the bar.

The noise was deafening as they entered the room. It was packed, a sea of animated faces, jostling bodies, touching, laughing and drinking. Jill searched urgently for Harry, spotted him a few feet away and shuddered. Max released his grip. "You've got it bad, haven't you?"

"Do you miss nothing?"

"I know how it feels to be in love. Let's go over and join him."

"Ah, Jill, you look fantastic." Harry beamed as they reached him. "Glad to see you're still walking after that exhibition by Max on the dance floor. Were you always so clumsy, Max?"

Max looked at Harry in disgust. "As there are women present, Sidenham,

I'll choose to ignore that remark. In any other circumstance I'd be sorely tempted to kick your backside."

Harry flushed. "Do you enjoy threatening me?"

"Enough," cried Jill. "Just for once shut up both of you."

Harry grinned at Max. "Do you hear the lady old man, shut up."

Max said nothing. His withering stare was enough to tell Harry what he thought of him. He gently released Jill's arm and walked away.

Harry blew out his cheeks. "Now we can go and dance."

"Not before she's had a dance with me," Tim's voice said from behind Jill. "Don't forget you promised to dance with me after my father had finished with you."

Jill blushed. She had forgotten. What was it with her? She stuttered, "I…I didn't see you there, and of course I hadn't forgotten. I'm sorry, Harry. I did promise Tim."

"Suit yourself."

"Or shall we have a drink first?" questioned Tim, knowing his intervention had infuriated Harry.

"Oh for God's sake, take the girl on the dance floor. I'm not going to wait all bloody night," growled Harry.

The two men squared up to each other, electricity flashing between them. They knew each other well. They were about the same size. Tim had lighter bones. Harry was a little bulkier. They probably weighed within a pound or two of each other. They were both handsome, attractive to women, but only one of them cared.

Tim made a huge effort to control his anger. "You're right Harry, I'm wasting time having a drink, and frankly I don't want to drink with you." He held out a hand to Jill. "Come on let's go."

"I can't wait," she said, feeling like pig in the middle.

"Good, because I hear one of my favourite tunes," said Tim glaring at Harry. "And as we haven't stopped for a drink we might have more than one dance."

"Please yourself. I like a woman to be warm," Harry mocked.

"You will wait for me," begged Jill.

"For you I'd do anything," smiled Harry.

Once out of the bar, she began to apologise. "I'm so sorry—I didn't really mean to say that. I love dancing with you. I just…"

Tim shook his head. "No apologies needed. Perhaps I shouldn't have asked you."

"Oh, Tim, for God sake!"

He kissed her lightly on her forehead. "OK…a stupid remark. But, what you see in *that* defeats me. He's a yob! Shit—I'm sorry, there I go again."

She smiled up at him. "That's okay, Tim; let's not fall out over Harry. You've never liked him; leave it at that. Let's just dance and enjoy ourselves. It will be good to be on a dance floor with you again, and I mean that—really, really good."

But as soon as they were dancing, he was left in no doubt where she'd rather be. The result was that they danced clumsily, like two strangers, and all the things he'd planned to say to her went unsaid.

As they walked off the floor, their silence embarrassed them both.

Harry intercepted them on their way back to the bar. "I was getting bored. That's your dance finished, Foster. Now don't bother us again. You ready Jill?"

Jill looked helplessly at Tim. "I'm sorry," she mouthed.

He gave her a frosty smile and turned away.

Jill forced herself to stay calm. "Did you have to be so rude to him, Harry? He's no threat to you."

Harry took her firmly by an arm and pulled her onto the dance floor. "How do you know?"

"Because I've known him most of my life, and he wouldn't behave like that."

Harry shrugged, bored with the conversation. "Okay, anything you say. Now I don't like sulky women, so what's it to be? Forget Tim, or are you going to spend the rest of the evening feeling sorry for him and in a huff with me? If so, you run back to your childhood friend now."

She felt totally ashamed as she replied meekly, "He's forgotten."

"Good, that's settled then. By the way, do you know that you're the most beautiful girl I've ever set eyes on?"

Not for the first time, she was taken by surprise at how quickly his mood could change. "You're a liar," she accused.

"I never lie to a beautiful woman."

"That's not what I've heard."

She was right. But this time he told himself he meant it, he really did think she was the most beautiful girl he'd ever held in his arms. The fact that he'd ditch her without a second thought was something that his amoral nature found totally natural. "Well, you shouldn't believe all the gossip you hear," he said with a smile. "Believe me, I don't flatter just for the sake of it. You *are* stunning, and all the more so when you're angry. You are angry with me, aren't you?"

"I was a little, but not anymore. In fact, I'm sorry I doubted you."

"Forget it. Now it's just you and me, as it should be."

She sighed as he pulled her close and ran a hand down her back. *God, he was quite something!*

He danced beautifully, his body so supple and his rhythm perfect. Any lingering guilt over Tim quickly disappeared. In fact, she found herself wishing he hadn't come back from London. He'd nearly ruined her evening. *Oh that is so unfair.* They danced a waltz, a rock 'n roll, and then slipped into each other's arms as the music moved into a more romantic mode. Jill felt the buttons of his hunt coat digging into her breasts and felt his hardness. She allowed her body to melt into his as they languidly moved around the floor. His arms held her tightly, and she never wanted to come out of them. But then her heart missed a beat. She saw her father glaring at her from the edge of the dance floor. *Go away. Stop spying on me; I'm a big girl,* she wanted to shout.

She closed her eyes, trying to forget he was staring at her, but when she opened them he was still there, a look of thunder on his face. "Damn!"

Harry pulled away. "What, what's the matter?"

"It's Father. Look at him, standing there with that disapproving look on his face. He'll have a real go at me when we get home."

"We can dance over to him and I'll tell him to piss off."

"No! Please don't do that, it would only make things worse. Just ignore him. He'll move soon. Let's move up by the band—then we can dance without him seeing us."

Harry was reluctant to move—he'd had enough to drink to readily accept a confrontation with the old goat. He'd just about had enough of old men trying to ruin his evening.

"I'll move if you promise me you will tell him about us."

She only hesitated for a second. "Okay, if that's what you want, but not tonight."

"You should have told him by now. What's the matter, ashamed of me?"

"No, of course I'm not. But we did agree that I would say nothing until we were sure about each other."

"Well, we are sure, aren't we?" Harry glided across the floor.

"Yes, yes, of course."

Harry abruptly stopped dancing. "Then tell him tomorrow. I'm getting fed up with discreet lunches in London, with your eyes constantly darting around the room like some fugitive." He started dancing again, but she could tell his mood had changed.

His rebuke hurt. She'd hoped he'd be a bit more understanding. "It's not that easy," she replied, showing her frustration. "I know he's a bit puritanical, probably a little possessive, which I don't blame him for. After all I'm all he's got left, but he's only doing what he thinks is best for me. He's been very protective since Mum was killed, maybe too much I agree, but I love him in spite of all his faults and I don't want to hurt him." Then she added boldly, "Let's face it, Harry, you wouldn't be his number-one choice as a son-in-law!"

Harry showed his irritation. "Well, fuck him, I say. You're old enough to make up your own mind. He lives in the past, his head buried in that beloved bible he's constantly quoting to people, and sees me as the devil trying to influence his daughter. But he has no right to say whom you can and can't see. Frankly, it's him or me."

It was Jill's turn to come to a halt. "Harry! That's brutal! I can't desert him."

"Tough, the choice is yours."

"Are you putting a pistol to my head?"

"That's exactly what I'm doing," Harry said callously, swinging her in a circle.

Jill looked at him defiantly. "It can't happen like that. I love you both." She was aware she sounded desperate. "I may be able to talk him round. But I need to find a quiet moment when he's in the right mood."

"That will never happen."

"Oh yes, it will! It has to! I don't want to lose either of you."

His smile frightened her, and as he guided her away from the band she felt his nails press into her back, making her wince with pain. Was this the Harry that Max and her father were constantly warning her about? She wanted to cry. It was so unfair. Why couldn't she be happy? Why couldn't Harry and her father bury their differences? "I'll sort things out," she said weakly as they reached the edge of the dance floor.

The pressure on her back eased, and he smiled down at her. "You do that. Now I feel we've exhausted that subject, and I'm parched. What about you?"

Jill's gut feeling was to say, "You can't leave it there," but thought better of it. She didn't want the evening sliding into total disaster. Instead she just nodded her head.

"I take that means yes," Harry snapped.

"Yes!"

He put an arm round her waist. "Do I detect a little temper?"

"No!"

"Good. Let's go to my table. The bar doesn't appeal to me at this time of night—always full of inebriated young men."

Once back at his table Harry filled two glasses with white wine from a half-empty bottle and handed one to Jill. "Sorry the glass is second hand."

"It doesn't matter," she assured him. "I'm not fussy what I drink from, and I need this."

He laughed. "Yes—a bit edgy, aren't we? Not at all what I wanted. Let's start again. To us." They clicked glasses and drank greedily.

"To us," said Jill, adding, "You dance beautifully."

"Thank you." Harry leant up against the table, stretching his long legs out in front of him. "My mother was a good teacher. She once said that I would never be short of a girl if I could dance." It was the first time he'd mentioned his mother. He'd talked a lot about his father—especially about his wild parties at Sidenham Hall and his solitary drinking bouts at the pub, which eventually caused him to drive into a tree on the way home for Harry's twelfth birthday. It took a power hose to wash the last remains of his father off the bark.

"Was she a good mother?" Jill risked asking.

Harry's eyes darkened. "Not was, is, and the answer is 'no'. She's a shit of a mother. I haven't seen her for the best part of ten years. Walked out of the house a week after my father was buried, saying she'd never come back, and she has been as good as her word. She left me to be brought up by my father's dreadful sister Maude, who it turned out was a lesbian. She was a tyrant. That's the only word to describe her. I threw her out of here five years ago." He grimaced. "Just to think of her makes my flesh crawl."

"Yes, I remember meeting her. I thought she was a bit odd, but I shouldn't have asked about your mother."

"No worry. I'd have told you sometime. I don't know who my mother hated the most, my father or me."

"She hated your father?"

"I think she would have killed him if she'd thought she could have got away with it. She couldn't stand his infidelity or his drinking. He humiliated her from the moment they got married. Do you know, he took an ex-girlfriend with them on their honeymoon? He screwed her more times than my mother. They hardly spoke to each other after that! Maybe that's an exaggeration, but when they did speak, it was normally to fight. I remember the house ringing to their angry voices. To my knowledge they never went anywhere together, and I'm sure the only time they slept together they conceived me! Christ, with parents like that, it's surprising I'm so normal."

That's not what I've been told, Jill reminded herself, but his handsome features and his self-assured manner overcame such reminders. She studied his dark eyebrows and the very white surfaces of his corneas. *He is a beautiful specimen of a man.*

"Your mother, where is she now?" she asked.

"She's living with some young guy half her age in Paris when I last heard. Always preferred young studs, did Mother. But it won't last. She's had so many lovers, I've lost count."

"Do you miss her?" Jill took a large swallow of her drink, thinking that no wonder Harry was a little strange.

"That's a difficult question. Perhaps the best way to answer you is to say that before my father was killed I felt terribly sorry for her, which led me to hope that we'd get on like a house on fire, once he was dead. What a little fool I was. I remember the day after my father's accident kneeling by my bed thanking God for relieving us of a monster, and imagining that my suffering was over. In fact, it was only just beginning, for to my horror I discovered my mother had no intention of loving "her bloody nuisance of a child," as she called me. Even now, after all these years, I can sometimes still hear her telling me that she cursed the day I was born and that she'd prayed for months she'd miscarry. How about that coming from your mother! But that's water under the bridge now," he said with a smile, "and it's time to knock back this tepid wine which is turning my stomach, and take the floor for the reels. I can see the others coming over here."

Quickly she asked, "What about Aunt Maude?"

"She died two years ago. She was drunk in Glasgow and got run over by her lesbian partner. As far as I know the lover is still serving out her sentence."

"I'm sorry, Harry; what a terrible story. I had no idea you'd gone through such hell. I can't imagine what a childhood must be like with parents that don't love you. Would you like to see your mother again?"

"No."

Jill sighed. "Well, it all sounds too sad for words, and now you have to put up with this gossip about your private life."

Harry shrugged resignedly. "It doesn't really worry me. The Sidenhams have always had a bad reputation. It's jealousy if you ask me. But we'll show them won't we? We'll be the happiest couple in the county and make all those doubting Thomas's out there eat their words."

A smile and a nod had to be sufficient, for at that moment they were surrounded by the rest of Harry's party. He made quick introductions and then hurried Jill onto the floor as the first reel was announced.

As they stepped onto the dance floor, any doubts that she might have had a few minutes earlier left Jill. She quite simply loved him. To hell with her father's disapproval and Max's dire warnings. It was her life and she'd live it the way she wanted to. If her father didn't come on board, well, too bloody bad. She shivered as Harry's fingers traced sensuously across her naked back and she felt her nipples harden against her bra. Life with Harry was going to be wonderful.

"Tonight?" he whispered.

"Tonight, Harry."

At last she was going to sleep with him.

······

She sat breathlessly on a marble seat in the conservatory where he'd led her after the last reel. If the evening had looked doomed, it was now positively the reverse. It had been a long time since she'd enjoyed herself so much. "This is my favourite spot in the house," Harry said with a hand laid nonchalantly on her thigh. "As a child, it was where I could hide from my father. Now it is where I come if I want peace and quiet. I never bring a telephone in here and won't allow the staff to disturb me." He took a long drink from his glass. "Thirsty work, these reels."

"Very," she replied, wiping her forehead with her lace handkerchief. "What fun Harry! I've even managed to forget about my father for a while."

"Glad to hear it. So while the mood lasts, how about one last dance?" He glanced at his watch. "It's two a.m. The band stops in about half an hour."

She jumped off the marble seat. "What are we waiting for then?"

Once on the floor, he drew her close immediately, and she laid her head on his shoulder. He smelt a little of sweat, but that only increased her desire. "Oh, Harry, Harry," was all she could whisper as she felt his urgency.

He gently took hold of her hair and tilted her head so that their eyes met. "Don't forget your promise."

"As if I ever would," she croaked.

"When can I expect you?"

"I'll take Father home and come straight back."

"I've a better idea"

She couldn't hide her disappointment.

"Don't worry I'm not going to sleep with anyone else. I just don't want you sneaking out of your house like some naughty child. Come over around ten for breakfast, that way he won't ask any questions. Besides, I like having breakfast in bed with a beautiful woman."

Could she wait that long? But what he said made sense. She didn't want to make love with him for the first time with her father's disgust ringing in her ears. And what did a few hours' difference make? Her head was spinning and her heart seemed to be fluttering out of control. She'd waited for this moment for what seemed forever. Now at last, she was going to feel the hardness of his body, not through his clothes or a fumble in his Aston Martin, but gloriously, sensuously naked.

"Well, are you going to come?" he was saying.

"Sorry, Harry, I was just wondering if I could wait that long! Yes, I'll be with you around ten."

He kissed the top of her head. "Has anyone told you that you have the most beautiful eyes and that you dance quite superbly?"

"Yes, you, only an hour ago!"

"Did I? Must be going soft then!"

She laughed a little nervously and held him that little bit tighter, thinking how wonderfully attractive he was, so sure of himself, so desirable. Could she give him what he wanted? Could the gossips be wrong or would she be discarded like so many girls before her? It was only a passing thought, as she felt his nails run down her back. She gave a long contented sigh and allowed herself to be transported into heaven, oblivious of nearly a hundred pairs of eyes watching her. When the music stopped, they stood unmoving in the middle of the dance floor for several minutes, neither wanting to break the spell.

"Wow!" Jill exclaimed, looking up at him with watery eyes.

"And soon we will be in bed," Harry whispered into her ear.

"I can't wait," Jill whispered back, spotting her father staring in their direction. "But before that I think Father may have something to say. He is not looking too pleased. Here he comes; stay with me, Harry."

Harry glanced in Philip's direction. "I think I may have ruined his evening, but I'm not going to give him the satisfaction of seeing me bolt like a rabbit. Leave this to me."

Alarm bells started ringing in Jill's brain. "Please, Harry, don't make a scene."

"It's tempting, but I won't."

Philip stood tall and dignified, containing the fury that was burning inside him. "Good evening, Sidenham," he said caustically. "It's time for me to take my daughter home."

Harry's eyes mocked Philip as he pushed Jill towards him. "Take her. Thanks for the loan." He bowed to Jill and turned away. She watched him disappear, fighting back the tears. She had not expected such rejection. How could he walk away and leave her? How could he change so quickly? Confused and hurt, she glared at her father.

"You behaved like a whore tonight," he said quietly.

"If you think that too bad, and I don't care." She was seething with anger. "You may have just ruined everything. How dare you do that?"

"Dare! I'll say what I like my girl, and what's this about everything? You got something going with Harry? Jill watched him shaking. "By God you've been deceiving me." He took her roughly by an arm. "I never thought you'd hide something like this from me. "It's time to go home, and have this out face to face."

Jill felt a strange, tight sensation in her chest as she looked at her father. She had never openly defied him before, but she was about to do so. It gave her an aching sense of loss and a strong desire to cry, and she realised why. Harry had been right. She couldn't have them both. "No, I don't want to go yet!" she said defiantly.

Philip glared at her, fighting to keep control of his temper. "Don't you dare defy me, child! What's more I forbid you to ever see Harry again. He's no good. He's an adulterer, a drunkard, and an atheist. And you...you are a disgrace."

Jill stared at her father, speechless, aware that they were attracting attention from couples standing nearby. Philip noticed the stares as well and pulled her towards the door. "No more arguing—you're coming with me! I don't want a scene here," he whispered with a biting urgency.

But Jill was high on champagne and sexual desire. She wrenched her arm away. "You can't order me around, Father. And don't call me a child. I'm old enough to make up my own mind. I'll leave when I'm ready. And don't insult Harry like that. I love him." There the words were out.

Philip's control snapped. In front of hundreds of shocked couples making their way out of the Hall, he struck his daughter twice across her cheek. A collective gasp went up from the watching crowd. A deathly silence followed. Jill didn't cry out, just stared at him, hurt and disappointment in her eyes. "You shouldn't have done that, Father." She looked around for Harry, saw Tim staring at her, mouth hanging open and then spotted Max. She made to run towards him, but Harry suddenly appeared in front of her, a smile on his face, and his arms held out to her.

"I see you have made your choice?" he said in a triumphant tone, loud enough for all to hear. For a moment, she allowed him to hold her tight, before she pulled away and turned to face her father. "I won't be coming home tonight, Father. I won't ever be coming home again."

The devastation etched on his face would haunt her for the rest of her life.

······

When she woke later that morning, alone in Harry's four-poster bed, exhausted and with a headache threatening, Jill regretted her outburst. It had been wrong. It had been hurtful. There was no way she should have humiliated her father in front of his friends. She anticipated his wrath, and despite the warmth of the bed, she shivered. She touched her cheek, remembering the shock as his hand had struck her, how she'd unforgivably forced him to act so out of character. She remembered her last words she'd spoken to him. "*I won't ever be coming home again.*" He'd have been devastated. In the heat of battle she'd not paused to think—she feared she'd opened a rift that might never be healed.

Now, here she was lying in Harry's bed, just like the whore her father said she was. She touched the indentation on the pillow where Harry's head had rested until a few minutes earlier, and hoped he'd prove to be worth the seemingly inevitable sacrifice. She sighed as she thought of their wild coupling once they were in his bed. It had been so exciting, so addictive. Her skin crawled at the thought of him doing it all again. For the best part of five months she'd been waiting for him to take her to his bed. She'd imagined it would be tender, soft and so deeply loving. Well, it hadn't been that! But, she was not complaining. No doubt once they'd worked the lust out of their systems, the tenderness would follow. She stretched her long lean body and thought briefly of her father, no doubt pacing up and down his kitchen, clutching his bible and praying for her salvation. He'd be wondering where he'd gone wrong. It would be in character for him to be blaming himself and that made her sad. It was a two-way thing. They'd both made mistakes.

She rolled over and buried her head in Harry's pillow, wondering if she could patch things up. But of one thing she was certain: She'd not drop Harry for anyone. Already she was yearning to feel his hardness again. Why did the stupid man have to go for a cup of tea? She wanted him beside her, telling her endlessly that he loved her. She tried to relax by running her toes up and down the silk sheets. It didn't work. She threw off the covers deciding to go to the bathroom to wash the remains of their lovemaking off her body. But as she moved past Harry's long mirror, she caught sight of her nakedness, her long hair caressing her breasts. She moaned and touched her hard nipples and moved back to the bed. She didn't want to wash Harry's semen off her body. She wanted it there forever. As her father had said, she was behaving like a whore. She'd thrown herself at a man with the worst reputation in the county. How could she have been so brazen?

What have I done?

There was still time to pull back. Just dress and run, she told herself. Surely her father would forgive her if she told him she was finished with Harry? She looked round for her clothes—spotted them in an untidy heap on the floor and started to laugh. She had no transport. Even if she had the energy, she'd look a bit foolish walking the six miles home in her ball gown! She'd have to ring Max—reliable Max. She jumped out of bed and started to unravel her underclothes from her dress. What a state she must have been in! She was a sensible girl from a conventional family, not the wild flirtatious type that Harry loved to have around him. She was not for him. *Max was right. I was a fool.*

But then she caught sight of a photograph of Harry sitting on his horse and thought of what she might be losing. For Harry wouldn't be rushing round to ask her back if she cut and ran now—not his style at all! What was she thinking of? Of course she didn't want to go home. She was not being honest with herself. She wanted Harry above all else. He had lit a fuse, exposing a side to her character that she hadn't known existed. She picked up her silk panties off the floor and pulled them on before moving back to the bed and stretching out on top of the duvet. She couldn't wait for Harry to pull them off again.

"Ah, what a sight," Harry said from the bedroom door a few minutes later. "It's pure perfection."

She rolled onto her side. "You might have knocked," she laughed.

"What, and miss the best sight I've ever seen? You look damnably sexy if I might say so, Miss Bennett."

He put the tray of tea down on the bedside table and threw himself down beside her. "My God, you smell incredibly raunchy."

For a second she stiffened at his touch. He felt her resist, suspected what was in her thoughts and gently rested a hand on one of her breasts. "This is not the time to have second thoughts," he whispered in her ear.

He kissed her on the mouth, harder and with more passion than earlier. Something in her moved then—something she'd never experienced before. She pushed her tongue between his teeth, moaned and knew she was lost. This time he was gentle, so slow, and just perfect. So absolutely wonderful! Jill allowed herself to be carried off the earth onto a different planet where life was an endless roller coaster of pleasure. Where warmth and love came wrapped in large, soft parcels. Where earth became an alien planet threatening this perfect place, this heaven that she'd often dreamed of, but had never believed she would find. Far beyond where her brain could think rationally, she was transported into ecstasy.

......

Three hours later, she was luxuriating in Harry's bath, steaming hot water lapping at her neck, a glass of chilled Krug champagne in one hand and a cold chicken sandwich knocked up by Harry in the other. He sat opposite her, his face red from the heat, gently massaging her feet, and every now and then, a hand would stray to her thighs. *Oh God, will this bliss ever end?* All thoughts of her father, of Max, of what people might think were drowning in the steaming water of the bath.

As she smiled back, she marvelled at the change that had crept up on her. Six months ago she'd been happy with her lot, content to be what she would call an ordinary country-type girl, helping her father, loving her horses, and working three days in London for a smart estate agent—the head partner a good friend of her father's. Her ambition in life had been to have children and eventually take over the farm from her father. Her horizons were limited, she knew that, but didn't care. And then she'd met Harry, and her horizons had exploded. It was heady stuff. She closed her eyes, and responded to his touch, reflecting that her innocence was over and that perhaps she had not changed for the better, but what did she care? Her mundane existence was gone forever.

Chapter Four

The sound of the huntsman's horn echoed across the wide valley, a hint of snow drifted with the clouds. Max and Philip, both eight, ran eagerly behind their fathers, excited by the sound of the horn and the cry of the hounds. But today there was an air of sadness surrounding them, for the next day they were off on what Max's father called *'a great adventure.'* So it was the last time they would be on the hill. The last time they would thrill to the huntsman's notes, or feel the excitement as the hounds scented their quarry. It was the last time they would run with their friends, battling against the elements, trying valiantly to keep up with their fathers. For, by the time the next hunting season came round, they would be hundreds of miles away from their birthplace. It was to be somewhere south of Birmingham wherever that might be, their fathers having been successful bidders for two neighbouring farm tenancies on the Sidenham Estate in Gloucestershire. Their world was about to change and both boys were filled with foreboding.

But who were they to argue with their fathers? Young voices made little impact. What did they know about financial matters? What did they care about a warmer climate where the lush grass would fill the bellies of their livestock? What did they know about the hardship suffered by their parents as they had tried to chisel out a living from three hundred acres of the unforgiving Cumbrian environment? It was a harsh place to live and made for a hard and uncertain existence, their lives dominated by the extremes of weather. They survived on the edge of poverty. But this meant nothing to the boys. All they thought of was what they would miss. Like searching up the hills for the first sight of the fox, laughing with their friends, the fights at school, the conker competitions in the autumn, and building a snowman when the first snow settled. It was all very well, being told they would be happier down south. As far as they were concerned, they were happy enough already.

· · · · · ·

Twenty-four hours later, as they passed Penrith in a heavy snowfall and headed south in the cattle lorry, with his mother following behind in the battered old Ford, Max felt his father's hand on his head. "We are doing this for you, Max. You wait. One day you'll thank me."

Max looked miserably across at his father and decided it would be wise to say nothing. His heart was broken. For the first time in his young life he did not believe his father. He was resigned to years of misery.

· · · · · ·

A few years on, he had to apologise. The Sidenham Estate had given both families all they could have wished for. They had financial security, fertile land under the bellies of their livestock, and the added bonus of a food-starved nation. Max even found 'the foreigners' as he and Philip had called them, surprisingly friendly. The hunting wasn't bad either, though they missed the music of the hounds echoing across the hills. Their fathers thanked God every day for His generosity, and as they slipped into old age, the two men never missed the chance of reminding their sons that but for the grace of God they would still be shivering on the hill. Philip's father, a deeply religious man, told him endlessly that, "God is smiling on us because we are good Christians. Remember that, boy, as you grow older, for God does not reward everyone on this earth." It was something Philip was never to forget.

· · · · · ·

Five years after the last of their parents died Max and Philip were summoned to see Harry's father, Jake, the third Earl. He was an overweight man with a shock of red hair and small bilious eyes, which peeped out from under heavy eyelids. He was a renowned philanderer, copious drinker and reckless gambler. The number of women he'd lured into his bed was legendary, and every now and then, his immoral ways landed him in trouble. This time, he was deeper in shit than usual. He was faced with the threat of court action and possible prison if he didn't pay a considerable sum to a distraught girl who was accusing him of sexually assaulting her. As he'd been drunk at the time, his defence was weak. If that wasn't bad enough he was under threat from his wife to go public over all his other misdemeanours, if he didn't settle. "And I'm sure the press would like the bit about your young whore on our honeymoon," she'd said with relish. With such unpalatable choices and no recollection of the supposed assault, Jake had little option but to agree a sum with the girl's father. How he was going to find the money was another matter. Always short of cash, he reluctantly decided he would have to sell some land. It would be a blow to his pride, but the alternative was too appalling to even contemplate. The estate encompassed nearly six thousand acres. Max and Philip tenanted two outlying farms of some thousand acres each, five miles from Sidenham Hall. Jake decided this was the perfect land to sell.

Sitting behind his desk in the Estate Office, he glared at the two men, making no attempt to be civil. "I've decided to offer you the freehold of your farms. This is the price I require." He passed each of them a sealed envelope. Unable to believe their good fortune, they asked for a few days to consider the price and talk it over with their wives. "It will depend if it makes financial sense," Max said.

"I understand. You have a week," said Jake, standing up from behind his desk and reluctantly shaking their hands, before waving them towards the door without another word.

By the time Max and Philip returned five days later, Jake's fingernails were bitten to the quick and his eyes more bloodshot then ever from lack of sleep and from his heavy hand on the whisky decanter. "Well?" he enquired, as soon as the two men were in his office, not bothering to offer them a seat.

Max smiled at him, enjoying his obvious discomfort. "We think your offer very fair, on one condition."

"What is that?"

"You include the sporting rights."

Jake nearly choked at the audacity of the man. "The sporting rights are not negotiable."

"In that case, there can be no deal," replied Philip, speaking for the first time. "It's all or nothing. Think about it, Lord Sidenham, and then come back to us." They left Jake as uncivilly as they had been greeted, leaving him with mouth hanging open and reaching for the whisky decanter.

The two men had known Jake would balk at selling the sporting rights but had made the decision to gamble, pretty certain that they held a winning hand. Jake was appalled. It was bad enough to have to sell the land, but to give up the sporting rights over two thousand acres was not something he'd bargained for. Surely, to be offered the land was good enough for two uneducated northerners? What on earth did they know about shooting? They probably didn't even have a shotgun between them. But it might take months to set up a sale, and he wasn't too sure his wife or the girl would wait. In spite of his many flaws, Jake was a realist, and the stark fact was that he was cornered. Muttering obscenities under his breath, he slammed his fist down on his mahogany desk and decided he'd have to ring the two men the next day.

At nine the next morning, they were back in the Estate Office to be met by Jake, still muttering obscenities under his breath and conceding defeat with ill-concealed bitterness. Unknown to them, he'd also decided that they would never have the guts to stop him shooting over their land.

This was a bad misjudgement, bred out of arrogance, because it was in order to keep him off their land that the two men insisted on the clause. They'd watched for long enough Jake treating their fathers like some inferior breed, hardly ever bothering to say as much as *'Good day,'* or *'I hope you don't mind'* as he drove his rich friends over their fields on shooting days. Perhaps, if he'd bothered to ring them up the night before or invited them out for a day, things might have been different. But Jake cared nothing for any of his tenants. The inferior class, as he called them. So Max and Philip saw this as a moment to be rid of 'the rampant Earl.'

It was not long after the contracts had been signed that Jake discovered his plan had failed. On a depressingly wet August day when the combines were sitting idle in the fields covered in tarpaulins, Max spotted one of Jake's game keepers driving towards a beech wood above his farm house pulling a trailer full with pheasant poults. Knowing what Jake was up to, Max phoned Philip.

"Looks as if our friend is doing exactly what we feared. I've just seen one of the keepers taking birds up to my beech wood."

Philip, who considered Jake a sinner and despised him even more than Max did, was quick to reply, "I think this calls for a meeting with Sidenham. No time like the present, I say."

"I agree. I'll meet you at the farm in half an hour. I've just rung the Estate Office—he's there."

Jake was furious. He huffed and puffed until he was blue in the face. He threatened, he swore loudly, and he nearly choked on his ex-tenants' audacity. But the two men held firm.

"You signed the sporting rights over to us and I want those birds off my land by sunset," demanded Max. "The alternative is court action. What's more, we never want to see any of your keepers on *our* land again."

Faced with such implacable opposition, Jake had no alternative but to concede defeat. But he never spoke directly to the two men again, relying on his solicitors to correspond on even the smallest matter.

So the seeds of a feud were sown, and although, as expected, none of Jake's threats came to anything, he refused to eat humble pie, treating his two neighbours like pariahs. After his untimely death and the departure of his wife, Max and Philip tried to mend bridges with the young Harry, but quickly discovered, that although he was only rising thirteen, he harboured the same bitterness towards them, even daring to publicly blame them for his father's slide into alcoholism, an accusation so blatantly untrue that no one took it seriously. It was an accusation that the two men found hard to stomach, even though they felt some sympathy for the young man's plight, and when no apology was forthcoming they reluctantly accepted that the feud would probably never end.

······

Time had changed nothing, and as Philip drove himself home from the Hunt Ball, his feelings towards Harry would have been unprintable. How had Harry managed to snare his daughter? How could she have fallen for such an arrogant and blatantly immoral womaniser?

Arriving back at the farm, he shuffled into the sitting room and slumped down in front of an unlit fire, his mind in turmoil, overcome by loneliness and resigned to remaining awake during what was left of the night. As the minutes ticked by, the horror of the situation grew like a cancer, until all his anger was levelled at his daughter's traitorous behaviour, rather than at Harry. It was unbelievable that she'd kept from him her infatuation for the ghastly man. It was a nightmare that he feared might run forever. How he yearned for Mary's calming influence, as he thought of Jill lying like some common whore in Harry's arms. What had possessed her to behave in such a disgusting manner? He had warned her many times of the man's reputation, and certainly she was aware of the animosity between the two families. He shivered, not only from the coldness of the room, but also from fear of the unknown. His guts churned as it dawned on him that he might well be close to losing her. That hurt. But however strong his love for her, he would not allow it to compromise his beliefs. God's teachings were quite clear, and if Jill chose to bed with Harry, she would not be welcome in his home. He gazed morosely at the black ash in the grate and wondered where he'd gone wrong. What could he have done to stop Jill walking into such a dangerous situation and putting their relationship at risk? He shook his head in bewilderment. He had no idea. All he could do was pray that before too long she'd see the error of her ways and come crawling back, begging his forgiveness. He stirred the ash with a poker and tried to convince himself that her love for him was too strong for her to defy him for more than a few weeks.

He heard the familiar hum of the milking machine starting up in the yard and was amazed to realise that he'd been home for over three hours and was still in his hunt evening dress. Normally, he would be down in the kitchen, overalls on, making himself a cup of coffee on the dot of four-thirty, preparing to go out to see his two cowmen. He was shocked that he'd spent so much time feeling sorry for himself. That was not his way. He jumped out of the chair, stretching his aching body. He would take a shower, grab a cup of tea, and be as right as rain. Jill and Harry would just be a minor irritant until she came home. As he hurried up the stairs to the bathroom, he remembered his father telling him at the age of seven that only weak men cried, and selfish ones felt sorry for themselves. "Any man worth his salt straightens his shoulders and takes disappointments on the chin," he'd said. Philip had never thought it would be Jill who would bring him to the point of forgetting such advice. He ran a cold shower, stripped off and stepped under the stinging water, its sharpness piercing his skin, reminding him of the times he and Mary had stood naked there together, gasping as the coldness enveloped them. He sighed and quickly turned off the shower. He didn't need such memories. Perhaps if Mary had been alive none of this would be happening. In his bedroom, he threw on his working clothes and moved to the mirror to brush his hair. It was at that moment he saw it—a tear rolling down his cheek. He put out his tongue to catch it and drew it into his mouth, tasting the salt. He slammed his fist hard against the mirror. It shattered, the glass tumbling to the floor. For several minutes he stood hypnotised by the blank space where the mirror had once been. He forced himself to look at the shards of glass at his feet, convinced that every piece forecast a year of misery.

······

"You have humiliated him," Max said. "What's more he has to live with the gossip which is sweeping the area, and you know how your father hates being the brunt of that. Let me tell you a few of the rumours going round. *She's gone off with that bounder. She's sleeping with that shit. She's already pregnant. Her father has thrown her out and he will never have her back, him being a religious man. She swore at her father in front of all his friends. She should be ashamed of herself. She's just another starry-eyed girl bewitched by Sidenham. It won't last, of course, and then what will happen to her? In my opinion Sidenham should be castrated.* Yes, you may well look at me with those wide innocent eyes of yours, but you and Harry are the topic of the moment and most of the stories are not complimentary."

They were sitting in Max's farm office. A dusty, chaotic room, white paint peeling off the walls, cobwebs hanging from the ceiling, and a strong smell of farm disinfectant. The room was cluttered with farm accounts, reference books about sheep, cows, and pigs scattered on the floor. The walls were hung with various trophies. Shields for best farm, photographs of prizewinning cattle and horses, paintings of all Max's hunters and of his beloved terriers, one of which was now sitting on his lap glowering at Jill, as if to say, *If you weren't here, we would be on a walk hunting rabbits*. On his desk was a large photograph of Jane astride her favourite hunter taken by Max a week before she was killed.

Jill sat on one of two chairs in the room, the other one occupied by Max behind his desk. It was a room Jill usually felt comfortable in and where she was welcome whatever the crisis. Today she wasn't too sure on either count.

"I never meant to humiliate him, Max," Jill said guiltily. "But he struck me and I lost my cool. I would love to apologise to him, but he won't even speak to me unless I swear on his damn bible never to see Harry again, and I won't do that. Oh, Max, it's too awful. Can't you make him see sense?"

"Not at the moment, I'm afraid. Not only did you humiliate him, but you also hurt him deeply."

"He's hurt me as well."

Max looked at the beautiful young woman from under his bushy eyebrows and saw the defiance in her demeanour. There was going to be no easy mending of bridges. Philip had already informed him of his conversation with his daughter.

Jill couldn't hold Max's stare and dropped her eyes to her lap. "I suppose you think I should leave Harry?"

Max shrugged his wide shoulders. "I would like you to, yes—expect it, no."

"I love him, Max. He's so different to the man you warned me about. He's insecure, not surprising when you hear his horror story of his childhood. Has he ever told you?"

Max shook his head. "I only know about his father, and that's enough for me."

"Well, you might think better of him if you knew the full story. Ask him one day or maybe I'll tell you now."

"Go on then, we have the time."

She told him. "And what's more," she finished, "He's gentle and loving. Does that change your mind?"

"Not really. Many people have had unhappy childhoods and turn out to be perfectly normal. I can't honestly say that about Harry. I'm sorry Jill."

"In that case you agree with my father?"

Max shook his head. "My loyalties are divided. Your father has been a friend since childhood. You have been special to me since you were born. You both supported me when Jane died. I understand how you both feel. Please don't ask me to take sides. I fear you are both going to be hurt. But of one thing I'm quite certain. Your father will never be able to understand how you could love Harry and neither can I, but I will never turn my back on you, and if this relationship comes to an end you can depend on me to support you."

"Will you understand if I stay with Harry?"

"I will always love you, and yes I will understand."

Max leant across the desk and stared at the large diamond ring on Jill's engagement finger.

Oh God, she's deeper in this than I thought!

He chose his words carefully. "But your father will not be so forgiving. I hope you realise that before you jump."

"But that is so unfair."

"Life is unfair a lot of the time."

"He's my *father*, Max "

"I know, and I understand your distress. But I have known him a long time, and he will not sacrifice his principles even for his daughter."

"Then he will have to live without me."

Max was shocked—he hadn't expected this. "Oh that is so wrong. Don't think a threat like that will change him. He's prepared to live on his own if you carry on with Harry. I saw him yesterday and he's already a changed man. He won't go out hunting, even talks about selling his horses. He is retreating into his shell and going through a deep depression, probably not helped by him breaking a mirror. I don't need to tell you how superstitious he is."

"Oh, that's awful, Max. Poor Father, he was always warning me of breaking mirrors. I used to laugh at all his superstitions although I knew how seriously he took them. But I will not give Harry up. He's my life now, and Father will have to live with that. If he won't have me home, then we must both learn to live with it. It may sound cruel to say that, but he gives me no choice."

"Are you going to tell him that?"

"I'd hoped you might agree to do that—you'd do it much better than me."

"I don't think so. This is something only you can do."

"I suppose you're right, only he may refuse to see me." Jill said back, her eyes radiating the sadness she felt in her heart. Then she said, "I think you may be the only friend I have left."

Max rubbed his unshaven chin. "Neither your father nor I have the right to try to force you to change your mind. Just because you marry someone whom we dislike is no excuse for throwing away a long friendship. I'm just sorry that your father can't see it that way."

Jill rose a little unsteadily from her chair and attempted to smile at Max. "You're a real brick, Max, especially as I know how you feel about Harry. Your support means so much to me, in what is obviously going to be a very difficult time with Father. I never thought he'd react the way he has, but I won't give up Harry just to please a cussed man. I have listened to you, I promise. I'm being careful, though I must say I find that difficult!" She gave a little embarrassed laugh. "You may not believe this, but I do have my head screwed on the right way, and I'm well aware of Harry's reputation. If it's any consolation to you, I won't jump into anything too quickly."

Max stared pointedly at the ring and smiled ruefully. "It looks as if you've already jumped."

Jill shrugged and fingered the ring. "You noticed then?"

"How could I miss it?"

"Well, maybe I've just told you a tiny lie!"

Max leant back and roared with laughter. "You, my child, are incorrigible! I wish you luck in your adventure—for I fear that is what it will turn out to be. No, don't glare at me like that; I hope you prove me wrong. And remember, whatever direction this relationship may take in the months ahead, there will always be a shoulder here for you. Now let's change the subject eh? How about coming out hunting again soon?"

"Harry and I don't think it would be wise. We are off to the South of France on Saturday and have no plans to return before the end of the hunting season. We feel it's best to disappear for a bit. Hopefully, a little of the dust will have settled by the time we get back, and we will be left alone to make our plans."

Max stared at the ring again. "Plans for what?"

"Max darling, don't be so stupid! We are going to get married of course."

He stared at her, openmouthed. To be struck speechless was a new experience for Max.

·······

The weather in Nice was surprisingly warm for early March, and Jill shut her eyes and let the sun caress her face as she breathed in the early scent of mimosa that hung in the air like an expensive perfume.

"Oh, Harry, that feels so wonderful!"

Harry sniffed the air and blinked in the strong sunlight. "I must admit it makes a change from the drab weather we've left behind," he said cheerfully, putting an arm round Jill's slim waist. It was seven months down the road since he'd made his move and he still enjoyed her company. She didn't fawn over him like some of his women, and she was amusing to talk to. No dumb blonde. At first it had been his intention to seduce her and then send her back to an enraged father. Some sort of revenge thing for times past, he told himself. But she'd got under his skin. Now, here he was taking her to France.

Harry, you're going soft, he chided himself.

He'd already spent more on her in a month than he had done in a year on his last girl friend. A diamond ring that had set him back two thousand pounds had been sheer extravagance. Then there had been dinners at numerous expensive restaurants when Jill had been in London. There had been several weekends at the Savoy Hotel, and now, here he was in France. But, as he glanced at her with her long hair blowing in the gentle breeze and her exquisite face held up to the sun, he had no regrets. He could think of nothing more wonderful than spending long, lazy days with a girl of such beauty, who possessed an innocent sensuality that he found most addictive. In fact, Harry considered spending several more months with her before discarding her. For, smitten or not, there was no chance he'd stay with her. OK he had sort of proposed to her, but he'd done that to other women several times before. It seemed to keep them in his bed until he was ready to end the charade and show them the door. His independence was far too precious. Not even the undoubted beauty or the amenable company of Jill Bennett could change the habit of a lifetime. She'd get over it. No doubt she'd call him a shit and burst into tears, hopefully throwing the ring at him before leaving. But what did he care; he'd witnessed it all before. For the moment she'd do very nicely, thank you.

"Harry!"

He jumped.

"You're dreaming."

"Sorry, darling. Always the same when I land here. It's a magical place, you wait and see."

••••••

Fast and expertly, he drove an open Mercedes, Hertz's most expensive luxury hire car, up the winding road that took them from the coast to the hilltop village of St-Paul-de-Vence, about fifteen kilometres from Nice. He was familiar with the road; St-Paul was his favourite place to take a girl. The staff of the Colombe D'or hotel knew him well and admired his taste in women. He tipped well for their tight lips.

Jill stared through her tinted glasses at the cloudless sky; her hair playfully tousled by the warm breeze flowed out behind her.

"You will love this place," Harry enthused as they approached the village up the steep winding road. "Perhaps a little overcrowded with tourists in the season, but at this time of the year it is magical. You wait and see—it will enthral you, I know."

For a moment, she felt a stab of jealousy. "You've been here with one of your girl friends," she accused.

"I most certainly have not! I use this place as a retreat from all the bitching that goes on at home. I wouldn't dream of taking you somewhere I'd been before with another girl."

She turned her head away not wishing him to see her discomfort. *Damn, I really must get out of this habit of being so suspicious.*

"You're still hearing Max," Harry accused.

"No, I'm not," she said just a little too emphatically. "It was stupid of me to ask you. I'm sorry, Harry. Oh, I'm making such a mess of this. Can't we just forget it?"

"We can, on one condition."

"What's that?"

"That you never doubt me again, and definitely never mention Max Foster or your father while we're here."

"It's a promise." It was not a difficult one to make. She'd been so wrong to doubt him. He wouldn't lie to her.

He laughed. "That's settled then. Now let's just forget the gossips and the snipers back home and enjoy ourselves. We are in one of the most beautiful spots in Europe, and you're deliciously desirable. Let's try and forget that this planet is hurtling towards destruction and live in our own bubble for a while. What do you say to that?"

Jill leant her head against the leather headrest and gave a long contented sigh. She'd read loads of romantic books—smiled a little cynically sometimes at the flowery prose, never imagining anyone said such things in real life. But here was a very sexy man proving her wrong, and *wow*, she loved it! She looked across at him with wide, adoring eyes. "I can't imagine a more wonderful idea Harry."

For the first time in his life, Harry felt a twinge of guilt.

······

On the Monday evening of their second week, they were sitting in the grill-room of the Carlton hotel in Cannes, enjoying the first course of what promised to be an exceptional meal and half listening to the tinkle of a piano being played somewhere in the hotel. As was the norm in March, the room was half empty and there was a low buzz of conversation. Jill was relaxed and happy.

"To us," Harry said, raising his glass of Chateau Talbot '70 (another extravagance.) Jill smiled and clicked hers off it.

She sipped the soft red wine and over the rim of her glass watched his steel blue eyes fix on her. She shivered uncontrollably. She'd die for him! "What a wonderful starter," she enthused, enjoying the receding taste of the scallops. "I can't wait to get my teeth into the duck."

"I'd like to sink mine into you now," whispered Harry.

Jill felt the electricity course through her body, and was planning a reply when a female voice behind her exclaimed, "Oh, my God, there's that shit Harry Sidenham!" Surprised, Jill swung round and saw two beautifully groomed and very attractive young women staring at her. Showing no signs of embarrassment at her outburst, one of them smiled at Jill, shook her head and pointed at Harry.

Flushing with embarrassment, Jill turned away and threw a desperate look towards him. "Do you know those two women behind us?"

He looked over her shoulder and the colour drained from his face. "I haven't a clue who one of them is, but the one smiling at me like Lucrettia Borgia is Henrietta Thompson."

"Henrietta Thompson!" exclaimed Jill a little too loudly.

"You don't know her surely?"

No, she didn't—well, at least not on speaking terms. But Henrietta didn't live too far from Sidenham Hall, and Jill knew enough about her to know she'd reputedly shared Harry's bed a few years back. *Oh God! Is this going to spoil everything?*

"No, I don't know her to speak to, but I've seen her out hunting and heard stories. I gather she's quite a girl with the men."

Harry thought back to his wild nights with Henrietta—the champagne washing over her body, her screams of delight as he sucked the drops off, and finally her wild, screaming orgasms. "I've heard the same," he managed to reply in a calm voice.

"You don't know her well, then?"

"I've met her at parties of course and seen her out hunting with her husband."

Jill had heard she'd gone through a nasty divorce and been comforted by Harry. But she bit her tongue, aware that things might be about to get awkward. She grabbed her glass and nearly choked on the liquid as she watched Henrietta Thompson walking towards their table.

"Oh, my God, she's coming over!"

"Keep calm. I'll handle this."

Henrietta oozed false charm. "Hello Harry darling, fancy seeing you here." She winked at Jill before bending over Harry and firmly kissing him on the lips. It was certainly not the kiss of a casual acquaintance. "Is this your latest?" she asked mischievously.

Jill watched Harry go very red.

"This, for your information, Henrietta, is Jill Bennett, who I'm going to marry, and I would ask you to apologise to her for butting in so rudely on our meal."

Unfortunately for Harry, Henrietta was a little drunk and not the least inclined to care how Harry felt. "Oh, you pompous old fart, Harry, don't be so high and mighty with me." She turned to Jill. "Watch him, darling. He likes proposing to girls and then ditching them. Gives him some sort of a sexual thrill, I suppose." She smiled at Jill's ashen face. "Oh, yes, he's a polished shit, mark my word! If you want my advice, get out now before he hurts you." Then raising her voice, she said, "This man is DESPICABLE!" The last word reverberated round the room and concentrated everyone's attention on Harry's table. Enjoying the interest she was causing Henrietta threw a smile at the enthralled company and, not attempting to lower her voice, she slurred, "Give this poor girl a break and tell her the truth. You remember the champagne Harry? Do you remember that time we coupled in your horsebox, and after we had brushed the straw off our sweating bodies you promised to buy me a ring the next day? Did you hell—you threw me out a week later."

As Harry leapt to his feet, there wasn't a sound in the room. "How dare you! Come on, Henrietta, you know damn well that's all a bunch of lies."

"But this little girl will never be sure, will she? Harry, you really are loathsome," Henrietta spat.

Jill watched him clench a fist. "Harry, *please,*" she said urgently.

Controlling himself with difficulty, he said, "You're right—this bit of trash is not worth getting upset about. Go away, Henrietta, you are spoiling our evening. Your lesbian friend is looking a trifle miffed." He turned to Jill with a sardonic smile. "This woman can't make it with a man."

It passed through her mind to ask, "How do you know?"

He laughed. "Go on, Henrietta, tell Jill what you like."

Henrietta rested a well-manicured hand on Harry's shoulder. "Now, now, darling, that's libellous." Then giving a little bow to Jill, she said, "Let me give you a piece of advice for free, darling, and I seldom do anything for free. Kick him in the balls and run; he's poison. His dick is really not worth the pain he'll put you through." Then with a theatrical wave to Harry, she slowly turned to the room and saw fifteen couples and all the waiters gazing mesmerised at her. She had centre stage—it was too good an opportunity to let slip. Never would she have a better chance to make a fool of him. She said, "Harry, *vous êtes un merde!*" There was a ripple of laugher. "And that," she said in English, "is being kind!" Then, giving him a withering look, she turned and walked a little unsteadily on her stiletto heels out of the room, holding on to her friend's arm for support.

Jill wanted the floor to open up and swallow her. A perfect evening had been ruined and the seeds of doubt, which were never far away, surfaced again. "Tell me Henrietta's lying," Jill begged.

"She's lying, the bloody woman," Harry growled. "She really is a roaring dyke. All that stuff about the horsebox and the champagne is a figment of her imagination. God, I wish she hadn't spotted us!"

"I wish she hadn't been here at all! She's ruined our evening. Suddenly, I don't feel at all hungry; in fact, I would really like to leave."

"Of course, I quite understand." He flicked his hand for the bill.

Jill forced herself to sound calm. "If you say she's lying, she's lying." She reached out and took his hand, puzzled by the look of surprise on his face. "I think Henrietta what's-her-name was trying to burst our bubble." Then emboldened, she took a deep breath and said, "But she's failed, Harry, although I do hope she doesn't hang around to goad you further." She gently touched his lips. "I've already told you, I believe you, and anyway I simply don't care what you did before you met me. Every man has affairs before they settle down. It's what Max calls a sort of sharpening-your-teeth thing. So end of story. What is important is that I know you love me—that is all I care about." Aware that many eyes were still fixed on her, she leant across the table and kissed him. "There, the final curtain. I hope the audience enjoyed the play!"

Harry could not believe his luck. He'd quite expected her to walk out behind Henrietta. "I do love you," he lied with a smile, reaching out and touching her face. "And I'm so sorry that our evening had to be ruined by that lying bitch. She chased me for a whole year. God only knows why because she really is a lesbian. I'm not lying, I promise you. I think she was disgusted with her sexuality, so she tried to give the impression that she was normal, marrying some poor ignorant runt, who couldn't read the signs. It all soon went sour and that was when for some perverse reason she started making up stories about us. With a reputation like mine, most of them were believed. Anyway, in the end her husband got fed up with being the butt of all the jokes about having a lesbian wife. He left her, got a job abroad, and as far as I know has never been back to England."

"So what happened to her after that?" asked Jill leaning her elbows on the table.

"She became embroiled with some very unsavoury people in London. Lived with various women, started to drink too much, went into a clinic, stayed sober for about a month after being released and then started drinking again. You saw what she was like tonight. Nowadays, she's seldom sober, so I hear, and spends most of her time wandering round the fashionable resorts trying to find rich old women to bed."

"You seem to know a lot about her."

"We have mutual friends, and they talk about her escapades."

"Yes, I know. But I don't always believe hunting gossip. It can be very vicious."

"And you of course would always give the injured party the benefit of the doubt."

"You know me. I'm just a little country girl."

"No more," Harry laughed, tilting back his chair.

"So you haven't seen her for ages?" Jill asked, daring to press him a little further.

"Not for ages. It's just bad luck she happened to be here tonight."

She drained her wine glass, happy to believe him. "Poor Harry, your life seems to have been an utter mess." She threw her napkin onto the table. "Come on, here's the bill; pay and let's get out of here. Your little country girl feels thoroughly embarrassed. I want to forget tonight and go back to where we where when we first walked in here. Do you think we can do that, still stay in our bubble?"

"With no difficulty."

"Oh, Harry, I hope you're right."

······

It was another of his lies. Each day from the moment they left the hotel, Harry did a good imitation of being a fugitive on the run. At every shop, every restaurant they walked into, he would look nervously around, terrified that Henrietta was going to jump out and confront him. Jill was upset, eventually plucking up enough courage to enquire, "That woman really has got to you, hasn't she?"

For a moment, Harry wasn't quite sure how to answer. "Mind your own fucking business," came to mind. But no, this was a time to control his natural instincts. So for once, he decided to be honest, or as honest as a pathological liar could be. "I must admit to not liking the idea that she's around here spying on us."

"Nor do I! But she'd have put in an appearance by now if she'd wanted to cause us any more grief. How long is it since our meeting at the Carlton? All of a week and there hasn't been a sign of her. My bet is she got the message. I think you are being a little paranoid."

"Maybe I am. But Henrietta is a bitch, and if she could put a spoke into our relationship she would."

Jill thought it useless to point out that it seemed she'd already succeeded.

"So let's forget her," Harry went on. "I'll drive you up to Mougins and we can lunch in a lovely little restaurant I know in the square. What do you say?"

Jill looked a little doubtful. "I hope it's not one where you took that ghastly woman?" No sooner were the words out of her mouth than she regretted what she'd said. It was tantamount to accusing him of lying. *And I don't think that…do I?*

. She held her breath, wondering what his reaction would be.

It was not what she expected. There was no swearing, no tantrum, just a smile and a shake of his head. "And afterwards, we will go back to St-Paul and go to bed. No arguing, Miss Bennett, do you hear?"

She shivered with anticipation, determined never to think of Henrietta what's-her-name again. After all, only a few days ago hadn't she been telling Harry that his past didn't matter? It was no good saying one thing and thinking another. She and Harry were an item, full stop, and no vicious old lesbian was going to ruin that. "Come on, race you to the car!" he cried, already impatient to see her wide excited eyes gazing up at him as he slowly removed her clothes.

······

Jill moved uneasily in Harry's embrace. Their lovemaking had been flat and she knew why—Henrietta bloody Thompson. She felt a little annoyed that if she could handle Harry's ex-girlfriends, why couldn't he? And *boy*, this one had certainly gotten under his skin. In the Mougins restaurant he'd been sulky—almost ignoring her, and although she put some of that down to her earlier crass remark, it didn't explain his apparent indifference to her. It had been an uneasy meal.

And now he's fallen asleep!

He began to snore. In normal circumstances, she'd shake him awake and they'd laugh and roll about on the bed like children. But she sensed this was not going to be one of those days. Leave well alone was written clearly on his chest. That was a worry. She didn't want it to become just another dull relationship, making love as a duty, Harry growing bored, moving away from her quickly and falling asleep. Or worse still straying into another woman's bed. She wanted their lovemaking to always be carefree and exciting, none of this 'bored after three years' nonsense.

"Damn you, Henrietta," she whispered as she propped herself up on an elbow and stared at Harry's face—it really was delicious, so smooth, so perfect. The temptation to risk waking him from his post-coital slumber was very strong, for she needed to talk to him urgently. The South of France had lost its appeal as far as she was concerned. She wanted to go home where there would be no Henriettas possibly hiding behind every shop or restaurant door. But had she the guts to say so? How would Harry react? She'd quickly learnt he didn't like being told what to do. She'd have to tread carefully—a thought only a few seconds old before she decided, w*hy the hell should I?* Their relationship depended on them leaving France pretty damn quick. She dug a finger none too gently into his ribs. "Harry!"

He groaned.

"Come on, sleeping beauty, wake up."

He groaned again and opened an eye. "What do you want?" he said irritably.

"No need to be irascible, Harry. It's time to wake up. I've got something to say."

"Can't it wait?"

"No."

Harry pushed himself into a sitting position, rubbing the sleep out of his eyes, and stared at her angrily, asking, "Well, what is it?"

Keep calm. Hold your nerve.

"What would you say if I suggested we went home?"

He was suddenly wide awake. "Why on earth do you want to go home?"

"Because I'm fed up with you behaving like a scared rabbit, and I don't want to spoil our relationship."

Harry scowled. "You mean fragile."

"NO! It is not fragile!"

"If you say so, but if that's how you feel, why are you so frightened of staying here?"

She fought to swallow her anger. "Stop putting words into my mouth. I'm not frightened, nor is our relationship fragile. I simply think we need to go home. The air around here has been poisoned."

"You think that, do you?"

"Yes."

"Okay, we go home."

It wasn't what she'd expected at all. "Oh, you were thinking the same, were you?"

Harry shifted uncomfortably. "Actually, I hadn't given it much thought, but perhaps you're right."

"Come on, Harry—admit it—you had given it some thought, otherwise you'd never have agreed without an argument."

In fact, he wanted to get away as quickly as possible. He was scared stiff of Henrietta. He'd been lucky so far—the lie about her being a lesbian had been one of his better get-out-of-jail ideas. But Henrietta had sworn revenge when he'd thrown her out. Which was a bit unfair, considering it was her bloody husband who had insisted..."Or else I'll fucking well castrate you, Sidenham," were his exact words. He reached out and pulled her close. "OK, I had been giving it some thought—we go home tomorrow."

Jill sensed his change of mood. "And we can be rid of that tiresome woman," she said, gently pulling his hair.

He kissed her hard before rolling on top of her. "And you find me irresistible."

"Foolishly, I do, Harry Sidenham," she said lightly. "In spite of Henrietta Thompson and all the other baggage that no doubt I will learn about one day."

He put a hand over her mouth. "Hush, no more, it's time you gave me your full attention." He squeezed one of her breasts. "You understand?"

She moaned and moved hungrily for his mouth, tasting the wine still on his breath. His hand smoothed her stomach, and he ran his tongue gently over her moist lips. She coiled herself round his naked body, luxuriating in their movements, their touching and their enjoyment. They brought each other to the heights and slowly, ever so slowly, they came down again, satiated and exhausted.

Jill lay back on the damp sheets, shocked by the force of her pleasure. The joy of travelling to places unknown in Harry's bed was quite breathtaking. The experiences she shared with him were of a splendour and richness she'd never forget. She didn't want to lose them, and in the afterglow of love, she made a decision. Harry had a bad reputation. Okay, he'd been a wild boy, and maybe he had played around with Henrietta, just as she'd claimed. But she would change all that. How many people who criticised him knew as much about him as she did? Certainly few knew about his disastrous childhood. If they did, perhaps they'd understand him a bit more and be a little less liberal with their criticism. She knew exactly what was wrong with Harry. His mother had never shown him love; he didn't understand the meaning of the word. Well, she'd show him. She'd give it to him by the bucket load. Jill smiled at the ceiling. That was all that Harry wanted. He loved her and she wasn't going to let him cock this one up. She was no love-struck teenager, as her father would call her. She was deeply in love with a mixed-up man, and she was the person to give him back his self-esteem and settle him down. She had absolutely no doubt about it. The solution was staring her in the face. Perhaps there was a slight element of risk attached, but what the hell! Girls were doing it all the time. She was in no mood to be bound by convention. She wouldn't tell Harry. It would add to the excitement, make a big surprise. A year earlier, she would have been horrified by what she was planning. *Boy, how I've changed!* She rolled over and pushed herself against Harry's back. He smelt delicious. She closed her eyes and buried her nose in the nape of his neck, imagining his whoop of joy when, one day in the not so distant future, she told him her news

Chapter Five

On an early September evening as well-dressed guests started to arrive, floodlights played on the Georgian façade of Sidenham Hall. Inside, a string quartet discretely played music from the sixties and Jill and Harry stood at the entrance to the ballroom greeting their guests. There was an air of excitement swirling round the gathering company. They had all guessed why the party was being thrown, even though the invitations had deliberately been vaguely worded. So there was that small element of doubt in everyone's mind.

Jill watched with some amusement at the chattering crowd around her, knowing they were on tenterhooks to find out if the rumours were true. Well, they would have to wait until midnight. She and Harry wanted to give nothing away, to keep them in suspense for just a little while longer. Jill smiled to herself, remembering what Max had said people were saying. Well, they were about to be proved wrong. She gave a low chuckle. She and Harry would show the doubters that they were an item that would last forever.

"Max!" she cried excitedly, as he came through the door. "How wonderful to see you; thanks for coming." Then sadly she added, "I see Father's not with you."

Max kissed her on both cheeks and bowed stiffly to Harry. "Sorry, darling, but I'm afraid not. I tried my hardest."

Jill felt a stab of annoyance with her father. Why couldn't he accept that she loved Harry? "I'm sure you did, and that's my father for you," she replied. "I'm not going to allow him to ruin my evening."

"And nor should you," Max said, holding her at arm's length. Even after a year with Harry, she still had an aura of innocent beauty about her. "You look quite stunning, if I may say so, and you have thoroughly put one doubting Thomas firmly in his place."

"Told you so, didn't I"

"Indeed. And that dress—quite lovely."

Jill refrained from telling him that Harry had paid well over a thousand pounds for the creation she was wearing. Max would not understand such generosity when it came to men buying their wives or girl friends presents. Jane had suffered his meanness with good grace, probably because he was normally dressed in what she would laughingly describe as 'scarecrow rags.' Jill stared at his threadbare dinner suit and smiled her thanks. "You are a darling, Max. I feel a million dollars."

Max beamed at her, before whispering in her ear, "I'd like to know how you tamed him?"

"I gave him my love Max, simple as that."

Max touched her arm as he went to move away. "Well, I hope you find the happiness you long for. You deserve it."

Jill watched him take a glass of champagne off a silver salver held by one of the dozens of tail-coated waiters before disappearing into the crowd. If only her father could have been so magnanimous.

He'd greeted her coldly on the day, six months earlier, when she'd gone to the farm to say she'd returned from France.

"Are you still with Sidenham?" had been his first question, standing by the front door, his arms folded as if barring her way.

"Yes, I am, Father."

"In that case you're still not welcome in this house."

Horror had been etched all over her face as he'd turned away without another word, slamming the front door behind him. For several minutes, she'd stood frozen to the spot, convinced that he'd come out and apologise. When he didn't, she'd felt her heart would burst. She'd never believed she could be so hurt. That her father, whom she loved and respected, could do this to her, turn his back on her with such absolute finality, was unthinkably cruel. She'd driven back to Sidenham Hall far too fast, and thrown herself into Harry's welcoming arms. He'd had enough sense not to gloat over her distress.

She'd not spoken to her father since. She'd tried, God, she'd tried—endless telephone calls, all cut off; numerous letters not answered. She'd even taken to spending some time sitting outside the farmyard in her car, sure that he'd be shamed into asking her into the house. After a month she'd given up. She'd made no more attempts to bridge the gap. He should be beside her now, not imposing himself on her conscience.

As Harry greeted two close friends, she watched his face creased in a smile, his eyes sparkling, and his long hair touching his dinner jacket collar, and she sighed with pride. She'd won him against all the odds. But to lose her father was a terrible blow.

Harry Sidenham, you had better be worth it!

For a brief moment they were left alone and she turned to touch him. "I love you, Harry, and soon everyone will know how much."

Was that a look of apprehension on his face? "Harry?"

"What?"

"Say something."

"What?"

"Well, perhaps 'I love you too,' might be nice."

"I love you too. Are you happy now?"

"You don't sound…oh, it doesn't matter."

How stupid could she get? She'd been mistaken. It was her imagination playing tricks. Of course he was apprehensive. It was a bold step for Harry. But he loved her. He'd told her so hundreds of times.

······

She found the beat of the music and the warmth of Harry's arms intoxicating. Added to that, several glasses of champagne had driven from her mind any nagging doubts she might have had over Harry's commitment. She glanced at the huge ornate clock hanging at one end of the ballroom. Harry's grandfather had brought it back from the roof of some remote railway station in India after a failed love affair with a Maharani. She felt a surge of excitement as she saw it was nearly midnight. "Not long now," she whispered into Harry's ear. "Don't you think we should make our way to the stage?"

He squeezed her waist and gently bit her neck—he wasn't going to make any more mistakes. "Okay, let's go." He took her hand. "Let's surprise this doubting rabble!"

They walked slowly towards the band, a path opening for them as they moved through the dancing couples. Those sitting at their tables rose quickly and made for the dance floor, eager to get as close to the lovers as was possible. By the time Harry and Jill reached the stage, the dancing had stopped and the floor was packed. Harry waved to the band and the ballroom fell silent. This was the moment all three-hundred-odd people had come to witness.

Harry looked down on the crowd with a smirk on his face. He guessed they'd give anything to read his thoughts. Ha, what a shock they'd have! Or would they? Probably they'd smile and say they knew the true Harry all the time. *A two-timing young bastard if ever there was one.* How right they would be, for he had no intention of getting married—this engagement charade was just an excuse to put the knife into that bastard Philip Bennett. Marry Jill? Oh no. He'd dump her when he was ready. But not just yet, for she'd got to him as no woman had before—he was quite fond of her really. So maybe he'd keep her for a few more months, or perhaps, yes perhaps, even a little longer if he could drag the engagement out a bit. Harry had no illusions about himself—he was a shit. But then, Jill was more the fool in believing him. She'd had enough warnings. He squeezed her hand a little harder and waved to the smiling faces. *You hypocritical lot,* he thought.

There were a few old county families whom he felt he'd had to ask, even though none of them had ever had a good word to say about him or his father. He couldn't resist a smile, as he recognised Marigold Philips, still looking good in her eighties, who he'd spotted as a boy leaving the Hall with a smile on her face after a late night assignation with his father.

Then there was the new money brigade with their wives or girl friends bedecked in designer gowns that had cost a fortune. They had no hangups over the Sidenham family. In fact, they liked being able to call an earl their friend, and the feeling was reciprocated—Harry had great admiration for their entrepreneurial achievements, likening them to his gambling skills, and they were refreshingly unstuffy. He saw several of the Sidenham staff gathered in a group staring at Jill. He knew they'd been gossiping in the pub about his latest girl friend, probably even taking bets as to how long she'd last, but he was far too arrogant to care what they thought. He scowled at a neighbouring farmer. What was the bugger's name? Ah, yes, Barnaby Jessop. How the hell had he worked an invitation? Harry was sure he'd told his secretary not to invite any of the local farmers. He knew they despised him for his inherited wealth, (in fact they disliked him because of his arrogance), and only spoke to him because he owned a large tract of hunting country. He made a mental note to make sure that Jessop and his ilk were removed from any further guest lists.

Yes, a very mixed bunch indeed, he thought.

"My Lords, Ladies and Gentlemen, pray silence for Lord Harry

Sidenham," bellowed the imposing voice of the Toastmaster.

Harry nodded his thanks before addressing the crowd. "Everyone, I would like to say how thrilled Jill and I are to see you here tonight. In a moment, we'll move into the garden for a firework display. I'm glad to say the weather has been kind to us." He stopped and smiled at the silent faces. "But first, the small matter of why you're here tonight. Looking down at you all lathered up with anticipation quite frankly sickens me." He watched the smiles freeze. "I jest of course." He turned to face a stunned Jill. "You tell them, darling, what they know already."

Jill swallowed and glared angrily at him. She knew he hadn't been jesting—he'd told her earlier what he thought of most of their guests. But his rudeness was inexcusable, especially in front of her. She felt her stomach turn, gritted her teeth and forced a smile. "Of course Harry jests, as I'm sure you all realise. The truth is we are delighted to have you here tonight."

"Not me," she heard Harry whisper behind her.

She surreptitiously kicked one of his shins and continued. "Now, I'm sure you have already guessed why you're here. But that won't spoil this moment for me and Harry." She heard a ripple of sympathetic laughter; determinedly she grabbed Harry's hand and pulled him beside her. "We want you to know that we are getting engaged."

So she'd kept her nerve. She was going through with it. What a bloody little fool! thought most of the guests. Then Max let out a shout. "Well done, both of you!" and the whole room exploded into cheering. Jill did her best to smile, but inside she was smarting. Once the crowd started to chatter she scowled at Harry. "Did you need to behave like that?"

"Like what? I was only speaking the truth."

······

As the clocks in the Hall struck one in the morning, and the guests slowly filed out into the night, Max found Jill to say good-bye. "It's been a wonderful evening, such a happy occasion." He was lying. What he really wanted to say was, "Now can't you see what you're letting yourself in for? Walk away before it's too late." But his heart ruled his head and he bit his tongue.

Anyway, he knew she wouldn't listen.

······

It took her two days short of three months to summon up enough courage to tell him. She'd wanted to surprise him the night of their engagement party, but Harry's boorish behaviour had upset her. So, although she loved the spectacular firework display and beamed happily at all the guests as they left, murmuring such words as, *best party we have ever been to...well done at taming Harry...we hope you have a wonderful life together...*For some unexplainable reason, she judged it was not the time for such a momentous piece of news. It had been a mistake, for as each day passed, she began to have doubts about the wisdom of her unilateral decision in France. She'd seen another side of Harry that disturbed her. But time wasn't on her side. Soon, very soon, he'd start to notice. Her news could wait no longer.

"Harry," she said a little nervously as she sat opposite him at breakfast one morning.

He looked over the top of the *Times.* "What?"

"Could you please put that paper down and listen to what I have to say. I want your full attention."

Irritably, he threw the paper to one side. "Well?"

She was tingling with excitement and the words came out in a rush "What would you like to hear most in the world?"

Harry smiled. "That I'd been left millions by an unknown relative who'd died in Australia."

"No, Harry! Please be serious. What would make you really happy?"

"How many guesses do I get?"

"If I said it was something to do with me, would that help?"

"Not much."

"Okay, something to do with an addition," she said, slight apprehension growing inside her. This was not going the way she'd planned.

"Haven't a clue. You can't be pregnant. So what's left? Ah you've bought me a new stallion."

"Oh Harry please! And why can't I be pregnant?"

"Because you promised me you were taking precautions."

Yes, yes, she had said that, but she'd decided he wouldn't mind her small deceit, once he heard the news. "Well, I am pregnant," she blurted out. "I made the decision in France. You need a child, Harry. You need to settle down. Have something to live for other than gambling and your horses. You need children to fill this vast house with their presence and laughter. You need..."

She never finished her sentence. His reaction was terrifying. Something that Jill was never to forget. He jumped to his feet, his coffee cup flying across the table, the black liquid splashing onto the blue carpet. "You're pregnant, woman?" he exclaimed, totally incredulous.

Jill's eyes widened in shock. She hadn't expected such a negative reaction. She was thrown into confusion. "Yes." She struggled to keep her voice cheerful. "Isn't it wonderful I'm carrying your baby, Harry?" She tried to smile broadly, but a widening of her eyes betrayed an element of fear.

If the table hadn't separated them, he'd have hit her. Instead, he slammed a fist down on the polished walnut surface and bellowed, "You stupid, stupid little bitch! What made you think I wanted to have a child? What arrogance made you think I wanted a child by you, the daughter of a northern peasant bogged down in religious claptrap that makes me sick and who stole land from my father? What right did you have to make such a decision on your own? Did you think it would tie me to you? Did you want to become the Countess of Sidenham that bloody badly? Well, I've news for you, my girl— get rid of the foetus or get on your bike!"

Jill reeled back in her chair. She couldn't believe what she was hearing. She'd been so sure, so confident of his love. Trying not to break up entirely, she cried, "Harry, how could you say things like that? And to bring my father into it is most unfair; you know damn well he paid your father a fair price. You've told me a thousand times that you love me. Surely you want our child!" Then, gathering what was left of her waning courage, she stated in a voice of conviction, "You can forget an abortion. I have no intention of getting rid of *our* child."

Beside himself with rage, Harry shouted, "Then we are finished, because I don't want the bastard. As for me, loving you—well, you should have known better than to believe me. Didn't Max warn you?"

Jill stared at him in disbelief. "Oh, that is so cruel, Harry." She was fighting growing panic. "This is not you speaking. Maybe I did bounce the news on you a bit. Maybe I should have discussed it with you, but you will love your child, I know you will. You will be a great father."

Harry's eyes narrowed to a cruel glint and his whole body was shaking, but his voice was menacingly calm when he replied, "You are deluding yourself. I don't want to be a father. I don't want to love a child that's been in your belly. Okay, you won't have an abortion, but don't expect me to provide for your bastard. I will deny I'm the father, put it about you've been unfaithful to me. And I suspect your father will be done with you once and for all. His God will call the demons down on you. You have played your cards wrong. No one treats Harry Sidenham like this."

A cold hand gripped Jill's heart. She didn't want to believe what she was hearing, but in the space of five short minutes he'd done a good job of shattering her dreams. Through watery eyes she stared at the man she'd die for. The man who she confidently assumed would be in her life forever. Was he, after all, the adulterous playboy her father had branded him? No! She was not yet ready to accept that. Harry was in shock—he'd come round. Their relationship was strong. She couldn't believe he'd never loved her. How could he deny he was the father? "Harry, darling?"

He threw back his chair and glared at her across the table. "What now?"

She sat frozen to her chair; he looked very threatening. She was terrified, filled with panic. She croaked, "Please don't ruin something that has been so wonderful. Take a deep breath. Remember all the little things we laugh at. All the fun we've had together. The love we've shared. Remember, Harry. Please, please remember."

"I remember nothing," he said brutally. "Already my mind is shut. You have destroyed us." He stopped short of telling her he'd never had any intention of marrying her. "And I want you out of this house." He glanced at his watch. "I want you gone by lunchtime. It shouldn't be too difficult. You came with nothing, after all." He gave her a smile that chilled her bones, picked up the *Times*, and walked towards the dining room door.

"You'll come back to me, Harry, you wait and see," she said defiantly to his retreating figure, but the last words faded to a whisper. He didn't bother to reply.

She was numb, finding it hard to believe that the last few minutes had actually taken place. It was a nightmare, one she'd wake from sweating, only to find Harry rushing around the table to take her in his arms. But as she gazed at the congealed fried egg on the plate in front of her, looked round the room, and saw the broken coffee cup on the carpet, she knew it was no nightmare. It was cold, horrible and frightening reality! Harry had, indeed, said all those hurtful things, and if she thought he was going to walk back through the oak door with his face creased in a delighted smile, she was deluding herself.

She rose slowly from her chair, her mind a caldron of conflicting emotions, and headed for the stairs. As she painfully climbed them, a flutter of hope returned. Perhaps, just perhaps, Harry was regretting his outburst and would be waiting for her in their bedroom, an apologetic smile on his face and his arms outstretched. But as she opened the door, she saw the room was empty. No Harry, no sound. A great black cloud descended on her. She'd never imagined she'd be unhappy in this room—the room where they had first made love, and the room where she had conceived their child. Why, why had he reacted so badly? She'd been so certain, and that had been her mistake. Had she never understood him? The truth hurt. The answers were staring her in the face. Harry had never wanted to settle down. How many women had made that mistake before her? She gave a rueful little smile. *Oh God, what a fool I've been. Probably he's already confined me to a dustbin marked 'discarded rubbish,' and the name of Jill Bennett already erased from his mind.*

"All right, Harry, I messed up, but you're despicable," she shouted defiantly at the closed door, before reaching for her two dusty suitcases on top of the wardrobe. Harry was right about one thing: There was little for her to take away.

The next thing she was aware of was putting her suitcases in the back of her car. As she started the engine, she wondered where Harry had gone. Would he appear to say good-bye? She shook her head. *Stop dreaming, girl.* That would not be his style. If he was nearby, no doubt he was waiting to hear her car move off down the drive. As she pulled away, she took one last look at the house she'd foolishly thought would be her home for the rest of her life. Now what? *Oh God, what am I going to do?* She'd alienated her father and was pregnant by a man who obviously had no intention of admitting he was the father. She was in crisis. When she reached the main road, she hesitated. Did she gamble that her father would welcome her back? That would be a bad bet, and she couldn't deal with another rejection right this moment. She shook her head. There was only one safe place to go, and only one person she could trust.

In the space of an hour Jill realised she'd finally grown up.

······

They sat together on Max's worn leather sofa, Nelson, his one-eyed terrier of undetermined age lying between them, his little head moving from one to the other of them, sensing as dogs can that something was wrong. Jill's ashen face mirrored her despair, and Max could feel her shaking. He made no attempt to speak, just held her tight waiting for her to break the silence.

"Max?" Her voice reminded him of her as a child.

"Yes?"

She pulled away from him and sat back in the sofa, laying a hand on Nelson's back. "Harry's thrown me out."

It was not the time to say, 'I told you so.' "Do you want to tell me what happened?"

"I've done the most stupid thing."

"Can you tell me?"

"I have no alternative."

"Whatever you tell me will just be between the two of us."

"Oh, how I wish that!"

"Meaning?"

"I think this will be difficult to keep quiet."

"Then the sooner you tell me the better."

"I suppose."

"No 'I suppose' about it. The sooner you get it off your chest, the sooner we can deal with the problem."

She began her shameful story, fighting back the constant threat of tears. Her pride may have taken a battering, but her situation was of her own making and she wasn't going to show her desperation to anyone. Max listened in silence, except for a gasp when she told him she was pregnant. When she'd finished she asked, "Are you going to throw me out?"

Max shook his head. "You must have a very short memory. You should know I don't break my promises. This is your second home."

"Only home," Jill corrected him. "But, oh, Max," she began a little guiltily, "I wish I was doing this with my father."

"Of course you do. It's only natural. I wish he could be more understanding. Perhaps, he might change now, if you really have split with Harry. Want me to give him a ring?"

"No, definitely no! He has his principles, and he'll never understand about the baby. What a terrible mess."

Max thought that an understatement, but he wasn't going to say, 'you foolish girl, why on earth did you dream up this stupid idea of getting pregnant without consulting Harry?' It was all water under the bridge, and anyway, she knew where she'd gone wrong. What she needed now was love and understanding. If her father wouldn't give it to her, he would.

He said, "A bit of a mess, yes. But the deed is done, as they say."

"I could have an abortion."

"That would end any hope of you mending bridges with your father, and knowing you I doubt if that is even on the agenda."

"Well, I did think about it for all of ten seconds after Harry had stopped shouting at me."

"No hope I suppose that he might relent and have you back?"

Jill's heart felt as though it had fallen into the crevasse of a glacier. Her head dropped into her hands and her body visibly sagged. "He will never have me back. He wasn't even prepared to talk. He even said he'd deny the baby was his, thereby insinuating that I'd been unfaithful. He was horrible. He was like a bomb being detonated. One moment our lives seemed perfect, and then all hell broke loose and I was left in the rubble, stunned. I was terrified. He changed in a second, and I'm not exaggerating. I can't believe that the man I love behaved like that. No, Max, I must accept I'm out of Harry's life for good. To do otherwise will just cause me more pain."

"But let's just say the unexpected happened."

"I'd go back. I love him."

"Enough to have an abortion?"

"I'd have to think about it for longer than a few seconds."

Max put a hand under her chin and gently lifted it so that he could look into her eyes. "He doesn't deserve you."

"I don't care."

Max gazed at the stricken face, the dishevelled hair, the shaking hands, and felt painfully sorry for her. There was little he could do to console her. He said, "Rest assured, I'll be beside you all the way. Together, we can get through this mess. Nothing is ever as bad as it seems. That may sound trite, but don't lose heart. Now, I hate to bring this up when you are so upset, but what are you going to do about your father? I really think you have got to tell him very quickly what has happened. It won't be a secret for long that you've left the Hall. It would be terrible if he heard from anyone else."

"Oh God, here we go again!"

"I'm sorry," Max apologised.

"No, no, you're right. I must face him. But not today, maybe in a couple of days."

"Don't leave it too long."

"I won't, Max, I promise. But I can't see him welcoming me back with open arms when I tell him I'm pregnant, and that Harry has dumped me and wants nothing to do with me or the child."

"Well, he might be glad to hear that Harry's dumped you, but I'm not so sure about the baby."

"And that will be so unkind."

Max gently ran his fingers through her hair. He remembered she'd loved him doing it when she'd been a child. "You can't be sure how he will react. He might surprise you. But first things first. You look dead on your feet. It may be only midday but I think you need a good sleep. When you wake, that will be the time to worry about your father and the baby. We shouldn't do anything while you're so wound up and exhausted. Now listen, I have some pills by my bed that will knock you out for several hours, at least until tomorrow morning."

"I don't know about that."

"Well, I do. You need sleep. One of my pills will ensure that. Come on Jill, it's for the best."

She rested her neck against the back of the sofa and closed her eyes. Max's fingers had already relaxed her. "I'm not in the mood to argue with you," she said. "I'll do whatever you suggest. Oblivion sounds a good idea, and the way I feel I wish I'd never wake up. That would solve all the problems."

"Don't let me hear talk like that," Max scolded.

"I know, but—"

"Hush. You know what I've just said—nothing is as ever as bad as it seems. Tomorrow is another day, and we will begin to think of solutions to your problems."

"Oh, Max, what would I do without you?"

"Manage perfectly well, of course."

Jill kissed him gently on the cheek. "No, I don't think so. Right now I feel I've really messed up, and I'm not too sure how I'm going to cope."

......

Harry held his third strong whisky of the evening in a well-manicured hand and swore loudly. Silly little bitch! He'd not been ready to dump her. He'd been enjoying himself. But to give him news like that! For God sake didn't a man have the right to be asked if he wanted to be a father! A father! He shuddered with horror. His childhood had put him off that idea a long time ago. He drank greedily. The rumourmongers would have a field day, but he'd be ready with his denial, accusing her of cheating on him. Then the shit would hit the fan! He smiled. He rather liked the idea. Perhaps, after all, he didn't care too much about losing her.

Of course, if she had any brains at all she'd get rid of the *thing*. But knowing Jill, he felt that wasn't an option he should treat too seriously. Anyway, what did he care? It was time to forget her. She'd been fun, very sexy and surprisingly amusing. But there were plenty of other fish in the sea, Henrietta for example. She obviously still had the hots for him, and now that her husband had divorced her—he smiled and refilled his glass. That would be the icing on the cake and really screw Jill up. With a bit of luck it would break her heart.

......

The ceiling was moving. Her legs felt numb; her heartbeat was rapid and her eyelids felt heavy. She saw a tall figure standing over her and she screamed.

"Jill, Jill, it's me, Max!"

She forced her eyes to open and stared, uncomprehending, at Max.

" Max?" Her brow furrowed.

"Yes, it's me," Max repeated, seeing the fear in her eyes.

"I thought you were Harry!"

"God forbid."

She sat bolt upright, still disoriented. "I'll second that."

Max put a mug of coffee down on the bedside table. "It's the drug, but you'll be OK soon. Here, drink this coffee. "Best thing to wake you up after those pills."

She stared at him, struggling to clear her befuddled brain. "Thanks Max. Those pills must be strong."

"Very, but they have done a good job. You've slept for ten hours."

"I don't believe it."

"Well, you have, and just what you needed."

"I think I could have slept for another ten hours. Might have been better if I hadn't woken…"

"Now, what did I say yesterday?"

"I know, and you're right, but…"

Max was quick to press the cup of coffee into her hand. "Come on, that's not the girl I know talking."

She took a sip of the hot liquid and lay back on the pillows, her eyes half closed. "I'm terrified of facing Father. I just don't know how I'm going to deal with him. He'll be so intransigent."

Max shrugged. "I can't give you any advice. This is something you have got to do on your own. I know he's an obstinate man, with very high principles, and as you've just said he can be intransigent. But to be fair to him, Jill, he has a point. You have been reckless—I'm sorry, you may not like to hear this, but you can't deny it, and I cannot tell you how to deal with your father. I repeat what I said some time ago—that must be solely between you and him. I suggest you leave well alone for today; think how you are going to deal with him, and then give him a ring tomorrow."

"Well, it won't take me long to work out what to say. I will just throw myself on his mercy." She sighed. "It will be a lost cause, I'm afraid. The first mention of the word pregnant and he'll be downright hostile. Oh shit, Max, what a mess!"

Max was lost for words.

"There you are you see, even you can't think what to say and I'm not surprised. Look at the facts. "I set out deliberately to have a baby. I deceive Harry; I don't tell Father, not even you. What hope have I got?"

"Well, maybe he'll surprise you."

"Forget it. Max, Father is not made like that, and you know it. He is not the sort of man to forgive a daughter's transgressions, especially when she turns up pregnant by a man he despises. Oh damn! Now look what I've done."

Max watched the coffee staining the blankets and gently took the mug out of her shaking hands. "It's going to be tough."

"And by the time this spreads all over the county, I won't have a friend left."

"You will have two."

"You, and who else?"

"Tim."

"Please, Max, don't lie to me; I really can't take it. After the way I've treated him the last thing he'll care about is me."

"I'm not lying."

"I think you are."

"I'll have a bet."

"You're lovely Max darling, and I know you're saying this to try and cheer me up, but right now I think all bets are off."

"Suit yourself Jill, but remember that Tim isn't a Harry, he will be a good friend." Then with a smile creasing his concerned face he added, "There's nothing more he'd like to do than go and knock Harry's block off."

"Somehow I don't think I'm worth it," Jill said sadly.

......

Jill's mother had often taken her to the end of the garden to stand under the walnut tree and look across the long valley stretching out as far as they could see. It was a breathtaking view at any time of the year. On a clear winter's day, you could see silent fields and ghostly woods, the oldest trees resembling tall intimidating skeletons. When it was spring, you could enjoy the landscape slowly coming into life like an artist's canvas. In summer, there was the smell of lush grass, the aroma from the breath of hundreds of cattle grazing in the green fields, and the smell of corn ripening. The air could be fresh or humid, and always there was the hum of busy insects. Whatever the season, whatever the weather, Jill's mother would take her by the hand and enthuse at nature spread out in front of them. "This is something to cherish, child, remember that. To own this is a privilege we must never take for granted. To be the guardian of the soil is God's gift. We must always be aware that we are His tenants. It is my opinion that everything else that happens to us in our lives pales into insignificance compared with the responsibility that God has given us. Many times I have stood here and gained inner strength. Much to your father's annoyance, I used to say it was better than going to church. Perhaps one day you may need to find that inner strength. Look no further than here."

Jill was remembering her mother's words as she drove into the familiar farmyard the following morning. She was scared. She hadn't even had the courage to make the call telling her father she was coming. Max had reluctantly picked up the telephone. She'd listened to his voice raised in anger, as he argued with the obstinate man on the other end of the line. *He's going to refuse to see me. He's going to refuse to see me,* she'd kept thinking. But Max would have no truck with Philip's intransigence, and cajoled and swore down the telephone until he relented.

The sight of Wellington looking over his stable door brought tears to her eyes. She'd neglected him terribly since meeting Harry, and it was an unpleasant reminder of how far she'd divorced herself from her home. She made a mental note to grab a carrot or two from the larder before she left. She blew a kiss towards the stables and braked to a halt. She breathed in deeply, trying to calm her jangling nerves, praying that she'd have a few moments to collect her thoughts, but it was not to be. Her father was standing by the garden gate, arms folded and a scowl on his face. She wanted to run.

But this is my home.

She forced herself to get out of the car and walk slowly towards him. The first thing that struck her when she was close to him was how ill he looked. There was little colour in his cheeks and he looked terribly thin, his tall frame a little bent. But what disturbed her most were his eyes. Normally so full of bright intelligence, they were now sunk deep into their sockets and looked lifeless, as if a mist had been drawn over his vision. Her natural instinct was to run towards him, take him in her arms and hug him close. But then she remembered the last time they'd spoken, the rejection, the slammed door. She stopped a few feet from him, feeling as if there was an invisible barrier separating them. "You look awful, Father," was all she could say.

"Hello, Jill." The voice was as dead as his eyes. "I suppose you better come in, and don't bother about the concerned bit. Of course I'm not well. How could I be, after you deserted me for that apology of a man?"

That hurt, but also pained her to see him in such bad shape. Which would win out, the desire to run or concern for her father?

Run!

She was close, so close, and it took all her will power to force herself to follow him into the house. He led her into the kitchen and pointed at a chair. "Better sit there. What's it to be, tea or coffee?" His voice might have been that of a stranger.

"You *know* I like tea, Father."

"Do I? It's been so long. And don't mumble. It annoys me."

The urge to run returned. How could he be so dismissive? She half rose from the chair, hesitated and then sank back onto the hard seat. It was a defining moment in her life. Ever since she'd been able to remember, she'd been in awe of him—allowed him to dictate how she ran her life, but suddenly she realised he couldn't be allowed to do it any longer. When she next spoke, there was a note of defiance in her voice. "I didn't know you were deaf."

Philip snorted with surprise. "I'm not. Just don't like you whimpering."

"I wasn't whimpering, and anyway, does it really matter? I thought you'd be pleased to see me."

"Then you delude yourself." Philip leant up against the Aga stove and stared at his daughter. At first he'd missed her. Told himself a hundred times he'd been too severe. But now it was too late. All the pain of losing her to Harry had drained every drop of emotion from his body. Only resentment remained. He'd have given anything to experience the old rush of love, to take her in his arms and say all was forgiven, but he knew the words would not come. His eyes filled with tears as he thought the unthinkable. As far as he was concerned, she'd walked away from him without even a 'sorry,' and she had broken his spirit. He could not accept that he'd been responsible for the split. All he'd done since she'd left was dream of joining Mary, and finding the peace his daughter had taken from him. He turned to look at the kettle so that she couldn't see the dampness of his eyes. A wisp of steam told him it was boiling. He dropped a tea bag into each mug and added water. It gave him the time he needed to compose himself.

"Milk and sugar are on the table," he said, putting a mug down in front of Jill, refusing to meet her eye, before taking the chair next to her. "Still with Sidenham?" he asked bluntly.

"That's one of the reasons I wanted to see you, Father. I've left him—well, actually he's thrown me out."

"Oh has he?"

"We had a terrible row. It's all over. I'm sure you've longed to hear me say that, but spare me the 'I told you so' lecture. I really couldn't take that right now." Was that a flicker of compassion she saw in his eyes? "I would like to turn the clock back. I know there's nothing I can say to mend the hurt I've caused you. But for what it's worth, I'm devastated. I can see now I should never have acted as I did, but I never thought my actions would cause such a split between us—never."

Philip's guess had been she was going to tell him she was about to marry Harry, certainly not beg his forgiveness. He took a sip of his tea. When he spoke his voice was not so harsh. "So you've left him. Seen him for what he is, eh? Naturally I'm very glad you've come to your senses. Might I say that a wiser head than yours could have prevented all this pain? But that's as it may be, and although I can't feel any sympathy for you, I do understand how much you must be hurting. To break up a partnership is always painful, however unsatisfactory it might be. What happened? No, don't tell me—let me guess. You caught him with another woman?"

"No!" There was anger in her voice. "It was not like that. He just didn't see things my way. I made a mistake."

"You don't just walk out on a relationship because you have a disagreement."

"Disagreement is the wrong word. This was a big time fallout, and I don't think he ever wanted our relationship to last. I was blind to this and made a monumental blunder."

"Go on."

Jill swallowed hard. "I'm pregnant."

Philip looked aghast. "You're pregnant by Sidenham?"

"Yes. You see I had this stupid idea that I could make him settle down. To have his child seemed the obvious answer. I misjudged him."

Any colour that Philip had in his face drained away and he stared open mouthed at his daughter, searching for words.

"Father, please! Say something!" There was a note of terror in her voice and her twisted features seemed those of a woman about to fall off a cliff.

Philip felt a dreadful heaviness in his heart. He was not angry, just terribly disappointed. He'd failed as a father. He could hardly believe it. When he spoke, his voice was surprisingly soft. "I'm sorry I've failed to bring you up respecting God's teachings. I tried so hard. It has not been easy without your mother, but I had hoped. Now we must both suffer. When you walked in here, I had made up my mind to have nothing more to do with you, but when you said you'd left Sidenham I nearly weakened; now I see that was a mistake. Nothing has changed. I feel great sadness for you, Jill. I don't know what you're going to do, but you're not welcome here. Not now you're…"—he choked on the words—"pregnant by Sidenham. I'm sure you understand."

Anger boiled inside her. "Understand! Of course, I don't understand. I'm carrying a child—your grand child. Whatever you think of Harry, the embryo in here"—she gently touched her stomach—"is a living being, an innocent little creature that deserves to be loved. Are you going to stand there and cold-bloodedly throw me out of my home for good?"

He hesitated for only a second, sinking in his chair and kindling a spark of determination in his eyes. "That is what I'm saying. If anything, my feelings are stronger now then they were after you went off with that man. Neither you nor your bastard child will ever be welcome in this house while I'm alive. Don't try playing the grandchild card; it will get you nowhere. You have sinned in the eyes of God, and in so doing have lost me. It hurts me to say this, but you disgust me."

Trembling and wild eyed with disbelief, Jill cried, "How can you say that! I'm your daughter. I've made a mistake—it's a mess I know, but this is a time I need your support, not rejection. Please, Father, don't do this to us."

"I'm sorry, Jill. I have no choice."

"No choice! Don't give me that rubbish. You know you have a choice. How can you sit there when I'm begging you for help and look me in the eye and say you never want to see me again? I love you. God would not want you to throw me out—what did you once tell me? God is compassionate. To forgive is a great gift. That's what you said, wasn't it? Well, I need loads of that compassion right now. You're the most important person in my life. I'll look after you like Mum did. I promise I'll give my life to you. We can have a future if we work at it; don't throw that chance away."

Philip got unevenly to his feet, shook his head and pointed at her stomach. "I'm not your life—*that* thing is. And we have no future. As for the compassion you ask for, I suggest you look to Sidenham for that."

Jill threw back her chair and said quietly, "Don't destroy yourself, Father, for at the end of the day it is you who will suffer the most and I don't want to see that happen. Think again, please." She edged toward the door, fearful of his next words.

There was silence. They took a break. Both exhausted by their emotions. Philip stood rigidly holding the Aga rail. Jill stared at him through watering eyes. They both waited, neither wanting to be the first to speak—the ticking of the kitchen clock and the hum of the fridge filling the empty void.

Eventually, Philip broke the silence, his voice determined, almost menacing. "You have already destroyed me. Get out."

Jill thought the devil had entered her father's heart. "You're a beast—an inhuman beast!" she cried.

He turned his back on her and said, "We have no more to say to each other. I no longer have a daughter."

"You can't do this to me."

Philip swung round, his eyes blazing. "Watch my mouth. Get out!"

She ran to him, stopped when she could smell his breath. "Now say that again, Father."

His eyes, so cold, bore into her. "Get out!"

She walked out slowly, determined to keep her dignity, but once she was in the farmyard her resolve broke. "Damn you, damn you!" she shouted, "I hate you!"

Philip watched her go, heard her anger and shook his head, a terrible sadness sweeping over him. "Please God, forgive me for what I've just done," he whispered and the mist settled again over his eyes.

······

This time, she didn't attempt to drive home. She ran to the farm office and rang Max. "Thank heaven, you're there," she choked as she heard his reassuring voice. "He won't have me back! Yes, I know—unbelievable! Can you pick me up, Max? I'm too shaky to drive. Please, please come as quickly as you can."

"I'm on my way. I'll bring someone to drive your car. Whereabouts will you be?"

"I'll be in Wellington's stable. You know where that is."

"I do. Where's your father?"

"He's in the house. Please hurry. Oh, Max, he was so horrible!"

"Hold on! Be brave."

"I'll try." She dropped the telephone and ran to the stables. She opened Wellington's door and laid her head gently against his velvet neck, the warmth providing the comfort she needed as she contemplated what an utter cock-up she'd managed to make of her life. Her future seemed bleak, because she'd misjudged two men. Despair swept over her. Harry had discarded her without a second thought, leaving her to fend on her own as a single mother. Her father had turned his back on her and so would most of her friends. She had no money and no home. How would she survive? She ran a hand across Wellington's wet nose and looked into his large inquisitive eyes. He snorted and shook his head. It was almost as if he were rejecting her as well.

Chapter Six

There was no walnut tree to comfort her, no swaying branches for her to dream under. No perfectly mown lawn running down to the house. No quiet pond where in summer she'd watch the swallows gracefully swooping down to drink. No ice to crack in the winter so that she could feed the goldfish. Instead, there was Max's weed-infested garden, the lawn a mass of white daisies, and what had once been two large herbaceous borders lovingly tended by Mary, a jumbled mass of wild columbine and choking bindweed. The contrast could not have been starker, and yet, within its chaotic boundary, Jill had found the solace she so desperately sought.

She sat with her face tilted towards the warmth of the sun, reminding her of that magical day at Nice airport when the Mediterranean heat had caressed her innocent face and she hadn't a care in the world. She'd been in love—still felt something for Harry. How swiftly life could change.

Six weeks had passed since Max had collected her from Wellington's stable, cold, confused, but with a new resolve in her heart not to buckle under the weight of her situation. She'd fought off the threatening shadows in the stable—she'd only herself to blame. Over and over she'd repeated the words, "I'm young, resilient, a long life in front of me." She had to face her problems head on. No one else could do it for her. So it was a resolute young woman who had met Max at the stable door—not the red-eyed, defeated girl he'd expected.

He'd led her to his car and they'd driven home in silence, Max deeming it better to talk once they were in his house. For three days he'd never left her side. He'd never pushed her to talk. She was calm, outwardly fine. She ate, she talked about his farm, about hunting, even managed a joke or two about the baby. But Max suspected that there was a lot of grief pent up inside her body, waiting for the right moment to ambush her. So he waited, ready to be there when the moment arrived.

It had happened on the morning of the fourth day. She'd not put in an appearance for breakfast. Max had flown up the stairs to find her bedroom door locked. She'd screamed for him to stay away. He'd not argued. He'd left her alone until dusk and then kicked the door open. She'd fallen into his arms and cried for an hour. He'd dried her tears with one of his large, coloured handkerchiefs, taken her hand and led her down to the kitchen where he'd put a mug of steaming tea in front of her. "Now it's time you got on with your life," he'd said.

What would she have done without him?

She watched him striding towards her. She smiled as he drew nearer and jumped off the rusty old bench that he'd thoughtfully pulled out of the ramshackle potting shed, so that she didn't have to sit on the grass. "We don't want you getting piles do we?" he'd chuckled.

"Max, you look worried."

He reached for her hand, fearful of giving her the news. She'd made so much progress, and she really could have done without the bombshell he was about to drop in her lap. "I've got some bad news I'm afraid."

"I have a feeling I know what you're going to say. Something has happened to Father."

There was no easy way to tell her. "I'm afraid he's had a stroke."

"Oh God, when?"

"I don't know, but probably some time in the night. Luckily, it's Hilda Danby's day to come in and clean. She found him in bed. She's called an ambulance. By now he'll be at the hospital."

"Do you know how bad he is?"

"No idea, but I don't think we should delay in getting to the hospital."

"Of course, we must go now. Where have they taken him?"

"To Bristol Infirmary."

"That will be a nightmare to get to at this time of the morning."

Max put a hand on her shoulder as they hurried down the garden. "I know. But try and keep calm, he'll be in good hands."

She stopped and turned to look at him, her eyes so sad. "I should have been with him Max." Then she added, "He must have been terrified all on his own."

"I doubt if he knew what was happening, and don't start blaming yourself. Remember he didn't want you at home."

"I know, I know. But, I just wish—"

Max interrupted her. "That's enough of that Jill, understand?"

"I'll find it difficult."

"I'm sure, but maybe this is the jolt he needed. If he recovers, he may see things differently."

Jill threw him a weak smile. "I wish I could believe that."

......

The frantic drive to the hospital brought back unwelcome memories of her father dodging in and out of traffic in his attempt to get to the hospital before her mother died, and today seemed a replica of that dreadful day when they had arrived too late. Every set of traffic lights seemed to be red; every pedestrian crossing had someone on it and parked delivery vans caused tailbacks. Jill cursed with impatience; each minute seemed like an hour, and at one particularly long hold up she felt like jumping out of the car and running.

Unlike her, Max stayed calm, weaving expertly in and out of the rush-hour traffic and judging when he could risk increasing his snail-like pace, but no one was more pleased when he screeched to a halt outside the casualty department. "I'll park the car and join you, he said urgently."

Once she'd announced herself at reception, Jill was swept up into the well-oiled machine of a department used to dealing with hundreds of such emergencies every day. Almost before she had time to catch her breath from the hectic drive, she was facing a young solemn doctor outside the intensive care unit.

"Miss Bennett, I'm glad to see you."

"My father, how is he?"

"I've just finished my examination."

"Is he very bad?"

The doctor took her hand, giving her a sympathetic smile. "He's seriously ill. He had another stroke in the ambulance. We're trying to stabilise the situation."

"Another stroke?" Jill cried. Then spotting Max, she ran towards him. "He's had another stroke!"

The doctor looked at Max. "It's quite common to have a small secondary stroke."

"I see."

"He was on his own when he had the first stroke," Jill said guiltily.

"So I gather."

"Is he going to die?" she asked fearfully.

"As I said, his condition is serious but he's putting up a fight."

"Would he have had a better chance if someone had been with him?"

The doctor shrugged his shoulders. "I can't say that."

"Is he conscious?" asked Max.

"I'm afraid not."

"Can I see him?" Jill asked urgently.

"Of course you can. I will get a nurse to take you."

Her father was in a coma. Jill stared at the tubes, the drip, the monitor, and her hand flew to her mouth. "He's dying," she said quietly to Max. "I only wish he could see me. Then perhaps he'd understand how much I love him. I'm sure he'd rest easier with his God if he knew that."

"He may recover," whispered Max with little conviction, as he stared at his closest friend.

"I don't think so," replied Jill. "And I helped to kill him."

Max shook his head. "Oh, no, that's not true."

She looked up into Max's concerned face and forced a smile. "You're the kindest and sweetest person in the world, but not even you can persuade me that I didn't bring on this attack. I caused him so much misery. He just couldn't deal with life anymore. He needed me so badly once Mum died, and what do I do? I go off with a man he disliked intensely. He'd every right to be very angry with me and I should have listened to him." Jill moved to the side of the bed and touched her father's hand. "He's so cold. Can you hear me, Father? Squeeze my hand if you can." The hoped for pressure never came. "I'm so sorry."

......

Philip died four hours later, never regaining consciousness, thus denying father and daughter the chance to reconcile.

Max led Jill away from the bed. "Come on, there's nothing more you can do here and you're exhausted. We'll get all the details sorted out and then we can go home."

"Just a few more minutes," Jill pleaded. "On my own, if you don't mind, Max."

Max looked at the nurse. "That will be alright, Miss Bennett. There's no hurry."

"I'll be in reception," whispered Max.

Jill nodded, waiting until he'd disappeared through the glass door before dropping to her knees by the bed. She'd known her father so well, known when he was happy, when he was sad, when he was tired, when he was in despair. She'd understood all his odd habits, and she'd loved him in spite of their disagreements. How was she going to say all these things to a dead man? How was she going to ask his forgiveness? But somehow she couldn't leave him until she'd spoken to him. She had to believe he could hear her. "I always loved you, Father. I never meant to hurt you or be the cause of your death. I needed you to help me, but if you can forgive me, I'll forgive you. I'm sorry I can't see you smile and tell me everything is fine between us again, but I sense your love and that is better than nothing. I can never forgive myself for hurting you so much, but I can survive because I know you always loved me. Go to Mum now. I know she'll be happy to see you." She slowly rose off her knees and kissed her father's forehead. "Good-bye," she choked, her face distorted beyond recognition by the power of grief.

······

She wasn't sure she wanted to go to the funeral. She'd said her good-byes in the hospital. She didn't want to stare for half an hour at the coffin. There was no way she wanted to see him buried. "I know you won't understand," she said to a horrified Max on the morning of the funeral as they stood in his kitchen.

"You can't not go to your father's funeral," he scolded. "What will people say? And I know Philip would want you to be in the church."

"He's dead Max!"

Max gave her a withering look and shrugged his shoulders. "That is not the point, but you do as you wish." His voice had an angry overtone. He turned to Tim as he came into the kitchen. "Come on then, son, or we'll be late."

"Give him my love," Jill said quietly.

"But he's dead," Max said sarcastically, immediately regretting it. But there was no time for him to apologise, they were already running behind the clock and he had no intention of being late for his best friend's funeral.

Jill waited until the sound of the car had faded into the distance before moving to an armchair beside the black kitchen range. It was where her father had regularly sat whenever he'd visited his old friend. It was here as a child that she and Tim had often sat on the floor with their backs to the kitchen range and listened to their fathers discussing farming business. The latest cattle and sheep prices and the prospects for the coming harvest dominated many of these conversations, as they were the backbone of their farming enterprises. It was here that she'd decided all she wanted in the world was to be a farmer at first to work alongside her father until she knew as much about the livestock and the crops as he did. Then in his old age, when he wasn't quite so active or willing to fall out of bed at four in the morning whatever the weather, she'd be his able deputy. She'd imagined it would be a wonderful partnership. Then she'd made one mistake—one stupid bloody mistake, and her world had been turned upside down.

Now her father lay in a dark forbidding coffin, his cold body stripped of all its dignity and she hadn't even the decency to go to his funeral. Christ, what was she becoming! She glanced up at the clock above the stove, so caked with grease that she could only just make out the hands. There was half an hour to go before the service. She could still make it. But she wasn't dressed for a funeral. Did that really matter—what was the most important? Twenty-five minutes to go! There was still just time.

......

She reached the church with seconds to spare. She sat down breathlessly next to Max aware that she was getting a few strange glances. She reached out to Max and felt the comforting grip of his hand fold over hers. "I had a change of mind," she said quietly.

"Well done," he whispered.

......

Max had arranged for a few of Philip's closest friends to come back to Walnut Farm after the funeral. Now Jill stood surrounded by these friends listening to words of condolence. How much they had respected her father, his religious beliefs and his rather old fashioned honesty, whatever that might have meant. They never mentioned he could be stubborn, so bloody hurtful. But she was happy to listen to the compliments, glad that they hadn't seen his darker side. And as she smiled, her thanks standing in the sitting room surrounded by all the things she'd grown up with she was filled with a longing to return. It would be the last act in her return to sanity.

After they had all gone, she said to Max. "I hope you'll understand this, but I'm going to stay here now. It's time I came home."

"Of course, I understand," he replied. "I'll go and collect a few things and keep you company."

"No, Max. You've propped me up long enough—I really want to be alone."

Max shrugged. "Well, I'm not too sure you're ready for this."

"Max!" Her tone said that she would brook no objections.

"Very well, but remember I'm on the end of the telephone."

......

Now at last, she was on her own. She looked round the room at the dirty cups, the odd glass that had contained whisky, the ashtrays full of cigarette ends and decided it could all wait until the morning. Though she was exhausted, she knew she'd never be able to sleep.

Waste of time going to bed.

Instead, she collapsed into her father's favourite chair, where he'd sat most evenings smoking his smelly old pipe. She smiled and wondered what he'd expect of her now. Certainly not waste time wracked with guilt. He'd expect her to get off her arse, regain her self-esteem and keep the farm running on an even keel. 'Prove your worth,' is what he'd have said. Well, she'd do just that. She'd always liked a challenge, and this would be one hell of a challenge.

......

"Hello Max."

Max sighed with relief. He'd spent a very uneasy night. "Jill darling, you okay?"

"I'm fine thanks. Sorry I pushed you out like that. I hope you haven't been too worried."

"Not a bit—well, perhaps just a little. Tim wanted me to ring, once I got back here, but I fought the urge—got the message, you see."

"It wasn't meant to come out quite so bluntly and I apologise. I needed to be alone. I feel better already. I've decided several things. One, I will never talk to Harry again, though that might be difficult. Two, is that I'm going to continue to be positive over the baby. After all, it's no disgrace to be a single mum these days. Third, I'm staying here, not being a wet weed and running back to you. There's so much to do. I know the men on the farm are very competent, but I suspect they're a bit lost without Father. I plan to see them this morning and tell them their jobs are safe. Then, I will sort out the house. How's that for starters?"

"It sounds good to me."

"I hoped you'd say that. However, I have a favour to ask."

"Ask away."

"Can you come over and help? You know, like with dad's clothes and things? I don't think I can do it on my own."

"Do you really want to do that now?" Max questioned.

"Yes. It's too morbid to keep drawers and cupboards full of his clothes, and it will only get more difficult to get rid of them if I delay. I want them gone."

Max thought back to the dreadful two days he'd spent burning Jane's clothes and broke into a sweat. He couldn't do it all over again. Not even for his goddaughter. "Would you understand if I said I couldn't do that?"

There was a slight hesitation before she replied, "I think so."

He could hear the disappointment in her voice. *You must be honest with her, Max*, he thought. "Look, this may sound very silly, but I don't think I'm the right person to help you. It would bring back terrible memories. Burning Jane's clothes was one of the worst times of my life, and I think I would become very emotional if I came over. Not exactly what you want at the moment."

"Oh, Max, I'm so sorry! How could I have been so insensitive? Of course I understand. You stay away. I'll do the job myself. Probably better that way."

"Tim will help."

"I'm really not too sure about that."

Max heard the doubt and said, "I'm not going to try and push you into something, but I'm sure, if asked, he'd really like to help. He still has a soft spot for you."

"I don't think it's the right time to be telling me that."

"I can't agree with you. Tim's friendship for you is cast iron."

"I can't ask him."

"Would you like me to?"

"I don't know."

"Well, I do. So I'm going to, anyway. Stop clicking your tongue. If he doesn't want to come, he'll say so."

Jill imagined Max waving a finger at the telephone. To argue would be pointless. "Okay, go ahead, but no pressure you hear?"

"I promise. I'll talk to him now and he'll ring you back. Don't go anywhere."

"I won't. And maybe it's time to find out if I can talk to someone other than you without feeling ashamed."

"Sometimes you talk a load of rubbish."

"Perhaps, but that's how I feel."

"No need to feel like that with Tim."

She steadied her breathing. "All right, I'll wait by the 'phone."

Max replaced the receiver and saw Tim had come into the room. "Did you hear all that?"

"Most of it."

"I can't go; it would crucify me."

"Dad, don't worry. I'd be delighted to go."

"She could get very emotional. Can you deal with that?"

"I think I can handle that. I'm more detached than you are. "

"I'm sure, and thanks Tim. I owe you one."

"No need. You know how I feel about her. She's part of the family, for want of a better word. Okay her fling with Harry was bloody stupid, but we can all make mistakes, and she's certainly paying for hers. She's had a terrible time and needs a friend."

"You can say that again. Taking on the responsibility of running the farm at the same time as having a baby is not going to be easy"

"She wants to stay, then?"

"Looks like it."

"I'm a little surprised. I thought she might like to get as far away from Harry as possible."

"She's always had a love affair with the farm. Ever since she could walk it's all she's wanted. I don't think anything will take her away."

Tim had a thought. "Unless, vindictive old Philip has struck her out of his will."

"That hasn't happened."

"Uncle Philip showed you the will?"

"He asked me to be a witness—told me the contents."

"He might have written another one since she took up with Harry."

"He hasn't. He told me so a few days before he died that it would be God's wish that he should forgive her."

"Well, I'm glad he did something decent towards her in the end."

"That's not very fair."

"It is by my book, Dad."

"He was a good friend to me."

"That's as it maybe. But he was so cruel to Jill."

"He was a very complicated man."

"I don't think that's any sort of excuse. Now, want me to ring her?"

"Yes."

"And you can take that self-satisfied look off your face, Dad. I just want to help her."

"Whatever you say, boy, whatever you say."

......

As she stood in the middle of her father's bedroom, Jill was shaking. The room was average size. There was the large double bed where as a child she'd curled up with her parents always at Christmas, sometimes on her birthday, and many times when thunder rumbled over the house. On one of the bedside tables was a paperback book spread open, which she assumed her father had been reading the night he'd had the stroke. On the other side of the room was a large wardrobe full of his clothes, which covered the whole of one wall. Opposite were three shelves of books—novels, various reference books on cattle and breeding horses, and of course, his well-worn bible. On the desk by the window were two photographs, one of her sitting proudly on her first pony, Topsy. Her parents had called it a stubborn, strong-headed menace, which had made her furious. The other, a rather faded picture of her parents smiling at a camera on their wedding day.

The room was very quiet, very simple and filled with her father's presence. She leaned against the desk, wracked by a dry sob. She'd left this room until last, knowing it would be the most emotional.

Tim put a hand on her shoulder. "You'll be okay, just breath slowly."

"I know, it's just..."

"Look, why don't you go down and put the kettle on. I'll clear the wardrobe and then we can have a much-needed cup of tea or maybe something stronger. I think you might find it easier."

She hesitated for a second, half shook her head, then threw him one of her smiles that had always gone straight to his heart. "Would you mind?"

"If I did, I wouldn't offer."

"I think I'm being pathetic."

"No you're not—just sensible. Now off you go. Put the kettle on or try and find your father's whisky. Whatever, just leave me to get on with the job. It won't take me long."

"Ok, but..."

"Yes?"

"Thanks, Tim."

He laughed, a little embarrassed. "I'm glad I can help."

She smiled for the first time since she'd entered the house. "See you in the kitchen." She turned quickly, not wanting to be in her father's presence any longer. It had been a traumatic few hours.

But she didn't go straight to the kitchen. Instead she walked into the area at the back of the house where rubbish was burnt once a week. Now the rubbish was her father's possessions. She gazed at a half-burnt shoe that had slipped off the fire, two smouldering ties covered in grey ash. She shuddered and picked up the shoe and threw it on the fire, before forcing herself to run back towards the house. She didn't want Tim to find her staring at a pile of ashes. At the door, she paused and looked up the garden towards the walnut tree. Was it her imagination or were the branches bowed in sadness? "You too?" she said quietly.

......

"It's done," Jill said with a sigh of relief and a weak smile. She was mentally exhausted. Drained of any emotion, she sat numbly at the kitchen table sipping her second mug of sweet tea, laced with a shot of her father's malt whisky which she'd found in one of the kitchen cupboards. She felt slightly shocked that in the space of two hours all evidence of her father's existence had been wiped from the house. It was so terminal.

Tim sat quietly beside her, content to say nothing, knowing she needed time to recover. He was happy to share her distress, quite surprised how comfortable he felt in her presence.

When she eventually spoke, her voice was strong. "Now it's time to look to the future." She touched her stomach self-consciously. "This little thing in here needs all my attention." She gave Tim a startled look. "What made me say that to you? I'm so sorry, Tim, I didn't mean—"

He interrupted her. "I don't mind a bit, honestly. I'm very happy to talk about the baby if you want to. Please don't feel embarrassed. You can say anything to me."

She reached over and kissed him lightly on a cheek, then quickly pulled back. What was she doing? Flustered, she stammered, "I don't know what came over me. It was a crass remark."

"Button that mouth of yours and stop apologising to me," Tim laughed.

Jill's eyes widened with surprise. "Then you don't find me repulsive?"

"Why on earth should I?"

She touched her stomach. "Because of this little creature."

He laughed lightly, sounding just like his father. "One small mistake doesn't need to ruin a friendship, for heaven sake."

"No, I suppose not, but a small mistake?"

"Well, okay, perhaps a little more than that. But what are friendships for if they can't survive the odd crisis? Listen, Jill, you have just said it's time to look to the future. So why not share a little of your new life with me? No pressure, I promise you."

This was not what she'd expected. She felt the blood rushing to her face. She'd convinced herself no one would ever want anything to do with her again. She should have known better with Tim. He'd never cared about convention, and had the same laid-back attitude as his father. She remembered it was something that had attracted her when they'd been younger. She found her voice. "I'm surprised, but so grateful—you have no idea how much better that makes me feel. I'll keep the door ajar," she laughed.

"Will it be open enough for me to squeeze through and ask you out to dinner within the next few weeks?"

"I think I'll need a little time to think about that. I need some breathing space, but thanks, it's a wonderful offer. But are you really sure or just being kind? Do you really want to be seen with a woman pregnant by another man?"

He caressed her with a broad smile. "You really do talk utter nonsense sometimes, Jill. What the hell does it matter? I don't care so why should you? Stop being so old fashioned. There are thousands of girls like you. So let me warn you now, I will not let this drop. I'm not doing this because I feel sorry for you. I'm back from agricultural college. The boy next door again, who is going to help you run this farm, or so my father tells me. So I will not just disappear. I will badger you until you agree to dinner. That's a promise."

"You're making me think there might be life after Harry."

He touched her playfully on the nose. "So there bloody well is—and a much better one, let me tell you. If you came out with me, you'd soon find out."

She pushed his hand away and laughed. "You haven't changed, have you, Tim?"

"I hope not."

"I don't want you to."

"Then I won't. So how about fixing a date now?"

Chapter Seven

She was terrified. Her fear of hospitals made her legs feel heavy and her heart hammer unevenly. If it hadn't been for a nurse firmly guiding her down a cold and intimidating white corridor, she'd have turned and fled, prepared to have her baby anywhere but in this awful place.

Then it might die—end of problem. She reproached herself for the thought.

If only this was a nightmare from which she'd wake up to find herself sitting under the walnut tree talking to Tim, her stomach flat and Harry, a figment of her imagination. She gave an involuntary gasp, encouraging the nurse to tighten her grip and ask, "Are you alright, dear?"

Jill nodded numbly, thinking, *what a stupid question.* Of course, she wasn't all right. She was scared. She gripped the small brown suitcase that she'd packed three weeks earlier in anticipation of a dash to the hospital. Each day since then, whenever she'd felt a pain, she'd been convinced the moment had arrived. But now she was well overdue and the hospital had decided that the baby needed to be induced. It all seemed so cold-blooded, in fact a bit like a production line. 'Come in on such and such a day, and you'll have your baby at such and such a time.' It was not what she'd imagined. But did it really matter? The end result would be the same. *A child I don't want. I'll hate it from the first moment I see it.* She was absolutely sure of that, but, again, she reproached herself. *And I didn't let Tim come with me.* How she was regretting that decision. But she hadn't thought it fair to expect him to hold her hand while she gave birth to another man's baby, certainly not one so unwanted. When she'd said this, he'd put his hands on her shoulders and stared into her eyes, "That's not the way I see it."

He'd been as good as his word ever since they'd burnt her father's clothes. He'd held back, never pushing his presence, content to wait. The result had been that she'd taken up his offer of a meal sooner than she'd expected, and grown used to him being around, not doubting his reasons anymore. Life had been on the up. Her positive attitude had returned. She'd started to laugh again—even at times forgetting the folly growing in her stomach. But now the dark shadows were threatening to return. The baby was about to come into the world.

Unless it's stillborn—oh, dear God, how can I be thinking this!

The nurse's voice interrupted her thoughts. "Here we are, dear. This will be your room for a couple of days. I'll be back with the doctor in a few minutes. You get yourself undressed and into the gown lying on the bed." Then, adding with a smile, "and my dear, you have a very persuasive boy friend if I may say so."

Jill gave her a questioning look. "What—what do you mean, Nurse?"

The nurse pushed open the door. "See for yourself," she said quietly.

Standing in the room, silhouetted against the window, was Tim clutching a large bouquet of pink roses to his chest. "Your favourite colour I believe," he said with a smile.

"Tim!"

He dropped the flowers on the bed, "You didn't think I'd let you go through this on your own did you?"

"I'm not sure how to answer that."

"Well don't; I'm here because I want to be."

Jill fought back the tears. "I'm not going to argue. It's just wonderful to see you. You've no idea how wonderful!" Then, without a second's thought, she threw herself into his arms and kissed him hard on the mouth. It was a moment that changed both their lives.

......

Emma was born at four in the afternoon on the fifth day of August 1977. When the small creature, weighing seven and a half pounds, was laid in Jill's arms, all her hostility vanished. She smiled at the puckered red face and felt a great surge of love flow through her entire body. "How could I ever have thought I'd hate you," she whispered, as the hungry mouth searched for her swollen breast. She looked up at Tim. "How could I?"

"I don't for one moment think you ever really did," Tim replied, looking down on Jill's white face. He felt proud. That confused him, for why should *he* feel proud? The small creature sucking at her mother's breast was the result of a union he'd been jealous of, and a disastrous one at that. And yet…he bent over and brushed his lips across Jill's mouth. "Can you believe I feel proud?"

She shook her head mystified. "No, I find that hard to believe."

"I can understand that, and certainly I don't think I can explain it either, at the moment, but later when I've gathered my rather muddled thoughts together I'll give it my best shot. But right now, I want to say I think she's beautiful and that I think we should call her *our* daughter. Forget Harry had anything to do with it. Since he threw you out, how many times has he shown any inclination to admit he is the father? Not once. To the contrary, he's told everyone who can be bothered to listen that you were having an affair with me all the time. I doubt if many believe him, but what the hell. Folk round here know how badly he treated you. All they want is to see you happy. So let's call Harry's bluff, and admit to the world she's ours. I bet you no one will question it."

Jill's face went slack with shock and incredulity at Tim's suggestion. *Should I take him seriously?*

"Perhaps not in public, but in private they might ask—"

"It won't matter. People will want to accept it, so they will."

"You'd do that for me?"

"I already feel she's mine. I want to share my life with you."

Choking with emotion as the reality of Tim's proposal sank in, Jill replied, "I can't take that on board right now." The slackness of her face was slowly replaced by a look of wonderment that the son of her godfather—the man she'd as good as rejected—wanted to, yes wanted to live with her. Never in her wildest dreams had she imagined this moment.

He put a finger to her lips. "I understand. Wrong time, I know, but I needed to say it, and you're tired. Oh yes, there's one other thing I want to say before I leave you to get a well-earned sleep."

"That is?"

"I won't take no for an answer."

She smiled at him with a mixture of weakness and affection and reached for his hand. "I promise you I will give it my full attention tomorrow."

"That's fine. I'm a patient man." He gently touched the small child on the top of her fuzzy head. "I must go now, let you sleep. I'll be back tomorrow first thing." He straightened up. "Got any ideas for a name?"

"Emma, yes, I want to call her Emma."

......

Later that evening, Tim confided to his father, "It was a very moving experience. Jill wanted me to be with her all the time. I actually saw the birth. I thought I'd be sick, but not at all—it was wonderful. I never once thought what am I doing here, watching another man's baby being born? I felt no jealousy or anger, just this great surge of pride, exactly as if the child was mine. I even remember calling her *our* daughter. A bit weird, I know, but that's how I felt. It was totally amazing."

Chapter Eight

From the age of nine, Jill had dreamt of her wedding day. Always, she was dressed in an expensive white wedding dress, the church filled with the intoxicating fragrance of hundreds of white lilies, her future husband, tall and clean shaven, with large blue eyes, staring at her as she walked up the aisle on the arm of her father. The ring being slipped onto her finger and she promising to obey the man she adored. The honeymoon in some romantic spot on the other side of the world spent making love and swearing they would love each other forever. How utterly stupid she'd been—life just wasn't like that.

Perhaps not quite like that, but the adolescent dream hadn't been completely destroyed, and here she was, three months after the birth of Emma just two hours away from marrying Tim. Okay, his eyes weren't a steely blue, (thank God) and she'd decided not to wear a white wedding dress. Nor was Tim going to whisk her off to some tropical island for a lustful honeymoon, because she had to get home to feed a hungry child. But otherwise most of her dream was still in tact. The church was full of white lilies, Tim was tall and clean shaven, and her friends, none of whom had deserted her much to her surprise, would be there. She could hardly contain her excitement.

She stood in the bedroom where she'd first had the dream and frowned at the mirror as she surveyed her naked figure, particularly the annoyingly visible stretch marks on her stomach. But this was not the day to dwell on things like that. Tim had said he loved the marks. Silly bloody man!

She glanced at her watch. It was time to dress. She moved across to her bed, piled high with fluffy animals collected over many years. Her favourite, the first teddy she'd been given, was showing signs of wear and tear. She felt a little sad that she'd no longer be sleeping in the room where she'd slept since a child, but she and Tim had decided to move into her parents' bedroom, a decision not made lightly. But there could be no place for ghosts now. She winked at her fluffy audience and picked up the blue suit (Tim's favourite colour) that she'd chosen a week before from Harvey Nicholls in London. Vanity played no part in Jill's life, but when she'd surveyed herself in one of the store's changing room mirrors she knew she looked good. The store assistant had said with admiration, "You look stunning."

Stunning. Well, she wasn't capable of being as conceited as that. But there was no denying that the sight of her blond hair hanging loose and flowing down to her shoulders, and her long, sculptured legs ending in a pair of delicately shaped feet in blue high-heeled shoes, certainly made her feel good, even though she wasn't wearing the long white dress of her dreams. She zipped herself into the skirt and hurried to the bathroom to put on her basic makeup. 'Why hide a pretty face under that expensive grunge,' her mother had said to her when Jill, like most of her friends, had wanted to plaster the makeup on. She ran a comb through her hair and then vigorously cleaned her teeth.

Could I be diving in too quickly? She rinsed her mouth. *Should I have waited a little longer before committing myself?* She shook the toothbrush. *Is he only marrying me because he feels sorry for me?* She spat the water angrily into the basin and shook her head. *What am I doing thinking like this? How could I be so negative? Of course he loves me.*

She stared guiltily into the bathroom mirror. It was bloody Harry raising his ugly head again. "Damn you Harry!" she yelled at her reflection. "I shouldn't be thinking like this. Tim won't let me down." She closed her eyes, determined to rid herself of Harry.

The timely intervention of Max's familiar voice shouting, "Hurry up Jill or we're going to be late, and I can't guarantee my son will wait at the church forever," did the trick. *Harry, you're out of my life forever!*

She loved Tim. She'd give him her life, her soul. They'd be like it was in her dream—inseparable. There, she felt better. She tossed her head and called out, "Just give me five minutes." There was just one more thing she had to do, something she should have done months ago, not minutes before her wedding. She rushed to her chest-of-drawers and searched frantically for the green bag that Harry had bought her at Nice Airport. She found it buried amongst some laddered tights. With shaking hands, she opened it and fumbled inside, before pulling out a small photograph of Harry smiling at the camera. *You insufferable shit,* she mouthed as she tore the picture into little pieces and threw them into her wastepaper basket. The bag followed a second later. Then she scooped up teddy and shouted, "On my way, Max."

One of the things that so endeared Jill to Max was her refusal to completely grow up, so he showed no surprise as she came out of her room holding the one-armed, one-eyed teddy in her arms. She saw Max smile. "He's one of the most important guests," she laughed.

"And he's a very lucky one as well, being so close to such a beautiful woman," chuckled Max, staring at Jill in admiration. "My son is a very lucky young man."

Jill threw him one of her natural smiles that always took his breath away. "No, Max. I'm the one who's lucky, and I promise you, I'll never forget it."

PART THREE
2000–2001

Remember me when I am gone.

Christina Rossetti, *Remember*

Chapter Nine

It would not have been Jill's preference to start hunting again so soon after Tim's death, and as she rode into the field below Sidenham Hall, she could feel the beads of apprehension on her forehead. She'd only agreed under heavy pressure from her children. "It's time to start the clock again,' Toria had said. "Besides, Emma goes back to Bristol tomorrow, so it might be the last chance we have to hunt together for some time."

Right on both counts, but it doesn't feel right.

She'd ignored her misgivings, telling herself that she'd overreacted at the funeral and that Harry presented no danger at all. In fact, by the time she'd loaded the horses into the horsebox, she'd almost persuaded herself that she might have misjudged him. After all, he'd been quite happy to deny he was Emma's father for twenty-three years, so what would he gain by blowing the whistle now? But the warning voice refused to be completely silenced. Harry was an unstable manipulator, and he hadn't come to the funeral wake just to give his condolences. Everything Harry did had a hidden agenda, and this agenda terrified her. She saw him sitting on one of his immaculately groomed geldings surrounded by the usual bevy of well-manicured women on smart thoroughbreds, though perhaps they were not as young as they used to be, nor in quite such large numbers. Could Harry's charms be slipping? *He certainly looked a trifle overweight at the funeral.* She smiled at the thought—saw he'd spotted her and she quickly looked away. It annoyed her that he still had the ability to fluster her. She was relieved to see Max ride into the field. He was untidy, as usual, raising his cap to everyone, and quick to move towards the nearest tray of port.

"Come on girls, let's go and join Max."

"Good idea," said Toria. "The air stinks round here."

Emma longed to say, "Don't be so stupid. You may not want to hang around, but I want to stay here and talk to Harry." Instead she said nothing, deeming this was the wrong time to rock the boat.

"Hello, girls," said Max as they rode up beside him. He gave them a generous smile and raised his glass of port. "What a lovely sight you three make."

Jill reflected that time and heartache hadn't changed Max one bit. He was still the good-natured man who laughed easily and was rarely seen without a grin on his face.

"Oh, you old flatterer," she said easily.

"It's easy to flatter when it's the truth," he laughed. "Besides I'm proud of my family of girls. Nice horse you've got there, Toria," he complimented.

"You should recognise it," she replied. "You bought it for dad a month before he was diagnosed with cancer."

"Ah, so I did, so I did," Max said a little sadly. "Well, you make sure you treat him right, young lady."

"I'll do that," Toria replied. "He's a lovely horse, Grandfather, but it's sad it's not Dad hunting him."

"Well, you'll do him proud I'm sure." Max saw the pain in Toria's eyes and quickly switched subjects. "Now, I better go and have a word with the police—got our usual bunch of antis out. Don't want them leaving my gates open again. Last time all my heifers were gallivanting down the village High Street."

Jill stared at the group gathered in an isolated corner of the field under a large chestnut tree surrounded as usual by police officers. She recognised the two middle-aged women carrying banners saying 'SCUM' in bold black letters. The four young men standing with them and dressed in combat gear were new to her. She frowned and looked away quickly. It was not that she was against other people disapproving of what she did, it was the way that some of them chose to do it.

And these four look dangerous.

She took exception to being spat at, called a bloodthirsty barbarian, or worse. What on earth gave them the right to abuse her? If she behaved the same way towards them in the street, she'd probably be arrested. She'd never been able to understand why the police were so ineffectual. It infuriated her that the antis seemed to be able to get away with so much violence in the name of saving a furry piece of vermin. Basil Brush had a lot to answer for. Well, if it ever came to a ban, she'd be one of the first to defy it and happily end up in prison. "It's freedom of choice," she told Emma one day when her daughter was questioning her. "Too much of our freedom has already been eroded and a stand has to be made somewhere. The fact that it's hunting is really irrelevant."

"Oh, come on, Mum," Emma had laughed, "it's all to do with hunting."

Jill glanced at Emma. Sometimes she was so like Harry.

Emma felt her mother's stare and reluctantly took her eyes off Harry. "I could do with a drink, Mum," she seemed to complain.

Emma's love of the bottle had started to worry Jill, and she was quick to say, "A bit too late, I think. We'll be moving off any minute now."

"Oh God," Emma said quietly to herself. Just recently she'd decided she could live without hunting, which saddened her in a way. It was not that she had a conscience over the cruelty bit, (that was reserved for ignorant townies), or had any feelings for the fox. It was just that she saw it as a complete waste of time coming home at her mother's behest to rush round the countryside on a cold wet day. It didn't make her any money, and delayed the moment when she'd reach her goal to be rich, really rich, in fact stinking rich. While sitting on a horse, risking a broken limb, she was endangering her source of income. By her own admission she wasn't particularly bright, but she possessed an uncanny nose for making a quick buck. In fact, she knew she wouldn't hesitate to be dishonest if she thought she could get away with it. She wondered how she could be so different from her conventional parents. Well, the sooner the whole day ended and she could get back to Bristol, the better. She'd stayed longer then she'd planned, and she was eager to get back to her thriving business. As she licked her dry lips—she'd have done anything for a slug of vodka—she hoped her customers hadn't gone to other ports of call for their pleasures!

The sound of the huntsman's horn interrupted her thoughts, and she followed her mother and Toria out of the field and into a position where they would be well placed if a fox was found immediately. She eyed a tray of glasses full of port and was tempted to hang back, but she knew if she wanted to get close to Harry, she had to be with the 'thrusters' rather than with those who just came out to trot around the fields and gossip. That was not Harry's style at all. Actually she was pretty pissed off with Harry Sidenham. She'd hoped he might have rung by now and offered her that promised ride in his Jag. She'd even rung him from her mobile twice and left messages, which had never been returned. *The rat's avoiding me because of that trouble with Mum.*

She petulantly dug her spurs into her horse's flanks. Since the funeral, she'd thought a lot about Harry, perhaps too much. But he'd always attracted her from afar. After talking to him, she thought he was something else. He was sexy, his manner mysterious, and his flashing steel blue eyes were to die for. But rumour had it that he was otherwise engaged in his favourite pastime: bedding married women. By all accounts, two at the same time! Well, she could hardly expect him to have taken a vow of celibacy after their short meeting, but she intended to have him one day—all six feet two inches, naked and panting for her. She swore loudly as she hit her left knee on a gatepost. Having erotic dreams out hunting could endanger her health and she'd get nowhere with a broken leg! *But Harry, I won't let you go.*

She broke into a canter and followed her sister. *Roll on tomorrow,* was all she could think of as her horse rose over the first jump of the day.

••••••

They had found a fox, as usual in the kale below the house, bringing back memories of her last day's hunting with her father. But Jill felt little sadness. To dwell on the past was no longer on her agenda. Besides there had been a screaming scent and she'd soon been caught up in the excitement of the chase. Now, late in the day, tired and weary, her bones aching from lack of hunting, she sat on the rise of a hill and surveyed the kaleidoscope of colour unwinding below her. The sight bewitched her. The steaming horses, the rolling fields, the ghostlike woods, the sheep gathered together, staring apprehensively at all the activity that was ruining their last graze of the day. The dark clouds passing swiftly overhead in the northerly breeze, the odd rook and pigeon on the wing, and the unmistakable call of cock pheasants as they prepared to go to bed. She patted her horse's neck and smiled, as she spotted Toria talking to Max. That girl could ride and she was brave, like her grandmother. Perhaps she'd been selfish in discouraging Toria from riding in point-to-points, but she wasn't prepared to risk another life and inflict more suffering on herself. *I was selfish,* she admitted.

But if Toria had ever resented her mother's cautionary hand, she'd never said so. She was special—so supportive since Tim's death, throwing herself into her new job with enthusiasm. Jill accepted there would be no return to university. Toria's future was on the farm. Secure.

But the same could not be said of Emma. Jill had a nagging feeling that things were not quite right with Emma. She couldn't put a finger on it, but for some reason she smelt trouble. As she sat running her gloved hand down the side of her horse's neck, she wondered if it had anything to do with Harry. Certainly, the drinking, the moods, the lack of interest in the countryside, and her worrisome curiosity about Harry (she'd noticed the glances towards him earlier) all gave her cause for concern. Perhaps, Emma had more of her father in her than was good for her.

She stood up in her stirrups as she heard hounds speak, setting the blood racing in her veins. A late hunt! Very often the best, when the scent hung low to the ground as the day grew colder. She was tempted to spur her horse forward and join those that were left in the valley. If she cantered, she'd catch up with them before they disappeared. But she held back, feeling the stiffness in her back and leg muscles. She heard hounds speak again, then silence before a loud 'Halloa' echoed up the valley. It was too much for her. She'd always hated missing a good hunt, and she'd been starved of the excitement. "Come on, old fellow, let's have one more go," she whispered, as she pressed her spurs into the gelding. He needed little encouragement, moving easily into his stride, perfect balance, perfect understanding, and the adrenaline flowing through his rippling muscles. Half way into the valley, Jill's eye caught sight of two horses going in the opposite direction. *Silly fools, missing the best hunt of the day*, she thought.

And then her heart missed a beat, for she recognised the grey horse. Emma! What was *she* doing going the wrong way? She pushed her mount for a little more speed, so as to get closer and see if there was a problem. A hundred yards further on down the valley she pulled up, her breath coming in gasps. Emma wasn't in difficulties. No, she was riding off with Harry! Jill felt sick, a little dizzy. The warning voice was hammering at her brain. Her shoulders dropped and she turned her horse away from the valley, even though she was tempted to ride after them. "Damn you, Harry, oh damn you!" she cried across the valley, before turning to ride home, her stomach taut, her eyes filled with tears.

The two riders rode on, oblivious to her presence.

······

It was dark when Jill heard the familiar sound of a horsebox pulling up in the yard.

"It's Emma!" she cried to Toria, as the security lights clearly picked out Harry's lorry and Emma climbing down from the passenger door.

Jill arrived in the yard, her stomach churning like the fast spin of a washing machine, just as Harry appeared from the back of the box leading Emma's horse, Chester. She had a wild desire to rush back into the house and hide, so certain was she that Harry would have told Emma that he was her father. But before she could move, she heard Harry calling to her, the lights clearly picking out one of those smiles that had once so captivated her.

"Sorry we're late, Jill." Not said like an apology. "Long hunt, you know, and we landed up several miles from the horse box." Harry winked at Emma as he gave her the reins of her horse.

With difficulty Jill refrained from shouting, "You lying bastard!" But she was eager to avoid a confrontation, at least until she'd found out if Harry had said anything. So instead, she forced herself to say, "I'm glad you had a good hunt, and thanks for bringing Emma back in one piece."

"I was watching over her. But she's a very capable rider, quite able to look after herself, you know. Want any help?"

Jill exploded. "Oh, Harry, you just don't get the message, do you? I don't want your help. I want you out of here NOW! I know Emma is perfectly capable of looking after herself, thank you."

"Mum!"

"Sorry, Emma, but as you know, Harry is not welcome here. Now are you going?"

His voice was dripping with sarcasm as he said, "What, no word of thanks?"

"Very well, thanks," Jill said with difficulty. "Now get out of this yard."

"Throwing me out is getting to be a very aggravating habit of yours." Harry spat. "However, might I suggest you try to control your temper?"

She didn't rise to his bait. She knew Harry too well. Instead, she gave a shake of her head and said, "Good night, Harry."

Without another word, he climbed back into the horsebox and gunned the engine. Relieved, as she was to see him go, she was fearful much worse was yet to come. She swallowed hard, smiled at Emma, and decided it would be best to play along with the charade for a while longer. "I'm glad you had a good hunt with Harry but I wish you'd come home with Max. I was getting quite worried. Now, if you can manage Chester on your own, I'll go and help Toria with your tea. Try not to be too long."

"I can manage," Emma called back as she led Chester to his stable. "And do you know, Mum, I don't understand what you find so awful about Harry. He's fun. At least not boring like most of those dickheads out today."

"Emma!"

Emma stopped and turned to look at her mother. "Oh, I know some of them are your friends, but wow, they certainly wouldn't set the world alight. All they can talk about is their children or their bloody gardens. Christ there's more to life than that surely? Harry is so different. He's alert, fun. Sorry, but I like him very much."

So he hadn't told her. But what had they been up to? Jill decided it was better not to ask. She should have felt relief, but instead, she was overcome with foreboding. She should have known Harry wasn't the sort to be straightforward. He was playing a subtle game, worming his way into Emma's affection, and then he'd strike like a cobra and swallow her whole. Poor bloody child! But she was powerless to stop him. She'd played the 'lying game' as much as he. She took care to compose herself before saying, "You may well find some of the people who hunt boring, but most of them are honest and have been good friends to us all, which is more than I can say for Harry. He may well seem fun, but he's untrustworthy, totally immoral and a compulsive liar. I would rather have any one of those people you call dickheads as a friend."

Emma stared defiantly at her mother. "You're wrong. How can you say that?"

"Because, young lady, I know a lot more about Harry than you. And tonight…" She stopped and shook her head. "Oh, it's nothing."

"You can't clam up now, Mum. What were you about to say?"

Jill hesitated for a few seconds before deciding the charade had gone on long enough. "I was about to say, let's take tonight, for example."

"What do you mean?" she said defensively.

"Harry's a snake, a manipulator *par excellence*. He made you lie to me just now."

"I didn't say a word."

"Your silence was a lie. I know perfectly well you and Harry didn't take part in that last hunt. I saw you both riding off in the opposite direction."

"You were spying on us!"

"Actually, no. I was coming to join the hunt when I saw you both riding off."

"Oh."

"Yes, 'oh' indeed, my girl! I think you owe me an apology."

"Okay, if it makes you happy I'll apologise for not saying anything, but since when has silence been a lie? Anyway, what does it matter? I'm old enough to ride off with Harry if I want to. And don't think we were up to something. We sat in his horsebox and talked. He has a fund of amusing stories."

Jill took a deep breath. "I wasn't suggesting anything, and I think this conversation has run its course. And I'm sure you think you're old enough to judge Harry for yourself. But I thought the same once. It didn't take me long to discover how wrong I was."

"Whatever happened to you won't happen to me."

The conviction in Emma's voice rattled Jill. This was real terrifying. Weakly she said, "When you come inside, I'll tell you a bit more about your new friend."

"Okay. I'll be interested to hear the dirt." Emma gave her mother a supercilious smile before lifting the saddle off Chester and walking to the tack room. As she reached the door, she said over her shoulder, "I'll be in for my eggs in say around fifteen minutes, and tell Toria I don't want them hard boiled."

Jill was cold, angry and tired. "Yes, madam," she couldn't stop herself saying as she turned back towards the house. "I'll make sure your eggs are ready for you."

Cursing herself for being churlish, she walked into the kitchen and saw Toria shaking the toaster and swearing under her breath, reminding Jill that she'd planned to replace it with a new one. "Sorry, I keep meaning to buy another one."

Toria turned with a smile on her face. "Oh, it doesn't worry me too much—getting quite used to its idiosyncrasies, really." Then she saw her mother's face. "You look awful. Trouble with Emma?"

"It's Harry. To think that only this morning I was sure he'd gotten the message to stay away from us. More fool me. Do you know he's just made Emma lie to me—or anyway acquiesce to his lie that they'd been at that last hunt? The man is insufferable."

"You saw them?"

"I was watching from the top of the valley."

"Oh dear, I'd hoped you hadn't seen."

"You didn't tell me," Jill admonished.

"I saw no point—knew it would only upset you."

"Well, I'm more than upset now."

"Mum, listen, I'm sorry."

"Oh darling, that was not meant as a criticism. But Harry is *so* dangerous. I just wish he'd go away. Die would be better."

"Mum, that's not like you!"

"I know, but he's always managed to bring the worst out of me."

"Perhaps if you told us why you dislike him so much, we might understand better."

"I don't think I can."

"Why not?"

"It's all too painful." A slight hesitation. "No, I really can't do it."

Toria rushed to her mother's side. "Alright, Mum, alright. I'm quite happy to drop the subject. Actually what happened between you and Harry doesn't interest me, but I don't think that applies to Emma. I think she'll ask lots of questions. You know how curious she can be, and she didn't ride off with Harry just to admire the scenery."

"No, and that's what terrifies me," Jill replied miserably, thinking of Harry lurking out there like some predator. "Damn Harry for coming on the scene again. Why after so long does he have to interfere with my life? It's just not fair. But then I suppose it's what I must expect from such a devious man."

Toria kissed her warmly. "I really do think you have got to tell Emma and me about Harry."

Jill gently pushed her away and looked sadly into her eyes. "You may be right. But not right now. It's not as simple as you may imagine. Emma is not going to stop seeing him whatever I say and she's bound to tell Harry every word of our conversation. And he wouldn't be Harry if he didn't manage to twist it to his advantage." She sank into a chair beside the kitchen table and buried her head in her hands. The truth was she felt the time had come to tell at least some of the truth and pray that Harry kept his mouth shut. Who the hell did she think she was kidding? All this chumminess with Emma pointed to only one thing. No decent man would go down that route, but Harry was not a decent man, he was evil. He wanted to inflict as much emotional damage on herself as he could and if Emma got hurt on the way too bad. He'd always blamed her for the breakdown in their relationship and was consumed by some perverse jealousy when she married Tim His bloated vanity could never accept that any woman, however badly he'd treated her, could resist him.

At that moment, a disgruntled Emma slouched into the kitchen, wet, cold and hungry, and harbouring an almost unbearable thirst for a large measure of vodka and a much-needed intake of nicotine. "It's fucking cold out there," she complained. "Bloody horse won't eat, and the bloody mud won't come off my tack. God, Mum, why can't you employ a groom?" Without waiting for the reply, (she'd heard enough of the boring old 'we can't afford it' talk), she flounced off to the sitting room to fill a glass with neat vodka and to pick up a packet of cigarettes she'd left on a table the night before. Five minutes later, she was back in the kitchen, the glass of vodka already empty and a cigarette in one hand. "That's better," she exclaimed, dropping down into the chair next to her mother. "And now, sister darling, are my eggs ready? Not too hard, I hope."

"If they are, cook the next lot yourself," Toria replied, slamming two boiled eggs in front of her sister.

"Oh, grumble, grumble, grumble," Emma spat, cracking open her first egg. "Actually just right, surprising as it may seem."

"Oh, I'm *so* glad," Toria retorted.

Emma chose to ignore her sister. She was hungry, and more interested in questioning her mother than getting into some silly argument. She polished off the eggs quickly, lit another cigarette, and fixed her eyes on Jill. "Now, Mum, I think it's time you told us what's with this Harry stuff."

Jill took a deep breath. "Has Harry said anything to you?"

"Only that he can't understand your attitude."

Well, if that's the case he's thicker than I thought, Jill was tempted to say, but knew it would only exacerbate an already awkward situation. So with a shrug of her shoulders she said, "I suppose he's entitled to his opinion, but I'll leave it to you to judge for yourself if his assessment is right."

"I'm all ears," said Emma.

Jill fiddled nervously with her empty glass of Sancerre and eyed Emma's cigarette enviously, even though she hadn't smoked for years. "I once had a disastrous affair with Harry. I was warned by both your grandfathers to keep away from him, but I chose to ignore their advice." She smiled sadly. "I suppose like all young girls I thought I knew best. But I was soon to find out how right they were. Although he said he loved me, Harry never gave up chasing other women. He lied, he was secretive, and he was unrepentant. But I loved him, so I believed his constant assurances that I was the only woman for him. All the others were mere dalliances. As you've just said, Emma, he's fun and he can dazzle women with that smile of his."

He does more than dazzle me, thought Emma as her mother continued.

"How stupid I was. Eventually we split up and I was left with no choice but to beg my father's forgiveness, which was not forthcoming. I was devastated. My life seemed utterly pointless until your father came on the scene."

"I think you should have told us this before now," admonished Toria

Jill hesitated for a second. "I saw no point. I thought Harry was out of my life, and so he would have been if your father hadn't died."

"Why did you split up?" asked Emma.

"We had a dreadful row."

"Did you sleep with him?"

Jill flushed. "I don't think I need answer that."

But you did, Emma thought, trying to imagine her mother in bed with Harry.

"No, please don't, Mum," Toria intervened, glaring at Emma. "We really don't want to delve into your past love life. It's too disgusting."

Well, I'd like to delve, thought Emma, sexually stimulated by the thought of her mother making love to Harry.

"I also think," continued Toria, "that we've heard enough about this affair with Harry. It was a long time ago and he was obviously a shit then and nothing has changed. All I can say is, thank God he threw you out, Mum. Harry as a father, yuck!"

Jill gagged momentarily on a piece of toast.

"Alright, let's drop the subject," Emma agreed, wise enough to realise it was the wrong time to fly to Harry's defence.

"Just one more thing," Jill said. "Until the funeral, Harry and I had only spoken on the very rare occasion since we split up. I didn't want to encourage him to be in our life in any shape or form, and both your father and I made that abundantly clear. That wish has not changed, so please, I beg you both not to encourage him in any way."

Emma scowled.

Toria asked, "Do you think he's trying to move in on you again?"

"I hope not, but I suppose it's possible, extraordinary as that may seem."

"Oh the sleazebag," Toria cried. "How could he, so soon after dad's death?"

"Harry is like no other mortal," Jill said.

"I'm sure you're right," Toria agreed. "If he starts poking his nose in around here, he'll have me to answer to."

"What a gutsy sister I have," exclaimed Emma, feeling slightly woozy from her large intake of vodka, and amused at how far off course her mother and sister were. *If only you knew, you'd shit yourselves*, she thought, before saying, "But I doubt if he'll be around again. If he hasn't gotten the message by now, he's an idiot."

"And what will you do, Emma?" Jill dared to ask.

"Tell him he's a liar and a menace to women."

"So you will see him again?"

"Only to tell him to piss off back to his bordello," laughed Emma.

Jill felt the tension lift. "Thank you, thank you both for your support and understanding."

Emma forced herself to look at her mother. "Well, I'm off for an early night. I'm knackered and need a hot bath. Hope you two don't mind. Oh by the way, darling sister, do you think you could make less noise in the bathroom at four in the morning?"

"Wouldn't do you any harm to come and help me," Toria bit back.

"You must be joking. I can't think of anything worse than having cows shitting over me at that hour. Good-night."

She left in a haze of smoke and hurriedly went to the sitting room to refill her glass with vodka, making a mental note to buy a fresh bottle in the morning. Once in her bedroom, she propped herself up on the pillows, and reflected on the thoroughly embarrassing ordeal in the kitchen. She wasn't sure which had been the most difficult, listening to her mother's confession or keeping her mouth shut over Harry. God, how she'd wanted to shout, "He's not after you, Mum, it's ME he wants! He excites me, he's dangerous, and he's so bloody sexy." She sipped her vodka—beautifully smooth, so addictive, a bit like Harry. Boy could she get hooked on him, a smooth-talking, immoral shit and no doubt very dangerous. She'd seen the cruelty behind his eyes. She'd had enough experience with men to know his type. But she liked dangerous men, and she felt sure Harry was attracted to her. They could have fun together. That was all she wanted in life, fun and money, and she was sure Harry would give her both. Nothing her mother said would stop her.

Chapter Ten

Emma didn't like to think of herself as a prostitute, no common streetwalker, nor did she advertise in contact magazines or on the net. She worked as an escort girl for an exclusive agency in Bristol. She was top of the range.

But her mother would have called her a prostitute.

She rented a flat in Redcliffe Street, just a few hundred yards from the Clifton suspension bridge, and within a matter of twenty minutes she could be in the centre of Bristol. She did not like taking men back to her flat—felt it was too risky and intrusive. Daytimes and nights with a client were spent in a hotel. The agency booked her punters, took a fee, and paid her the balance. What she earned after that was up to her. It was easy and lucrative pickings. She'd made her choice of profession on purely financial grounds, accepting that her parents would never be able to provide her with the lifestyle she hankered for. There were those that would say it was dangerous and downright degrading, and how could a nice girl like her sink so low, but two fingers to the lot of them! The money was what she was after—wads of lovely money! And she was doing very well, thank you.

Once men set eyes on her sleek five-foot-five body dressed always in designer clothes, they were hooked. Her short blond hair was cut like a man's. A few punters said it smelled like summer. Her long, thin legs were always elegantly encased in sheer stockings (she never wore tights), their colour varying with her mood; her eyes flashed with mischief. She could ask any

145

price for her 'extra' services and afford to be fussy. She was, as her employer called her, "One very classy whore." The danger didn't worry Emma too much either, for normally the punters coming through the agency had already been screened. Okay, even the best dressed, well-spoken male could go berserk when his dick was aroused, but Emma reckoned the risk was no greater than walking alone on a public street late at night. Now after a little over two years of work, she had her 'specials' anyway. Most of these were wealthy, married businessmen. They were reliable, generous and safe, never prepared to go over the edge. There was too much to lose at home. But some broke the rules and saw Emma as a prospective bride and as the basis for starting life anew without 'that bitching wife.' They thought she'd be eternally grateful for being rescued from such a humiliating profession. Others saw her as a mistress, set up in a flat conveniently close to their place of work. With a smile, she showed these types the door. No way did she want to marry some bastard who was cheating on his wife, and nor did she want to become the plaything of one man to be discarded when the excitement of keeping a mistress wore off. She was in the business for money, nothing more, and when she'd amassed enough to keep her in the style she desired she'd get out as quickly as possible. It was nothing for her to earn in excess of two thousand pounds a week, and if she spent a weekend with a man, she would get nearer three thousand. So far she'd earned very nearly three hundred thousand tax free.

But there was a price to be paid. The long hours, the drinking, the stress of having always to smile and then perform well in bed with a man, who more times than not made her feel sick, with his fat belly and the furrows in his skin damp with sweat was beginning to take its toll. The moment to quit was very close. But like so many girls before her, she was learning the stark truth that it was an easier profession to get into than to get out of. Money could prove as addictive as any drug.

It was raining hard as she climbed out of her MG. After so long away, the flat would be cold, but the money she'd splashed out on a new central heating system would soon have her warm and snug. With the ready agreement of her landlord, she'd lavished a considerable sum on the three roomed flat. When she dragged her tired, misused body home, she wanted to be able to relax in a Jacuzzi and wash off the stink of the man who'd been panting all over her. Recently, a large glass of iced vodka had been added to the therapy.

Head down against the rain, she ran up the drive and punched in the security code to open the door into the lobby. She dragged her suitcase up the two flights of stairs to her flat, inserted her key in the lock and swung the door open, switching on the lights as she moved into a small hallway. It was cold. She shivered, dropped her suitcase on the thick pile beige carpet and ran to flick on the heating. In less than half an hour the flat would be warm. She moved to the sitting room, sparsely but comfortably furnished, with two white leather sofas, several occasional tables and an armchair given to her by a dodgy antique dealer now serving a few years for fraud (who'd fancied her rotten and assured her the chair was worth a fortune). Shitty little bastard! She'd taken it in lieu of payment. When she'd tried to sell it she'd been told it was as good as worthless. But then what else had she expected, silly cow. On the walls were six garish modern paintings depicting God knows what, but which Emma liked to think were in the spirit of free expression. They had not come cheap. In one corner of the room was a table on which rested eight tumblers and two large bottles of vodka. She smiled at them as she moved towards the bedroom—a little smaller than the sitting room with a king-sized bed taking up most of the space. She liked to spread out in her own bed. A door led to the bathroom. She swore loudly as she put her suitcase on the bed, remembering that she'd forgotten to have her heated blanket mended. Ah well, there was a hot water bottle in the broom cupboard. Or maybe it was time to start work again. She hurried to the telephone and flicked in her ansaphone—she'd rung the agency before leaving home to tell them she was back in business.

The boss's familiar voice filled the sitting room, oozing gratuitous charm. "Dahling Emma, glad you're back. Sorry to hear about your father. SO many people have missed you. You really are one of my star girls. Now to business, dahling. Philip M (clients were only known by their first name and then a capital letter), is in town tonight and won't see anyone else but you. Don't let him down—one of our best clients. He's at the usual number after six this evening. DO so hope you can make it."

The inference was clear. A good client was worth keeping, and even her best girls couldn't expect to pick and choose when they worked. The boss would only stand so much and Emma had witnessed tearful girls leaving the old bat's office, knowing that she'd see they never worked again anywhere in the Bristol area.

Emma dialled the agency.

Philip was loaded, not bad looking, married with two children (cheating bastard), and was very generous. She smiled at the bed, knowing tonight she wouldn't freeze after all. She'd be in another, warmer one. She looked across at the photograph of her father, sitting smiling on the steps of his new John Deere combine and felt a brief stab of guilt. "Sorry, Dad," she mumbled. What would he have done had he guessed her career? Wow, that would have been a big bust-up! Journalist! She laughed. How had she thought that one up? But it had worked, which though it seemed a miracle, was probably only because of her parents' powerless financial state, their minds elsewhere, fighting to keep their heads above water, and then the dreadful threat of the cancer. God, how she hated the idea of poverty and the problems it caused. Well, she was doing okay, but for how much longer could she keep her profession a secret? Now that her father was dead, her mother was already growing more curious—the MG hadn't helped, mind you. Probably would have been wiser to have hired an old banger. That's what most journalists drove round in wasn't it? It dawned on her that she didn't really care what her mother thought. Bad, bad girl! What did worry her was if Harry ever found out. How would he react? Oh shit! "Quit!" she shouted across the room.

Wrong, don't be so impulsive! You don't have a clue at the moment which way the relationship is going. Be sure of him before chucking away a gold mine.

She felt aroused by the thought that Harry might be her next meal ticket. A delicious lip-smacking meal. She glanced at her watch—still three hours before she had to ring Philip M. She had time to slip into the warm churning water of her Jacuzzi with a large vodka in one hand. But first she'd make a call. She picked up her mobile and selected the number.

"Harry," she purred as she heard his voice.

······

"Do you think Harry's up to something with Emma?" Jill asked.

Max shrugged his wide shoulders. "I wouldn't like to say one way or the other. He's capable of anything, and you've made it quite clear to him that you don't want him sniffing around you. So your guess is as good as mine, but if he wants to get at you, what better way than through Emma? It would be his style."

"That's what frightens me. And then I ask myself, why didn't he say something to her that evening he brought her back from hunting."

Max gave her a knowing smile. "With Harry, you can never be sure what he's up to. His mind works in a devious way. I hate to say this, Jill, but don't drop your guard. I have a nasty feeling that worm is up to something, and it's not going to be good. He could ruin your life and smile while he was doing it. If he wants Emma bad enough he may well go all out to get her regardless of whom he hurts."

"I'm sure you're right, Max. Harry has always thought he can have whatever he wants, and as he used to say to me, 'fuck the consequences.'"

"I'm sorry I brought it up."

"Don't be, it's as well to be prepared, not that I will be able to deal with it when the time comes. All I can do is hope the nightmare will never materialise."

......

But the nightmare was already threatening.

For if Jill had been a passerby in Redcliffe Street at about the same time she was talking to Max she would have seen a silver Jaguar Coupe pull up at Emma's block of flats and a tall blond man wrapped in a thick camelhair coat ease his way out of the car, his head lowered against the biting wind. There would have been something familiar about him that would have made her stop and stare, and a few minutes later as he lifted his head to check the street numbers, she would have recognised him and known that all her worst fears were about to be realised.

......

"Harry!" Emma bounded out of the block of flats and threw herself into his arms. "Fab to see you!"

"Likewise," Harry said breathlessly.

"I didn't think you'd come. That was stupid of me wasn't it?"

"Very. I always keep my promises."

"That's not what I've heard," Emma teased

Harry gave a sarcastic laugh. "Of course, I forget that you've probably been told lots of bad things about me by your mother, especially since our little hunting adventure. Well, don't believe them all. I'm not half as bad as I'm made out to be."

"Couldn't care less anyway," Emma said with a dismissive wave of her manicured hand. "I like my men a little dangerous. Now where are you taking me for lunch?"

"Oh, it's lunch now is it, not just a ride in my car?" Harry winked. "That sounds deliciously decadent. Not often these days that I get the chance to take out a girl less than half my age and beautiful at that. Come to think of it Emma, you look stunning."

Emma had grown used to such compliments, but coming from Harry, it was something else. She blushed, feeling surprisingly confused, and said, "Thank you. Harry, just keep saying things like that, will you? And yes..."—

she gave him a delicious smile—"it is lunch *and* a ride in your car."

Harry shrugged. "Well, who am I to refuse such a beautiful woman, and lunch sounds a great idea. Have you anywhere in mind?"

"I know every restaurant within a five mile radius of this place," she was tempted to boast. Instead she said, "I believe there's quite a good restaurant by the theatre in the centre of town. Will that do you?"

"Sounds great." Harry glanced at his watch. "Come on then, let's go. Have you got to lock up or anything?"

"No, but I need to get a coat, I'm freezing out here. Want to come in?"

"No. I'll wait here for you."

"Okay, won't be a mo."

Good as her word, she was throwing herself into the passenger seat within the space of five minutes. "Jesus Harry, this is some car; my bum's feeling warm. Heated seats I suppose?"

"Not too hot?"

"Oh no, just right."

"Fine. Now, lunch first, drive later?"

"Definitely. I'm starving and need a drink. Anyway the drive to the restaurant will be enough for the time being."

"So, where are you taking me?"

"Harvey's in Denmark Street. I'll direct you. I'm told the food's to die for."

Harry looked across at his daughter sitting beside him, and wondered where this confident and sophisticated young woman had come from. He'd obviously missed out on a lot. He laughed as he pulled away from the kerb. "Okay, I'm in your hands."

It was Friday and Harvey's was buzzing, mostly with middle-aged management, enjoying themselves before heading home for the weekend slightly worse the wear from drink. There were murmurs of appreciation as Emma entered the room. Harry noticed she took it all in her stride. Though unknown to him, she was feeling uneasy, not so sure Harvey's had been such a good idea after all. In her desire to impress, she'd been careless. While they stood waiting to be seated, she searched the admiring male faces gazing at her and breathed a sigh of relief—not a client in sight. Unfortunately Charles, the headwaiter was about to expose her lie. "Miss Foster, what a pleasant surprise, we've missed you. I'm so sorry to hear about your father. Tragic."

"Thank you, Charles. It was a shock. Have you a table?"

Charles nodded sympathetically. "For you always, and as luck would have it your favourite one is free." He took her coat, handed it to a young waiter and with a "follow me" walked them to the table. "Your usual as an aperitif?"

"Thank you, Charles, two."

Charles bowed and gave Harry a knowing smile. He knew Emma's profession, but turned a blind eye. She oozed class, not like some of the other whores who had tried to use his restaurant as a pick-up joint. They had been quickly evicted. Emma had not been slow to learn the score. Be discreet, look a million dollars, tip well, and Charles would be putty in her hands.

Harry stared at his retreating back before saying, "You little minx, you know this place well. Might I ask how well?"

Emma reached for his hand. "I'm sorry, Harry. I like to play silly games. It's a place where we journalists come to gossip and, you know, spend some of our hard-earned loot."

Harry looked around him. "Never seen journalists so well dressed."

Emma thought quickly. "Friday is not their day. Too busy writing articles for the Monday editions. This is the business crowd, anaesthetising themselves before going back to their wives, girl friends or whatever for the weekend."

Harry looked at Emma with renewed interest. This was a streetwise young woman as well. He'd been around long enough to know the signs. "What exactly *do* you do?" he asked curiously.

"I'm an investigative journalist."

"Meaning what exactly?"

"Oh, you know, prying into people's lives and things. You know, a bit like you are doing now."

Harry chose to ignore the rebuke. "Like what?"

"People's indiscretions, like adultery, fraud, shady businesses, that sort of thing. Not much dangerous stuff, just gossip, really."

"And what paper do you write for?"

"I'm freelance. Go around the local papers offering them stories. The best offer gets my story."

"Not the nationals?"

"No."

"And you make enough money to drive an MG, rent a flat, and eat at places like this?"

Emma screwed up her face. This was getting difficult. It was time to bluff—convincingly, of course. "I get enough, what with an allowance from

Mum."

"She must be very generous, for I don't think local journalists make much money, at least not to live the way you are."

"My stuff is in great demand. I'm good at my job. I get paid top whack."

Harry shrugged. He didn't want to spoil the afternoon. He could voice his doubts some other time. "So I'm impressed. Your stuff *must* be in demand—like to see some of it sometime. I might be able to get you a job with one of the nationals."

"I'm very happy here, Harry."

Harry shrugged again. "Well, it's your choice, but I think you should have more ambition. If you're as good as you claim, and with your looks, you could go far given the right connections. And I have those connections."

Emma drummed the table irritably. Why, she wasn't quite sure. Probably because she hated people being nosey and Harry was getting pretty damn close to sticking his nose a little too deep into her business, and that wouldn't do at all—not one fucking bit.

"I don't need your help," she snapped, then fluttered her eyelids at him. "Sorry, that sounded ungrateful. But honestly, Harry, I don't need your help. I'll make it on my own, and don't think I'm not ambitious. I am just cautious."

"Fair enough, I didn't mean to interfere. Just thought you could do with a helping hand, and Bristol's a bit of a dump, isn't it?"

"Not when you get to know it. I'm happy here, okay? Let's leave it at that."

Harry smiled. "Of course, and here comes our aperitif. So no more talk of work, I promise, so boring; let's talk about other things."

Beaming all over his face, Charles placed two large glasses of vintage Bollinger champagne in front of them. "Best in our cellar. Enjoy. I'll be back in a moment to take your order."

"Wow!" Harry said, impressed, taking a sip of the cold liquid from the fluted crystal. "They do look after you well here. I hope you're paying."

"The champagne is on the house."

Now that really did blow her journalist crap clean out of the water, but Harry just raised an eyebrow. "All I can say is, this place must be making a lot of money or the head waiter is in love with you."

"Bit of both," laughed Emma, raising her glass. "Here's to us."

"To us, and a long friendship," added Harry, reminding himself to look a little deeper into Emma's line of work. "Now, shall we order?"

They ate half a dozen rock oysters each, followed by grilled Dover sole, boned with loving care by Charles. They washed the meal down with a

Sancerre. They finished with filter coffee and a brandy for Emma. Harry sat back in his chair, watching her sipping her drink.

Journalist, my foot!

They were the last ones to leave the restaurant. As they walked out into the cold late afternoon air, Emma, feeling slightly intoxicated, was floating on a cloud. "That was the most wonderful fun," she commented, putting a cold hand on Harry's arm.

"I enjoyed it as well," Harry confirmed. "I think we should do that again, and next time I'll pay."

"Yes, please. How about tomorrow?"

He gave a light laugh. "Not possible. But I'm free in a fortnight. What will it be, lunch or dinner?"

Emma would have loved dinner. It was so much more romantic, but she needed her evenings to be free, especially as there was a big conference beginning in two weeks' time and Philip M had already booked her for most evenings. "Lunch would be better."

"Okay, lunch it is, a fortnight from today. That's two days before our Hunt Ball. Are you coming this year?"

"No."

"Want to join my party?"

Emma pursed her lips. "I'd love to but I think that would be unwise, don't you?"

"Is this something to do with your mother?" Harry couldn't keep the annoyance out of his voice.

"Oh, come on, Harry, don't be like that. You know you upset Mum. Just let it rest."

Harry gave her a smile that had drawn many women into his bed. "Darling Emma, I'm sorry. I won't mention the subject again." In fact he was boiling inside. Fucking Jill was still managing to get in his way, but he had plenty of time. It would be wrong to show his peevishness; things were going far too well.

They walked in silence the short distance to his car. It was not an uneasy silence, more a silence of being at ease with each other. Once again, Emma had the strange feeling that she knew this man well.

In the car, he asked, "Home now or a little spin?"

Emma looked at her watch. "I think home. The rush hour in Bristol is horrendous, and it's gone four. I wouldn't leave it too late to get on your way if I were you. But you probably know that already."

"Indeed, got stuck a few weeks ago. OK, home it is. Next time I'll come earlier and you can drive. Would you like that?"

"Cool!"

"In that case we'll do it before lunch. It's a good idea to drive this car when sober."

......

He drove home in a thoughtful mood. His meeting with Emma had gone better than he could ever have wished. There had been none of the expected antagonism, given that by now he was sure Jill would have told Emma that he was strictly off limits. It was a little too early to say he was on the brink of being able to do some serious damage, but he wasn't far off. *Take it slowly*, he thought again. *Don't blow it.* As he turned onto the M5, he allowed himself a satisfied smirk. Timing would be of the essence. He wanted Emma gagging for him before he told her he was her father. He couldn't wait to see her face. He gave a loud shout. How he'd like to be a fly on the wall when she told her mother—it would blow Jill's mind. He gave little thought to the damage it might inflict on Emma. One thing was certain; the mother-daughter relationship would never be the same again. "No one," he said to the car, "gets one over on Harry Sidenham." He began to sing 'A long winding road' tunelessly. Life was improving; he'd been a bit short of excitement recently, and the women weren't flocking to him like they used to. Emma would give him back some of the excitement and the end result would be like no orgasm he'd ever experienced before. He whistled loudly, switching to Neil Diamond's 'Sweet Caroline'—he couldn't wait. He settled comfortably in his seat, enjoying the feel of power beneath the bonnet. Power—he'd always been in love with all its forms, and now he had the most lethal power of all within his reach: the power to destroy someone.

......

Emma sat in the antique armchair, a tumbler full of vodka in her hand, her mind a maelstrom. Her body was a coiled spring, the adrenaline still pumping. Her day had gone better than she could ever have hoped for. She'd forgotten what it was like to feel goose pimples creeping over her body when a man smiled at her. How great to be reminded! Harry had really got to her. *Oh boy, what a day!*

She raised the tumbler to her red lips, and a few seconds later felt the warmth of the alcohol settle in her stomach. She wondered if she'd had the same effect on Harry. Certainly, he liked her, no doubt about that. But did he *want* her? That was what she needed to know. Being honest with herself, she felt a little disappointed that he'd made no attempt to kiss her, seemed reluctant to touch her, although she'd touched him. Well, there was time. She mustn't push him; she wasn't planning this to be a one-night stand. Harry would be for life, and in the short time she'd known him, he'd given her no sign that she bored him. *So calm down and dream about a fortnight's time.* In the meantime she'd smile at the overweight bulks panting on top of her, open her legs and try to imagine every man was Harry.

Which reminded her. She glanced at her watch. She'd better stop dreaming and get to work. She had an appointment in just under an hour in the middle of Bristol She rose slowly out of the chair, stretched lazily, and ran her hands through her short hair. Yes, it had been a good day. She toasted Harry and drained her glass. "Here's to my future husband," she slurred, realising she was halfway to being cut. A cold shower was definitely called for.

......

It was a crisp December morning, two weeks before Christmas, and the wintry sun shone down from a cloudless sky. Jill was in the garden sweeping up the last of the walnut tree's leaves. Whatever the weather she'd taken to spending a few minutes in the garden every morning before Toria came in from the cattle shed for her breakfast. It was then that she could be at peace with herself. It was a time when she could lose herself in the all-enveloping solitude and feel Tim beside her, a time when she could reflect on her anxieties without the usual panic setting in. She glanced at the old tree, so still, so calm in the cold air. It was this aura of calmness that she found so contagious. She noticed a rabbit had been busy in one of the rose beds, eating the few remaining leaves hanging bravely to the plants. Her father and Tim would have shot the invaders, and once she'd have done the same, but now all life seemed too precious. If the rabbits wanted to feast on the meagre pickings of a winter garden then they were welcome. .She scooped up the fallen leaves from under the tree into her wheelbarrow, noticing that the tyre was flat. Like the toaster, it needed replacing. She smiled as she heard the familiar rusty squeak of the garden gate. It was Toria back from milking. Her time of solitude was near its end. As usual a busy day stretched in front of them. In a few moments she'd go back to the house and get Toria her breakfast while she showered the smell of cows off her body, and then they would go their different ways until the work was done. It was an easy relationship, one that Jill cherished, one she hoped would never be broken. But therein laid her concern. For she was absolutely sure that Harry was out there hovering, waiting for the right moment to cause mayhem in her life.

155

It was not a pleasant thought. Just recently she'd had an almost overpowering desire to share her secret with Toria, but had drawn back at the last minute fearful of causing cracks in their friendship and trust. She stared into the bare branches of the tree and wished the unthinkable: that Harry would die. She was shocked by the strength of her feelings. She ran a hand over the rough bark of the tree and wished that the future could be more predictable. Apart from her nagging doubts about Harry, Christmas was fast approaching, her first without Tim. He'd been so much part of Christmas for her and the girls. Now he wouldn't be pouring the first glasses of champagne as they prepared to open their presents. They would go to church without him, pull crackers without him, carve the turkey without him, and miss so many small things that were just Tim. But she could not allow those thoughts to ruin Christmas. It would be difficult, she dreaded it, but she knew what Tim would want.

And the New Year, what would that bring? She wasn't even prepared to hazard a guess.

Chapter Eleven

There was a thin sprinkling of snow on the ground as the guests arrived at Sidenham Hall for the annual Hunt Ball, and the threat of a heavy fall before morning. "No bloody hunting tomorrow if the forecast is right," one of them grumbled as he walked into the Hall and was engulfed in a crowd of more than three hundred people all seemingly talking at once. The noise was deafening.

Harry surveyed the gathering crowd of revellers with a jaundiced smirk on his face. Every year since he'd hosted the Ball, he'd stood on the balcony overlooking the reception hall and watched the hypocrites arrive. Nothing had changed since he and Jill had stood together greeting their guests twenty something years ago. They still slated him most of the year, never asked him to their parties, gossiped endlessly about his 'appalling behaviour,' and shred his newest girlfriend to pieces. Yet without the slightest sign of a conscience, they would hunt over his land whenever they felt like it and get drunk in his house once a year. He'd often thought of closing his land and his doors to the lot of them, but in a perverse way he rather enjoyed their ingratiating gratitude.

Surprisingly for a man of his vanity, it didn't worry him one jot that most of them disliked him. In fact he revelled in his notoriety, and was a little disappointed that tonight he couldn't add to his reputation by having Emma by his side. He imagined those that could remember his fling with Jill saying, "First he had the mother and now the daughter; has the man no morals?" His

lips curled in a smile. Soon he'd really give them something to talk about—
the biggest surprise they'd had for years. He couldn't wait! He ran a hand
through his thinning hair and grunted in disgust. It was just one of the many
signs these days that pointed to him getting old. Age worried him—actually
it terrified him. His rakish good looks, his thick mat of hair and his
penetrating eyes had long been his best assets. But now, as he surveyed his
features every morning whilst brushing his hair and saw the cluster of hairs
in the sink, he had to admit that he was ageing prematurely. His life style was
taking its toll. The morning-after bags under the eyes, the red veins on his
cheeks and the thickening paunch bore testament to too many glasses of port,
late nights in smoky casinos, and insatiable women. No wonder bored
housewives and curious young women failed to buzz round him like they
used to, and those that did come to his bed, looking for long forgotten sexual
stimulation, were almost as fat and desperate as he was. New adventures were
in short supply, so Tim's death had come at an opportune moment. He'd
never given much thought to Emma. If he was honest with himself, he didn't
care a damn about her now, but she was a means to an end.

At that moment he spotted Toria entering the hall with a crowd of her
young friends. He waved a 'hello' as she looked up and frowned. How pretty
she was. She ran Emma a close second. She had good features and her eyes
flashed an independent spirit. She was a cheeky young madam, rather as he
remembered her mother at the same age, and the little cow made it abundantly
clear that she had no time for him. Well, tonight he had plans that would wipe
that disapproving look off her face. She wouldn't be smiling for a long time.
First he'd dance with her. She could hardly refuse, and it would rile her. Then
later he'd make his move. She wouldn't be the same happy young woman
when she left. The thought brought a smile to his face.

Right, Harry, time for your entrance.

He straightened his white evening tie, adjusted his watch chain over his
stomach, checked his trouser zip, and slowly walked down the stairs into the
hallway, aware that close on three hundred pairs of eyes were staring at him.

How he loved that.

······

Emma sat opposite Philip M in the restaurant. He'd bought the most
expensive wine, and brought her a present, as he always did when he was
going to spend the weekend with her. One of the things that attracted him to
her was her bubbly personality, with no hint of boredom so obvious in other
escort girls he'd taken out. But tonight he sensed that she wasn't quite

switched on to his chatter and compliments. Had he upset her in some way, or worse was she growing bored of him? "Are you alright?" he asked, concerned.

She gave him the smile that had melted his heart the first time he'd set eyes on her. "I'm so sorry—I haven't been paying you nearly enough attention, and yes, I'm fine. Oh, you naughty man, Philip, you really shouldn't have," she exclaimed, as she opened the present and saw a diamond broach nestling in the box. "You must stop being so extravagant!" She leaned across the table and kissed him. "Now you will have my full attention, I promise."

"You seemed miles away."

"I'm sorry."

The truth was she *was* miles away, thinking of Harry dancing with some beautiful girl when it could have been her. Philip was okay, but he was just another client, not Harry. Money, she was learning, was not everything after all.

......

Toria watched in horror as Harry approached her. There was no escape. She was the only one sitting at the table. Her friends had gone to buy more wine or visit the loos. Why hadn't she had the sense to go with them? She gritted her teeth.

"Toria! What's a lovely girl like you doing sitting on her own?"

Her mother was right; he was a creep. "Just waiting for my friends to come back with more wine," she said back.

He stood over her, smiling down at her, so that he could see her cleavage. *Your stomach's too large,* she thought.

"Well then, how about a dance?" He held out a hand.

"Oh, I don't think—"

"I won't take no for an answer," he laughed, but his eyes were cold. "Your mother never refused me."

What a shit you are, Harry.

"You're insufferable, Harry Sidenham!"

"That's what everyone tells me." He was enjoying himself now. He liked a sassy woman. "I'm sure your mother would tell you to never refuse your host. All I want is one dance."

And that is all you're going to get!

"I should kick you in the balls," she whispered angrily and totally out of character. "But I can do that better while dancing."

He looked at her, nonplussed. "To think I considered you a well brought up girl!"

"Surprise then," she stated, as she rose from the table and offered her hand "So you'd better remember not to come too close."

"Ha!" was all he could say.

......

He might have put on weight, been a little slower on his feet, ageing prematurely, but he knew he could still dance, and Toria, despite her determination to get off the dance floor as quickly as possible, found herself enjoying his accomplished rhythm. "You can certainly dance," she said reluctantly.

"Your mother said the same." He held up a hand in mock surrender. "Sorry, that was uncalled for."

She pulled away from him and stood with hands on hips in the middle of the floor. "What's this thing with my mother? Are you obsessed with her or something?"

"Something like that," he replied, pleased that she was annoyed.

"But surely not after all this time? Your affair, or whatever you want to call it, was over years ago. In fact you've hardly spoken to each other since. If you're trying to muscle in on us, get this into your head: We don't want you around. Mum thinks you're wasted space and I'm inclined to agree. Have you gotten the message?"

She gasped at the enmity radiating from his eyes. He reached out and crushed her to his chest.

"That hurt!"

He didn't apologise. "You can't tell me what to do, young lady. I have every right to see your mother, ask her. Go on, ask her why, and see what she says. Perhaps she's keeping a deep dark secret from you," he added maliciously.

Toria struggled out of his clutches. "The only secret she kept from us was her affair with you. So don't try that tack with me."

Harry's lips curled in a sardonic smile. "Is that all she told you?"

Toria shook her head. "*That* was enough. How she could have loved you beats me. You're a nasty man, Harry, and this dance has gone on long enough. Thanks for nothing."

"My pleasure," he laughed. "Well, let me tell you there's lots more locked in your mother's cupboard. In fact, I'd like to prove to you that I'm not the liar you think I am. Hear me out, that's all I ask, and then go and ask her. She won't deny it. I suggest we meet in my library around eleven." He glanced at

160

his watch. "In about an hour's time."

"Go take a jump in the lake."

"You'll be there."

"You'll have a very long wait."

"I doubt it."

"Oh for God's sake, Harry, good night."

He gave a grunt of satisfaction as he watched her hurry off the floor. She'd come to the library—he was certain of that. Her curiosity would get the better of her. But telling her about Emma could wait; he had other things on his mind. He pulled out a monogrammed white silk handkerchief and wiped his sweaty palms.

Toria hurried to the ladies intent on composing herself before she returned to her table. She felt tearful, unsure of herself. Harry had unsettled her. Of course, she told herself, she wouldn't go to the library, but in the same breath she asked herself why not? Could her mother possibly be guarding another secret, one far more shattering than her last revelation? Wouldn't it be easier to call Harry's bluff and laugh in his face? Of one thing she was sure; she wouldn't feel at ease until she knew the truth. She washed Harry's sweat off her hands. She rinsed her face, ran a comb through her hair and stared at herself in the mirror. She looked shattered. *And this is supposed to be a party,* she thought miserably as she turned and made her way out of the Ladies.

Once back at her table she glanced at her watch.

．．．．．．

"So you came." His voice was smooth, self-satisfied. He was standing with his back to her, staring at the curtained window. He didn't bother to turn round. Toria's first thought was how intimidating the room seemed with the high shelves of books on three walls, the other covered in dark green wall paper, and heavy green velvet curtains. She felt claustrophobic. If she hadn't had that extra drink or two she'd have turned and fled.

"Yes, I came," she said, her voice cool. "I don't want to spend a moment longer with you than I have to, but I need to know if there really is something haunting my mother after all these years."

"Oh, I won't keep you long," Harry said, turning slowly to face her. "This will be over very quickly." His voice softened into a mirthless smile. He held two glasses of wine. He handed her one and pointed to a sofa. "Let's sit over there."

She followed him to the sofa. He sat down, smiled and patted the seat next to him. "Come on, nothing to be frightened of. I won't eat you."

Reluctantly she sat down. Immediately he put a hand on her arm. She jumped. He laughed. "Why so nervous?"

"You give me the creeps."

His eyes flashed. "You shouldn't say things like that when you're alone with a man."

This is where I get out, she thought, starting to rise from the sofa. "I don't know what you mean by that, but I'm out of here. You haven't got anything to say about my mother, have you? I made a mistake in coming. Thanks for the wine."

"Oh no, not so fast," Harry said, grabbing her arm. "I've changed my mind—it can wait. I have another idea and we both know what it is."

"You are very wrong there. Let me go, Harry."

He ignored her. "Has anyone told you that you're very pretty, that you have a very sexy mouth, and that you're very desirable?"

"Please, Harry, I want to go."

"Oh, come on, Toria, stop playing the innocent. Kiss me."

Inside, she was panicking, but fought to keep calm. "Kiss you! Listen, Harry, just let my arm go and we can forget this. You tricked me into coming here. I should have guessed you had an ulterior motive, but luckily I don't know anyone else as despicable as you."

"The little girl's twigged!" He pulled her arm. "Come on, let's have that kiss."

Alarm bells were deafening her. She looked round the room, searching for an exit. There were two doors, the one she'd come in by and another to her left. She hadn't a hope of reaching either of them before he'd stop her. She was trapped.

"And don't try to run," he laughed, reading her thoughts. "You'd never reach either of the doors and the French windows are closed."

"OK, one kiss, that's all, and then I can go?"

"It's a promise."

He leant forward. He smelt of alcohol. She threw the glass of wine in his face and jumped up. "That's the nearest your going to get to me, Harry."

Unperturbed by the wine staining his white shirt, Harry just smiled. "That was very stupid." He moved quickly for a big man and grabbed her arm. "Not so fast, my little beauty. Now the game begins."

She tried to pull her arm away. He threw his wineglass over his shoulder and grabbed her round the waist. She whimpered. With absolute clarity she knew what was going to happen next.

He picked her up and threw her back on the sofa, then landed heavily on top of her. She was trapped beneath him. His hands moved up her thighs and she felt her knickers tear.

"Please God, no!" she screamed, fighting to get out from under him.

He laughed as he worked his trousers down. She screamed again. "Shut up, you little bitch," he said breathlessly and slapped her across the face. She cried out in pain; he drove a fist into her stomach. She fought for air. He was strong, driven now by wild sexual desire, imagining he had Jill underneath him. Toria was powerless to stop him.

Everything that happened after that was like a nightmare.

It was over in minutes. He stood up, breathing heavily, zipping up his trousers and straightening his clothes. Through misty eyes Toria stared up at him, numb, feeling terribly cold and utterly humiliated.

Harry leered down at her. "That's what you came for, that's what you got. Now I suggest you stay here until you can control yourself and then leave by the French windows. We wouldn't want anyone knowing what a whore you are, would we?"

Toria stared at him, bemused. Harry turned away from her and walked out of the library.

She didn't move for several minutes, fighting the nausea, the pain and the overwhelming feeling of humiliation. But slowly her eyes began to focus, and the nausea and pain were replaced by the desire to run, run and run. She struggled to her feet, swayed and pulled her dress down, aware that she was without her knickers. "Oh God!" she cried, limping towards the curtains covering the French windows. She pulled them open and found the catch to open the windows. The cold air made her suck in her breath. Her cheek stung where Harry had slapped her. She stood still in the cold darkness frightened that someone might see her silhouetted against the light from the library. But there was no shout, no welcoming voice, and she breathed again. She shook off her inertia, realising every wasted second could lead to her discovery. She hitched up her dress and ran to the well-lit car park.

······

She crept into the house, careful not to wake her mother. She ran upstairs whimpering and locked herself in the bathroom. She tore off her clothes, ran the hottest bath her skin could stand and then started to scrub every inch of her body with a nail brush. She winced from the pain, but never once stopped the frantic scrubbing until all her skin was red and stung from the soap. Only then did she feel she'd erased Harry's sweat from her body. She lay back in the bath and closed her eyes. The initial hysteria had died down and her heart was beating normally for the first time since she'd fled the Hall. Waves of shame and anger washed over her. She was angry with herself for being so gullible, angry with her mother for reasons that she could not quite fathom, but which she felt had led in some way to the humiliating happenings of the last few hours. She was ashamed at being raped, and fearful of dangerous emotions that Harry had stirred within her. She glanced at her watch still on her wrist. She'd been in the bath for over an hour. She sank down in the water and wished she had the guts to drown.

......

"Breakfast is on the table, Toria."

Toria sat up on her bed. She was cold, covered only by the damp towel from the bathroom. "I don't want any, Mum. Please leave me alone. I've a bad hangover—I'll be down soon."

"Must have been a good party," Jill said through the door. "I'll see you later."

Toria rolled off her bed and staggered to the mirror. She threw off the towel and stared in horror at the large bruise on her stomach and the contusions around her thighs. There was only a slight reddening on her face where Harry had slapped her. Thank God, for after dragging herself out of the bath she'd made the decision to say nothing to her mother. She'd fight the humiliation and the awful feeling that she'd in some way asked for what she'd got, on her own. She knew it would be the hardest thing she'd ever had to do in her life, but she'd win through. She'd toyed briefly with the idea of going to the police, but it would be her word against Harry's and who would believe her side of the story? She had a girl friend who had been raped coming back from a party at college. Her parents had taken her to the police. "And that's when it really started to get bad," she'd told Toria. "If I'd known what I know now I wouldn't have gone near them. The rape was nothing compared to the humiliation the law put me through. I was made to feel as if I'd been to blame. And then the trial, the indignity of it, and then the man got acquitted—his word against mine. I can still hear his laugh. 'The man nearly always wins when there are no witnesses,' my lawyer told me afterwards. 'Why did you put me through such hell if you knew that?' I asked. Do you know what his reply was? 'You pressed ahead with the case. You didn't need to.' 'Well, why didn't you bloody well tell me that,' I shouted at him. I still feel sick thinking about it. God forbid it ever happens to you, Toria, but if it does, button your mouth and fight it on your own. Tell no one, least of all your parents. It'll be hard but less traumatic in the long run."

OK, Toria told herself, *this is where I start.*

......

But it was not going to be easy, and if she was pregnant, well, she'd have no choice but to come out in the open. And what if Harry had some disease? His dick had been everywhere. As she moved slowly down the stairs, she could hear her mother singing in the kitchen and that made her angry. It was time to confront her with her fears. In the bath she'd had moments of rational thinking, and had worked out why this anger was festering within her. She'd reluctantly decided that Harry hadn't been entirely bluffing. And if this was true then her mother was in part to blame for the dreadful events of the night before. But halfway down the stairs, any thought of confronting her mother vanished as she was consumed by the desire to lock herself away in a darkened room, alone with her self-loathing. It was a feeling that would unexpectedly creep up on her many times in the months ahead. But she gripped the stair rail and fought the panic. She took a deep breath, controlled her breathing and carried on down to the kitchen. There would be no questions today.

"Toria, you look a bit under the weather," her mother greeted her.

She found it difficult to meet her mother's eyes. "I'm fine, just feeling a little shaky."

"Well, it's not like you to overindulge."

Without saying a word Toria moved to a chair by the kitchen table. God, the bruises hurt. Her eyes filled with tears. How on earth was she going to get through the day, or tomorrow, or the next day? How was she going to contain her anger with her mother, an anger that was perhaps unjustified? After all why should a mother tell her children all her secrets?"

"Are you all right?" asked Jill. "It's unusual for you to be so quiet after a party."

Toria clenched her fists together and forced herself to look at her mother. "Actually I didn't enjoy last night."

Jill frowned at the puffiness of her face. "I'm sorry. Do you want to tell me about it?"

"It was Harry. He was very unpleasant, tried it on with me."

"Harry tried it on with you!"

"Yes, Mother, he tried it on with me, got that?" Then Toria jumped up from the chair, controlling her anger with difficulty. She wanted to shout, "What are you hiding, Mum? Harry hinted it was something pretty damn serious last night." But she couldn't bring herself to open up another emotional front. Instead she mumbled, "I don't want to talk to you at the moment. I'm going out."

"Has Harry been telling you things?" asked Jill weakly.

"I told you, I'm going out."

"Please, Toria."

"No!"

"Will you be back later?" was all Jill could say.

"If I had somewhere else to go, the answer would be no, but as I haven't, I suppose I might be, but don't bet on it being today."

Jill stared at Toria's retreating figure, guilt washing over her. She had a pretty good idea why Harry had moved in on Toria. It would be one of his games. She doubted if he really wanted to have sex with her, more likely to tell her about Emma when she was at her most vulnerable. Was this the beginning of his avowed intention to destroy her family?

......

"I want to know what her line of work is." Harry was speaking on the telephone to a private investigator he'd used before. "Follow her and report back as quickly as possible. It shouldn't be too difficult."

......

"She's a prostitute."

"She's what?"

"I'm sorry, Lord Sidenham, but the young lady is a prostitute. She works for an escort agency in Bristol. Very posh, but nevertheless, the girls sell themselves for sex."

"Are you sure about this?"

"There is no doubt. Shall I send the bill to you as usual?"

"Yes, yes." Harry slammed the receiver down and collapsed onto the sofa where he'd raped Toria. This was something he'd not anticipated. His guess had been that Emma was into drug dealing. The last thing he'd have thought of was prostitution. He wasn't the slightest bit shocked, but she had surprised him. This called for a stiff drink. Once he'd a glass of whisky in his hand he settled down to think. Did this startling revelation make any difference to his plans? He stroked his chin. No, in fact it played into his hands. He could make Jill out to be the useless mother—that would really hurt her. What a case he could make. *You have no parental control. When I learned the truth of what Emma was up to, I realised that you were a rotten mother, and with Tim dead, what alternative did I have but to tell her I was her father?* Well, that was a load of balls, but it sounded good. A prostitute! He picked at a tooth—he still found it hard to believe.

I bet she doesn't come cheap.

He thought of her designer clothes, expensive shoes, jewellery and the MG. Well, at least she wasn't working from the street. A posh agency, eh! That didn't mean much. There were some very weird people out there, and money didn't guarantee her safety. In his time he'd consorted with some strange people with money who had some very devious tastes. He wondered why she'd chosen that profession. A quick buck came to mind. *A chip off the old block*, he thought.

He looked round the room at the collection of books stacked to the ceiling. They were priceless, collected by his grandfather and father. There were many beautifully bound first edition classics and books on the great military campaigns of world history. There were modern books on specialist subjects, and a whole wall containing the best of erotic art. He'd not added one single book to the collection, preferring to spend his money on gambling and women. He'd once thought of selling them but stopped short of that because he'd discovered he had a conscience! He couldn't bring himself to destroy something that two men had so lovingly collected over many years. How fucking stupid could he get? The money would have come in useful. Perhaps one day he'd have to sell—his overdraft was causing his bank concern. He reached for the pack of Gitane, always on the left-hand side of his desk, a box of Swan Vestas by its side. He lit a cigarette and inhaled deeply, blowing what smoke was left towards the ornate ceiling (copied from a Florentine house where his grandfather had once stayed with one of his lovers), and reflected on the word 'destroy.' There was something wonderfully sinister about the word.

Destroy! He ran it slowly over his tongue. He inhaled deeply and thought of Jill. He wondered if Toria had told her he'd raped her. He suspected not, and that was how he liked it. He thought it would be rather amusing to tell Jill himself. Ah, what pleasure he'd get. It would be the first nail in her coffin. Emma would hopefully provide the rest.

••••••

"I'm not pregnant!" Toria shouted at the bathroom wall. "Not pregnant!" It was two days to Christmas, three weeks since she'd been attacked. She almost fainted from the relief. She unlocked the bathroom door and walked unsteadily back to her bedroom. She needed a little time to compose herself. What better way than to wrap up her mother's present. No longer was her anger focused on her. Once she'd got over the initial feeling of betrayal, which she accepted was wide of the mark anyway, she realised it was unfair to blame her for what had happened. She'd decided that if rolls were reversed she wouldn't feel obliged to tell her children about something that didn't concern them—well, that was not quite true, but Toria was in no mood to hear grubby details of her mother's sex life with Harry. So the silences, the glares, the blunt answers, the reluctance to eat at the same table had been superseded by a new awareness of how much she needed her mother. From that moment on the black cloud that had been hanging over her head began to slowly dissipate. She still felt dirty, and humiliated, but she'd stopped reliving the horror every minute of the day. She'd fought countless lonely battles, mostly in the darkness of her bedroom. But now at last there were signs that she was winning, and she didn't want to risk falling back into the darkness, and the pregnancy bit made that far less likely. At last she could go out in the car alone without driving home within fifteen minutes, terrified that she was being followed. She could talk to people without thinking that at any moment she'd be attacked. But the dangerous emotions that had stirred the day after Harry's attack had grown, filling her brain. They were totally alien to her gentle nature. They were targeted at one man, and they bit very deep.

She jumped off her bed and moved to the window. Her mother had put Christmas lights on the walnut tree. She smiled, remembering last Christmas when the ladder her father was standing on had slipped from under him and he'd been left hanging from a branch until she and Emma had heard his cries and rushed to his aid. She wondered what Christmas would be like without him. It would certainly not be easy. But in some ways she was looking forward to it. It was something that never changed. It brought families together. It represented stability in a changing world. Never had her world changed so much in the last twelve months. And right now she craved stability more than anything else on earth.

She heard carols being sung somewhere in the village. As had happened every year since she could remember they would soon be at the door. Her mother as usual had made a punch, and baked dozens of mince pies, which the choir would enjoy round the Christmas tree after they'd sung their carols. Toria decided she would be first at the door to welcome the choir in.

Chapter Twelve

Max breathed in the cold air, relieved that it hadn't snowed over night. Although he enjoyed his lonely stint in the early hours of Christmas morning, he could do without the inconvenience of a fall of snow. It had been his practice to give all his farm staff the day off, believing it was the one day of the year when, if possible, families should be together. He enjoyed talking quietly to each cow as he attached the milking cups to their teats, their warm breath mixing with the pungent smell of their dung. It was not a smell that worried him, in fact the opposite. Milking finished, he'd move on to the calf pens where dozens of hungry calves bleated for their food. Finally, he'd take the quad-bike up to the pastures to cast a critical eye over the out-wintering stock. He had never worried that time was passing. He always knew he'd be back in time for church.

But today was going to be different. There was no Tim to celebrate Christmas with. It would be the first time he wouldn't be going to church since the family had come down from Cumbria. The first time, he'd be hurrying through his workload. It had the makings of a day hard to bear, but Max had no intention of allowing himself to become depressed. One of the many things he remembered his father saying was, "The dead must take second place to the living. Mourning can't go on forever. Otherwise, life becomes like death, nothing moving and nothing changing; the world becomes a skeleton." Max went along with that. Life was a precious thing. A gift from God, and a vibrant ever-flowing stream, and even a death as painful as Tim's could not be allowed to change that. He had to make sure that he didn't get caught up in the slack water and become stuck in mourning for the dead. It would be a difficult day, yes, but with Jill's help, he'd get through it.

••••••

Toria's alarm woke her at four in the morning. Just because it was Christmas day didn't mean she could lie in bed—there was a heavier workload than on most mornings. She allowed herself to luxuriate in the warmth of the sheets and blankets tucked tightly round her for a few moments, imagining the frozen water troughs and buckets, and her ice-cold hands as she struggled with gates that she had to open to let the cows into the milking parlour. She let out an audible moan as she pushed back the bedclothes with her feet and switched on her bedside light before running to the bathroom. Already, she could hear her mother in the kitchen. Although she was looking forward to the day, it was going to be difficult. At some time in the day Harry would force himself into her thoughts, as he had done every day for the last three weeks. But she was learning to push him to the back of her mind. And today there was no way he was going to intrude on the memories of her father, who had been so much part of all her Christmases. She thought of her father's smiling face at the breakfast table, his laughter as he watched Emma and herself wolfing down their porridge so that they could rush into the sitting room and by a roaring fire start the 'present opening ceremony,' as he'd called it. She'd still been sleepy; he'd already been up for hours. They were allowed a sip of champagne, and then, present opening finished, he'd walk his family down the road to church, where they'd share the third pew from the front with Max's family. Normally, either he or Max read the lesson. As the years had moved on, the champagne glasses had been a little fuller. They'd sung lustily and happily in church and it was a ritual she'd imagined would never end. It had been her favourite day of the year. Then death had intervened and spoilt the party.

••••••

Emma woke to the noise of her sister in the bathroom. She rolled over and looked at her bedside clock. Four in the morning! Shit, her sister must be mad! She pulled the bedclothes over her head and went back to sleep.

••••••

Jill watched the kettle boil and thought of Tim. If he'd been alive, he'd have already rung Max to make sure he was awake and to remind him he had to wear a tie in church. Then he'd have added with a laugh in his voice, "Also, Dad, if you have time, please wash the smell of cows off your hands. The vicar's nose seems to curl more every year when we go up for communion." Angrily, she wiped away a tear. There was no point in going down that road. She could not allow herself to be sad on Christmas day. She might miss Tim, but Max and her two daughters would be with her. Much to her surprise Emma had unexpectedly turned up the night before, having originally informed her that she would not be able to get down. 'I'm covering a very important story, Mum,' she'd lied. The fact was she was on line to earn a very fat cheque for spending Christmas with a client. But at the last minute the cheating bastard had cancelled. "You know," he'd informed her, "children and all that." Oh yes, she understood! So the next best thing was to go home and perhaps devise a way to sneak off and see Harry.

Jill had been tempted to ask Emma what story was so important that she couldn't come down and spend Christmas day with her family, but she'd thought better of it. Emma was coming, that was all that mattered. Questions could be asked at a latter date if the mood took her. She smiled as she made a pot of tea. She was so lucky. Toria had got over her anger and they were back on good terms and Emma hadn't mentioned Harry for weeks. It could after all be quite a good Christmas. But she'd miss Tim.

The ringing of the telephone made her jump. It would be Max. He'd said he'd ring. *Just to see you're all okay.*

She picked up the receiver. "Max?"

"None other. Everything okay your end?"

"It's fine, just making a cuppa before Toria and I go out. I imagine you're on your way to the cows?"

"I'm already in the office checking a few things. Thought I'd get to you a bit earlier this year. Felt you might need a little cheering up."

"Max, you're really thoughtful. But I'm really not too bad. Had my moment I admit, but now I'm looking forward to the day."

"That's what I like to hear. I can't wait to hear the first pop of the champagne cork. You did buy some, I presume?"

"There were a dozen bottles in the cellar; I can't see us drinking our way through that lot. By the way are you going to church?"

"No. Thought I'd give it a miss. You know, what with having to walk past Tim's grave. Stupid?"

"No of course not Max, but I'll go. I've bought some flowers. I'll say hello to Tim for you. So see you here around twelve."

"You can bank on it—and Jill—thanks."

"It's no problem, Max." Her heart went out to him. He was such an ebullient laid back character. He had no truck with public shows of sadness, so it was very easy to forget how he was suffering. To lose a wife and child must be devastating. Tim had been as much a part of his life as hers. She had never wanted it any other way. "Oh, Max."

"Yes?"

"Thought you might like to know Emma turned up last night. Looks exhausted and—"

"What?"

"She seemed a bit distant, rather strange actually, but probably nothing."

"I shouldn't worry. She's probably just tired."

"That's more than likely. Now I must go. I've a lot to do. Take care. See you for lunch."

"I'll be there." Max hung up.

······

Harry woke in a foul mood. He was alone in a vast house, just his housekeeper to keep him company. He'd struck lucky with a very delectable about-to-be-divorced thirty-year-old, who he'd first met watching polo on Smith's lawn, Windsor, back in the summer. They'd dined and bedded four times since their first meeting, and she had agreed to spend what Harry had anticipated would be a wonderfully debauched Christmas with him. But an abrupt telephone call the night before had informed him that his about-to-be-divorced lover had suddenly been overcome with remorse, and decided to try for a reconciliation with 'my boring fart of a husband.'

"For the sake of the kids, Harry darling. I'm sure you will understand."

Actually no, he didn't understand, but he knew it would be no good saying so. He'd slammed the receiver down in a pique of sexual frustration. It was a letdown of vast proportions and left him cursing his luck. He was sure the reconciliation would fail, but in the meantime he was facing a lonely Christmas unless he did something about it. His dream of caressing the soft flesh of a thirty-year-old might be in tatters but somewhere out there must be an old flame, wrinkles and all, gagging for a bit of fun with the 'adulterous old roué' as he'd become known recently. He'd lost count of how many he'd rung and he was still facing Christmas alone. He was pissed off. He looked at his gold Rolex. It was only nine; after his morning ride, what was he going to do with his day? Several unbelievably tiresome ideas came to mind, like going to church, taking a walk, visiting his staff—God! But he'd have to do something or he'd go mad. Perhaps sitting in front of the fire with a drink in his hand dreaming of Emma would be the best idea. Yes, that would pass the time. His lips curled in an evil smile as he wondered what Christmas would be like at Walnut Farm. Pretty uneasy would be his guess. He decided to take a shower before his housekeeper, Mrs. Banks, arrived with his morning cup of tea. He showered into a semblance of humanity and moved back to his bed like a sloth and waited for Edna Banks.

A few moments later he heard the familiar knock. "Good morning, Lord Sidenham, happy Christmas." He scowled and grunted, which didn't wash with Edna. She'd been with him for seven years and was immune to all his moods. She also despised him, but he paid well. Her husband Tom was the groom and they had a lovely little cottage on the estate. They didn't want to lose the sunsets. They knew when they were well off, so she ignored Harry's rudeness and insufferable behaviour.

"Happy Christmas," she repeated, thinking she'd like to drop the tray in his lap and hopefully injure the parts most dear to him.

"Oh, yes, yes, happy Christmas to you, Mrs. Banks."

The smell of lavender water wafted round the room. Edna always applied it generously to her plump little frame every morning. "Are you not well, your Lordship?"

"No, I'm bloody well not. All my plans blew up in my face last night. I'll be on my own. Mrs. Sedgefield won't be coming."

Serves you right, you randy sod, Edna wanted to say, having listened in on most of his telephone conversations planning his Christmas of debauchery. Instead, she put the tray gently down on his lap and said, "I'm so sorry, it will be a bit lonely for you."

"How did you guess?" The sarcasm dripped from his mouth.

"Well, that's a shame indeed, you poor man. So I'll only lay for one for lunch?"

"That's right, unless something drops from heaven."

Edna thought of a good reply but asked, "The usual time?"

Harry glared at her. "Yes, yes, the same time, woman. Now go."

Once again Edna ignored his rudeness and left the room a little slower than usual. She could hardly wait to spread the news that Harry had been stood up by his latest bit of stuff. "Losing his touch," she would say to her husband later.

The thought of eating on his own was almost too much for Harry. He'd hardly slept all night thinking of sitting beside his lover still warm from his bed, a glass of one of his best clarets in one hand, while the other strayed over her soft thighs under the table. "Damn. Damn. Damn!" he shouted, and sent the tea tray crashing to the floor as he jumped out of bed. He'd ride off his temper and frustration, gallop across his land, work himself and his horse into a lather and come back and drink the claret on his own—the first step towards obliterating what promised to be a dreadful day.

······

At ten o'clock, Emma stretched lazily in bed and wondered what Harry would be doing. She felt a wave of jealousy sweep over her as she imagined him in bed with one of his women, before rising late to host a large lunch. But she could be wrong, as from all accounts, Harry was running a bit short on girl friends, he had few friends, and she knew he had no family. *Could he be on his own, longing for me as I am for him? Dream, dream on...*

Which she did, imagining his hard body pressed close to hers. What music they'd make! Then a thought struck her. It was one hell of a temptation. Would he be angry? Actually, why should he be? She was sure he loved girls ringing him. If he was in the middle of something, she could always apologise. She smiled and reached for her mobile. After a few rings, his voicemail clicked in. *Fuck!* She hesitated for a moment before leaving a message.

······

Harry returned from his ride flushed and ready for his first drink of the day. He'd galloped his horse flat out for over two miles, driving him on as a man possessed, determined to clear his brain. Not bothering to change out of his riding gear, he hurried to the whisky decanter and poured himself a stiff drink. His temper might have eased, but the loneliness was still all around him. He looked at his Rolex—ten minutes before Mrs. Bank's summoned him to the dining room for his solitary lunch and the inevitable slow slide into drunkenness. Later, he'd struggle up the stairs and fall fully clothed onto his bed, cursing his lot and knowing he'd never make the hunting field for the Boxing Day meet.

Then he saw the red light of his voicemail winking at him.

······

Jill missed Tim in several ways but she hadn't shed a tear, and the chatter round the table lifted her spirits. She watched Toria and Emma laughing and teasing Max as he told yet another of his stale jokes and missed the punch line. Jill smiled across the table at him as they stood up to pull the crackers, and felt that they had all weathered a storm. Tim would have wanted it no other way. She reached out for a one of the green crackers. "Right, let's do the business," she laughed.

"One, two, three, pull!" Max called, and they strained and laughed, as, arms outstretched, they endeavoured to wrestle the largest piece of the cracker away from each other. The winners smiled in absurd triumph. Then they did it all again until everyone had a hat. Toria stuck a gold paper crown onto her head and laughed, "I think we look a right lot of idiots!"

"Speak for yourself," joked Emma." Now I think we should read some of these appalling jokes."

"Before that, Emma," said Toria quietly, "I think we should drink to your father."

They raised their glasses and gazed at the ceiling. "To you, Dad," Toria continued. "Just to let you know Mum's given us a lovely day." It was said with a smile and a light chuckle, and no one shed a tear.

Two hours later Jill found herself alone with Toria. "Thank you, darling, for being so special today; I know it can't have been easy."

At that moment Toria was tempted to pour her heart out, but quickly thought better of it. Why spoil what had turned out to be quite a good day? "It was fine, Mum, really fine. I thought we all did very well."

Jill smiled her agreement, and then for a brief moment thought she saw a flicker of pain pass over her daughter's eyes. But it was not the time to ask questions or to disclose secrets.

It would prove to be a fatal mistake.

......

It was dark as Emma accelerated onto the road. "I must go and see Hannah," she'd explained to her mother. "She's off to Australia next week, so last chance to see her. Back soon." With a wave of her hand, she'd hurriedly left, not wishing to be questioned too intensely as to why she wanted to say good-bye on Christmas day to a girl she'd hardly spoken to for a year.

"I didn't know she cared that much for Hannah," Toria said.

Jill said, "Nor I."

Max happened to know Hannah was going over to have Christmas tea with her aunt. For some reason, Emma was lying, but he chose to say nothing. He didn't want to spoil the day. But where was she going? What was so important that she had to go out on a freezing night? The answer he came up with made him feel quite sick.

......

Harry heard her car approaching and opened the front door just as Emma brought the MG to a halt. "You got away, then," he exclaimed, a smile crossing his face as she eased herself out of the car.

"No problem."

"What excuse did you make?"

"I'm visiting Hannah Roberts. As you probably know, she's off to Australia tomorrow."

"So she is. I didn't know you were so friendly."

"We're not, but I had to think of some excuse."

Harry laughed and put an arm around her shoulders. "As good as any, I suppose. Now let's get out of the cold. Don't imagine you've got too long?"

"Sadly not. Seems silly, but I don't want to upset Mum today. She's been fantastic, so happy. It could have been a dreadful day, us all thinking of Dad, but instead she's managed to get it just right. So it's back home fairly soon."

"I understand," said Harry grudgingly. "Come on into the library and we can enjoy a drink together." He shut the front door behind him. "It's lovely to see you. I was getting very bored."

"Fancy Harry Sidenham, the famous stud, being all on his own for Christmas," she teased, her eyes shining wickedly. Harry wagged a finger at her. "But I'm glad," she continued. "I wanted to see you, but didn't fancy butting in on a party." She stopped in the library doorway. "Wow, have a few books!"

"My grandfather and father collected them."

"Very impressive. Worth much?"

"A small fortune. Thought of selling them several times, but then I imagined the two old buggers turning in their graves, so relented. At least until I'm broke, that is."

"If they were mine I think I'd do my best to hold on to them."

"If push came to shove, I wouldn't hesitate to sell them. No point in having a stack of old books collecting dust when I'm broke."

"Are you nearly broke, Harry?"

"Let's put it this way, I'm getting short."

"From what I hear, you spend money very freely. Gambling *and* women are two very expensive pastimes I would think. But then, I suppose these books are a bit special," Emma said, pulling out a beautifully bound first edition of Charles Dickens. "Do you know the quotation by Mark Twain?"

"I don't think so."

"He said, 'A classic: something everybody wants to have read and nobody wants to read.'"

"Mark Twain had a point, but first editions of Charles Dickens are worth a fortune. Whether they are read or not is immaterial," Harry observed.

"Rarity, I suppose, said Emma."

"Probably, and I suspect Mark Twain wasn't quite right—lots of people have loved reading Dickens over the years."

Emma shrugged her elegant shoulders. "I don't much care either way—I didn't come to talk about the classics, Harry."

"No, of course you didn't. So let's open the champagne nestling in ice over there."

Emma gave him one of her sparkling smiles. "That sounds a much better idea."

Things are going my way, he thought. With a warm glow in his stomach he moved across to the table where Edna Banks had only a few moments earlier placed the ice bucket. He thumbed the cork out with a pop and carefully filled two silver goblets, his crest engraved on one side. Handing Emma one he raised his and said, "Happy Christmas, Emma, and many of them." They clicked glasses.

"Mm...not bad, not bad at all," she said appreciatively, moving to kiss him on the lips. "Now, tell me why you're alone?"

"I was let down at the last moment. I think that's all you need to know. Your call was very welcome. I was beginning to feel a bit lonely. But this makes up for everything. I wouldn't want anyone else here but you."

"Oh, what a load of claptrap, Harry," she said amiably. "I bet you were let down by a gorgeous woman." For a second she thought she saw Harry blush. She chuckled, "I'm glad she stood you up. It's nice to be here. Well worth coming out on such a freezing cold night."

"You're too observant for your own good."

"In my profession you have to be," Emma nearly let slip, checking herself just in time. "Maybe I am, but what the hell. I'm here now with you and the champagne. What more could a girl ask for?"

"I'm glad someone enjoys my company," Harry said. "Now let's relax for the short time you've got. Come on, sit beside me on the sofa and we'll do our best to knock off this bottle."

They sat close together, sipping their drinks, talking about his horses, her ambitions, and his thoughts on life. As the champagne took effect, their conversation took on a more intimate tone, bantering good humour mixed with the odd innuendo. Both found it difficult to hide their excitement.

Emma glanced reluctantly at her watch. *If only, oh if only I had more time,* she thought. "I must go, Harry. I don't want to raise any suspicions."

"Why should you?"

"What? Go?"

"No, raise suspicions, I mean."

"Because my excuse for leaving was pretty thin. If any of them remember how much I dislike Hannah, I could face some awkward questions, especially from my sister."

"Nosey Toria," Harry quipped.

Emma laughed. "That's my sister for you"

He looked at her over the rim of his glass. *If only you knew,* he thought, but said, "You know, when you laugh you are most attractive. A little like your mother."

"I don't think I want to be compared to mother right this moment," said Emma. "I hope you're not going to go on about her for the little time we have left. That would be *so* boring. Tell you what," she said, deciding not to give him the chance, "if you're free on New Year's Eve come to Bristol, and we can see the New Year in together."

Harry never hesitated, even though he'd have to cancel a party. "That's a brilliant idea; I'll come. Got anywhere special to eat in mind?"

"We could go back to Harvey's. I know they're having a special evening."

"Okay, but they could be full."

"I can always get in."

I bet you can.

"Harvey's it is. Now how about finishing this bottle before you go?"

She laid a hand over her glass. "Very tempting, but no thanks. I've got to drive home and I can't arrive back pickled! Oh God, I really must go."

"I know." He rose unsteadily from the sofa and held out a hand. "I'll see you to your car."

"Thank you, Lord Sidenham," she said with a laugh. "Most gallant of you!"

His laughter echoed in the hall. "I'll count the days until I see you again," he said, opening the front door and shivering as the cold air rushed in.

"We might meet tomorrow?"

Harry looked up into the dark sky. "I doubt we'll be hunting. Frost didn't go off today. It's got well into the ground. Pity really, but there you are."

Emma tucked her long legs into the MG and started the engine. "Not to worry. See you in Bristol, anyway. Give me a ring the day before. Oh, and Harry."

"Yes?"

"Thanks for the champagne. Glad you were on your own. Bye now." She slipped the car into gear and roared off before he could reply.

He stood watching the rear lights until they disappeared. Then he ran back into the house and punched the air. "Yes!" he shouted, his voice echoing around the hall. His heart was singing. She was hooked. It was nearly time to put the knife in. He'd make his move on New Year's Eve.

......

Emma drove home in a wild state of excitement. Going to Sidenham Hall had been a brilliant idea. Thank God she'd been brave enough to pick up her mobile. Harry had been lonely. That had been *so* good, making him aware of how he needed someone for more than just a casual relationship. She'd had so many men, she'd lost count. Some who lusted for her, others who fell in love. It was the endless procession of these losers, these pathetic specimens that were beginning to get her down. Now the prize was almost in her grasp—her release from the grind of unwanted sex into the arms of a man she knew she could love. *Oh, my God, this is something else!* She pushed hard on the accelerator and felt the back of the car twitch. She swore quietly, easing her foot off the pedal.

Ice.

She wasn't ready to die. Her life could be about to take a new and exciting turn. She had never been one for having a conscience. Her philosophy was you took what you wanted and to hell with everyone else. In fact, she and Harry were probably of like minds. But as she drove back into the farmyard a tiny voice was saying, "What about Mum?" She cut the engine and reached for the cigarette packet on the passenger seat. Well, what about her? There was no way her mother would be able to accept her and Harry as an item. She had made her feelings for him quite clear, and who could blame her! Her daughter sleeping with her ex-lover. Let's face it, it was a bit bizarre. She drew the smoke deep into her lungs and gave a slight shake of her head. It was like the roll of a dice—someone was going to be the loser. But this time the dice were loaded. She coughed on the smoke. Did she care enough about her mother, when a vibrant and exciting relationship was beckoning? She shrugged. It was no contest. Harry was her future. She couldn't live her life around her mother forever. She let out an audible sigh and ground out her cigarette in the ashtray. "Shit. Sorry, Mum," she whispered.

Chapter Thirteen

Harry's stomach was churning as he eased the Jaguar into a parking spot outside Emma's flat. Tonight was going to be quite an evening. Tonight he was going to drive the dagger in and twist. The outcome was what excited him. He suffered no conscience at his actions. He hunched his shoulders against the cold and walked towards the building. Somewhere in there Emma was waiting on tenterhooks for her doorbell to ring. The little whore was in for a shock. He took a deep breath as he read Emma's name on a white card beside one of the buzzers, and his hand shook as it dwelt by the button before he pressed it.

Almost immediately her excited voice came through the intercom. "Is that you, Harry?"

"It's me, and freezing."

"You've come!"

"I said I would didn't I? Now get the bloody door open!"

"Sorry! It's just that I thought this weather might put you off."

Oh, I had every intention of turning up, even in a blizzard, he thought. He heard the lock release.

"OK, door's unlocked. Come on up. Third floor"

She was standing at the door of her flat, her wet hair dripping on the floor, her green eyes bright. "Harry," she said with a smile, and threw herself into his arms. He kissed her softly on her cheek. She smelt clean, no perfume, something he wasn't used to, and he liked it. He pushed her away and gave her a generous smile. "So you're a doubting Thomas?"

"Not really, but I know you don't always keep your promises and this weather would have given you a good excuse."

Harry laughed. "You have been doing your homework well."

"Something I always do."

I bet you do, young lady! he thought as he gently put a hand over her mouth. "Enough. It's wonderful to see you. Just finished your bath?"

She smiled. "Okay, enough, and yes, I've been scrubbing the dirt of Bristol off my body. Yuck, it's so filthy." She looked pointedly at her watch. "Anyway, you're early. You really mustn't arrive when a girl's in the middle of her toilets."

Hanging his head in mock apology, he said, "Oh, I'm *so* sorry. But if I might say so, you look terrific like that."

She blushed, probably a first, but Harry seemed to have the knack of making her do things she hadn't done before. "Thank you, Harry. Now come on, it's freezing out here, let's move into my flat. It's lovely and warm, and I've got a bottle of guess what on ice?"

"Vintage Bollinger"

"Wrong." She pulled him out of the cold hallway.

He laughed. "Then what?"

"A bottle of first-class vodka. Not your supermarket stuff, not even the best you can buy in Britain. This is the real stuff, straight from Russia. Potent, and believe me, very, very good. I know you like vodka, but you wait 'till you try this."

"Sounds wonderful," Harry enthused, following Emma into the flat thinking, *I bet you've had a Russian client. Is this really my daughter?*

......

The sound of sixty inebriated revellers singing at the top of their voices threatened to lift the roof off Harvey's as the last chimes of Big Ben faded away. Emma clutched Harry's hand and kissed him. "Happy New Year, Harry," she shouted above the noise.

As he leaned to kiss her she moved so that his lips touched her mouth. He quickly moved away and ignored her questioning look. "It will be the best year of my life," he assured her. "No doubt about it, it's going to be a wonderful year."

"I hope that it will turn out the same for me. This year's been a bit of a bitch."

"I know. It's tough to lose one of your family." It wasn't time to say 'father.' "But I'm sure things are about to change."

"Whatever, things can't be any worse. My father dying was a terrible shock. So here's to the New Year." Emma raised her glass.

"To us," added Harry, clicking glasses and pleased to get off the subject of Tim. Actually he was rather drunk. Emma had insisted on picking up the bill as soon as they had arrived at the restaurant, saying, "Just so you can't moan when we drink good champagne." And the good champagne had kept flowing.

"I'm going to sit down," Harry shouted. "I'm incapable of standing up any longer. The vodka and champagne, you know."

"I know." Emma laughed and collapsed into her chair. "I think I'm drunk too."

"Who said I was drunk?" laughed Harry. "But it might be a good idea to get a taxi."

Emma stifled a yawn. "Oh, you boring man, can't you live dangerously?"

Harry was about to snap, "Not when there's a risk I might kill someone," when he realised he was indeed being boring—he'd driven drunk more times than he could remember. He didn't care a fuck about the legal limit. So why start getting all righteous now? Not the right moment. "Okay, I'll drive. Just thought you might disapprove like a lot of your age group. Say when you're ready to go. In the meantime let's get some water."

Emma placed a hand on his thigh. She was feeling hot. She hadn't felt like this since dancing with...oh, God, she'd forgotten the man's name! She didn't want to hang around any longer than necessary. "I'm ready to go any time," she said, waving at a waiter and asking for a bottle of mineral water and the bill. "I bet we get home without a blue light flashing up your arse," she laughed.

"That might be uncomfortable!"

"I'd like to see it though."

He decided to play along. "Maybe you will."

Emma winked at him and tightened her grip on his thigh. "Oh, you naughty man," she giggled. "I'd like to see your arse very much."

"In that case, I suggest you pay the bill on the way out. No point in wasting time."

Emma jumped up, swayed, recovered her balance and held out a hand. "Come on then."

Harry followed her to the restaurant door, where she paused to sign the bill and smile her thanks. "Happy New Year," she called back into the restaurant before grabbing Harry's arm and weaving her way up the stairs into the street. "Now take me home, Harry, and show me you're the man I've been told you are."

Luckily for Emma it was too dark for her to see his smile.

······

He drove slowly, imagining Emma's face when he told her. He could visualise it collapsing in grief, her carefully applied make-up running down her cheeks. He was not the sort of man to worry about shattering his daughter's life. He had no affection for her. She was a means to an end.

By the time he drew up outside the flat he was sweating. Emma leant over and kissed him. "Come on, Harry, let's not hang about." She stretched lazily. "Oh God, I think I'm a little pissed. Help me out, will you?"

He jumped out and moved quickly to open her door. It was too bloody cold to hang around.

"Oops, I think I might need a hand."

He caught her just before she pitched onto the pavement. "Look at the pair of us, a couple of real old soaks!" she giggled and gave a loud hiccup. "Sorry. Hope I can remember the code to the frigging door!"

Harry's laugh was mirthless. "I bloody hope so."

"Ah, we're in luck!" Emma cried as she heard the welcome buzz of the lock releasing.

"Thank God for that!"

"Wow, that was difficult," she laughed. "Now we have to negotiate the stairs."

"I'll carry you."

Emma broke into another fit of the giggles as he picked her up and started to climb the stairs. "Just like a newly married couple!" she managed to say. "Here, you better have the keys. Don't think I'll be able to find the hole." With that she gave a shriek of drunken laughter.

As soon as the door of the flat was closed, Emma made a drunken lunge at Harry. He swayed out of the way and she fell at his feet. She hiccupped loudly and swore.

How he hated women who couldn't hold their drink. None too gently, he dug a foot into her ribs. "Come on, you drunken whore, stand up."

She pushed herself into a sitting position. "What, what did you call me?"

"A whore and you look ridiculous. Stand up."

Her mind scrambled by alcohol, she failed to pick up Harry's tone of contempt. She giggled as she struggled to her feet. "Okay, Harry, you have your fun. If you want me to act like a whore, I will. But I'm not into pain. How's this for starters?" She lifted her short skirt, showing her long legs encased in sheer nylon stockings. She wore no panties. "Like that, Harry?"

Harry snorted with disgust. "I'm not playing perverted games. I'm telling you that you're a whore."

A cold hand touched Emma's heart. What was he playing at?

"Are you trying to tell me something, Harry?"

"You're a whore. All this"—he waved a hand round the room—"is paid for by sex. Your lifestyle is supported by prostitution. I've had a private detective following you, so don't deny it." He gave a low chuckle. "I must admit I never thought I'd have a whore for a daughter."

Emma was suddenly very sober. "Why, you two-timing bastard!" Then his words sank in. "What's all this daughter crap?"

"You're my daughter."

She moved swiftly, her eyes blazing and stopped inches from his face. "What a load of shit, Harry. Tim was my father."

"No."

"You and Mum…"

"That's what I'm saying."

"You're a liar, a fucking liar!"

Harry moved quickly. He wanted to end it, he'd come to destroy, and he didn't want to waste time trying to convince her. He grabbed the telephone, shaking the receiver in front of her startled face. "Go on, ring your mother. Ask her. She won't lie."

Emma knocked the receiver out of his hand. "I don't believe you. My mother has always said you were a pathological liar. I don't know what your game is, but you will never get me to believe you're my father. My mother would never have lied to me all these years. You're cruel, Harry, so very cruel. I have misjudged you just like my mother did. I thought we had the beginning of a relationship. God, how could I have been so stupid! Get out before I scream the place down."

Harry held up his hands and smiled. "I'll go, but you'll sweat tonight thinking about what I've said. You'll ask your mother. And the—"

"Get out, get out!"

Harry moved towards the door. "I'm your father, Emma, get used to that, because I'm part of your life now."

"Tim was my father. He loved me, cared for me. You've done fuck all except try to mess us about since he died. Why did you lead me on? You knew

I was falling for you. Was it a plan to hurt my mother? What's with you, Harry?"

"I told you, ask your mother."

"Fuck off."

"I'm going, but I'll be around to haunt you. Your life will never be the same."

Emma turned and fled to her bedroom. She didn't hear him slam the flat door, nor the sound of his feet on the wooden stairs, or the outside door closing or the screech of his tyres.

She could hear nothing above her screaming.

......

The shrill ringing of the telephone woke Jill with a start. Confused, she threw out an arm and knocked the bedside light flying. "Damn!" In the dark she groped for the receiver, found it and managed to get it to her ear. "Hello."

"Mum!"

Jill's brain rapidly unscrambled. "Emma!"

"Yes, it's me."

Jill felt a rush of panic. "What's happened? Are you all right?"

"No, I'm not all right!"

Jill heard the despair. "Hold on just for a second. I knocked the light over when you rang. I'm in the pitch dark. Must find the light. You hear me?"

"I'll hang on. But don't be too long."

"I won't be." Oh God, what had happened? Jill fell out of the bed, banged her head against the floor, and dragged herself to the light switch.

"Mum!"

"Yes, still here—just fallen out of bed. Ah, found the light. It's three in the morning! What's the matter?"

Silence.

"Emma! Are you still there?"

There was still no answer.

"Emma, please say something to me." Visions of her being raped flashed past Jill's eyes. "Darling, have you had an accident or has someone attacked you?"

The reply was just audible. "Neither of those two things."

"Then for God's sake, what?"

"It's Harry."

Stunned, Jill croaked, "Harry, Harry Sidenham?"

"Yes."

"What about him?"

"I've been seeing him. He came here tonight to celebrate the New Year."

Jill nearly dropped the phone. "Is he with you now?"

"No! I've thrown him out. I thought I was falling in love with him. What a mistake—he's just been using me to hurt you, I think. I don't know what he was trying to do really. I'm too mixed up to think straight—had a lot to drink."

"Oh God, I'm so sorry."

"He's not my father, is he?"

Jill felt as if a fist had struck her in her stomach. "Is that what he told you?"

"Yes. He's lying, isn't he, or is that another one of your secrets?"

Jill's throat was dry.

"Mum, please."

"I don't want to have this conversation over the 'phone—come home."

"You can't wriggle out of this, Mum. I want to know now! He's not my father, is he? It's quite simple—yes or no?"

There was no way out. "I'm afraid he is."

"No! For Christ sake, why haven't you told me? You've messed me up big time. I should hate you."

Jill just mumbled, "I'm so sorry."

"Sorry! Sorry! Is that all you can say!"

"What else can I say? I was going to tell you. I wanted to at Christmas but it seemed the wrong time."

"The wrong time! That's rich! What about the right time?"

"I know that's what I should have told you years ago, but I funked it. Come home now and we can talk. I need to explain."

"I think you should have done that a long time ago. I can't believe you've lived a lie for all these years."

Jill could hear the anger in Emma's voice. What was she doing to her children! "I understand your anger—in fact wouldn't blame you if you never spoke to me again, but please give me a chance to explain."

"I'm not coming home, not yet at any rate. I need a little time on my own to get my head around yours and Harry's deceit. I'm not sure I can handle you at the moment, and I might say things I'd live to regret. Besides, it's terrible outside—thick, freezing fog and I've had too much to drink. I'll see how I feel tomorrow."

"I think you should come home now."

"Don't you dare push me; at the moment, I'm angry, Mum—with you, with Harry and with myself. By tomorrow things may be different."

"I don't know what to say."

"Then shut up! You should be ashamed of yourself."

"I am. Oh, Emma, I am."

"I just wish it hadn't been Harry who told me—that's fucked me up more than anything. One minute I'm crying the next I'm swearing at you, and the next I'm so angry with myself!"

"I could come to you."

"No!"

"Why not?"

"Didn't you hear me? I'm sorry, but I don't want to see you. Leave me alone."

"Very well. But remember, I love you."

"Right now I don't think I care."

Jill choked back a sob. "That hurt."

"I very much doubt if it hurt as much as you've hurt me."

"I've made a mistake," Jill said quietly.

"You sure have. Now I don't want to talk anymore."

Jill felt a wave of panic. She didn't want to break the connection. "No wait, darling."

"No. I'm stopping now. See you sometime."

"Tomorrow?"

"Don't bank on it."

"Emma, please! Emma?"

The telephone was dead.

Jill replaced the receiver. She was sitting on the floor, her back resting against the bed. The room swam in front of her eyes, she felt as if her body was being battered by a giant wave, and every muscle was screaming. Then very slowly her vision cleared, the room stopped spinning and her body relaxed. But it was only a brief respite before the mental anguish clicked in. She stood up unsteadily, her legs reluctant to take her weight. Negative thoughts battered at her brain. But one constant theme repeated itself: Emma should not be alone in her flat. She fumbled for the telephone and frantically dialled 1471, then the number 3. All she got was the engaged tone. She looked round the room wondering what to do. She had no idea where Emma's flat was—how could she have allowed that to happen? Sleep was out of the question. Maybe she should ring the police. They might be able to trace her. No, that was too drastic. What she needed was someone to calm her down. Someone to tell her she wasn't the lying, uncaring bitch she felt. It was no good going to Toria. She picked up the telephone and dialled Max.

"It's me," she said as soon as she heard his voice. "Sorry to wake you, but I need to talk to you urgently."

"I was awake anyway. What's happened?"

"Something terrible—far worse than I'd ever have expected. You won't believe this but Emma has been seeing Harry. She told me she was in love with him, and tonight he told her he was her father. She's devastated—not making a lot of sense. She's angry at the world. It's like a horror story, and I don't know what to do. She doesn't want to see me. She refuses to come home, and I can't go to her because I'm ashamed to say I don't know where in Bristol she's living and she won't tell me. Max, I'm worried sick."

"I'll be with you in half an hour," Max said.

......

Terrified that Harry might decide to harass her, Emma dropped the receiver onto the floor. It would be in character for him to try something like that. "Arse-hole!" she shouted to the empty room. *Christ, I need a drink.*

She moved out of her bedroom to the table in the sitting room where she'd put the vodka before she and Harry had left for the restaurant. She poured herself a stiff measure from the half-empty bottle and dropped down on the sofa. What a shit of an evening it had turned out to be! She felt as if every ounce of breath had been driven from her body, leaving her weak and defenceless against the conflicting emotions thumping away in her brain. She was angry with Harry, the two-timing bastard for leading her on. She was angry with her mother for her lies. She felt sick at the thought that she'd had the hots for her bloody father—Jesus Christ! She drank greedily from her glass. She was worried about what Harry was planning next. He'd made it abundantly clear he was not going to go away. So what could she do? She threw her hands into the air, forgetting she was holding the glass of vodka and the liquid spilt all over her. It was the last straw. She turned onto her stomach and buried her head in one of the cushions, tears streaming down her face, her make-up staining the blue silk cover. Life was a bitch. She'd cocked-up badly, foolishly thinking that Harry would be her ticket to freedom. How fucking stupid could she get? She wiped some of the liquid off her dress and considered her options. Perhaps it was time to go home after all.

But my mother's a liar.

Perhaps it was time to forget her dreams of being rich and settle down to a mundane life just like Toria. Go back to horses. Go hunting, and marry a local boy with as much character as a cold fried egg and be constantly pregnant.

But my mother's a liar.

And Harry would be just down the road. His evil presence would haunt her. So no local boy, no babies. Okay, what was the next option, move to London and sell herself? She'd heard the Arabs paid well. She lifted her head off the cushions, her makeup ravaged by tears. Through half-closed eyes she spotted the picture on the mantelpiece of her mother and Tim sitting under the walnut tree. She let out a cry, rubbed her eyes, and jumped off the sofa. She swayed a little, found her balance, and walked towards her bedroom. She had an overpowering desire to go home. Her mother might be a liar, but she was the best option she had.

......

Darkness engulfed the MG as she drove the little car across the Clifton suspension bridge. She'd always been frightened of the dark, and to make matters worse, she guessed visibility was down to about fifty metres. If the fog was as thick on the motorway, the journey home could take a long time—and she was in a hurry. She strained to see in front of her. The fog wasn't the only problem. Her eyes were not focusing, as they should have been. But she told herself there would be little traffic at nearly four on New Year's morning, so no problem. But she soon discovered that was not to be. The lack of traffic on the road left it dark, and several times she clipped the curb and had to fight the steering wheel to stay on the road.

By the time she reached the roundabout leading onto the M5 she was already tired, her eyes burning from lack of sleep, and a headache thumping at her forehead. A voice in her head was shouting, *Turn around!* But she was in no mood to think rationally. She wanted to go home, face her mother, and find out if she could forgive. Nothing else mattered. The lights of a solitary car blinded her and she put a hand up to her eyes. The fog seemed thicker here and she felt disorientated. Frustration coursed through her body. It was as if the elements were conspiring against her.

How many times have I done this trip? Christ, I can make it home with my eyes shut!

Swearing loudly, she searched for the slip road onto the motorway. The first time round she missed it, swore again, and retraced her steps on the roundabout. On her second circuit the fog seemed to lift for a moment and she found the right route at last. She drove into total blackness, no lights from traffic, no overhead lights on the road. She shivered, feeling isolated as the great expanse of darkness enveloped her. Once on the motorway she put her foot down hard on the accelerator. She thought it was safe even with the patchy fog. There seemed to be no traffic on either of the carriageways. She glanced at the speedometer—it read ninety. She pushed the accelerator hard to the floor.

......

The Range Rover was doing fifty. The driver judged that this was the maximum speed he could safely drive in the conditions. He was relaxed, sober, his wife asleep in the passenger seat. He was heading back to their home in Bristol after visiting his mother in an old people's home in Cheltenham. He loved Christmas and New Year with his mother, and there might not be many more. She was becoming infirm, her eyesight failing, her heart growing weaker. His wife, supportive as ever, had never complained about these few days spent in the old lady's company, in spite of it meaning she'd miss Christmas at home with their children and grandchildren. "There will be plenty of time for that," she'd say, every time he brought the visit up around October. She knew how much it meant to him.

He glanced over at the woman sleeping peacefully beside him. His life would have been nothing without her, and now they were looking forward to his early retirement and the end of these annual early morning dashes back to Bristol, so that he could be in his office by eight in the morning. He smiled contentedly. He was looking forward to more time together, the holidays without the inevitable telephone calls. He risked another look at his wife.

It was a fatal move.

When he turned his full attention back to the road, lights apparently coming towards him blinded him. He screwed up his eyes. Something wasn't right. The lights seemed to be straight in front of him. "Jesus!" he yelled, a split second later, realising with terrible clarity what was happening. He swung urgently on the steering wheel. "God!" he shouted. It was the last word he spoke. Emma's MG ploughed into the front of the Range Rover and exploded. The driver and his wife, trapped inside their car, screamed for four minutes as the flames licked round their legs, burning the flesh off their bones, until the fire intensified and engulfed their bodies. By the time the emergency services arrived the two vehicles were burnt out wrecks, both unrecognisable, a twisted mass of metal.

"Christ, what happened here?" exclaimed a shocked fireman.

"Looks as if some idiot was going up the motorway the wrong way," came back the reply from the first policeman on the scene. "Must have been going like shit out of shovel by the look of it."

"Crazy bugger," said the fireman, wrinkling his nose at the smell of fried flesh. Half an hour ago he'd been reaching the end of his shift, and looking forward to going home to his wife of four months and enjoying a well-earned four-day break. Now he knew that would be postponed for several more hours.

......

By the time Max arrived Jill was frozen to the marrow.

"You're so cold," he said concerned, wrapping his large arms around her.

"I've been out here waiting," Jill said through chattering teeth.

"Why in heaven didn't you wait inside?"

"I don't know really—I just felt I needed to be out here."

"Well, let's get you warm." Max said, leading her back into the house. "A hot mug of tea is what you need."

Jill smiled weakly as Max made for the Aga. "I'd rather have coffee. Actually, come to think of it, a good slug of brandy wouldn't do me any harm."

Max looked at her distraught face. "Good idea. Is the bottle in the usual place?"

Jill nodded and moved to get two tumblers from a shelf. "Are you going to join me?"

"Actually I think I might."

Max filled the tumblers with generous measures and gave one to Jill. "So, we have a problem?"

"A very big one. Can you believe it!"

"I can believe anything where Harry is concerned and I was expecting something to happen like this after I caught Emma out on her lie at Christmas."

"What lie?"

"Forgive me for not telling you, but I felt it would ruin the day, and I planned to tell you later."

"But you haven't."

"No. Emma has beaten me to it."

"What was the lie? Oh no, don't tell me—she went to see Harry?"

"I suspect she did, but I can't prove it. All I know is she certainly didn't go and see Hannay. She wasn't at home."

"How naive I have been. I should have realised something was up. Emma hasn't been herself the least few months"

"You must not blame yourself."

"But if I'd told the truth years ago."

"There's no good going down that road. You and Tim made a decision, nothing can change that. The fates have conspired against you, Jill; Harry would have gone to his grave without saying a word if Tim hadn't died. Now his vindictive mind sees the chance to hurt you."

"I know, and he's succeeding. For all I know Emma may want him as a father."

"Did she say anything about how she felt?"

"Just that he had deceived her, and that she was angry with me. That's not surprising is it?"

"Not at the moment. But she loved my son, and she won't love Harry after this. Try not to worry too much, oh I know that's easier said than done, but ones she's had a night to think about it I'm sure she'll come back here. This is her home Jill. Harry was just an infatuation, and he's destroyed that. Anyway don't tell me he wants her around. He doesn't want a daughter. I doubt if he even loves her. He just wants to destroy this family. Emma's no fool, painful as it might be, she will have realised that by now."

"I hope you're right Max. If not I've lost her."

. "I very much doubt you've lost her. She's confused, angry, and needs time to get her head in order. She'll come home Jill—just be patient."

"But why Max after all this time is Harry's doing this?"

"He's full of envy and bitter at losing you. He never thought you would pick up the pieces of your life and be happy. When he threw you out, he thought he'd destroyed you."

"And when Tim died, Harry saw his chance for revenge. What a sad man he must be."

"And a man like that is very dangerous."

"He's already proved that. Poor darling Emma, what can she be thinking? I'm really worried about her alone in that flat."

"Have you tried ringing her?"

"There was no answer."

"I could ring—you know, just to wish her happy New Year. She's no reason to know you've spoken to me."

"She'd know you would be the first person I'd turn to, but you can try. I'd feel so much better."

Max moved to the telephone. "Got her number?"

"I wrote it on the pad."

He dialled. There was no answer.

"You sure this is the right number?"

"As sure as I can be. I was pretty panicky."

He dialled again. "No good, she's not answering."

Jill controlled the panic building inside her. "Maybe she's had a change of mind and be on her way here?"

"Change of mind. Who has had a change of mind?" Asked Toria, as she walked into the kitchen rubbing the sleep out of her eyes. Then seeing the two sombre faces staring at her said, "Must be something serious. You two look dreadful."

Max intervened. "Sit down, Toria, please. We have something to tell you."

......

Dawn found the three of them still huddled over the kitchen table. The bottle of brandy sat empty, as did the tumblers. Now three mugs of coffee had taken their place. Toria, white faced, was shaking her head in disbelief. "So that was your secret Mum. I couldn't have got it more wrong. No wonder Emma's upset. It can't be easy knowing your Harry's daughter."

"Hopefully she'll come home and we can talk," Jill said.

"She'll do that," Toria said with confidence. "Emma's no fool in case you haven't noticed. Harry's used her, played on her emotions without a second thought. She'll hurt for a bit, be angry like I was, but in the end she'll recognise this as her home, not Sidenham Hall. Be patient Mum, and you won't lose her. Emma loves you. She'll understand your reasons for not telling her. She was happy with you and dad. She'll want to keep it that way. She'll want to talk—get the anger out of her system, and forget that bastard as quickly as she can. There is no way she'll accept him as her father. She'll be on her way already."

"I pray you're right. I just wish it had been me who told her. At least it would have denied Harry the pleasure. How he must have enjoyed the moment. I really didn't think he would be so cruel."

"Harry's capable of anything," Toria said quietly.

"What do you mean by that?" asked Jill.

Toria glanced at her mother. "I, I've been hiding something from you since the Hunt Ball. I swore to myself that I'd never tell you, because that is what Harry wanted. But now I think I've got to."

"If it's something between you and your mother, perhaps I ought to leave," said Max rising from his chair.

"No stay," Toria said. I think you should hear this." She shook her head.

"This is not easy. It brings back too much, far too much. But…"

Her distress was palpable and Jill was quick to say, "You don't need to say a thing."

"Yes I do. Harry would take great pleasure in telling you one day, and he's probably already told Emma. I can just see him embellishing the whole disgusting affair." Toria took a deep breath, stared at her mother and said quietly, "Harry raped me at the Hunt Ball."

Jill froze—sat openmouthed staring at her daughter

"He what?" asked Max.

"He raped me in his library."

"No! I don't want to hear this!" cried Jill, burying her head in her hands.

Max stood up and gently put an arm around Toria. "You don't need to say any more. I can understand how painful this must be for you."

Dry-eyed Toria looked up at him. She'd done with crying. "There's nothing more to say. I fell into a trap—simple as that. I was gullible, a fool." She saw the anguish in her mother's eyes. "Don't blame yourself Mum. I was angry with you, but what's done is done. I've been to hell and back. It's really shitty, but I think I'm coping—well just."

"I can't imagine what you must be going through," said Max. "Keeping it to yourself all this time. Did it cross your mind to go to the police?"

"Never. It would have been Harry's word against mine, and I went into his library willingly. It was not telling Mum that was the hardest."

Jill's eyes were wet with tears. "I don't know what to say. It must have been horrendous."

Toria gave a weak smile. "I think that about sums it up. I was longing to tell someone but I felt so guilty, and I blamed you for it all. But I'm okay with you now and it's better shared between us, and don't you dare say '*sorry*' again, Mum; I've heard that enough times."

Jill stared at her hands, rather than meet Toria's stare.

"You're a very brave young woman," said Max admiringly.

"No, I'm not Max. I've cried until I have no tears left. I close my eyes every time I pass a mirror. I hate my body. No, I'm not brave Max, just determined that Harry is not going to ruin my life."

"That takes guts," said Jill finding her voice.

······

The fog was dense, holding Walnut Farm in its ghostly embrace. It was cold—the sort of cold that ate relentlessly through your clothes and into your bones. Jill was half frozen and apprehensive. "I can't bear this much longer," she said nervously reaching for Max's hand. "I don't think she's coming. I knew it was wrong to be too optimistic."

"She's coming," said Max keeping the growing doubt out of his voice. "But we don't need to wait out here."

"I know, but let's give it a little longer."

Max looked at his watch. "Very well, another half-hour. If she hasn't come by eight-thirty, we go inside and I'll give her another ring."

"Okay."

They heard the sound of a car at the same moment. Their eyes turned to stare down the yard towards the road, praying that at any moment the MG would appear out of the mist. They stood still, their ears straining, their nerves jangling, every second seeming like an age.

"Please God let it be Emma" Jill said breathlessly. "I'm sure it will be Emma."

The police car came to a halt a few feet from where they stood.

Jill's mouth fell open as her mind raced among the reasons that might have brought the police to her home. "I was so sure. How stupid of me," she whispered.

"She'll be here soon," Max said soothingly, as a police Inspector and a young WPC got out of the car. Jill gave the Inspector a weak smile—she remembered seeing him out hunting several times. "Inspector?" she said evenly, while a sense of impending disaster began to grow in her mind.

He touched his cap. "Mrs. Foster."

"Good morning, Inspector," Max said, stepping forward. "What brings you here on such a miserable morning? Not more trouble with those damned hunt saboteurs?"

The inspector shook his head. "Not this time. We came to see you, Mrs. Foster. Perhaps it would be better if we went into the farm house."

Feeling her unease surge into fear, Jill said, "No need. Whatever you came to say, you can tell me here. Now, Inspector, what's so important that couldn't wait until the fog cleared?"

······

Jill's screams echoed around the farmyard; they were heard in the village houses nearest the farm. The horses in their stables became agitated by the unfamiliar noise, the cows shifted in their stalls. Toria recognised the sound and froze. A puff of wind caught the last withered leaf on the walnut tree. It had obstinately clung to its branch all winter. It spun gently down to the frozen ground.

Chapter Fourteen

Harry had chosen not to go on the motorway. His journey home would take longer, but he hated motorways in the fog, and besides knowing he was over the legal alcohol limit, he reckoned he was less likely to attract attention from the police if he stuck to the minor roads. He drove slowly, fighting to keep his eyes open. The adrenaline surge had abated and he was very tired. In spite of this he smiled to himself. What an evening! He could still see the look of horror on Emma's face. His plans had gone well—first Toria, then Emma. As for Jill, he was certain she'd never recover from the double blow. He'd waited a long time.

He stared at the black wall in front of him, blinked, and knew he was within an ace of falling asleep at the wheel. He didn't want to risk having an accident. He drove slowly until he found a lay-by, turned off the ignition, huddled down into his overcoat and within a few minutes he fell into a restless sleep.

When he woke, the fog was thicker. He was cold; his mouth was dry, and he was dying for a pee. He forced his stiff limbs out of the car and urinated against a nearby tree. Back in the car he glanced at his watch. It was just gone nine. He was amazed. He'd slept for a little over five hours. No wonder he was frozen. He felt his stubble and thought of the warmth of a hot bath and a black coffee. Urgently, he put the key into the ignition and caught sight of his mobile. Someone had called. Not bothering to look at the number, he pressed the redial button. It was Max.

He asked irritably, "Good God, man, what are you doing ringing me!"

"Where are you, Sidenham?" Max's voice demanded.

Harry hated the way Max called him 'Sidenham', and he felt his temper rising. "What the hell has that got to do with you, Foster?"

"Because there's an emergency here, and you need to get your arse back here pretty damn quick."

"Oh fuck off, Foster," Harry shouted, and rang off.

Before he could pull out of the lay-by his mobile rang again. He thought of disconnecting it, decided against and asked, "What the hell do you want, Foster?"

Max knew he had to keep calm. If he showed his anger Harry would ring off, so with some effort he said, "This is very serious. You need to get back here."

Harry picked up the urgency in his voice. "Don't tell me my bloody house has burnt down?"

"Unfortunately nothing like that."

Harry grunted but ignored the insult. "Then what, for Christ's sake, man?"

"Emma's had a terrible accident."

"Oh my God, how bad?"

"She's dead, Sidenham. She was killed on the motorway. She was on the wrong carriageway. It seems she was coming home. She should never have tried it. And do you know what?"

Harry guessed what was coming but asked, "What?"

"You as good as killed her."

Harry broke the connection.

······

Harry scowled as he saw Max's Land Rover parked outside the Hall. Max was the last person he wanted to see. He was tired—a little shocked, he had to admit. After all Emma was his daughter. The last thing he'd wanted was for her to die. Come to think of it, it rather ruined his plans. Now here was this boorish old man arriving uninvited. He jumped out of the Jaguar and walked towards the Land Rover. It was empty. He whirled round to stare at the house and caught sight of Max standing by a window. The man was in his house! That stupid woman Mrs. Banks would get the sharp end of his tongue. Swearing under his breath, he walked slowly through the front door to be met by Max standing arms folded behind his back, a look of thunder on his face.

"Just walk in uninvited, won't you," Harry spat.

"Edna let me in. I want a word with you, Sidenham."

"Mrs. Bank's had no authority to do that. So say what you have to say right here and then get out. You're not welcome"

"Very well, as you wish. This won't take long. I know it's a complete waste of time appealing to your better nature, to ask you to go and beg Jill for her forgiveness. I know you don't care who you hurt. I know you're eaten away by envy. I know you couldn't care less that your daughter has been burnt to a cinder. You behaved like an animal with Toria, and now, because of your utter disregard for anyone's feelings, you have Emma's death on your hands. Did you really want to hurt Jill that much?"

"As much as I possible could." Then a self-satisfied smile crossed Harry's lips. "So Toria spilled the beans did she?"

"You're insufferable Sidenham. How can you live with yourself? I know it's no good appealing to your conscience because I doubt if you've got one. So just stay away from all of us and leave us to grieve without your odious presence anywhere near us. Do you understand that simple message?"

"Get out, Foster! Get out before I take my fists to you!"

Max stood his ground. "You don't understand at all do you? Well, I'm going to enjoy giving you the beating of your life and maybe that will get my message through."

Max hit him then with a large clenched fist. It sank deep into Harry's soft stomach. He hit him again, harder this time, and watched Harry sink to the ground, clutching his stomach and coughing violently. He kicked him hard in the groin. "I should have done that several years ago," Max said menacingly, before turning his back on the stricken man. The last thing he heard as he hurried outside was the satisfying sound of Harry being very sick.

Once in the Land Rover, his anger evaporated. He was shaking—shocked by his violence. He'd never struck a man before. He silently cursed Harry for bringing out the worst in him. *But then,* he thought, *Harry has the knack of being able to do that to anyone.*

PART FOUR
2001

Within your shadow I am bound.

G. Apollinaire

Chapter Fifteen

For the second time in less than a year, Jill was sitting by her bedroom window, rereading the faded letters from her mother that had given her strength while she was away at boarding school. This time, the letters did little to raise her from her depression. The exposure of her jealously guarded secret had opened the floodgates of misery. Emma's tragic death and Toria's shocking experience had wrought havoc with the fabric of a family already under stress. It would be difficult to stitch the fabric together again. What had she done? She wondered if her normal robust constitution could ever rebound from these hammer blows.

To make matters worse the police had informed her that Emma had worked for an escort agency in Bristol. To Jill this was just a polite way of saying that her daughter had been a whore, selling her body for money to men unable to keep their pricks under control. When the police had told her, she'd shaken her head in disbelief that she had been so blind. Since then, she'd chastised herself again and again for failing miserably as a mother. Why hadn't she suspected that something was not right with the journalist story? The secrecy about the flat, the weekends away, the flashy clothes, and finally the new MG should have alerted her to the fact that something didn't quite add up. She should have been asking questions. It was no good using Tim's illness and their financial worries as excuses. A mother should always have her eye on the ball, especially when a young one sets out on her own for the first time. She stared at the letter she was reading, but her eyes were unable to focus on the writing and the letter fluttered to the floor. She knew she'd feel better if she cried; anything would be better than the tight pain in her chest that threatened to burst out, but she didn't have the strength even to cry. She'd lost too much sleep, tossing and turning every night since Emma's death, haunted by uninvited images of burning cars and Harry mocking her. Now she was near to exhaustion. She just wanted to curl up in a ball and sleep forever. Her eyelids closed and her head nodded forward, fatigue enveloping her. Then, very gently, she slid to the floor.

She began to hallucinate. She heard a noise like thunder crack above her head and felt as if she were being swept down a fast flowing river, the angry water bearing her on and on and then hurling her over raging rapids. She was tossed about like a piece of matchwood, her arms flailing, and her mouth filling with water. She tried to scream, but the water was choking her.

A few moments later, alerted by strange noises coming from her mother's bedroom, Toria burst in and stared in horror at her mother writhing on the floor, clutching the leg of a chair, and making funny gurgling noises. "Mum, Mum!"

There was no response.

Toria clasped her hands together and breathed in slowly, trying to control herself. "Mum!" she yelled; this time louder, bending down and grabbing one flaying arm.

Jill tried to fight her off.

"Mum, what on earth are you doing? It's me, Toria!"

Her voice cut through the noise of rushing water, and very slowly Jill came out of the trance. She stopped fighting Toria and, gasping for breath, her eyes began to focus. Her head cleared; the noise of rushing water fell silent. She stared up at Toria, a questioning look on her face. "What's happening?" she asked, searching Toria's face for an answer.

Toria pried her mother's fingers open and gently helped her onto the bed. "You're going to be fine, Mum. I think you've just had a nightmare. Try and relax. I won't leave you."

Jill grabbed Toria's hand in a vicelike grip. "I felt I was drowning."

"Poor Mum, you're exhausted. You must have been hallucinating."

Jill shuddered. "I must be losing my mind."

"That's rubbish. It's just that everything has suddenly got on top of you, and you really must see the doctor. You know, just let him check you out. No, don't look at me like that. Sometimes, even you need a little medication. So please no arguing, okay?"

"I'm too exhausted to argue."

"Well, that's one good thing," Toria said, forcing a laugh. "I'll ring the doctor now before you change your mind. I reckon you need a few good nights' sleep and something to see you over Emma's funeral. After that, things can only get better."

Jill thought of the pain she saw every day on Toria's face and wondered if that would ever happen.

......

Max sat in the snug of The Drunken Duck, a pint of best bitter in his hand. Walter Stibbens the publican sat opposite him, swaying on an old wooden chair pockmarked by woodworm and threatening to collapse under Walter's weight. The pub smelt of age, stale tobacco, spilt pints, and chips. At precisely eight every evening the sound of Neil Diamond's gravely voice came from three old and cracked speakers spread haphazardly around the two bars, his voice fighting to be heard above the hubbub of animated chatter. Walter's love of Diamond was tolerated with good humour. The locals would have it no other way, and anyway Walter would change none of his habits for anyone. His kitchen had been threatened with closure a few times by the health and safety officer. "Interfering sods," Walter moaned after each visit, and then went about the necessary changes with a hangdog expression as if his last penny was being coerced under threat from "those bloody lackeys from Whitehall."

Both men had known each other for years, but after Max became a widower they had forged a close friendship, built around their shared love of hunting and a good pint of beer. There were not many evenings after a day's hunting when the two of them could not be found huddled over a table in the pub reminiscing on the events of the day while enjoying a pint of their favourite bitter. But today the atmosphere was sombre. "So there you are," Walter was saying, moving his large bulk uneasily in his groaning chair. "Now you can alert Jill to the danger that before Emma's funeral tomorrow Sidenham is going public with the story. I assure you I wouldn't worry you with this piece of news if we weren't dealing with a snake like Harry Sidenham."

Max saw the concern in the friendly eyes half hidden by the largest pair of eyebrows he'd ever seen. "No, you did the right thing," Max assured him. "Nothing would surprise me when it comes to that man, and this sounds just the sort of thing he'd do."

Walter nodded, scratching his chest through his green woollen shirt. "I'm not trying to pry, old friend, but I assume you knew about this?"

"I've known for years."

"What a thing to expose, now that the poor girl is dead. It can only hurt Jill more."

"That's Harry's intention."

Walter nodded sombrely, before breaking into his familiar smile. "Well, rumour tells me you have already made Harry abundantly clear about your feelings. You gave him a good hiding so the story goes."

"It only took one uppercut and a well-aimed jab into his groin, but I'm not proud of what I did Walter, especially as there was a moment when I felt like killing him."

"A view shared by many. But watch him, Max, he's a dangerous man to cross."

"I'm not frightened of a coward."

"They can be the most dangerous," Walter warned, wagging a finger at his friend.

"Well, he certainly doesn't frighten me," said Max, rising reluctantly from the table and eyeing Walter's second pint. "I think I'll forgo my refill tonight—better hurry over to Jill's, just in case events move quicker than we expect."

"A wise move," Walter agreed.

Max left the pub and drove the short distance to Walnut Farm. Walter's news was disturbing, and he knew he had no alternative but to tell Jill. That concerned him, given her present state of mind.

••••••

Harry sat behind his desk, a whisky in one hand a non-filter Gitane cigarette in the other. Opposite him, perched uneasily on a hardbacked chair, sat Giles Taylor. "That unpleasant young reporter from the local rag," as Harry disdainfully called him to one of his dwindling band of friends.

Giles Taylor had no time for Harry either, and for good reason. Not only because he insisted on calling him 'Taylor' in a derogatory manner, which deliberately implied that he was inferior. But also because of a past incident which had blighted his chances of promotion within the paper. So when the telephone call had come through from Lord Sidenham, his editor had said with a wink, "This sounds just the ticket for you, Giles. That was your old friend Sidenham. From the little he told me, there's a good story to be had up at the Hall. There is nothing like a bit of aristocratic scandal to whet our readers' appetites. Get over there and see what's going on."

Giles had realised it was pointless trying to wriggle out of the assignment. He'd shuffled his feet, run a hand through his greasy black hair, and cursed his luck at being in the office when the call came through.

He'd hoped to never be reminded again of his humiliation at the hands of 'Shagger Sidenham' as he was known in the office. There had been a tip off that a van load of thugs from Brixton London were going to descend on the Hunt and 'dust up those fucking toffs.' Giles didn't carry any hard or fast opinions about hunting one way or the other—most of his colleagues on the paper would say that he had very few opinions about anything. But he'd covered enough hunts to know that if there was going to be a story it would more than likely come from the anti side. So on this particular Saturday he'd opted to run with the antis, and had the misfortune of being ambushed in a wood by a gang of Hunt stewards led by Harry Sidenham. Before he'd had a chance to explain that he was a reporter he'd been thrown along with the antis into a foul-smelling pond by some large and very angry men, all at least a foot taller and much fitter than himself. "The bastards tried to kill me!" he whined later to his editor." He'd been the laughing stock of the office for a week, and a month later was passed over for the job of sub-editor.

Now he was once again face to face with Harry. Nothing had changed their opinions of each other, but the story erupting from Harry's mouth was sensational, and with a little embellishment could restore his fortunes at the paper. He licked the tip of his chewed biro, did his best not to meet Harry's disdainful stare, and scribbled enthusiastically, his eyes darting enviously every now and then at the cut glass decanter containing the whisky.

Shit, the bastard might at least offer me a drink.

......

"Walter Stibbins is very reliable. As I'm sure you know, he's no gossip monger," Max said, as he and Jill stood by the calf stalls where Toria was coaxing a newly born calf to drink. "If he says that little creep of a reporter Giles Taylor has been up at the Hall, we can assume Harry's about to play the grieving father denied access to his daughter all these years. The fact that he didn't care one little bit about her is immaterial. He wants to cause trouble before the funeral."

"Can you be sure of this, Max?"

"Yes."

"Who told Walter?"

"Edna Banks. She overheard the whole conversation. Went straight to Walter because she felt you should be forewarned."

"Now the whole village knows," Jill stated.

"No, she'll keep her mouth shut, but the local paper won't. They won't take into consideration the hurt they will cause you and Toria," Max said. "I know the editor, John Franks, quite well. He's an overweight, chippy young man, eager to make his mark and has little regard for the pain his articles might inflict on people. He will make a meal of this one, hoping to increase sales and maybe catch the eye of a big national paper and sell the story."

"It's not fair," whispered Jill. "Hasn't Harry done enough damage already without going public? Emma's dead, can't he leave it at that?" She ran a hand nervously through her hair. "Would it do any good if I appealed to his better nature?"

"He hasn't got a better nature," Toria said bitterly. "If he can be so callous about Emma, when will he go public about me, I wonder? I can just see the story. *She threw herself at me. She was panting for it. I'm just like any other man after all. Offer it to me on a plate and I'll take it.* How humiliating, but it would be his style. He'd love to hit us with a double blow while we're down. If that happens I just want to die. I don't think I'd have the strength to deal with something like that."

"He won't go down that route, I'm sure," said Jill. "He raped you, for God's sake."

"My word against his and you know the man is almost always believed."

"He's got to be stopped," said Jill. "He's done us enough damage already. He's a parasite."

Toria gave her mother a knowing look. "You or me?" she asked only half joking.

······

Later that day Jill was driving her Volvo Estate car towards Sidenham Hall. The weather was dreary, rain threatening, low cloud hung over the hills. It suited her mood. She'd had time to reflect on the conversation in the calf shed and decided there was only one course of action she could take: have it out with Harry, try to make him feel sorry for her. Beg him to understand. Already she suspected her appeal would fall on deaf ears, and all he would do was mock her, but she had to try. Seeing Toria's stricken face had made up her mind. It was time to try and put a stop to Harry's games. Persuade him he had nothing to gain. Of course, that was the problem—Harry obviously thought he had a lot to gain. Did he care what people thought of him? She knew the answer. As long as he had the means to hurt her, he'd be happy. Not for the first time in her life she wondered what on earth she'd seen in him in the first place.

The rain battered at the windscreen, the wind howled around the car. It was scary; a storm was brewing, and her resolve weakened. She could be about to make a fool of herself, exposing her fragile state of mind to a manipulator par excellence. Tears of frustration threatened to blind her, and she slammed her foot on the brake, encouraging furious hooting from a car behind. As it passed her, she raised a hand in apology. She wiped the tears away, angry with herself for showing weakness. But she felt so impotent. For several minutes she sat staring out of the window at the familiar peaceful countryside shrouded in mist. A sense of reality was returning. She'd been consumed by anger, and acted on impulse. Better to admit she'd made the wrong decision. There was no point in going further; she'd be playing straight into Harry's hands. But her anger hadn't abated. There would be a time when Harry would rue the day he'd involved her daughters, but it would be a time of her choosing. For once Harry would not be setting the agenda.

She decided to go home.

......

It was a beautiful day for a funeral, a late January day sparkling from the crisp overnight frost. The air was bitterly cold and cirrus clouds scudded across the upper reaches of the sky. Every now and then the sun broke through and cast shadows over the churchyard.

Jill looked round at the sad faces, many of whom had come to Tim's funeral, and couldn't help thinking they must be getting used to coming to the churchyard to bury a Foster. What on earth had she done to God—the all-loving God that her father had encouraged her to embrace? What had she done to deserve His wrath? She remembered Toria once asking, "How can you believe in God, Mum? It's a big fairy story especially that bit about a virgin birth. Surely no one can believe that?" She'd been horrified by her daughter's atheism; now she was beginning to think she might have a point. She stared at the coffin as it was lowered into the ground. The final resting place for a daughter she felt she'd badly let down. She would have liked to turn to God to ask him where she'd gone wrong, even ask Him for His forgiveness, but she could not bring herself to talk to Him.

And then she saw Harry.

Harry! He seemed to have a habit of turning up at funerals. She turned away quickly from his gaze. How dare he invade her space at this time? She wanted to rush at him—beat at his chest—scream *'murderer'* into his face. That was exactly what he'd want her to do. She forced herself to turn and hold his stare, her eyes radiating her anger.

The vicar ended his prayers and Jill broke the eye contact and picked up a handful of earth and threw it onto the coffin. "Goodbye, Emma darling, I'm sorry I let you down," she said quietly.

When she looked up, Harry was gone.

......

That night a great storm swept up from the West.

The wind was gusting to gale force eight at times, and as it rushed up the valley it uprooted the more vulnerable trees in its path. The rain lashed the fields and beat angrily on the windows of the houses, and the sheep on the down huddled under the hedge, their heads buried in each other's wool. The walnut tree bent its back against the gusts and its roots fought to keep their grip on the earth. The tree had witnessed many storms like this, and in its youth had treated them with contempt, holding its branches high, its trunk as straight as an arrow. But the years had taken their toll. Scars were beginning to appear on its bark. But nowhere was the damage greater than on the large branch that overhung the garden seat. It had taken more than its share of the howling winds and driving rain, and it had been sorely wounded. Water was seeping ever deeper into its cracks, and decay had set in. For four hours the branch resisted the gale. But in the final hour of the storm, its defences finally surrendered, and with a mighty crash it fell to the ground, missing the garden seat by inches.

Jill heard the noise above the wind, and fearing the tree had been uprooted, buried her head under the bedclothes.

The sound also woke Toria. Grabbing the torch she always kept by her bed, she rushed to her window. The beam picked up the tree and the fallen branch. She blew out her cheeks and smiled; perhaps it was an omen.

The next morning, the air was still. The sun shone down on the chaos left by the overnight gales. Jill sat on the damp seat under the walnut tree, the debris from the fallen branch all around her. She was tempted to think that if the old tree could survive such a battering, so could she. Wounded they both might be, but they were far from dead. They were tough, two seasoned fighters, able to bend against adversity and fight on. She pushed her hands deep into the pockets of her woollen skirt and walked purposefully back to the house, smiling as she passed Toria. She ran up the stairs and made for the bathroom cabinet. She reached for the packet of sleeping pills which the doctor had prescribed for her. Startled at the new determination flowing through her body, she emptied the contents into the lavatory pan. She wouldn't need drugs anymore.

······

"What on earth has come over her?" Max questioned Toria two days later.
"Would you believe it if I said it was the walnut tree surviving the storm?"
"I think I might."
"There's your answer then. She's already ditched the pills and been out
for her first ride since Emma died. She's a different woman, Max."
Max smiled and blew a kiss towards the garden. "Well, God bless that
warty old tree, I say!"

······

Things were not working out as Harry had planned. Since his revelations
had been front-page news in the local paper, he had suffered several
humiliating reversals. Firstly, the chairman of the Hunt had written a
downright insolent letter asking for his resignation as joint master of the
Hunt, and then to add insult to injury, the silly old fart informed him that they
no longer wished to hold the Hunt Ball at Sidenham Hall. Harry had enjoyed
writing, "You've just shot yourself in the foot, you pathetic old man, because
you are no longer welcome to hunt over my land. If one member of the Hunt
sets foot on it I'll take you to court. Fuck the lot of you, I'll hunt elsewhere."
But when he'd rung round to the neighbouring hunt secretaries asking if he
could come out on a day's hunting, the replies had all been polite but in the
negative. *Well, stuff 'em,* he thought, *I'll do my hunting in Ireland.* And then
the next morning, the telephone had rung and Walter Stibbins had told him he
was not welcome at The Drunken Duck. Not welcome! He'd sold the fucking
pub to him in the first place. Walter had ended by saying, "In fact, Sidenham,
if you dare walk through the door, it will give me great pleasure to personally
throw you out." Harry had blasphemed loudly to a dead connection.

He was a little puzzled by these rebuffs. In his arrogance it had never
crossed his mind that the reaction to his story would be so negative. He'd
imagined he'd be engulfed in a great tide of sympathy. The father denied
access to his daughter for twenty-three years, the father who had unselfishly
allowed another man to bring her up as if she were his own. It had not
occurred to him that most people would brand him as a liar.

······

"Which is exactly what you are," said Jill.
"How dare you say that in my house," Harry blustered, looking at Jill with
undisguised hatred. "You come here unannounced…"
Moisture beaded on his upper lip and she relished his discomfort. "You

didn't expect that did you? It's taken me a long time to pluck up the courage—I've aborted several times"

"I'm, I'm surprised," Harry stuttered, fighting to regain his composure. "I didn't think you had the guts, frankly. But then you've never failed to surprise me, Jill. So why are you here? Not to commiserate with me, that's for sure."

"You're right on that count. I'm delighted that you've fallen flat on your face. It was cruel to print that story, so vile, so unnecessary. I'm surprised you thought people would believe you. But as I said that's not why I'm here. I'm here to ask you to give an undertaking that you'll not go public over raping Toria. You have already done her enough damage."

Harry smiled. "So she's said it was rape has she?"

"I believe her, so don't try and tell me otherwise. You raped her. Count yourself lucky you got away with it. Oh Harry how low can you sink? Wasn't it enough that you were going to mess up Emma's life? For God sake, have you no conscience about Emma's death?"

"Ha! Don't try and swing the blame on to me. As for Toria—she threw herself at me."

"I knew you'd say that. Come on, Harry, it's me you're talking to."

"She walked into this room bold as brass and dropped her knickers. I took her on the sofa where you're sitting. She was compliant, very soft."

Jill felt sick, a picture of Toria struggling building up in her mind. She wouldn't have stood a chance. "God Harry, how I hate you! How can you look at me and lie like that? Toria would never throw herself at you; she's not that sort of girl and besides she's always thought you were an apology for a man."

Harry half rose from his chair. "Enough! I've had enough of you, Jill."

"You said that a while back Harry. But it wasn't true, was it? You didn't want me to go; you thought I'd crawl back after I'd had an abortion. You were so sure. That's what this is all about. You wanted to possess me—and if you couldn't you didn't want me to be happy with another man. You've been eaten away with jealousy ever since."

Harry's face flushed with fury. "Oh, fuck off, Jill!"

"It's true."

"Get out!"

"I'm going. But before I do, remember this. I can only take so much provocation."

Harry moved to within a few feet of her. "What will you do, Jill, kill me?"

"Don't tempt me, Harry! Now get out of my way. I don't want to be in your odious presence a moment longer."

••••••

The light was going; the winter sun was sinking behind the hills overlooking the vale. Harry sat in his leather chair with the familiar glass of whisky in his hand. The library was almost dark, but he didn't hurry to turn on the lights. Since Jill's visit, which had disturbed him more than he was prepared to admit, he quite liked the dark. It suited his mood. She'd slipped under his guard—injected thoughts into his brain that he'd managed to ignore before. He stared through one of the large windows at the dying light. He did not believe in salvation, and even if he did, he'd long used up his credit with God. Jill had been right. He'd cheated, intrigued and lied his way through life. No wonder he had few friends left. Well, fuck it! Who was he to care? There was always a woman around somewhere who would be glad to come to his bed.

He thought of the point at which the paths of good and evil had crossed his life, and he'd chosen the easy route towards greed and immorality. If he was honest with himself there was a touch of regret that he'd led such a debauched life; it might have been different—oh, yes, he hated to admit it, but if he'd handled Jill carefully his life might have taken another course. But he didn't believe in dwelling on what might have been. He was what he was, and he could still make waves. All he had to do was pick up the telephone and speak to Giles Taylor and Toria would be front-page news. He reached for the whisky decanter, conveniently placed within his reach by Mrs. Banks, and poured a large measure. He was already halfway to being drunk. Sod Jill, sod everyone. No one was going to change Harry Sidenham.

He thought of Emma, so vivacious, so beautiful. It was a pity she'd died. He'd credited her with more sense than to drive after so much to drink and the weather conditions. She'd been a mindless stupid girl and now he was getting all the grief. His eyes darted round the room coming to rest on Emma's flat keys lying on the top of his desk. He'd forgotten he had them. He should return them. He had an appointment with his accountant in Bristol the next morning. He'd push them through the letter box of the flats. He took them in his hand remembering the time Emma had handed them to him. "You're welcome any time Harry," she'd smiled, brushing her lips lightly on his cheek. He should have realised then he was playing a dangerous game. He stood up, swayed and fell back into his chair, the whisky working its magic.

That was where Edna Banks found him in the morning.

••••••

That same morning Jill eased the Volvo into a vacant parking space opposite 14 Redcliffe Road. Her nerves were jangling, and she bit nervously on her thumbnail, a habit she thought she'd cracked years ago. She was alone by choice, having rejected Max and Toria's pleas for one of them to come with her. She took several deep breaths to control her racing heart and reached for the bunch of keys lying on the passenger seat. Attached were six black numbers scrawled in Emma's writing on a white card, with the words 'code for front door' underneath. Reluctantly, she left the security of the Volvo and looked up the tree-lined street. The houses were mostly Victorian, set back from the road by small gardens and sheltered by tall lime trees. It was obviously an affluent area, and Jill couldn't stop herself from wondering what Emma's neighbours would say if they knew she'd been a prostitute. She pushed open the metal gate of number 14. Grey flagstones led up to a blue front door. The grass on either side of the path was neatly cut, and manicured hedges divided the property from its two neighbours. There was tightness in her chest as she punched out the numbers and pushed the door open. The interior was bright. The walls were a pastel green, and there was a large bowl of white lilies on a table. On her left was a large glazed window, with tied back plain green curtains. She hesitated for a moment, gathering her courage before taking the stairs to flat 2. The third key on the ring released the lock. She walked in and shut the door behind her before walking through the small lobby into the sitting room. She stopped, and stared in disbelief.

She didn't move for several minutes, her eyes taking in the green pile carpet, the expensive furniture, the handmade curtains, and what she thought were rather garish paintings on the walls, signed by the individual artists.

Probably clients!

It must have all cost a fortune. She moved across the sitting room, glancing at the small kitchen on her way to the bedroom. The king-sized bed was unmade, an empty hot water bottle lying on the sheets. There were clothes chucked everywhere, all pointing to Emma's quick exit. A row of wardrobes took up one wall, and after a cursory glance inside, Jill realised her daughter's affluence hadn't only been spent on fixtures and fittings. She stared round the room unable to stop herself from wondering how many men Emma had romped with on the bed. She moved to the bathroom. It was as opulent as the rest of the flat. A thick white carpet covered the floor. In one corner was a white Jacuzzi with gold accessories. There were wall-to-wall mirrors. Jill let out weak gasp. She returned to the bedroom and dropped onto the bed and looked round the room. What was she going to do with the contents of the flat? If she took it home, it would be a constant reminder of what Emma had become. It only took her a few seconds to decide. Nothing in the flat except for the odd photograph, and a few bits of personal jewellery had anything to do with the Emma she knew. So she would take the photos and the jewellery. Give the clothes to Oxfam. The paintings and furniture she'd arrange to sell locally. The landlord could have the rest.

Her mind made up, she hurried back into the sitting room, keen to get arrangements settled and get out of the flat as quickly as possible. She saw the telephone on a table cluttered with various bottles of alcohol, and noticed a small blackboard hanging from the wall with names and numbers written in white chalk. It looked rather out of place amongst all the affluence. As she moved to the telephone, she spotted a red light blinking. It was Emma's ansaphone. She hesitated. It would be best to wipe out the messages without listening to them. To hear people talking to Emma as if she was still alive would be very distressing, and for some reason, she felt she would be intruding on a life she'd been ignorant about. She bit her lip and decided that was nonsense. The messages had to be listened to. Apprehensively, she pressed the playback button.

The first message was a cryptic reminder from an electrical shop that Emma's heated blanket was still awaiting her collection. "And we can't store it forever, Miss Foster." The second was from a garage telling Ms Foster that her MG was due a service. The third was from a Helen Barclay at Freeke and Massey, estate agents, requesting that Emma get in touch with her within the month to tell them if she wanted to renew the lease. "If not, please let us know in good time." The fourth message made her heart skip a beat. "Dahling Emma, where the bloody hell are you? No news for over a week now and I'm beginning to think you've left me. As you can imagine, M in particular is going crazy. Please make contact ASAP or I will be forced to take you off my books." The next message was a plaintive plea, which Jill guessed came from M. It went, "Emma, this is Philip. Mrs. K doesn't know what's happened to you. I'm missing our dinners and much more. I know I shouldn't contact you direct, but I'm lost without you. Please ring Mrs. K and she'll get in touch with me. I think I love you."

There were no more messages. She jammed a finger on the stop button and removed the tape, dropping it into her handbag. Philip was missing his shag!

Well, too bad Philip, no more shags with MY daughter!

She ran to the kitchen and with shaking hands poured herself a glass of water. She drank greedily. Refilled the glass and returned to the telephone. She scanned the board. All the numbers she required were on it. She wouldn't bother to ring the electrician or the garage. They would surely have heard of Emma's death, and she didn't want their sympathy. That left Freeke and Massey and—she hesitated—perhaps Emma's madam, Mrs. K. Had she the courage to ring her? Why would she want to ring her, morbid curiosity? No it was more than that, much more. She wanted to hear the voice of the woman who had controlled her daughter, who had corrupted her, who, she shamefully acknowledged, might have known Emma better than herself.

······

Harry drove fast, one eye keeping a look out for the police and speed cameras. He didn't want to be late for his meeting, and he had to add the extra few minutes it would take him to drop off Emma's keys. He felt scruffy. He hadn't had time to wash or shave. He'd thrown on a suit and drunk a cup of coffee Mrs. Banks had brought him. He felt fractious—not in the mood to have a lecture from his accountant. He had a headache and his mouth was dry.

······

Jill was put through to Helen Barclay.

"Hello, Mrs. Foster, so kind of you to call at a time like this. All of us here are devastated by the terrible news. Your daughter was such a lovely young woman. I know nothing I say will help to reduce the pain, but please accept our condolences."

"Thank you, Helen—you don't mind me calling you that? Yes, it was devastating. It's not easy to come to terms with such a dreadful death. I'm sorry it's really not your problem."

"I don't mind a bit."

"You're very kind, but why I rang is because I don't want to spend much time here. I want to end the chapter and close the book, if you know what I mean. So I wonder if you could see you're way to arranging the sale of the furniture and paintings? I will remove my daughter's clothes and personal things. As for the carpets and curtains I'm sure the landlord won't mind me leaving them."

"I'm sure they will be only too pleased to have such good quality carpets and curtains to offer a new tenant. As for the furniture and paintings, if you are sure you don't want them I will be happy to arrange to have a local auction house dispose of them. The paintings should be of special interest."

"They are ghastly."

"I agree, but then we can't all have the same tastes can we? They are all by young and rising stars, so your daughter told me. "

That probably wasn't all that was rising, Jill thought.

"Now rest assured, I will do everything I can to help you, Mrs. Foster. Oh, by the way, we owe you a month's rent. Your daughter paid six months in advance."

Jill fought to keep her voice steady. It was little things like this that seemed to bring home her dreadful loss. "Thank you. Do you have my address?"

"I have. Your daughter gave you as a guarantor."

Emma never told me that!

"Okay, and take off any expenses."

"I'll do that, and I presume you would like the cheque from the auction house sent to the same address?"

"Yes, please."

"That will be arranged then. Is that all, Mrs. Foster?"

"I think so. If not, you know where I am. Oh yes, the keys—where do you want me to leave them?"

"I have spares here. You should have two sets. Can you post them to me? It's probably the safest."

"I've only found one set. The police found them next to my daughter's burnt-out car. If she had the other set with her, I'm afraid to say they have probably been incinerated along with my daughter." Jill heard a sharp intake of breath. "But I'll have a look around here and if I find them I'll leave both sets here if that's all right with you? I'd rather not take them back with me to post. You know this closing the book bit. It sounds stupid—but if I take the keys—you understand?"

"Mrs. Foster, don't worry, I completely understand. Just leave them in the flat and the other set are not important. We always change the locks when new tenants take over. I will come over and pick them up later today."

"You're very kind, Helen. Now I've taken up enough of your time, and there's a lot to do here. So must rush."

"Good-bye, Mrs. Foster, and good luck. My thoughts are with you."

Jill slowly replaced the receiver and tried to conjure up a picture of Helen Barclay. She would be a caring woman without a doubt. Perhaps even someone who knew what it was like to lose a child. She sipped her water and took another look at the board. Mrs. K's number stared out at her. It was now or never. She tried to imagine what sort of woman she'd be talking to. A large, big bosomed middle-aged tarty sort, who'd once been a hooker herself, or a younger version who had the sense to sell girls rather than herself? In the end, it didn't really matter. Hopefully she'd never set eyes on Mrs. K and it was all a case of making money out of young girls' bodies. What she looked like was immaterial. She dialled and held her breath.

"Hello, Executive Escorts. Can I help you?"

"Mrs. K?"

"Who's that?" The voice was suspicious.

"It's Emma Foster's mother. Does that mean anything to you?"

The voice was very wary now. "Emma who?"

Jill took a deep breath. "Mrs. K, I'm no threat to you. But I know my daughter worked for you, and I just want to say she won't be coming back."

The voice was gentler. "Oh, Emma, our best girl. I'm sorry. I heard the news. Absolutely tragic. I will miss her." The connection was broken.

Jill dropped the receiver. It had been a mistake to ring.

......

Harry screeched to a halt outside number 14. No parking spaces so he double parked. He wasn't planning to be long. He jumped out of the car juggling the keys in his left hand. He ran up the path to the door, punched in the code, pushed open the door and ran up the stairs. The door to Flat 2 was open. He shrugged. He didn't want to have to explain to anyone why he had the keys. He quietly stepped into the hall and dropped the keys on the floor, looked up and gasped.

"Harry!"

Standing in the sitting room doorway was Jill. "Christ, what are you doing here?" she asked incredulously.

He quickly regained his composure. "Dropping off the keys Emma gave me. I assume you're clearing out the flat. Quite opulent isn't it. She must have been doing very well."

Jill ignored his last remark and held out her hand. "You can give me the keys, and then you can leave."

"You can pick them up off the floor, and I don't know that I'm ready to leave. Come to think of it I might like to give you a hand. It would be nice for the parents to do something together."

Suddenly Jill felt very angry. "Oh God you're a shit, Harry. Please go!"

"You're beginning to sound like a stuck record," Harry laughed, enjoying seeing Jill's anger, as he pushed past her into the sitting room. "I see you've started. Where next?"

"Get out!"

Harry moved threateningly towards her. "I've no intention of going. Oh, isn't that a sweet photograph of you and Tim with Emma on that table. Perhaps I might take that—you know, as a memento."

216

"You're sick, Harry."

He raised a fist.

"That's right, hit a woman. You've been doing that all your life. That's the only way you'll get this picture." She moved too quickly for him and grabbed the frame off the table.

"I'm going to have to take it from you."

She was very frightened—shaking. But she stood her ground. "If you move another inch towards me, I'll phone the police." With her free hand she fumbled for her mobile in her pocket.

Harry lunged towards her, but again she was too quick for him. She ran into the bathroom and locked the door. Then she dialled the police. "You have about five minutes, Harry, before the police arrive," she shouted through the door. "I should run if I were you. Attacking a defenceless woman is a serious offence. And your breath stinks of whisky."

"You bitch!" he screamed.

"Piss off, Harry!"

"You're bluffing, Jill. I'm going to break the door down."

"You haven't time." God, she was terrified. The door shook. She sat down on the floor and closed her eyes. How long would the lock hold? It was going to be a very close run thing.

And then she heard the siren.

......

"I don't ever again want to feel fear like that," said Jill.

"Poor Mum. I'm so sorry. I knew I should have come with you."

"Thank God you didn't. I'm a little shocked, but that will pass."

"Did the police arrest him?" asked Toria.

"No. I didn't press charges. I apologised for wasting their time. I told them it was a domestic."

"What did Harry do?"

"He kept very quiet. I think he was terrified of being breathalysed and worried I would press charges."

"I think you should have done, that would have really shaken him," said Toria.

"What charges? He hadn't touched me. Besides, his humiliation was enough for me. And he didn't get the photo."

"I'd give anything to see that man in jail," said Toria bitterly.

"Join the club. On the other hand perhaps we should be more forgiving."

Toria gave her mother a withering look. "Forgive! Forgive the man who nearly fucked up my life and killed my sister? You can't be serious!"

Jill wilted under her gaze. "No, perhaps you're right. But you're far too young to carry such anger inside you for the rest of your life."

Toria didn't need to reply. Her silence testified to her unswerving hatred.

Chapter Sixteen

On the 18th February, Max was sitting watching the lunchtime news when his heart missed a beat. The sombre face of the Minister of Agriculture stared from the television set announcing a suspected outbreak of foot and mouth disease. Memories of the day in 1967 when he'd had to call the vet and heard his herd of prize Friesians condemned to die was etched on his memory. Sometimes, even after so many years, he would lie in his bed at night and imagine he could still smell the pungent odour of his herd going up in flames. If the disease came knocking on his door this time, he wasn't sure he could live through such hell again.

......

Jill's stomach lurched as she watched the news. "I don't believe it!" she exclaimed to a shocked Toria.

"It's been a disaster waiting to happen," said Toria. "Only last week at the young farmers AGM our vet was warning us that the disease might be coming to the UK. He said it was utter madness that this country still imported meat from countries where the disease was endemic."

Jill raised her eyebrows. "Is that true?"

"It's true. There's a lot of illegal importing as well, and I'm told there are a few characters not too careful about boiling swill for their pigs. It's a miracle it's taken so long for the disease to arrive here."

"I had no idea," Jill said, totally incredulous. "I wonder how many more people are ignorant of the facts. Anyway it's not confirmed yet. So keep your fingers crossed."

"Bet you it soon will be. A Minister doesn't appear on the news and say something like that unless it's serious. I'd say it was ninety-five percent certain that this country is now in an epidemic situation."

"Poor Max, having to go through this all over again."

"Didn't he lose his herd in 1967?" asked Toria.

"Yes. I think I might pop over. It's not the sort of time you want to be on your own."

"Yes, I agree, Mum."

"Are you going to come?"

"Sorry, too much to do here and I think we should start taking a few precautions, like putting straw and disinfectant down at the two farm gates. We can't really do much else."

"Can you manage?"

"I've got plenty of help."

"Well, if you're sure I'll dash over and see Max."

······

Max was sitting staring at the TV when Jill arrived. "Good of you to come over, Jill," he said with a smile. "I was not enjoying the prospect of spending the rest of the day on my own."

"You know you are always welcome at home."

"Yes, but I thought you might have a lot to do."

"Toria's looking after that."

Max grimaced and switched off the TV. "This is very serious." He pointed at the TV. "The Ministry of Agriculture going public like this means they are pretty sure. But you never know it could be a false alarm. Fingers crossed, because if it isn't I can see the disease sweeping across the whole country. For the last few hours I've been telling myself it's no good panicking. Know something?"

"You're panicking."

"Yes. Want a drink?"

······

It was on the early morning news. It was February 22nd, a date few farmers in Britain would ever forget. 527 pigs confirmed with the disease at Heddon on the Wall in the county of Essex. The country had its first outbreak since 1967. The catastrophe had arrived and most farmers felt it had been a catastrophe waiting to happen. Forced onto the back foot, the government had no option but to admit that meat from third-world countries where foot and mouth was endemic had been pouring into the country.

"It's confirmed!" Jill shouted to Toria above the hum of the milking machines.

"I feared it would be," she said, removing the milking cups none too gently from a cow's teats and standing up to look at her mother. "It's nothing short of criminal! From what I hear, this is the virulent pan-Asiatic type O strain of the disease—no stopping this one in its tracks, apparently. Spreads like wild fire. What's more, I bet you there is no coherent policy ready to deal with this outbreak. Even after what happened in 1967, recommended safety measures still haven't been taken."

"If this blows up into a major outbreak," Jill moaned, "it will bring many of us to our knees."

"It *will* be a major outbreak Mum, you wait and see. But we have done the best we can. Entrances disinfected and gates locked. We are in a state of siege. Our animals have been brought in from the fields. All we can hope is that the winter rations last."

Jill looked at the few cows left waiting to be milked. "It looks as if you've nearly finished. I think we both could do with a walk."

"Give me five minutes."

"OK. I'll wait by the walnut tree."

Half an hour later Toria joined her mother. "Let's walk down to the steam. I want to check we haven't left any of the ewes out," she suggested.

"Good idea."

They left the garden and crossed into the pastures where in a normal year the milking herd would be grazing in about six weeks, released from their winter confinement.

"I doubt if we will be putting the herd out in April this year," Toria commented, kicking angrily at the grass.

"I think you're right. It would be far too much of a risk."

"Won't make a lot of difference," Toria added gloomily. "If the disease spreads, no amount of precautions will keep it at bay."

"Let's try not to think about it," Jill said, taking hold of Toria's hand. "It's too horrific to imagine all our stock being burnt in front of our eyes. I can still remember watching Max's herd go up in flames. And after the flames, the dreadful silence, the empty fields. It was horrendous."

"It must have been terrible," Toria agreed.

They walked on in silence to the bottom of the pastures where the wheat land began. They looked up towards the downs where the sheep should have been grazing, and saw the shepherd on his ATV checking that all the ewes were accounted for.

"Lambing will start in a week or two," Toria said. "It's one of my favourite times, but I wonder if this time there will be any ewes to lamb."

"After all that has happened to you this is so unfair."

"That's life, Mum. Now come on, I know it's difficult, but let's try not to dwell on our problems for a little while. And look at it—the vale—so beautiful, so peaceful. I can't imagine the peace being shattered by the noise of bulldozers, Lorries, and heaps of rotting carcasses lying on the turf."

"The thought makes me want to vomit," Jill said sadly.

······

In the two months that followed, the countryside hurtled into crisis. The Ministry of Agriculture and the Government collapsed into a state of panic. All footpaths, wild life parks, Zoos, Theme Parks, National Trust properties and stately homes were closed to the public. Hunting's own governing body had already brought all forms of hunting to a close a month before, and the Jockey Club had done the same with the majority of horse racing. The countryside fell silent, almost deserted.

The farmers moved around in fear.

As the epidemic spread, the beleaguered rural communities grew used to the daily crack of the slaughter men's pistols, the rumble of the Lorries carrying the dead carcasses through the villages for burial. The roar of the burning pyres, and everywhere the noxious smell of burning or rotting flesh pervaded the nostrils. Swiftly and without mercy, the disease was devouring the livestock of a nation. Belatedly, the army was called in, and the public stared at their television screens in horror at the slaughter of millions of animals. They watched the Prime Minister telling the nation to keep calm, only for him to announce a few days later that he was postponing the general election. Slowly but surely, the countryside began to wither, and the prospect of financial ruin became a reality for many rural businesses.

The farmers were powerless.

The Ministry of Agriculture was powerless.

The disease ate its remorseless way through the countryside.

······

Toria sat alone in Emma's bedroom. She knew it was unnatural to spend every moment of her free time talking to a spirit, but she missed her sister more than she could ever have imagined. She was heartbroken, still inclined to fall into periods of depression, and her anger against Harry Sidenham festered in her mind. It was a dangerous cocktail of emotions. She smiled at the photograph on the bedside table of her and Emma standing in the farmyard proudly holding their ponies. Life had seemed so simple then. She reluctantly rose from the bed. She could hear her mother calling. "I'll be back soon," she said to the photograph, as she made for the door.

······

The vast echoing rooms of Sidenham Hall did nothing to improve Harry's bad temper. Hunting was cancelled, the Cheltenham festival postponed, and severe restrictions had been imposed on everyday life. He kicked angrily at Ben, his seven-year-old Labrador, who retreated whimpering into a corner of the room. "Damn bloody dog," muttered Harry. The whole country had come to a halt, and that was bloody inconvenient. What did it matter if a few fucking farmers lost their livelihoods? Most of them were struggling to make ends meet anyway, and the compensation cheque would probably be one of the largest they'd ever receive in their lives. Jesus, he could do with a dose of the disease amongst his animals. The fat cheque would help pay off some of his mounting debts. Of course, he would take a much-needed holiday as well. In fact he might not come back. Just recently he'd been thinking more and more about selling Sidenham Hall. It made sense. It was large, expensive to keep up, fucking cold in the winter and the estate was losing money. There seemed little hope of children's laughter filling the house, and being financially restricted didn't suit him one little bit. Anyway soon the whole country would be one big national park, if the Prime Minister and his government had their way. So what was the point of owning land just so that the masses could swan all over the place, leaving their litter while he paid the bills? Maybe it was time to move on. He quite fancied the idea of a house in France. Every now and then when he'd had a few too many whiskies he admitted that he'd badly misjudged the Fosters. They had proved far more resilient than he'd expected—gathered the sympathy vote that he'd thought would come his way, and he was growing bored with being shunned by the locals. And then there were the threatening letters.

He heard the sound of a car on the gravel drive and moved to a window. It was the postman, no doubt bringing another one. For the past month they'd been arriving at regular intervals. He'd toyed with the idea of going to the police, but quickly abandoned the idea. If news of his concern leaked out it might exasperate the situation further. Instead he'd decided to hire a private detective. After several weeks of fruitless work, the detective reported he'd drawn a blank. Furious at the man's incompetence, Harry had refused to pay his bill. In desperation he'd turned to Giles Taylor by that time not caring if his predicament was made public. He needn't have worried. "You have your ear to the ground most of the time round here," he'd said. "Perhaps you might hear something."

Most of Giles's reply had been unprintable, but the gist was, "Do your own dirty work, and leave me alone to do more important things. You're past history, Harry, and personally whoever is threatening you gets my vote. Besides you may not have noticed but we have a crisis on our hands in the countryside. So..."

Harry had slammed the telephone down. Jumped up, little prick. After that he'd tried to ignore the letters, but that was not proving easy, as they were becoming more threatening. He knew he had many enemies, suspected quite a few might like to give him a black eye, but could someone really want him dead? It unnerved him. He moved to the front door and picked up the pile of mail from the floor, urgently scanning each envelope. There was no telltale white envelope with his name and address written in large black capitals. He blew out his cheeks with relief, noticing with disgust that his hands were shaking. "Come on," he shouted, "it's all bluff, and no one frightens Harry Sidenham."

His voice echoed round the great hall.

......

Toria stared at the lesions. She rested her head on the side of the cow, a five-year-old, and one of her favourites. "Oh God!" she exclaimed.

"Something the matter, Toria?" asked Frank the herdsman standing by her side. He'd heard her shout.

She lifted her head off the cow's side. "Look at that Frank. What do you make of it?"

Frank moved to the side of the cow and patted her flank. "Steady, old girl. Just let me take a look." He stood silently for a few minutes and then looked up at Toria's ashen face. There were tears in his eyes. "I think we've got trouble."

......

It took two hours for the men in white overalls and green Wellington boots to reach the farm. By then Max had arrived with a hastily packed suitcase. "I won't be allowed off your farm if the disease is confirmed, and I thought you and your mother might need some support."

"Max, you are a star," said Toria, her eyes wide with despair. "But you could be putting your herd at risk."

Max shrugged. "If your animals have the infection, they will cull my herd anyway. So it doesn't matter a damn where I am."

"Oh, that's so unfair," cried Toria.

"It's government policy."

"I don't know why they won't consider vaccination," said Jill looking questioningly at Max.

He put a hand on her cheek. She liked the feeling. "I don't think that's an option now," he said. "Too bloody late. Maybe at the beginning, but we are too far down this slaughter policy to change. Besides, for once I agree with the ministry. I don't see vaccination as the answer. It only hides the disease, especially in sheep."

Toria wasn't sure she agreed, but said nothing. It was utterly pointless getting worked up over something she had no control over. To have Max around was what mattered.

······

Three days later, a Ministry vet confirmed it was foot and mouth. It was what they had all expected, but it didn't make things any easier. It was a day Jill and Toria were never to forget. The police had already sealed off the farm. No one had been allowed to leave or enter since the disease had been suspected. To all intents and purposes, they were cut off from the outside world.

Jill found it eerie and quite terrifying.

Toria thought her world was falling apart.

Max sat on Jill's sofa, his head in his hands. Confirmation of the disease at Walnut Farm meant that for the second time in his life he was about to lose his herd. The first time he'd been thirty-four years younger, resilient and confident that he could rebuild. But now, alone, his son and wife dead and his life span almost used up, he wondered whether he had the fight left in him to start all over again.

······

Toria stared at the humane killer, noticing how steadily the slaughter man held the gun in his hand. She hated him for being so calm. *These are my friends that you're about to kill: how dare you feel nothing,* she wanted to shout, knowing it was unfair. He was only doing his job.

But damn you nevertheless!

She glared at him, wanting to hit his impassive face.

"I really don't think you should stay here," a concerned voice said from behind her, and she whirled round to see a tall young man with deep brown eyes and long black hair almost reaching his shoulders. His face was tanned; he carried no extra weight, and was dressed in the regulation white overalls and green Wellington boots worn by all the MAFF vets. On his hands, he had a pair of bright yellow rubber gloves. He was looking at her with something akin to pity. She thought he resembled someone out of a horror movie.

"Who the hell are you to say that?" she snapped.

"I'm the vet who will supervise the slaughter of your animals."

"Not without me by your side you won't," spat Toria. "If you think I'm leaving while you murder my cows you can think again."

Her defiance took Mark McIntyre by surprise. Since arriving from New Zealand six weeks earlier in answer to the frantic calls for help from the British Government, he'd witnessed many heartbreaking scenes. Hysteria, tears, outright anger, even the threat of violence, but never a beautiful girl defiantly insisting she was going to watch every animal shot. It brought home to him what a mistake he'd made in volunteering to help. It had been the most disturbing time of his life. He was a vet, for God sake! His job was to try and save lives, not to condemn thousands of animals to death and, worse, watch them being shot. He was mentally exhausted from the experience, and despite the girl's obvious contempt for him, his heart went out to her. But no matter— this was not a time he could afford to be soft. He had no choice but to be brutally blunt. "I think you are being very stupid. You have no idea what it's like to watch hundreds of animals shot in front of you. It turns my stomach, and I'm supposed to be trained to deal with this sort of thing. It will affect you for the rest of your life. So, I'm sorry, but you cannot stay here. You must go back to the farm house."

She stood her ground, hands on hips. "No way, vet."

"Mark, Mark McIntyre."

Toria caught his accent. "You're not from this country."

"New Zealand."

"Well, Mr. McIntyre, by the time we've finished this argument I suspect you will wish you had never left your home shores. If you think I'm going back to the house to calmly sit down and sip tea while you and your henchmen slaughter our stock, you've got another think coming. I'm not a weepy little schoolgirl. I look after these animals day and night, and if they must die I'm going to be with them."

"Those are admirable sentiments, but misplaced."

"Don't you dare patronise me vet! You will have to use force to move me."

"Miss Foster, I personally won't use force, and believe me, I'm sick of doing this job, sick to my stomach. I hate seeing animals die. This is not the reason I became a vet. I understand, I really do, but please save yourself the misery and leave now. I promise you the job will be done well."

Toria saw the concern on his face. She became less confrontational. "I'm sorry Mr. McIntyre, I'm sure you're very competent, as no doubt are your men—and so they should be after so much practice, but I'm not budging."

"I really must insist."

"You're wasting your breath. You're a vet, you should understand. I have lived with many of these animals for a good part of my life. I know the cows, the calves and the bulls by name. Since my father's death, I have milked the cows three times a week and I've never missed the birth of a calf. The ewes I have sat up with for hours during lambing, and you stand there and expect me to walk away and drink cups of tea or whatever while I hear the shots ringing out from your murder squad? No way! I know what a terrible job you have to do, and I'm prepared to accept you hate doing this. But I'm going to be one big problem unless you are prepared to have me around."

"I think we should start," one of the slaughter men interrupted, glaring at Toria. "Unless we get moving now, we won't be finished by dark."

"Oh, you poor sods!" Toria said dismissively.

"Now, please, Miss Foster!" Mark admonished.

"Too bloody bad—that's how I feel."

The slaughter man ignored her. He looked at Mark, "Well?"

"Give it a few more minutes."

The man looked at his watch. "Five, that's all, then we'll move into the cubicles. Best place to start. Then we will work our way round the rest of the buildings, ending up with the ewes and the lambs."

Toria gasped.

Mark risked putting a hand on her shoulder. She shook it off angrily. "Please," he begged, "Please go. Let me walk you back to the house."

"No! Forget it, Mr. McIntyre, I'm not moving! So what are you going to do about it? Get one of your murderers to drag me back to the farm house?"

"No."

"NO?"

Mark stared at the defiant young woman standing beside him. She looked lithe and strong, in good shape, and she was incredibly attractive under stress. He had a strong urge to tell her this. *Wrong place, wrong time*, he thought. But she was the sort of girl he'd like to ask out for a drink. "All right you can stay," he said reluctantly. "But I warn you, make a fuss and I will personally carry you to the house. We have a job to do and it's going to be done. There is nothing you can do about that. Understand?"

"Yes, yes, I know that."

"Good. Then follow me and God help you."

······

The crack of the first shot caught Jill standing in the garden. She cried out, put her hands over her ears, ran into the house and headed for the sitting room, hoping that the thick walls would cut out the sound. But the next shot reverberated around the walls, sounding if anything louder—and the next, and the next. She realised there was no escape. She sank down onto the sofa and stared at the window, wincing each time a shot came. But even in her distress she had time to think of Toria. She was outside, in the thick of the slaughter, watching, alone. But she couldn't bring herself to join her; she hadn't the stomach to stand and watch the stock fall bleeding to the ground, to die where they stood. She felt bitter, somehow betrayed, and totally useless.

For two agonisingly long hours, the slaughter went on. Jill didn't move off the sofa, counting each shot as it rang out. 374. Only one more than there should have been. The slaughter men were marksmen. It was difficult to miss at a few feet. When at last there was silence Jill felt numb—her brain ringing from the noise. But she didn't stay still for long. There was someone out there who would need her.

······

Toria watched every animal shot, staring mesmerised as they gave their last shudder. First the cows, their innocent eyes watching the pistols move towards them. Then it was the turn of the two bulls. Onto the calves, and finally the ewes, their bellies bulging with lambs due to be born in a few days' time. She managed to stay dried eyed until the last ewe fell to the ground. Like her mother she'd counted every shot. She looked at Mark, his overalls splattered with blood. His long hair soaked in sweat. She spoke in a hoarse whisper, "You were right—I will never forget that. It was the most awful thing I've ever seen. It will be etched on my memory forever, but I'm glad I stayed, and just in case you go away thinking I hate you, please don't. I know you were only doing your job."

Before he could reply, she was running across the yard towards the house. He could hear her sobbing as she ran. She'd been foolish, but he understood. If the animals had been his, he had no doubt he'd have done the same. He swore under his breath, turned to look at the carnage behind him and slowly walked away, thinking how sad it was he'd met her under such dreadful circumstances. He'd never forget her pretty face, creased in despair.

......

As she burst into the house, Toria flew past her mother. She bolted upstairs to the bathroom, stripping naked and stood under the hot shower for a good half-hour. The first thing that was clear in her mind was going downstairs with her blood-soaked overalls and throwing them into the dustbin. She stood for a moment at the open door and listened to the silence— the all-embracing deathly silence. She would never be able to forget the horror of what she'd witnessed.

"That was the most terrible thing, Mum," she said tearfully as she gulped down a mug of coffee. "I wish I'd died with them."

Jill could understand exactly how she felt.

......

Five hours later, Toria was lying awake in her bed still haunted by what she'd witnessed: the stench of shit, the noise from the panicked animals, the determination in the eyes of the slaughter men as they went about their gruesome task, and then finally the eerie silence. She knew it was a day that would change her life.

......

The first of his cows fell twitching to the floor. Max, like Toria two days earlier, stood alone, his large shoulders slightly stooped. His normally gentle eyes were dull. His large frame shook. The herd he'd spent years breeding and nurturing were about to be destroyed. He was an isolated figure amongst all the activity.

When the last bullet had been fired, he thanked the slaughter men and shook hands with Mark McIntyre. "I'm sure you will be glad to get back to New Zealand, young man. This is a task I wouldn't wish on my worst enemy," he sympathised.

"You can say that again," Mark replied. "I wish to God I'd never come."

"But you did, and I hear you have handled delicate situations with great tact. Thank you." Max pulled his large blue handkerchief out of his pocket and violently blew his nose. "Damn, now look what's happened."

"You're not the first man I've watched cry this last month," said Mark, "I doubt if you will be the last."

"Thank your lucky stars if that's all you witness," suggested Max. "Last week one poor sod shot himself in front of the vet."

......

A week later, the pyre was finally finished. It would burn the livestock from five farms in the neighbourhood. The army had built it in one of the pastures half a mile away from Walnut Farm, but clearly visible from the house. Jill and Toria stood hand in hand under the walnut tree and watched the final load of wooden sleepers being put into place by the bulldozers. They had been assured the burning of the carcasses would begin in three hours time. It was not a moment too soon. The house stank of the rotting carcasses, still lying where they fell, rats nibbling away at the putrefying flesh. The smell clung to their clothes; everywhere they moved the stench invaded their nostrils. The horses confined to their stables, breathed in the polluted air and grew restless. The village was almost deserted. Those that had friends elsewhere had fled the stench of the rotting animals that surrounded them. But there was no such escape for those on the stricken farms. The occupants were prisoners, with no choice but to watch piles of animals that had once been their livelihood vanish in the flames.

A way of life was being destroyed.

......

That night, with the light from the pyre flickering behind closed curtains, Jill and Max sat together on her sofa, Jill wondering where the next disaster was going to come from. "I'm scared."

"I understand how you feel," sympathised Max. "You've certainly had a basin full of trouble."

"And Harry's still lurking out there, like some predator waiting to make his next move. I saw him the other day in the post office, ignored him, but his eyes followed me everywhere. I couldn't wait to get out; he made me feel very uneasy, and if I feel like that what about Toria?"

Max nodded. "I think of her a lot. Must be terrible having Harry down the road. I'm surprised how well she's coping; it can't be easy. Perhaps she should go away after this is all over. In fact why don't you take her away? It might be just what you two need—time away to finally banish any sort of fragility that remains in your relationship. There won't be much to stay here for."

"I'll think about it, Max, but I'm not sure she'll be too keen; she's changed so much."

"Who can blame her, but give her time, Jill. No need to push—wait your moment."

"You're a very wise man Max. I don't know what I'd do without you."

Max stayed silent, reaching for her hand—it was all that was necessary.

She smiled and closed her eyes, happy to have him close. He sat very still and thought back to the times when she'd been a child and she'd sat on his knee and he'd run his fingers through her curly blond locks. He'd loved her then like a father, but as she'd grown into a beautiful girl there had been a subtle change, easily controlled, but always there under the surface. Now those underlying emotions were tugging at his heart. They would come to nothing. He was far too sensible. He'd never mention them to anyone. He moved into a more comfortable position and rested his head on the back of the sofa. Within minutes he was asleep.

······

An hour later, Jill eased herself off the sofa. Max didn't move. She smiled at his weather-beaten face relaxed in sleep, and decided to leave him where he was. She went to fetch a blanket and laid it over him. He grunted but did not wake. She touched his hand before moving away.

In her room, Jill hastily closed the curtains and began to undress—her mind on Harry. It was never a good time to think of him, but he was never far from her thoughts. He would know that, the sadistic bastard. She watched the patterns of the flames on the curtains and wished that it was Harry burning on the pyre. Somehow Harry had to be silenced. She climbed into bed, longing for the comfort of deep sleep, but knowing, as with so many nights before, that sleep would prove elusive.

······

That same night, Toria lay on Emma's bed, her head buried in her pillow so that she could not see the flames from the window. The door was locked. She didn't want her mother coming in. Her thoughts were not for sharing. Her violent emotions were scary. They hammered at her brain. They were exhausting her. She knew there was no way she was going to get relief from their constant pounding until she faced them head on. Only then would there be any hope of her life returning to something like normal. She could envisage the solution—it was so simple. But could she carry the solution through to its conclusion? Did she possess the courage, or for that matter the cunning? Nor would it be easy to come to terms with her conscience. Nothing in life seemed easy anymore. She rolled over in the darkened room to stare at the moving light behind the curtains, knowing she faced another sleepless night.

······

Half a mile away at the far end of the village to Walnut Farm, Mark McIntyre tossed restlessly in his bed in The Drunken Duck. Not for the first time he was thinking of Toria. It surprised him, but she intrigued him. He liked a gutsy woman, and she'd certainly proved that. And she was very beautiful, and gave off an aura of innocent sensuality. *You're smitten, Mark McIntyre*, he realised with a chuckle. It was a new experience. Back in Auckland he'd had several girls on the go at the same time. Never felt very much for any of them and was quite happy to enjoy their company and the odd night in bed. He'd never considered himself ready for a serious relationship, valuing his independence too much. So his feelings for Toria mystified him, especially as he'd met her in the worst of circumstances, and only spoken a few words to her under the most stressful conditions. He'd probably been in her company for three hours at the most, and those were hours he'd rather forget. Yet, there was something so attractive about her, so challenging. Of course he was making a complete fool of himself. He'd be the last person she'd ever want to see again. Anyway he'd soon be heading back to New Zealand and into the arms of one of his many admirers. He'd forget her. He beat the pillows into the right shape and closed his eyes. But sleep did not come easily, and when it did, he was plagued by dreams of burning cattle, the terrified cries of dying pigs, and the heartrending sight of small lambs bleating before they died. Mixed up in all these pictures was Toria on her knees, covered in blood, begging him to spare her animals. He sat up several times to drink water from the glass by his bed, sweating in spite of the cold room, and then fell back to try and fall asleep again. But she wouldn't go away. Always she was there, her blond hair tangled with sweat, her wide eyes staring at him accusingly as she knelt in the filth of dying animals. At four in the morning he could take the torment no longer and quietly went down the corridor to run himself a bath.

Tomorrow he'd ring the farm and ask if she was okay.

······

As the clock moved towards midnight, Harry sat by the fire in his library a worried man. It would be another sleepless night. The latest letter would play on his mind. He swore loudly and tossed the piece of vitriol into the fire where all the others had gone. The suspense was getting to him; the bottle was becoming his only solace. He scratched at his unshaven chin—it had been days since a razor had touched his skin. Dandruff lay on his collar, and he no longer manicured his nails. There was no spring in his step; his arrogant confidence had taken a knock. His life was becoming one long drinking session. He felt an outcast where once he'd reigned supreme. Now he was confined to his estate while his animals were slaughtered. Well, at least he'd soon get a fat cheque, and then—yes—and then he'd sell the Hall and move to France. He couldn't wait. He jumped as the clocks in the house struck midnight. A man going nowhere Jill had said. Well, fuck that! He had a few more tricks hidden in his closet. He wouldn't go without making waves, no way. It didn't pay to underestimate a man like Harry Sidenham.

He jumped at the ring of the telephone. Who would ring at this hour? Once it might have been a girl. With an unsteady hand he picked up the receiver.

"Harry?"

"Who's that?"

"Never you mind. This is just to tell you that there will be no more letters. It is time to move on."

"Fuck you! What do you mean by move on?"

"That would be telling Harry."

"Who are you?"

"An avenging Angel."

"Go to hell!" Harry cut the connection.

He moved back to his chair and stared at the fire. He was shaken. It had been a woman's voice, obviously disguised. He tried to bolster his sagging moral by telling himself it must be some nutter, but to no avail. There were several women out there who would love to inflict mental suffering on him and he was pretty sure he knew which one would be in the front of the queue. He gave a none-too-confident laugh. Had she the balls to cause him physical harm? Was that what she was threatening when she said it was time to move on? Could he be in danger? It all seemed very unlikely if his guess was right. He threw the stub of his Gitane cigarette angrily into the fire and refilled his glass from the decanter on the table by his chair. He was frightened, and he'd never been frightened before. He'd move his plans forward. He drained his glass and refilled it immediately. An hour later the decanter was empty.

······

That night, like so many before it, the countryside should have been in darkness, but it was burning. The light from the pyres lit up the trees, the fields and the sky. The foxes, used to killing at night, moved cautiously in the half daylight wary of this alien world that had suddenly arrived to disrupt their lives. The deer grazed uneasily, and the rabbits chose to remain in the undergrowth rather than run in the fields. The badgers stayed close to their sets. Everywhere, there seemed to be danger, and anxiety was a constant companion.

Chapter Seventeen

As midnight struck, heralding the end of General Election Day, a figure dressed totally in black with its face hidden by a balaclava, crept along a bridle path on the Sidenham estate. It was a path the figure knew Harry often rode, and since the outbreak of foot and mouth had curtailed his other rides he took this same route every morning, seeing no reason not to ride it, as it was entirely on his land. The figure was confident that no one else would take the path as it had been shut to the public since March. But the time for heart searching was over; it was time to act—the restrictions might soon be lifted. The figure carried a coil of strong wire in a gloved hand, in the other a small torch. It moved slowly, very deliberately, ears alert, knowing there would be only one chance. It stopped at a point where the path narrowed between two oak trees and smiled. This was the spot reconnoitred three days earlier. It seemed the perfect place. There were two low branches on each tree enabling the figure to climb and reach the required height. The wire was pulled tight between the two trees, high enough to take Harry in the chest and send him crashing to the ground. The figure knew to an inch where the wire had to be.

It was designed to maim, not kill. He had to suffer.

The task completed the figure stood for a moment surveying its work, checking that the height was just right, and that the wire was taut. Satisfied, it moved carefully into the undergrowth on one side of the path. It put a backpack silently down on the damp ground and pulled out a ground sheet and then a thermos containing coffee laced with brandy. The figure dropped onto the sheet and unscrewed the cap of the thermos, hands steady and heartbeat regular, and prepared for a long wait. There was no rush of conscience, no regrets.

••••••

Harry mounted his horse as the stable clock struck seven. In the summer he rode early, avoiding the flies and enjoying the early stillness of the countryside. He preferred to ride alone so that he could push his horse to the limit without the disapproving look of a companion. As usual, he shunned a hard hat, preferring his battered old tweed cap. He was suffering from the now familiar hangover, made worse this morning by the landslide victory in the election, and the knowledge that he'd have to put up with the same shower of incompetent politicians running the country for another four or so years. He hadn't bothered to vote. He'd decided it would have been a waste of time. Besides, ever since the letters had stopped, he was uneasy when away from Sidenham. He just couldn't rid himself of the feeling that he was being stalked, but for some unexplainable reason he was fearful of finding out whom his antagonist might be. The truth was he was like the ostrich, head buried deep in the sand.

He growled a "thank you" to the young girl holding his horse, whose name still escaped him, even though she'd been working with the horses for six months.

"Rude bastard," she said quietly to his retreating back, "Sarah is my name as if you care!" She was a little less than five feet one, but she was strong of mind and surprisingly tough. She had small pert breasts and she had cropped her hair very short and dyed it blond with red streaks. It was not her style, but she knew it annoyed Harry even if he couldn't remember her name. She wanted to annoy him very much. She despised him; she hated his lecherous behaviour with the other two stable girls, and she had nothing but contempt for his total lack of love for his horses. In fact she would have rather liked Harry to make a pass at her so that she could kick him in his overgrown genitals. She'd have been long gone if it hadn't been for foot and mouth. It had been a miserable few months.

Harry took the route dictated to him by the disease restrictions and headed for the bridle path that intersected his land. It was flat, better grassed than most years due to the lack of other horses, and would give him a good gallop for at least three-quarters of a mile before he reached his boundary. He dug his spurs unnecessarily hard into his horse's flanks and broke into a trot. It took him ten minutes to reach the path. He reined in his horse, checked the tightness of his girth, pulled his cap down firmly on his head and patted his horse's neck. "Right, you old bastard, let's see how fast you can go this morning."

Within the space of five minutes he was galloping flat out, the wind whipping into his face, and the fresh air forcing its way into his tobacco-laden lungs drove the effects of his late night boozing out of his brain. He felt the exhilaration of having a good horse underneath him. It was second only to a woman. The sheer poetry, the balance, the understanding between man and beast was something he'd never get tired of. He let out a great whoop of joy.

He never saw the wire.

He felt an almost imperceptible tug on his chest as the reins were torn from his grasp and he was ejected backwards out of his saddle, turning a somersault in the air before crashing to the ground behind his horse, his head thudding against a stone. The alarmed horse galloped on.

The dark figure waited a few moments before breaking cover. It moved swiftly to Harry's side. One glance was enough to see he wouldn't be moving anywhere in a hurry. There was blood trickling from his nose, his breathing uneven, and a jab in the ribs with a toe confirmed he was unconscious. The balaclava was ripped off and a smile crossed the figure's face. That was good. If he survived, he'd suffer for the rest of his rotten life. That would be justice.

Satisfied, the figure moved to climb the branch of one of the trees and loosened the wire—likewise on the other tree. There was only the smallest mark to be seen on the barks. Once on the ground the wire was carefully rolled up and put in the backpack. The ground sheet was folded and followed the wire and the torch. The figure looked round to be sure there was nothing left to raise suspicions that someone had been lying in wait. Then it turned and disappeared into the undergrowth as quietly as it had arrived.

······

The sound of hoofs clattering across the yard alerted Sarah. She ran out of the tack room to meet the horse covered in sweat circling the yard, his nostrils distended, and eyes radiating fear. She knew the old fellow was normally the calmest of customers. She looked round for Harry. It was not unusual for him to dismount by the stable yard gates, tie the reins over the horse's neck, slap his wide rump and leave him to wander into his stable, shouting as he walked back to the Hall, "Cut the bugger's food down, he bloody nearly killed me this morning." Or, "He went like a cart horse this morning—no fucking life in him—so up his feed, for Christ's sake." With Harry you learnt his mood swings very quickly and just got on with your job. But today she spotted the reins were broken and that a stirrup was missing. Sarah sensed that something had gone badly wrong. "Whoa, boy, whoa," she coaxed, walking up slowly to the horse, who recognising her soothing voice came to a standstill blowing froth from his nose.

"Done his usual, has he? Let the old fellow loose again?" the disgusted voice of Tom Banks sounded behind her. "That bloody man—"

"No, I don't think so this time, Tom," Sarah interrupted. "I didn't hear the usual invectives. Not like the man, and look, the reins are broken and a stirrup is missing. This fellow has been frightened; look at the lather he's got himself into. My guess is that his Lordship must have had a fall somewhere."

Tom despised Harry for the same reasons as Sarah, his continual harassment of the stable girls and the way he treated his horses. So his first reaction was to feel a certain satisfaction at the thought of Harry covered in dust, painfully walking back to the Hall. But then it struck him that Harry might be injured, and much as he would like to see Harry with a few cuts and bruises, he was not the sort of man to wish his boss a bad injury. The horse was reliable, not likely to shy at much, and Harry was a good horseman, unlikely to fall off even if inebriated, unless something out of the ordinary had happened. Sarah was probably right. He made an instant decision. "Put the old fellow away quick, Sarah. I'll get the Land Rover. This doesn't look good. If the bugger is in trouble, we'll more than likely find him on the bridle way. If he's not injured, and we meet him covered in dust swearing blue murder, we can all have a good laugh."

......

They found Harry twenty minutes later, and it didn't take Tom long to realise he was badly hurt. "He's unconscious, and his pulse is weak," he said to Sarah. "I don't like the look of him at all. See the blood oozing from his nose, and he looks a nasty colour."

"He looks awful."

Tom nodded. "Bad idea to try and carry him to the Land Rover—might do a lot of damage if we try and move him. I think this is a job for the paramedics. I'll see if I can phone the emergency services from my mobile, but I doubt if there'll be a signal from here. Probably have to use the radio to contact the estate office. If there's no one there, one of us will have to drive back to the Hall."

"He could be dead by the time we get back there," said Sarah, gazing at Harry's ashen face.

"I know, but there's little else we can do."

"It will have to be a four-wheel-drive ambulance," advised Sarah, as Tom rushed to the Land Rover.

"Or a helicopter," Tom added as he opened the Land Rover door and grabbed his mobile. "No signal." He reached for the radio. "Be there, Annabel, for Christ's sake, be there!"

Annabel was sitting behind her desk painting her nails waiting for the kettle to boil so that she could have her first cup of coffee of the morning. She was not the brightest girl on Harry's staff but she was friendly and a looker. She'd been his secretary for nearly a year and knew the form. A low-cut blouse, a demure smile, and eyes that said, 'I'm yours anytime you want me,' guaranteed her job was secure. Tom blew out his cheeks with relief when she picked up the radio. She was not someone Tom would like to depend on in a crisis so his voice had added urgency. "Listen, Annabel, we have a crisis. The boss has had a nasty fall, could be serious, matter of life or death. Now listen carefully, this is what you must do."

Annabel listened to the details. "Right Tom, I understand. I'll get back to you as soon as I've got the emergency services organised."

"Good girl, and don't hang about."

The urgency in his voice galvanised Annabel. "Don't worry, Tom, I'll sort it out."

......

Max walked disconsolately into his farmyard at around eight the same morning. There was no need. The farm was like a ghost town, but he was finding old habits hard to break. The awesome stillness surrounded him. How he missed the hum of the milking machines and the shuffling and complaining noises coming from the cows waiting to be milked. Inadvertently he looked round for his two stockmen, waiting for their friendly greeting. He swore under his breath; his imagination was playing hell with his emotions these days. As he shuffled into the empty milking parlour, he kicked angrily at a white plastic bucket and watched it roll across the floor to come to rest against the empty milk tank. Cobwebs were already decorating the ceiling and he stared in disgust at rat droppings by the door. He made a mental note to come back later in the day and clear up the mess. In 1967 he'd not allowed standards to drop, but he was finding it much more difficult this time to adjust and his staff had caught the mood. He sat down on his father's old wooden milking stool, which he'd never found the heart to throw away. He liked to remember his father, fingers working dextrously as he nursed every last drop of milk from the cow's teats. He wondered what the old man would have to say about the way the outbreak had been handled by the government. He managed to smile—it would not be very complimentary!

He stood up impatiently. He needed fresh air, away from the lingering smell of disinfectant and the ghosts of so many animals. He crossed the lane that divided the farm from the fields and climbed over the gate, dropping down into the fresh grass that his herd should now be grazing. A wave of despondency washed over him. He felt old; battered was a word that came to mind. His way of life was in tatters and he wasn't sure he had the desire, or the courage to begin again. He climbed towards the beech wood overlooking the village and dropped down onto a tree stump. From his vantage point he could see figures moving around in the village, the first of the children hurrying towards the school. He heard the church clock strike the half-hour, and watched Walter Stibbins step out of the Drunken Duck, as he did every morning at eight-thirty except on Sundays. It was such a peaceful scene, but it was deceiving. The village had suffered badly from the foot and mouth outbreak. In March, the Drunken Duck should have been full of Irish punters come over for the Cheltenham festival. This year the bars had been depressingly quiet, and Walter's six guestrooms had stayed empty. At this time of the year, the village was normally bustling with tourists and Julia Stubb's little teashop would be doing a roaring trade. She'd lost heart after looking at her empty tearoom for weeks, and gone to stay with her sister in Hampshire. The village shop was suffering too, and nearly all the nearby farms had been forced to lay off staff. The new moneyed townies, who over the last few years had bought farm cottages surplus to the modern requirements of a farm business, had all fled back to the cities, wrinkling their noses in disgust at the constant smell of burning flesh. Max doubted if they would return before summer was out. It would take more than soothing words from the government to repair the damage to rural communities.

His eyes shifted to look across at Walnut Farm, just visible through the trees. He could see the field where the pyre had devoured so many animals. What devastation—nearly nine million animals destroyed since February and something like seventy-six thousand in his county alone. He stamped out his cigarette. He'd walk across to Walnut Farm and have a cup of coffee with Jill. It would cheer him up. He'd be welcome. Both of them were lonely and undecided about their future.

He was climbing the gate onto the lane when he heard the sound of a siren coming from the far end of the village. Curiosity made him hurry down to the village. He was standing in the main street when the post van appeared by the school, followed closely by a police Land Rover its blue light flashing urgently. A second later he heard the whirl of a low flying helicopter.

Walter Stibbins joined him. "The air ambulance," he informed Max. "Harry Sidenham has taken a tumble from his horse. The postman says his life is threatened. Bloody good thing if you ask me," he added with satisfaction. "Bloody parasite, that man. I don't suppose you will be too upset, eh, Max, if he fails to recover?"

Max smiled, and put a hand on Walter's shoulder. "It's a terrible thing to say, old friend, but no, I won't be shedding any tears."

......

Jill heard the siren and saw the helicopter pass overhead. She ran down the garden and rang Max. There was no answer. Of course he'd be outside somewhere. Why couldn't he have a mobile like everyone else? She rang the village store. "Hello, Mrs. Clark. Any idea what's going on? Harry Sidenham? How terrible! Thank you, Mrs. Clarke, sorry to bother you."

She walked thoughtfully back to the house, the beginning of a smile creasing her face.

......

The news spread through the village and surrounding areas like wildfire. Local radio and television carried it by lunchtime. "Lord Sidenham, the owner of Sidenham Hall and several thousand acres, suffered a serious fall out riding early this morning. He was found unconscious on a bridle path by one of his staff and flown to the hospital by air ambulance. First reports indicate that he has broken his back and sustained serious head injuries. He is in a critical condition."

Toria sat with her mother in the garden. She felt as if a great weight had been lifted from her shoulders. "I just can't bring myself to feel anything but satisfaction over what has happened to that man. In fact, terrible as it sounds, I hope he dies." She decided not to add that she was bitterly disappointed that someone had got to Harry before her.

Jill put an arm round her shoulders. "I know I've said we should forgive, but I understand how you feel. Harry might not be the Devil, but he's certainly the most evil man I've ever met for sure."

Chapter Eighteen

A week later Jill sat under the walnut tree, as the June sun set behind the vale. There was a stunning red sunset and the long evening shadows played across the garden. Swallows were performing their aerial ballet for the last time that day. She could see the gold fish rising in the pond and two butterflies seemed to be taunting them as they gently fluttered over the water. She heard the horses behind her in the paddock having their evening gallop. She should have been at peace with the world. Harry was no longer a threat. He was desperately ill, almost certainly facing life as a cripple. But there lay the problem. She was disturbed by her feeling of satisfaction that Harry was lying paralysed in the hospital. No one cared. Not even his mother could be bothered to come over from Paris to see him. He'd spend the rest of his life locked in a hell from which there was no escape. She could find no compassion for the man she'd once loved. She rose slowly from her seat ashamed by her thoughts.

······

"**I'm** going away."

Toria's bluntness took Jill by surprise. A cold hand touched her heart. She was incredulous. "Do you mean you want to give up all this?"

"What's there to give up Mum?" Toria asked sadly. "There's nothing and no one left. Dad and Emma are dead. The farm is an empty shell without livestock. There is nothing for me here except terrible memories."

Jill gasped. "I had a gut feeling you might one day say this, but I hoped that perhaps with Harry no longer a threat and the possibility that it won't be long before we can restock that you might have been tempted to at least give it a go"

"I haven't made this decision lightly. I've thought long and hard, tried to tell myself I'll wake up one morning and think differently, but it's no good. I know what I'm saying will hurt you. I know you had a dream for me. But now I don't want to be part of your dream. Everything around here in some way reminds me of either Harry or Emma. And when I'm not thinking of them, I'm hearing the crack of the pistols and smelling the fear of those poor animals. I don't want to farm anymore. I don't want to live here with all the ghosts. I want to be free of them, not live in a poisonous atmosphere. I have to go."

"There is no way I would want to stop you," said Jill "I believe I would have done the same had I been in your shoes, but I will miss you so much, so very much. Have you made any plans?"

"Yes."

"Are you going to tell me what they are?"

"I'm going to New Zealand."

"New Zealand! That's half way round the world."

A trace of a smile crossed Toria's face. "I'm not going alone."

"You're not?"

"It's funny really how some things work out. You know, good coming out of a disaster. You remember Mark McIntyre?"

"The vet?"

"Yes. I've been seeing him quite a lot recently."

"You didn't bother to tell me."

"I didn't think it necessary. I never imagined it would come to anything, least of all move so fast."

"But there was plenty of time—that is if you'd wanted to tell me."

"Yes, you're right, there was. I'm sorry. I'll bring him over soon."

"This young man is the person you are planning to go to New Zealand with?"

"He goes back next week. I'll follow soon. He thinks he can find me a job."

Jill looked at Toria in disbelief.

"He's very kind, Mum. That's all I can say at the moment. I doubt if we'll ever have a relationship, because if we do, I would have to tell him I'd been raped, and at the moment all I want is a friend—a friend who doesn't know all the dirty details. If I tell him I will feel the same as I do in the company of my friends here—an object to be pitied."

"I'm sure they don't think like that."

"You don't spend time with them. Trust me, they feel like that."

"But if the relationship grows you will have to tell him. You can't hide it away from the man you love. It may be terrible, degrading, and a horrific experience, but if he loves you he will understand. Really, I promise you he will."

"I would give anything to believe you, but right now it's not an issue. Mark need not know. As I said, he's a friend prepared to help me out. We're not in love, and if things don't work out I can always come back, can't I?"

"Of course you can," Jill said weakly. "I'd love to see you back. I've lost your father and Emma in a very short space of time, but up until a moment ago I thought I had you. Now—oh God, I can hardly bear to think about it—I am going to lose you. Just like that, going halfway round the world with a man I don't know."

"It's a bitch Mum, but I'm going."

"Will nothing change your mind? Can't we talk this over? Perhaps go away for a week or two, and see how you feel?"

"That is not an option. I'm gutted, I really am, but I have to get away. My life here is a misery."

Jill looked crestfallen.

"Mum! Oh God, I'm so sorry. Please try and understand."

Jill felt her last drop of energy drain out of her body. "I understand, and I'll get over it." She smiled at Toria. "The most important thing is for you to be happy, and I can't hold on to you forever."

"Thanks Mum."

"Well, there you go then."

"As you say, there you go. You okay?"

"I think I want to be left alone for a while."

"Mum, just wait."

"What, not more bad news?"

"I hope you can find happiness again."

"I hope we *both* can"

Suddenly Toria was in her mother's arms. "There is nothing, absolutely nothing I could wish for more, than for our lives to be different. Then I wouldn't be here in your arms telling you all these hurtful things, but that can't be. So here we are about to say good-bye. It's time to try and put my shattered life back together."

......

Mark stared at Toria through a haze of cigarette smoke. The Drunken Duck was buzzing. It was quiz night, and on quiz night even Neil Diamond was silent. Toria was captain of the home team. She was laughing, her eyes showing a rare flash of enjoyment. But Mark's intuition told him that behind the smile there dwelt another Toria, which had nothing to do with her father or Emma. There had been the odd occasions when he'd thought she was going to open up to him, but then she'd shrugged and moved on to another topic. Tonight she looked good, sitting beside him concentrating on the questions being fired by the quizmaster standing in the middle of the saloon bar. Close up, he could smell her sweetness. See her perfect skin, her great eyes, her long lashes, and that entrancing little nose. *Angels must look like that*, he thought. He wondered what it would be like to hold her close. Go to bed with her. Perhaps that was moving too fast—he mustn't rush things, but boy was he tempted to try.

An hour later, after the home team had finished celebrating a hard-fought victory, she turned to smile at him. Not for the first time making Mark think it was something she should do as often as possible." A drink," he suggested, noting the little beads of sweat glistening on her brow.

"That sounds great."

"Do you want wine, beer?"

"A glass of dry white wine would go down well, but not Chardonnay please."

"No Chardonnay as ordered and I'll join you." He stood up, stretching his tall frame, and walked across the floor to the bar. When he returned, her smile had gone and she seemed distant. "What are you thinking?" he asked, concerned.

"That I've hurt my mother—gambled on going halfway round the world with a man I hardly know. I feel I should forget the whole idea, and yet..."

"And yet?"

"I feel comfortable with you—God that sounds so old fashioned, but it explains perfectly how I feel. You don't ask intrusive questions. You take me as I am, ride my moods with skill—I like that. In fact I like you—actually very much—but I want you as a friend, Mark. Do you see what I'm getting at?"

"I think so." He raised his glass. "Well, here's to us in whatever form." Then he put his glass down on the table and kissed her, very gently on the cheek. "I'll be your friend forever I hope."

"I would like that very much. You're kind. Not many people would have rung me after an altercation like ours. Now here I am really glad you did." Her rather sad eyes rested on him. "Do you know something?"

"No, but you're going to tell me."

"If anyone a few weeks ago had asked me whom I would most like to be having a drink with, you would have been the last person on my list."

"I never felt like that. I confess I even found your anger attractive."

"Isn't that a little bit bazaar given the circumstances?"

Mark shrugged his wide shoulders "Yes, I thought so too."

"So why did you ring me?"

"I was very worried about you, and because I thought you were amazingly brave."

Her eyes darkened. "Actually I was shit scared. It was the most awful moment of my life so far, but I knew I had to be there."

"I can understand that."

"I was also very angry, though wrong to take my anger out on you. I was angry at the world, the unfairness of life. I was about to suffer another terrible loss. But deep down, I was grateful to you, if you can understand that. You told me you hated doing what you had to do. In a funny sort of way, I felt empathy towards you, and—" she hesitated for a second—"I was very touched when you rang. Not that I was too sure about taking you up on your offer, but I'm glad I did."

"I'm glad too, because I really like you. Oh that sounds so naff, but I really do. And although I swore to myself earlier tonight that I would keep my mouth shut I have this great urge to tell you that you're the first girl I've ever thought I might like to spend the rest of my life with. Have I said too much?"

He saw shock register on her face and hurried on. "I know we haven't known each other long, and I certainly won't push you—in fact I'm very glad to stay a friend if that's what you want, but—and this may sound very adolescent and stupid—I feel something most exciting."

"This is all a bit sudden," Toria said nervously. "I'm not angry—in fact I'm very touched. However you know nothing about me, and I think it's better if it remains that way." Then she heard herself saying, "At least for the time being. I feel this could become like an express train out of control and I don't want that. I'm sorry Mark to dash your hopes but give me more time please."

"But you will come to New Zealand?"

"Yes, I will."

"That's all I want to hear. Take your time."

Had he seen a flash of fear in her eyes confirming his intuition? He couldn't be sure, but he'd have to tread very carefully or he might lose her, and he didn't want to do that. She was so fragile, like a piece of fine Chinese porcelain, so easily broken. But he wanted to be there to put the pieces together again. Never had he been so sure of anything in his life. It wasn't going to happen over night. It might not happen for several months, but he would be there. Then when she had no burdens to bear, no hangups left, they would be together.

That was how it was going to be.

Chapter Nineteen

She turned left onto the A46 at Evesham and half an hour later joined the M5 at junction 9. The road was busy, Lorries taking up nearly all the nearside lane. She'd have to concentrate, which was probably a good thing—it helped to take her mind off the purpose of her journey. It was the twenty-second of August, warm and rather oppressive. It heralded the end of a long dry spell. Thunder had been forecast by the end of the day. She had all the windows of the car open; the sound was deafening, but she was sweating. It was not entirely the heat, for she had no illusions about what the next few hours would bring—they were going to be harrowing. She felt wretched, uncertain about her motives. They were certainly not Christian and that horrified her. How on earth had she arrived at a situation where she was going to gloat over another person's misfortune? She'd always thought she could control her emotions, turn away from confrontation, sort of take it on the chin, but no longer—Harry had seen to that.

A black MG flashed past her, reminding her, if she needed reminding, that she was not far from the spot where Emma had died. It helped to strengthen her resolve. She drove past the turning to Cheltenham race course, silent from the buzz of crowds since the foot and mouth outbreak. She left the town of Gloucester on her right and much too soon she was turning off the motorway at junction 17. She pulled into the next garage and filled the car with fuel and asked the attendant behind the cash desk directions to The Royal Infirmary. *You can turn back now,* she thought. That would be the merciful thing to do, but after a few moments of reflection she realised she'd used up all her reserves of compassion months ago. She gunned the engine and pulled out of the forecourt.

She drove slowly, following the attendant's instructions. It was not easy in the crush of the Bristol traffic. Twice she had to turn round, swearing under her breath. She wanted to get to the Infirmary before her resolve deserted her. She cursed silently at a car driving too close to her rear bumper which forced her to miss a turning. Luckily a few yards on she spotted a traffic warden. She pulled over to ask the way.

He was friendly. "Take the first turning left at the roundabout up there, dear—takes you into Marlborough Street. Go past the Bus Station on your left and you'll see The Royal Infirmary on your right. It's difficult to park, mind you. It might be easier if you parked in the bus station and walked from there."

"Thanks." She found the bus station easily—decided to do as she'd been advised, and walked. It seemed the longest walk she'd ever taken—in fact it was less than a quarter of a mile.

The Royal Infirmary was not a building an architect would be proud of. It was forbidding, dark and unwelcoming. She moved to the reception desk, her whole body shaking. *Do I really want to do this?*

"Can I help you?" a bored voice enquired.

"Can you tell me which ward Lord Sidenham is in?"

The bored receptionist consulted a list behind the desk. "Fleming ward."

"Could you tell me how I get there?"

The girl looked at her as if saying, "God we get idiots all the time." She pointed to the wall behind Jill. "Follow the signs."

"Thank you."

This was it—this was the moment she'd dreamed of ever since Harry had crashed off his horse. But faced with the imminent prospect of seeing him she felt in a blue funk. It had not been easy coming to terms with her revengeful act. She'd committed a premeditated crime for which she could go to prison. That was unlikely unless she chose to confess. The police were satisfied it had been an accident. Harry had been riding recklessly, tanked up with alcohol. But a persistent little voice was saying she'd committed a heinous crime. *Christ! Come on! No chickening out now!* She stopped, took a long breath, ran her tongue over her lips—she'd have killed for a cup of tea—gave a low laugh—but no time. She looked up and forced herself to follow the signs.

......

Harry was in a cubicle at the end of the ward. He was lying on his back, eyes closed, a tube in one arm, and another in his mouth. He looked dead. A young doctor was standing by the bed.

"Oh, sorry, Doctor, I'll wait outside."

"No need—I've finished here. May I ask who you are?"

"A very close friend."

"It's relatives only really, but no one has been to see the poor man since he arrived here, so I guess on this occasion we can make an exception."

"Thank you, Doctor. How is he?"

"I'm afraid he's still in a coma. Nearly eight weeks now. It's not looking good. He's also paralysed from the waist down. Not much more we can do for him. Just have to hope he regains consciousness. Then we can ship him off to Stoke Mandeville to get treatment for the paralysis."

"Is there a chance of him regaining consciousness after so long?"

"There's always a chance, and he has at times shown small signs of life, which has given us some hope. I wouldn't like to say more than that."

"If he doesn't regain consciousness, how long will he live?"

The doctor was surprised by the blunt question. "Hard to say. Some difficult decisions will have to be made, and as you are not a relative I can't discuss them with you."

"He has a mother in Paris."

"So I gather from his housekeeper, but no one seems to be able to trace her."

"I'm not surprised. I don't want to bore you with a long story, but I wouldn't place much hope on her coming to see him, even if you do find her. They haven't spoken for years."

"I see. Well, we've contacted his solicitor. It's his problem."

"I suppose it is."

The doctor looked at his watch. "I must go now. I've a lot of patients to see. My advice is to talk to him about things he might remember. Say his house, his horses, and normal things like that. Something may click—it does happen. We've had patients recover and remember quite a lot of what has been said to them. It never ceases to surprise me what the human brain can do. Don't expect anything, but if you get a reaction press this button by the bed. A nurse will come immediately."

"I understand. Thanks, Doctor."

The doctor smiled a good-bye and left the cubicle.

Immediately she turned to Harry. "So it's you and me, alone again," she said, dropping down onto the chair by the bed. "I won't keep you long." She braced herself and reached for a hand—it felt clammy—she shuddered. Thoughts swirled in her head. Had she really done this to a fellow human being? She waited a second for the tide of grief, but none came. He'd got his just deserts. She tightened her grip on his hand and leant forward so as to be closer to him. "I did this to you Harry. I set up a wire between two trees on the bridle way, the right height to catch your chest. I knew you'd be galloping— pushing your horse hard. I waited all night. I didn't want to kill you—I wanted you to be like you are. Paralysed—dependant on other people. I wanted you to sit for years smelling your shit, unable to feed yourself. I wanted you to pay for what you've done to my family. I look at you now and feel nothing. You've turned me into a revengeful woman and I hate you for that. I hope you can hear this because I want you to know that it is my greatest wish that you suffer for the rest of your miserable life. You're evil, Harry."

Was it her imagination or did she feel his hand move? She wasn't sure enough to ring for a nurse, but she felt a surge of something akin to excitement—he'd heard her; she was sure of that. It fascinated and horrified her at the same time. She pushed the chair back violently and it crashed backwards onto the floor. She turned and ran from the cubicle. A startled nurse watched her fly past her towards the stairs. She hurtled down them, fighting for breath. She felt as if she was choking. She didn't stop running until she was outside in the fresh air. The street swam in front of her eyes and she had to lean up against a wall of the hospital to prevent herself sliding to the pavement. She was oblivious to the curious stares, oblivious to the hot sun beating down on her. After a few moments her heartbeat returned to normal, her vision cleared and she became aware of the stares and the heat. She pushed herself off the wall feeling the sweat between her armpits, and threw an apologetic smile at a couple looking concerned. "Just the heat," she said. They nodded and moved on. She steadied herself, and started to walk back to the bus station. *Dear God was that really me in there?* Jill asked herself.

......

She had regained her composure by the time she reached the Volvo. Her hand was steady as she inserted the key into the ignition. She pushed her head hard against the headrest and briefly closed her eyes. . What she'd done had been loathsome. It was a day to be forgotten as quickly as possible. She started the engine and eased herself out of the car park onto the main road. There was more traffic now—the start of the notorious Bristol rush hour she assumed. She hoped she wouldn't get lost. She needn't have worried. At the roundabout there were directions to the M5. She relaxed. She couldn't wait to get home. There was something she had to do. Ever since she'd watched Harry ripped off his horse she'd kept her secret to herself, but now she knew that was no longer possible—she had to confide in someone close to her. She'd ring Max as soon she got home.

••••••

She recounted every little detail—her conflicting emotions—the build up to her fateful decision. All the time she watched Max's face waiting for him to interrupt and tell her she had to go to the police. But he sat silently on the bench, perspiring gently, even though the walnut tree protected them from the late afternoon sun.

"That's it," she said finally. "Nothing left to say. I will never be quite sure how I managed to do it. I know I should be overcome with remorse—perhaps even change faiths and confess, but it's no good. Remorse won't come. Oh, Max, do you hate me now?"

"Hate you! Don't be so stupid Jill. I understand the pressure you were under, and I can see that Harry could drive you to do something so out of character. You must have been desperate to be driven to such an extreme act."

"I was. So if you don't hate me, and I thank God you don't, how do you feel?"

"Harry's a parasite. He had it coming. I just feel, well, a great sadness, is what comes to mind."

"I think I'm in shock."

"Of course you are, but you can depend on me. What you've just confessed to me does not affect our friendship. What you did was wrong, but there's an end to it. I understand absolutely, and your secret is safe with me. In time you will heal, perhaps never quite able to forget, but life must go on."

"I think I can live with that. I knew what I was doing; it was no spur of the moment thing. I planned it carefully. If I have to suffer a bit well that's tough. It was all of my own making."

"I will always be here for you."

"As you always have been darling Max."

"As we always have been for each other," he corrected.

Chapter Twenty

As soon as the house fell quiet Toria crept along the passage to Emma's bedroom. She shut the door behind her, switched on the light and sank onto the bed. It might be the last time. All being well she'd be leaving tomorrow with Mark for New Zealand. She hadn't wanted to stay in England without him. But she had a big hurdle to climb first. She had to tell Mark about her rape. Would she lose him? That was a gamble she felt she had to take. They were at the divide between being friends and becoming lovers, and it was not fair of her to go to New Zealand with such a secret locked away. She'd been surprised with the ease she'd fallen in love. She'd thought she'd always feel soiled—that she'd recoil from any man who wanted to touch her sexually, and once they knew her story they would recoil from her. Love had crept up on her unexpectedly. She'd fought it—not easy with Mark continually dancing his favours on her, and she'd discovered love was hard to ignore. Adding to her deep concern was her remorse at deserting her sister, although she knew that was totally irrational. But irrational or not, it would be a huge wrench not to be able to spend a part of every day in the company of her sister's spirit. "If I leave I'll miss you," she mouthed. "Forgive me."

She stretched out on the bed, remembering the times as children when they'd lain in the dark swapping stories. They'd laughed a lot then, carefree enjoyment before adulthood had changed all that. Toria closed her eyes and imagined that they were together in the room saying their farewells. She felt the pressure of tears and curled up into a ball, thinking of Mark lying awake in the bedroom at the end of the landing wondering why she was so slow to come to his bed.

......

A knock on the door woke her with a start and she sat bolt upright on the bed.

She didn't answer, fearful it was her mother.

"Toria, I know you're in there."

Toria flew to the door. "Mark! I thought it might be Mum." In the dawn light filtering through the landing window she could see he was dressed in a pair of pyjamas at least a size too small. In spite of how she felt she couldn't help but giggle. "Where on earth did you get those from?"

"The local shop didn't run to anything bigger."

"You told me you slept naked."

"I do, but not when I'm sleeping in your mother's house for the first time."

"Well, come on in quickly before she hears us."

"Anyway what are you doing in here?" Mark asked surprised, noting she was still fully dressed. "I was worried—thought I might have said something to put you off me."

Toria led him to the bed and patted a spot next to her. "Nothing like that, I was just being childish, irrational, and probably a little stupid. I must have fallen asleep. You see I spend a lot of time in this room—don't laugh—talking to my sister. Crazy?"

"Not at all. You miss her very much, don't you?"

"Like mad, even though she could be a pain in the backside and bossy. We had this strong bond, which is impossible to explain to an only child such as you. When we were younger, we used to meet in here after our parents had gone to bed and spend hours telling each other stories. It was magical. That's what I do now. Tell her stories and imagine her sitting where you are, smiling and laughing. You see our stories were never sad."

Mark very gently ran a finger across her lips. "So what happens when you come to New Zealand? Can you bring her with you?"

"No. It's time for me to let go. Emma will understand."

He nodded, a smile growing on his face. "Will she understand I love you?"

For a second Toria felt irritated by his frivolity, but then she saw the softness in his eyes and knew he hadn't meant it like that. She felt a warm glow in her stomach. "I, I think so. But will you understand?" She hadn't meant to ask that—too soon—but now she'd have to explain."

"Understand what?"

She took a deep breath. She could be about to ruin something special. But she had to give him the chance to leave without her. She would burst with pain, but she couldn't live a lie with Mark.

"What I mean…I hadn't planned to tell you tonight—sometime soon, not tonight, but now I think I have no choice, but it won't be easy."

"Take your time. Come here, let me hold you."

She held back for a moment—saw the questioning look in his eyes and a little hesitantly moved into his arms. She shivered. The die was cast. She spoke slowly, her voice steady, but her heart was turning cartwheels. "Harry Sidenham raped me. Want to hear about it?"

He did not leap up and run for the door as she'd expected. Instead he touched her hand and said," Only if you want to tell me, because it will make no difference to how I feel about you."

"How can you be so sure?"

"Trust me."

This is exactly what she did.

Mark listened, held her tight. He watched the tears slide into the little grooves below her eyes. Every now and then, when she stopped for breath, he'd wipe away a tear perhaps ask a question, always germane. He didn't want to rush her or divert her. He just wanted her to unload in her own time.

Toria watched him as intently, and slowly she began to realise a truth. Mark was not going to sit in judgement on her. He was not going to walk away from her. When she'd done, she was exhausted. "That's it—the whole story. I should never have trusted him, but it's too late to say that now."

"I can never imagine the terror that must have consumed you Toria. Maybe you were a trifle naïve to trust a man like Sidenham, but it's easy to say that now. Maybe that sounds as if I'm sitting in judgement on you. Nothing could be further from the truth." He gently pushed her away and stared into her eyes. "Now listen up. None of this makes any difference I promise you. Now that's an end to it, okay? "

Toria fought back the tears. "Is it as simple as that?"

"Yes."

"I can't find words to say how wonderful that makes me feel. I never thought I'd ever be able to say to any man, "I love you. But now I can."

Mark hitched up his pyjamas. "Just make sure you only say that to me. Now can we get on with our lives?"

"Let's hope so. Maybe at last I can see a future without nightmares, without the fear of Harry, without the constant worry that another catastrophe is around the corner."

"No more 'maybes' you hear. Of course you can."

"To think only a few moments ago I was certain that I'd lose you. And Mark…"

"Yes?"

"Thanks. You're great." She felt his muscular body through the pyjamas. How lucky she was to have found a man so full of compassion. "I think I'm falling in love with you," she whispered in his ear. "Do you mind?"

"I fell in love with you some time ago."

"You did?"

"It was that night in the pub when you were leading your team to victory."

"Well, you might have told me."

"I knew it was the wrong time—you seemed a bit screwed up."

"I was." She stared at him and started to giggle again.

"What this time?"

"It's those pyjamas; you look quite ridiculous, Mark McIntyre."

"Then why don't you come and take them off?"

"I will, but not here. In my room."

······

She was quite shocked by the violence of her feelings towards him. Surprised that in such a short space of time she could rid herself of the fear— the feeling of being dirty, and be able to enjoy such a great dynamic force of pleasure, emotion and sheer physical joy. He was careful, so gentle. Careful too, in the time he took, the long, long time leading her into her excitement until she could hardly wait, hardly bear it. Finally when he entered her, she felt herself easing around him, confident, so close to him. "I love you so."

"I love you too," Mark said, "so very, very much."

They moved into another world altogether—a world that Toria had imagined only existed in her most erotic dreams. She knew without a shadow of a doubt that she was lying next to the man she wanted to spend the rest of her life with—*"The whole of my life!"* she shouted.

······

Jill made no attempt to hide her tears. She'd lost so many people close to her and now here she was at Heathrow about to see Toria off to New Zealand with a young man, who Toria had only introduced to her a few weeks earlier. On the way to the airport she'd felt the onset of loneliness, which was daft she'd told herself. After all she still had Max down the road, the farm to help Max run, her horses, and many friends. But they were no replacement for a husband and two daughters.

In contrast to her tear stained face Toria was looking radiant, holding Mark's hand, laughing with him and Max, and obviously looking forward to what she called her great adventure. But in spite of her sadness, her reluctance to see Toria go, Jill was happy for her. She accepted that Mark had given her back a little of her confidence and a reason for living once again. She understood better than anyone the reasons for Toria wanting to leave England.

"Well, here we go," Toria exclaimed as they stopped opposite the departure gate.

Jill struggled to smile. "Good luck, darling."

Toria ran into her arms, "Good-bye, Mum, and thanks for understanding. I promise I'll write, and I'll be back to visit before you know it. Take care." She pulled away, brushed a tear off her mother's cheek, grabbed Mark's arm, waved to Max, and hurried away. As they reached the departure door she turned and smiled.

It was a moment Jill would never be able to forget. In a relatively short space of time she'd lost all her family.

Chapter Twenty-One

The church bells pealed their joyful music over the village. It was a day of unbroken sunshine. It made the community smile. It was a day to celebrate. The last foot and mouth restrictions had been lifted, and the village could start the painful process of getting back to normal, though many things would never be the same again. "A day to thank our Lord," said the vicar to his packed congregation.

"It's a day I thought would never come," Max told Jill as they left the church.

"Well, it's here, and we can start to plan for the future," she said. "I can't wait to get cattle back on the farm. It's been so silent."

"Terrible," said Max, starting to walk up the Village street.

"Oh, yes, one other thing, you miserable old pessimist," said Jill, walking beside him. "Look, the teashop has reopened, the church was full, the new money has returned, and Walter Stibbins has a smile on his face again. There's a future here after all."

"And you are full of new ideas."

"Some. But they can wait until we've rebuilt our enterprises," Jill assured him. "Remember we are a partnership, and without Toria, you will need all the help you can get, so don't sound so glum."

Max marvelled at the way Jill had recovered from Toria's departure. She admitted to moments of extreme loneliness. "But they're getting shorter," she'd told him two days earlier. "And I've always got your shoulder to cry on—I can't begin to tell you how much that means to me. Sometimes I feel I'm being so selfish burdening you with my problems and being guilty of forgetting you've lost a son."

"There's no need. I like you coming to me. Makes me think I'm still some use to someone."

"You don't need to worry on that score, Max. I will always need you."

At the gate to Walnut Farm they paused. "I'll see you for supper then," Jill said, opening the gate.

"Look forward to it," said Max cheerfully. "By the way, I've been meaning to ask you, any news of Harry?"

"Last I heard he was still in a coma."

"Hope he stays that way."

So do I. Dear God, so do I, thought Jill. She said, "I feel the same. See you about eight, and the topic of Harry is off the menu from now on."

"That's a promise."

She watched him walk to his car, waved as he drove passed her before closing the yard gate behind her. She thought how different it would be in a few weeks time—the smell and noise of cattle wafting across the yard. She felt excited for the first time for months—a part of her life was returning. She unlocked the front door and stooped to pick up her mail from the mat, then headed out of the house for the walnut tree. She dropped down onto the seat beneath the tree. She relaxed, enjoying the light breeze brushing her face. She could feel new vitality coursing through her body. She'd got plans. Now at last she'd be able to make a start. She was aware of a new determination nurturing in her heart, and that brought a belief in herself that she realised had been lacking all her life—even in her marriage to Tim. Men had sculpted her life. No man would do that again. She'd try to persuade Max to diversify on the farms, suggesting turning some of the redundant farm buildings into holiday cottages and perhaps she'd even run a B & B in the house—there was plenty of room now. But her most exciting realisation was that now she would have time to write—or at least try. It had been a long held dream.

She had many stories to tell.

She looked up into the branches of the old tree, smiled at the woodpecker's nest industriously chiselled into the stump of a fallen branch. She watched two blackbirds drinking from the edge of the pond and reflected that little had changed in the garden since she'd been a child. That was where her book would begin—with the first story she could remember her mother telling her under the tree. There had been so many stories since. Enough to fill a book, and she wouldn't have to look far for a title. There was something magical the way the tree had supported her at every turn of fortune in her life, and it was in the old tree's honour that she'd call her book, 'Stories from under The Walnut Tree.'

She stretched lazily. It was a long time since she'd fallen asleep in the garden. She closed her eyes.

And then she heard the phone ringing in the house.

......

"He's regained consciousness!" Jill's voice shook as she greeted Max at the garden gate. "I can't believe it after all this time. But it's happened before apparently. He's paralysed from the waist down—always will be, I gather. Next week he goes to Stoke Mandeville, and then—oh God—he could be home in a few weeks. I knew it—I knew things looked too good. I don't think I can bear the thought of Harry coming home."

"Let's sit down," Max said guiding Jill towards one of the chairs on the patio. "This needs thinking about."

"Thinking about. Christ, Max, I've nearly killed the man! I don't want him a few miles away reminding me of what I did."

"I know, I know, but there's no good getting hysterical. You must have thought this through. You must have realised there was a chance he'd come home."

"That was something that slipped through my planning!"

"At least he doesn't know it was you."

"Oh but he does Max—at least there's a chance. What a mess!"

"What do you mean? Max asked appalled."

"I went to The Royal Infirmary to gloat—yes to gloat. I held his hand and told him that I'd strung up the wire."

"Why haven't you told me this before?"

"I didn't think it would be necessary."

"You went to the Infirmary to see Harry and you thought it wasn't necessary to tell me!"

"You don't need to say any more. I was so full of bitterness, I couldn't stop myself. Now I'll probably spend the rest of my life in prison."

"That's pure defeatism," Max protested.

"What if he remembers what I said? It is possible you know."

"A chance in a million."

"No, Max, the odds are much shorter than that, and if it does I'm in deep trouble. Harry won't let this pass. And to think I thought life was on the up!

Just shows you should never count your chickens."

······

A week went by, another week, three weeks past and Jill was beginning to hope. *Hope what?* She thought. *That he's too ill to leave Stoke Manderville, that his memory hasn't come back? Stop kidding yourself.* But she kept hoping.

······

"He's coming back in a fortnight." Jill's voice came down the line.

"Are you sure?"

"Of course I'm sure, Max. Edna Banks has just rung. He's going to need twenty-four hour nursing and she and Tom are moving into the house to coordinate everything. Tom's been told to sell the horses, and for the time being he and Edna plan to stay. You know, see how it works out."

"I'll come straight over."

"No, Max, not this time. I want to be alone."

······

Harry came home at midday on a Tuesday. By then Jill had bitten her nails down to the quick worrying whether he had any recollection of her visit to the hospital. If he had, would he go straight to the police or enjoy taunting her? Whatever, she knew he'd make her life hell.

······

The call came five days later. "It's Edna Banks here, Mrs. Foster. Sorry to bother you, but his Lordship would like to see you."

Jill's heart started pounding. "Right away, Edna?"

"No, tomorrow at around eleven. He's quite good then—gets a bit tired later, slurs his speech."

"All right, Edna, I'll be there. How is he?"

"Bad tempered, very frustrated. Not much has changed. He seems a bit confused at times. He's better in the mornings before he's had a drink. He can't walk, of course. His arm movement is restricted and he's incontinent. It's not very pleasant. I'll say one thing, which I know I shouldn't, but he won't be bothering any ladies again."

"Poor man," was all Jill could say.

"Indeed, poor man, Mrs. Foster, but wickedness never pays."

"No, Edna, you're right, it certainly doesn't. I'll see you tomorrow then."

"Tomorrow it will be, Mrs. Foster."

"Oh, Edna?"

"Yes?"

"How's his memory?"

"I don't really know. He says very little. The doctors say he's made quite a good recovery."

So all hope was gone.

......

The autumn rain made the morning grey and mizzly. It was washing the first of the fallen leaves down the road. The tarmac glistened in the morning gloom. Jill felt detached from the world, already in her mind a prisoner. She drove slowly as if time would intervene, and Harry would be long gone to his Maker. *The dreams of a desperate woman,* she thought, but then what else did she have left? She thought of Max begging her to take him along. Her swift rejection had met with a nod of understanding. But as each minute past she wished she hadn't been quite so dismissive.

It was still raining as she drew up outside the Hall. She sat for a few moments gathering her wits about her. She was determined not to show weakness. She'd face him, listen to his loathsome voice condemning her to a life of incarceration, but never allow him to think she felt any regret. She'd no intention of giving him that satisfaction.

She ran through the rain to the door and pressed the bell. Edna had heard the car and opened it almost immediately, saving her from getting a soaking.

"Mrs. Foster, how nice to see you. What a dreadful morning. I regret to say it matches Lord Sidenham's mood. Proper nasty he is this morning—thoroughly upset one of the nurses, and they are not easy to get around here. To tell you the truth, I'm not sure how long Tom and I can stand it here."

Jill managed a smile. "I can understand that, Edna. I think you're a saint. I don't know how you've put up with him for so long."

"In the past most of his tantrums have gone over my head, but now it's different. He's very demanding, wants me around him all the time. 'Can't stand the fucking nurses messing with me, Edna,' he grumbles—if you'll pardon my language, Mrs. Foster. I tell him I have to sleep sometimes and all he says is that I'll have plenty of time after he's dead. I'm exhausted."

"I'm sure you are, poor woman."

"But we'll see," Edna said as she shut the door. "Tom and I will assess the situation in a few weeks time. Don't want to do anything precipitous. I actually feel sorrow for the miserable man. I wouldn't like to have ended up like him."

"I'm sure."

"Ah well, no good moaning about something that I can easily alter, is there? Now mustn't waste any more of your time. He's in the library. You know the way. If you want anything, he's got a bell on the left-hand side of his chair."

"Thank you, Edna. I'll go on through."

As she walked slowly towards the library she felt as if an invisible magnet was drawing her nearer and nearer to the edge of a cliff, where she'd teeter on the edge and then plunge to her fate. By the time she reached the large oak door she was shaking with fear. She stopped as her hand touched the brass handle—somehow she had to compose herself. She inhaled slowly, regulating her breathing, until some semblance of control returned. She acknowledged it was the best she could do. She turned the handle and walked in.

There had been a big change in the room since her last visit. One wall of bookshelves had been removed to make room for a low hospital type bed. Harry's large mahogany desk was also missing, allowing room for the clutter of necessary items needed to look after a paralysed man. A commode, two oxygen cylinders, a large chest of drawers, a jug of water, a glass, and a roll of toilet paper, all sitting on the top of a white table. There was a smell of urine lingering in the air, and by one of the French windows was Harry, dressed in a blue shirt, a pair of worn beige trousers, sitting in a wheel chair. Jill swallowed a cry. He seemed smaller, hunched up like an old man. There was a tray of what looked like baby food on a table by his right side. It seemed he moved his head with difficulty as he looked up to stare at her. She was shocked by the deadness of his eyes—his bloated face—his shaven head, which exposed a long angry gash running from just above his left eye to disappear somewhere behind one ear.

I did this to him, Jill couldn't help thinking. "Hello, Harry."

She watched him struggling to move his right arm. He pointed a finger at himself. "You satisfied now?" His voice was weak.

He'd remembered. She stood rock still in the middle of the room, frightened to move in case she collapsed. "What—what do you mean?"

"Don't play the innocent with me. It was not hard for me to deduce that you were the person who did this to me. The nurses told me that you were the only visitor, and I remember every word you said."

"I—"

"Shut up! I can see the guilt in your eyes. Regret gloating over my bed? Never thought I'd regain consciousness, eh? Want me to show you mercy, just like you did to me? Ha! Want me to say I deserve it? You should know me better than that." Harry's voice rose. "Look, look what you've done to me! I'm as good as dead! Fuck you, woman!"

"Do I regret it?" Jill moved swiftly to his side, all fear and shock gone. "Regret it, Harry—never! I hope you suffer and suffer. Look what you've done to my family. Emma's dead. You raped Toria, and all because you wanted to get back at me. You're a sad case, Harry. For Christ's sake, what sort of monster are you?"

"What are you?" Harry spluttered. "Do you look upon yourself as an avenging angel? What right have you got to judge me and pass sentence? You're just a common criminal—you can't say that of me."

If Harry could have gotten out of his chair, he'd have hit her. Instead saliva ran down one side of his mouth, and his pallid features turned puce. Jill could feel his anger like an electric shock, but she didn't flinch. Harry was where he deserved to be. If that meant prison, at least she'd have the satisfaction of knowing he was in his own type of prison as well. She crossed her hands in front of her chest and smiled grimly. "So what are you going to do about it?"

"I wondered when we'd get round to that." Harry dug his nails into the plastic sides of his armrests and sneered at Jill. "It's occupied all my thoughts since leaving the hospital. You see, I don't want to make you into some sort of martyr. I don't want to give you the chance of gathering sympathy. So I've been thinking of other ways of making you pay. I'm not going to the police—at least not yet—thereby denying you the chance to tell your story in court. You're going to come and live here, work every hour of the day and night looking after me, and if you refuse or ever try to leave, then I'll shop you to the police. So you see, Jill, I've got my wish after all. It has taken time, but you've come back to me, and do you know what my greatest pleasure will be? It's knowing that you will suffer far more here than sitting in prison."

"I will never live here!"

"Then pass me the telephone."

"You really mean it!"

"Oh yes, I mean it."

Fighting to get her wits about her, Jill asked, "How long have I got?"

"For what?"

"To make up my mind."

"I wouldn't have thought you needed any time."

"Well, there you're wrong."

"Twenty-four hours, then."

"You're the dregs."

"Call me what you like, I'm past caring. But you're trapped, Jill."

"You make me sick, Harry."

"Good—I like that. You don't do much for me either. Now, before you go and no doubt talk to that common farmer friend of yours, be a good girl and light me a cigarette, will you? There's a packet on the floor by the commode."

"Stuff you," Jill felt like saying, but what was the point. Harry was right, she was trapped. She might just as well do as he asked. She moved over to the commode, found the packet and pulled out a Gitane.

Harry was enjoying himself now. "Light it for me. The matches are on the table here."

Without saying a word Jill lit the cigarette.

"Now put it in my mouth."

"I should ram it down your throat!"

"Now, now, that's no way to talk to a defenceless man and your future employer."

Jill put the cigarette between his teeth. "I hope it chokes you."

Harry pointed at the door. Jill quickly made her exit, slamming the door behind her. "Plg," she shouted, and then caught sight of Edna Banks standing by the front door. "Oh, Edna, I'm sorry."

"Don't apologise to me, Mrs. Foster. Tom and I call him a much worse name than that. Are you all right? You look very pale."

"I just need fresh air."

"I know exactly what you mean," said Edna, opening the door, "and it has stopped raining. Will I see you again soon?"

"I don't think I'll be coming back."

······

Harry heard the front door close, a feeling of satisfaction flowing through his body. His life might well be descending into hell, but he'd take Jill down with him. It never occurred to him that she might choose otherwise. He chewed on his cigarette and breathed in deeply. A mistake—the smoke made him cough. He tried to lift a hand to reach the cigarette, but he hadn't the strength; it fell from his mouth. He swore loudly and pressed his bell.

"The bloody man is summoning us again," said the nurse to Edna. "And here we are just having our first coffee of the morning."

"Leave him be," advised Edna. "It won't do him any harm to wait. If he shits himself too bad."

Harry smelt burning and realised the cigarette must have fallen into his trouser turn-ups. He tried to look down, but couldn't see his feet. He pressed the bell more urgently.

"He's getting very angry," said the nurse. "I think one of us ought to go and see what he wants."

"A few more minutes won't hurt," said Edna, twisting her spoon in the coffee. "I'll go then; you had a rough night."

Harry choked on the smoke. He realised he was on fire. Terror engulfed him. He saw a flame, felt the heat and opened his mouth, but the smoke cut off his scream. He fought for air, fumbled for the bell, but already he was growing drowsy. A searing hot pain forced its way into his mouth and burnt his lungs. He made one last effort to press the bell, but by then he was too weak. By the time the flames caressed his face, he was already dead.

······

Max drove. "Are you sure about this?" he said as he threaded his way through the town traffic to the police station.

"I am."

"Is there no alternative, call Harry's bluff, perhaps?"

"He wasn't bluffing. He gave me two clear choices. I've chosen the least horrific"

"Dear God, you must hate him."

"I don't think I need answer that."

"At least you'll have your chance in court, I suppose."

"I'll plead guilty, Max. I'm not going to try and find excuses. It was a pure act of revenge—end of story."

"You'll go to prison for a long time. Harry could die any day. Your time with him could be short."

"Even a few weeks would be worse than a life sentence."

Max drew up outside the headquarters building of the Gloucester Police.

"Well, this is it, Max. Don't leave me."

"Of course I won't. I'll stand bail. Get you a good lawyer. We can win this."

"No, Max. I must pay for what I've done."

Jill opened her door and stepped out, waited for Max to join her. They walked slowly, holding hands. They were close to the entrance when Jill's mobile phone rang in her bag. "I can't answer that now."

"I will." Max took the bag off her shoulder and pulled out the phone. "Hello. Edna! What? Christ! Of course, right away!" He grabbed at Jill's arm. "Hold it! Don't go in, it's Edna Banks. She wants a word urgently!"

Printed in the United Kingdom by
Lightning Source UK Ltd., Milton Keynes
138725UK00002B/58/A